UNBOWED

LEE HARDEN SERIES

BOOK 5

★

D. J. MOLLES

The characters and events portrayed in this book are fictitious. Any similarity to real persons, living or dead, is coincidental and not intended by the author.

Who are you, Lee Harden? Are you wrath? Are you vengeance? Are you just a man of violence, always seeking an outlet for your anger? Is that all that lays at the center of you? Is your core just a vicious animal, trained to go for the throat, looking for opportunities to be let off the leash?

Or are you, perhaps, something a little bit more than that?

ONE

KILLERS

GREELEY OR BUST was painted in big, white letters on the side of the utility van that took up the rear of the convoy as it snaked its way north, away from the refinery.

How many yards between Lee and the back of that van?

200, maybe. Now 250. Now 300.

In the course of the ten days since Lee had lost his left eye—and his depth perception with it—he'd developed an obsessive habit of forcing himself to estimate distances. What had come almost instinctively to him over years of ranging targets with both eyes now became an exercise in in focus.

Eventually the van, and the convoy ahead of it, followed the slow turn of the long road away from the refinery, and disappeared into the scrubby trees in the distance, flickering in the late morning sun that blazed through the branches.

And then Lee was alone with Corporal Ryan.

He was mostly confident in his distance assessment. That wasn't the problem. The problem was that it took him *time* to calculate that distance. Which meant that any shot that required a hold-over was not something he could make quickly.

It was like being a champion sprinter, and then finding one day that you had trouble simply walking.

Which, coincidentally, Lee also had trouble with.

They had broken his body. Lee was determined to gain back some of his physicality, but it had become exceedingly clear that he would never get back to where he'd been.

It left him with a gaping hole, an ache that seemed to reside just beneath his sternum, lodged between his heart and his guts. His confidence in his body had been cut out of him, leaving only a crippling and utterly foreign sense of vulnerability.

Half the man I used to be.

One working eye. One working arm. One working leg. The left half of his body belonged to some invasive stranger. Some old and battered creature that gave him nothing but pain, and robbed him of the fluidity with which he was accustomed to moving through this world.

"Major…sir…" Corporal Ryan's voice trembled.

Lee took a breath and bore down on it. He turned—his right leg first, nice and easy. Then his left leg, stiff and aching at the hip-joint. He squinted his right eye against the sunlight streaming between the pipelines, and looked down at the man before him.

Corporal Ryan. On his knees. Hands bound behind his back. Sweat from the humidity, and from the stress, beading across his pale forehead, and glistening in the stubble of his two-week beard.

He looked like shit. And it almost roused a sense of pity in Lee.

Almost. But not quite.

Corporal Ryan was dead to Lee. He just didn't know it yet.

Who are you, Lee Harden?

"Listen," Ryan whimpered. "I'm sorry. I understand that what I did was wrong. I was only confused by…by the command structure, and how everything has changed. I understand now that what I did was insubordinate. I've thought a lot about it. I'm ready to follow your lead, sir. And Sergeant Ryder, too. I understand that he's my superior now. I can follow orders."

Lee listened. Oh, he listened. He gave himself time to digest it, and, as his eye ranged across Ryan's fearful face, he wondered if the words would get through the barrier that Lee had erected around his heart and his mind.

He gave those words a chance.

But they just crashed against Lee's walls, ineffective.

Lee shook his head. "I don't trust you anymore, corporal. I tried. I gave you a second chance. But when you refused to follow Sergeant Ryder's orders a week ago, that was it."

"No," Ryan pleaded. "No, I learned my lesson. Why else would you have kept me locked up for a week, if you didn't think I could learn my lesson?"

Lee laid his hand on his holstered pistol. "Ryan, I was never going to let you live."

Reality crashed through Ryan's face. Obliterated vain hopes. "But…but…"

Lee laid his gnarled and uncooperative left hand on Ryan's shoulder. "I just didn't want the others to see this happen."

Ryan squeezed his eyes shut. Tears seeped out from the corners. "Please!"

Lee felt his nose curl. Corporal Ryan was more than just insubordinate. He was a coward. Here he was, an able-bodied young man, half the age of the battered fuck standing over him, with twice the physical capabilities. If the situation had been reversed, Lee would have launched himself at his captor, used his teeth if he had to. Bit his throat out. Stomped his head to mush.

He wouldn't have simply knelt there, begging.

"I can't trust you," Lee said again. "You have no place with us."

He drew his pistol. He needed no range estimate to hit his target.

Ryan opened his eyes. He saw the muzzle of the pistol pointed at his head. His mouth gaped soundlessly. Paralyzed by it.

Lee's finger tightened on the trigger. Brought it back to that stiff wall, beyond which another ounce of pressure would break it. Firing pin into primer. Propellant igniting. Bullet racing, blooming through skull and brain matter.

A distant ringing in Lee's ears, threatening to crescendo into the all-encompassing inner shriek of tinnitus.

Ryan's eyes left the muzzle. Found Lee's.

Whatever he saw there terrified him more than the muzzle.

What are you, Lee Harden?

Lee almost flinched away from that expression. But instead he pressed the trigger until it broke.

***

Lee opened the back door to the Humvee and found Deuce keeping his seat warm for him. Not that he needed it warm—the sleeves of his combat shirt were rolled as high as he could get them, and the so-called "sweat-wicking" fabric was plastered to his back, not wicking much sweat at all.

Seated behind the driver, Abe lifted his head. His black hair was nearly as long as his black beard now, and about as bushy, shot through with an even sprinkling of wiry gray. He gave Lee a quirked eyebrow, but didn't say anything. Between them passed a tacit acknowledgement of what had just happened.

There was no judgement in Abe's eyes. Not about this, anyways. He and Lee's hands had been dirty long enough that neither thought it was worth mentioning anymore. Simply par for the course.

Are you a killer? Are you still Mr. Nobody?

Deuce stuck his muzzle in Lee's face and gave him a lick, and a wag of the tail. Lee didn't immediately oust him from his perch. His commands to the dog were slower these days. He gave Deuce the deference the dog had earned.

Deuce didn't need his pity. But looking at the dog, with the crusty remains of his own ruined eye—just like Lee's—he had a hard time just slapping him on the rump and telling him to get down.

Instead, Lee put his fingers into the dog's fur and gave him a scratch behind the ears. His right hand moved just fine, but the tendons of the left still ached and smarted in his wrist, and the fingers only moved a fraction as far as they used to.

"Good boy," Lee murmured, noticing the burgeoning tinnitus beginning to fade. Then pointed to the back, where a little niche had been left open in the fastback amid piles of gear. He clicked his tongue, and Deuce obediently relinquished the seat.

Lee used his right leg to hoist himself up, and then maneuvered his left into position and sat down with a huff.

"You ready?" Abe asked, as Lee shut his door.

Lee settled into his seat, looking out the window, back towards the refinery. Was he ready? Were the people ready?

"Did you sink the boats?" Lee asked.

"Perforated the hulls. Ripped random shit out of the motors. They're back in the surf somewhere. Even if someone finds 'em, they're not getting to the drilling rigs. Not in those anyways."

Lee nodded. Through the tangle of pipelines that ran about the refinery, he could just make out the glimmer of the sea beyond. "And you're comfortable with what Pez did to the rigs?"

"Hell, Lee, I don't even understand half the shit he said. But he says they're plugged up or something. No one's getting any oil out of them without a shit-ton of work."

It was the best they could hope for. Lee had toyed with the idea of permanently disabling the drilling rigs with explosives. But sometime in the future, they might want to get those drilling rigs and refineries working again. Right now, they only needed to deny resources to the enemy.

Because they were coming. Whoever had taken Butler from them wouldn't stay in Georgia forever. They'd come after Lee. And when they reached Texas, Lee didn't want them to have a supply of fuel to continue their chase.

Lee had drained every drop he could squeeze out of this place before giving the orders to sabotage it. There were eleven tanker trucks in that massive convoy that had just lit out. Mostly gasoline and diesel, but some JP-8 to run the Blackhawk as well. And any other aircraft they might come across.

"Lee."

He had to turn his head all the way to be able to see Abe with his right eye.

"Everything's taken care of," Abe soothed. "It's time to go."

Lee nodded. "Just checking boxes, Abe. It makes me feel better."

"Well, if you're feeling warm and fuzzy enough, I'd like to catch up to the convoy."

Lee looked to the driver, one of Breckenridge's soldiers. "Private Turner, you can go ahead and get us out of here."

Turner nodded, cranked the wheel around and started driving.

Lee glanced at Abe again. "Pez is in love with you now."

Abe chuffed. "Been following me around like a puppy."

"Loyalty is good. You saved his family."

"Didn't save everyone. Couldn't."

"Can't save people that are already dead."

"Nope. Suppose not."

"Hey."

Abe met Lee's earnest gaze.

"You did good work down there."

Abe nodded. "I know. I'm not mad about it. I gave those fucks what they had coming."

Lee let it go. He'd already debriefed Abe fully when he'd returned only a few short nights ago. He'd gone to rescue the families of the refinery workers being held captive by the cartel. He hadn't been able to save everyone's family. Several of the families were already dead, their husbands at the refinery just hadn't known it yet. But, at the very least, Abe had delivered them vengeance. And for that, every single one of those refinery workers now looked at Abe like he was some wrathful god made flesh. They both loved him and feared him.

They were loyal to Abe. And Abe was loyal to the cause. It amounted to the same thing.

Lee found it hard to trust in many people these days, but Abe was an exception. If there was anyone in this world that Lee trusted fully and completely, it was Abe Darabie.

Which didn't mean they never argued. Arguing between them had become a given. Abe was one of the few people who didn't pull punches with Lee, and for that, Lee actually trusted him more. As tiring as he could sometimes be.

Case in point: Abe's chagrinned expression as they passed through an intersection, staring out to the east, where the road led back towards Butler.

"You're a stubborn fuck, you know that?"

Abe frowned at him. "Hey pot, I'm kettle. Nice to meet you."

Their arguments almost had a call-and-response feel to them now. It was both irritating and comforting to be back with Abe, and have his old friend second-guess every damned thing he did. But Lee reminded himself that he'd missed that when he'd been all alone in Butler.

"This is the right strategy," Lee said with a confidence that was not so much invested in the end result of that strategy, but rather that it was the best of a set of shitty options.

"I didn't say anything," Abe replied.

"You sighed."

"I sighed? What are you, my wife now? I can't sigh?"

"If we'd split our forces to ambush whoever comes in from Georgia, then our push towards Greeley would be that much less effective. We need everything we have moving north. And even then, we're looking at hard odds."

"Sure, Lee. We've already gone over this."

"Well, I'm not the one mooning out the window, fantasizing about shitty strategies that aren't going to happen."

"A shitty strategy is *not* placing a rear-guard and getting your ass pinched between an army in the field and a fixed and fortified objective."

"We won't get pinched. We'll get into Greeley."

"You hope." Abe fixed him with a serious look. "And if Sam doesn't come through for you? If he doesn't get into Greeley? If he can't convince people to turn on Briggs?"

"He will."

"You sent a half-boot to do a special forces job."

"And I've got an army that's seventy-five-percent civilian guerillas. Any other obvious shit you want to point out to me?"

Abe sniffed. Scratched at his beard. Never let his eyes leave Lee. "Are you just being contrary because you like to screw with me, or do you really have that much faith in Sam?"

Lee considered that. Did he really have that much faith in Sam? When had the kid that had hidden under a stump, crying for his dead father, become a man that Lee could trust? Did he really think that Sam could pull this off?

Maybe he didn't. Maybe he wasn't *sure*. But you can never be *sure* about anything. Not in life. And certainly not in war. The future was unknowable.

And deep down, Lee knew that his faith in Sam had nothing to do with whether or not he thought Sam could actually accomplish his mission. Rationally, he *did* think that Sam could, or he wouldn't have sent him. But really, the reason why he'd sent Sam, and not one of the more qualified people, was that he didn't *know* those more qualified people like he knew Sam.

Lee looked out the windshield. "How many times have I been betrayed, Abe? How many times have *you* been betrayed? How many plans have gone tits up because the person we trusted turned on us?"

Abe gave no response to that. Because the list was too long to even consider.

"I can count on one hand the number of people I *know* won't stab me in the back. Everyone else is subject to suspicion. So if you want to know why I sent a half-boot to do a special forces job, it's because I know—*I know*—that Sam won't betray me."

Abe took a heavy breath, and when he pressed it out, he seemed to relinquish the argument. "Well. I hope he can get the job done."

Lee felt a winch in his chest tighten another notch. “Yeah. Me too.”

TWO

SAMEER

"I THOUGHT COLORADO WAS SUPPOSED to be all mountains and cool, crisp air," Jones griped, wiping sweat off his brow. "The fuck is this?"

Sam shuffled forward a few more steps, the hot concrete starting to burn through the thin soles of his worn out sneakers. He glanced to the side of the roadway, where two men in black polos and body armor watched them from the bed of a pickup truck, their rifles slung, but ready and in hand. He couldn't see their eyes behind their sunglasses, but Sam was pretty sure they were looking at him and his group.

"This look like the mountains to you, Jonesy?" Sam muttered. He glanced to his left and could just barely make out a hazy ripple in the distance that rose up above the flatness of the horizon like a jagged wall.

The Rockies. But Greeley wasn't in the Rockies, despite the image he'd had in his head this whole time, which he guessed was something more like Aspen. When you think of Colorado, you don't think *flat.*

But Greeley was flat.

Not that they were in Greeley proper just yet. This was the southern edge of what was called the

"Red Zone," which was actually a little town called La Salle, according to the battered map they'd left in the old Honda Civic they'd ditched ten miles back.

One of the operatives in black polos held up his hand. "Y'all stop right there."

Sam's spine stiffened, his heart jerking into high gear. He squinted against the sun, expecting the Cornerstone operative to level his rifle at them. But the man simply stood there, looking bored.

Sam let his breath out slow. Best not to appear too nervous. Best to just look like the desperate, worn-out refugees that they were supposed to be.

Jones shifted beside Sam, giving the operative a sideways glance. His grip tightened on the strap of the rifle he had slung on his back.

There were six of them in the group. Sam's squad—Jones, Pickell, Frenchie, and Johnson—and Marie. She'd been a last minute add on. Five military-aged males might still cause some uncomfortable questions to be asked, but the presence of a middle-aged woman diffused that suspicion. Or so they hoped.

They were all dressed in tattered and filthy civilian clothes. They'd intentionally worn the most threadbare items they could rustle up, the most worn out backpacks they could find, and fitted their feet into sneakers with split toes and soles that were paper thin—if not downright holey.

They certainly *looked* like they'd been travelling on foot for weeks.

They smelled like it, too. None of them had washed themselves since the day this plan had been decided on. All for the mission.

The operative that had ordered them to stop looked up the road, where the actual checkpoint stood, maybe fifty yards ahead. There, another group of haggard civilians was being inspected and questioned by a mix of soldiers in US military uniforms, and Cornerstone operatives in their black polos.

Highway 85, through La Salle, was the only entry point on the south side of Greeley. The signs on the other roads in made that much explicitly clear: ANYONE APPROACHING GREELEY ON THIS ROUTE WILL BE FIRED UPON. IF YOU ARE SEEKING ASYLUM, TAKE HIGHWAY 85 NORTH TO LA SALLE.

The Cornerstone operative in the pickup bed traded a few comments over a radio, and then returned his attention to Sam's group. If he found them suspicious, he didn't show it. This was just another day at the office for him. Another group of pathetic peons to be dealt with.

But he did heft his rifle. As did the operative next to him.

"You six," the first operative said, projecting his voice at them, unnecessarily loud, as they were only ten yards away from him. "First thing you need to do is raise your hands up above your head."

Sam felt the eyes of his squad flit to him, but he stayed focused on the operative in the truck. "Uh, sir, why do we have to--?"

"Raise your hands if you want to get into Greeley," the operative said, sounding annoyed. "If you're not going to comply with the security procedures, then you can just turn your happy ass around and get the fuck out of here."

Sam raised his hands, and the others in his group followed suit.

"Alright, one at time, starting with the Macho Man with the big mouth, step forward."

Sam assumed that was him, so he stepped forward, out of line with the others.

"Do you have any sidearms on your person?" the operative said.

"No, sir. Just my rifle."

"Roger that. Listen to my commands very closely. The rest of you listen as well, so I don't have to repeat myself. You're going to take your right hand. You're going to use that right hand to take the barrel of your rifle and hold it straight out in front of you. Go ahead and do that."

Sam did that. They all had their rifles slung on their backs, rather than across their chests, in yet another attempt to look less like the squad of soldiers that they actually were.

"Now, take your left hand and remove the magazine of your rifle."

Sam complied with that as well.

"Stow that magazine in your back pocket. Now, with your left hand, work the bolt and eject the round from the chamber."

Sam slid the charging handle back and the brass cartridge clattered out onto the roadway.

"Good. You can sling your rifle now. Pick up your cartridge and fall back in line. Next—the lady."

It proceeded like this for all six of them, until their weapons were emptied and their magazines stowed.

The operatives in the pickup bed lowered their rifles. The one that had been doing all the talking pointed down the road. "You may proceed to the checkpoint. Do not touch your weapons until you're instructed to do so by the soldiers at the checkpoint. If you don't comply with that, they will chew you the fuck up. Have a good day."

Sam did his best to look meek and started walking towards the checkpoint, his group jumbled up around him.

"What a douchebag," Jones murmured once they were out of earshot. "Is that like a Cornerstone requirement? Part of their training regimen?"

"Just be cool, Jonesy."

"I'm always cool. Just sayin'."

Sam glanced over his left shoulder to Frenchie and Johnson. "You guys alright?"

They looked worried. But they both nodded.

"Yeah, we're good," Frenchie said, trying on a rickety smile.

Frenchie and Johnson had been a sticking point between Sam and Lee. Lee didn't know them. Didn't trust them. Didn't want them on the op. But Sam had bled with them. He knew they were solid. And so he'd vouched for them. Gave Lee a guarantee that he'd make sure they got the job done, that they'd be assets, and not liabilities.

Sam turned to his right, where Marie strode beside him. Her sharp eyes watched him shrewdly. She didn't look worried, exactly. More…circumspect.

"How about you, Marie?"

She shrugged her narrow shoulders, her lean features drawn into a pursed expression. "Right as rain. Just another refugee, looking for a safe place to stay."

"That's all we are," Sam agreed quietly.

Sam took stock of Pickell last, but he needn't have. Pickell looked as calm as ever. His expression was that same neutral good humor with which he navigated everything. He could've been in the turret of a Humvee driving through primal-infested countryside, or hanging out around a campfire. His attitude seemed to always remain the same.

God has fixed the time of my death, he'd told Sam. That was how he made his peace with everything.

Maybe he was a little off in the head, but it seemed to work for him.

The only thing that Sam could tell from Pickell's sweaty, slightly pale face, was that he was hurting. The wound he'd taken during the fight for Butler wasn't even close to healed. Sam had tried to get him to stay behind, but Pickell insisted he could hack it.

Up ahead, the group of four refugees that had preceded them had made it through the checkpoint and now continued on towards the squat little sprawl of buildings that made up La Salle. Sam saw people moving about in there. Thin smoke trails rising up from cookfires. The scent of woodsmoke and latrines, faint on a light breeze.

The soldiers at the checkpoint turned their attention onto Sam's group as they approached. Sam took a quick count, though he was painfully aware that there was nothing he could do to fight them at this point. He and his entire group was at the mercy of ten men. Five soldiers in OCPs. Five Cornerstone operatives. One of the soldiers covered them with an M249 from behind a barricade of sandbags on the left side of the road. Another covered them from an M2 on the top of a MATV on the right.

Sam didn't like staring down all those muzzles. He felt powerless. Vulnerable. Subjected to the will of others, his life in their hands. It hung upon a few ounces of pressure from ten triggers. It was not a pleasant situation in which to find yourself.

Two Cornerstone operatives stood in the very center of the road, waiting for them. To either side of them stood concrete Jersey barriers, bottlenecking the road so that a vehicle couldn't get through—only people.

One of the operatives stepped forward and put a hand out for them to stop. He held a clipboard. His rifle was slung to his chest. He didn't wear sunglasses like most of his compatriots. His dark eyes ranged across the group, evaluating them, taking a reading from their expressions.

He must've been okay with what he saw, because he looked down at his clipboard and thumbed a pen. "Names."

They gave their real names, one after the other, giving the operative time to scribble them down. The only change was from Sam. He gave his *actual* real name. Not the Sam Ryder he'd become. But Sameer Balawi.

It felt strange to let those words out of his mouth. He hadn't introduced himself by his real name in so long, it didn't even feel real anymore.

Sam expected some sort of remark from the operative about his ethnicity, but the operative just wrote it down, then raised his eyes to the group again.

"Any doctors, nurses, paramedics or EMTs?" he spoke quickly, rattling them off out of rote habit.

No one spoke. He didn't seem surprised.

"Engineers, electricians, or metal workers?"

Silence.

"Anyone with military experience?"

This time the silence felt strained. At least to Sam. Was it his imagination or did the operative stare at them for a few beats longer than he had after his other questions?

He clicked the pen a few times. Then grunted. "Any of you got family inside Greeley at this time?"

Sam shifted his weight. Again, no one responded.

"What state are y'all coming from?"

"Oklahoma," Sam answered.

The operative fixed his eyes on Sam. "You speak for everyone?"

Sam shrugged. "We're all from Oklahoma."

"What part?"

"Little settlement on the eastern side."

The operative's eyes cinched tighter. "What was the name of the nearest town to your settlement?"

Sam found his throat getting dry. "We were about an hour outside of Tulsa."

The operative's lips flattened. "Don't dance with me, kid. Gimme the name of the nearest town to your settlement."

"Centralia."

"What happened?"

Sam felt his chest flutter, feeling a wrong answer might swing things into areas he didn't want to go. "What do you mean?"

"I mean what happened to your settlement, kid? Why are you standing here in front of me right now?"

"We ran out of food," Marie broke in.

The operative turned his attention to her.

"Crops didn't come in last harvest," she continued. "Settlement broke up over the winter. Didn't have enough people to keep it running this spring. So we left. That's why we're here."

The operative bobbed his head. "And what are you? Like, the mom of the group or something?"

Marie managed a smile. "Something like that."

"Any of y'all relations?"

"No, sir. We just all decided to make the trip here together. For protection."

The operative regarded her for a moment, then gave a look to all of them in one sweep of his eyes. "Have any of you, at any point in time, been a part of, or know someone that has been a part of, a group calling themselves the United Eastern States?"

They had all agreed beforehand that the safest answer to a question like this would be dumb silence. But now, with the question hanging in the air between them, Sam felt his skin prickle with nervous heat, like no matter what he did, he looked suspicious. As though something as stupid as how he held his hands might be a dead giveaway.

"*Those* communist fucks?" Jones suddenly belted out. "Fuck them. I heard they eat babies and cornhole each other."

Full-on panic engulfed Sam's head like feedback in his brain. For a moment, everything was nearly too bright to see. He didn't dare look around at Jones, even as his hands suddenly twitched with the urge to slap the shit out of him.

The operative looked at Jones, his brow furrowing. "That a fuckin' joke or something?"

With the operative's attention off of him, Sam shot a wide-eyed glance at Jones, but found him standing there, staring at the operative with wild eyes, shaking his head with a sort of fervent hysteria.

"Nah, man," Jones said in a spooky voice. "Ain't no joke. Fuckin' horror show out there, that's what people say. Never been. Never want to. Hope y'all nuke their asses or something. Why haven't y'all nuked their asses?"

The sheer, earnest insanity with which Jones threw these words out seemed to have the opposite affect that Sam had expected. Rather than grow more suspicious, the operative seemed to lean away from Jones, with an expression that said he wanted to move things along a little quicker now.

"Right." The operative looked down at his clipboard and gave a minimal shake of his head, as though clearing it. "Well. I regret to inform you all that, unfortunately, none of you have any of our fast-track skills."

Sam felt his stomach plummet.

The operative held up a hand. "That doesn't mean you can't get into Greeley, but it means you'll have to wait until we can find a place for you. Don't ask me how long the wait might be, because I don't know." He hiked a thumb over his shoulder. "That lovely little burg behind us is what we call 'The Tank.' You'll have to find yourself a place there while you wait to see if we can fit you into Greeley. No, there's no food there. You'll have to fend for yourselves—"

A shout in the distance cut the operative off.

Sam's eyes focused past the checkpoint, down the quarter mile of roadway to La Salle. Movement caught his eye on the northwestern corner of the sprawl of buildings. People running.

Just three of them. What looked like two adults and a child.

Running towards Greeley.

"Christ," the operative muttered, shaking his head.

An amplified voice lilted over to them across the distance: "Stop, or you will be fired upon."

It wasn't shouted. Whoever said it just...said it. Casually. Like you might tell a kid to stop jumping on their bed.

The figures didn't stop running.

A single burp of automatic gunfire rattled through the air.

Dust sprouted around the figures. And they toppled.

Sam stared at where they'd been. They'd fallen so flat that he couldn't even see them anymore. He kept waiting for them to get up, to raise their hands over their heads, to surrender. But they didn't. A gust of wind swept across the ground and pushed those little dust clouds away, and then there was nothing there.

The operative let out a heavy breath. "And there was a fucking kid in there. Who the fuck takes their kid with them to pull a stunt like that? Buncha fuckin' animals." He turned back to Sam, his expression severe. "That brings up my next point. There are fucking ground rules in The Tank. Don't try to make a run for Greeley. When we're ready to come get you, we will come and get you. You try to run for it and we will take that as hostile intent."

Sam's eyes drifted out to the little empty spot in the fields between La Salle—AKA The Tank—and Greeley. Then he dragged them back to the operative. Words rushed into his mouth with the sudden force of a burst pipe. None of them were wise things to say.

Remember the mission. That's what you're here for. That's your only reason for existence right now. Nothing else matters.

He clenched his jaw to prevent himself from speaking, and nodded his head to indicate that he understood.

The operative sniffed. "Moving on. You need to turn over your weapons."

Sam's hand went involuntarily to the sling of his rifle, but remembered the warning given by the other operative and pulled back before he touched it. "We gotta give you our guns?"

The operative huffed. "Yeah, that's what I said." He jerked his head to the left. Sam looked and found a stack of weapons leaning up against the back of the sandbag wall. "Everyone gets disarmed before entering The Tank. Those are the rules."

Sam grimaced, looking over to La Salle. Refugee camps weren't known for their civility. A lot of desperate people crammed in together, with no food and no prospects, and no idea how long they would have to remain in that purgatory.

The operative let out a dry chuckle. "If it makes you feel any better, no one else in there has guns. But we do let them keep their knives. So…you know. Watch your back."

Sam glanced back at his group and found their faces as doubtful as his. But he forced himself to nod. "Go ahead, guys. Give 'em up."

The operative pointed to the left shoulder of the road. "Just stack them up right there."

With a slow, mournful clatter, six rifles were laid on the shoulder of the road.

"Alright, last thing," the operative announced. "Take off your packs, lay them at your feet, and open them up."

This just keeps getting better and better.

Sam's heart kept a steady, hard rhythm in his throat as he laid his pack down on the ground and opened it up, and prayed to whoever might by listening that he'd disguised the contents of it well enough. They'd known they'd likely be searched. But that didn't mean his attempts at camouflage were going to work out.

The other operative that so far hadn't done anything but stand there and stare at them, now stepped forward and began to pat each of them down, while the one that had asked all the questions rifled through their packs.

Sam stood, spread-eagle, but the guy frisking him kicked his ankles anyways, so Sam spread them a little further, even as his gut tightened with anger. *Fuck these people. Fuck every one of them.*

He didn't make eye contact with them for a moment, because he knew that his eyes would betray what he was thinking. And he was thinking that he was going to burn their house down.

"The fuck's all this?" the operative said, hefting a jumble of electronics out of the bottom of Sam's pack. Sam stared at them, instead of at the man. He saw what was in them. But did the operative?

"Just…stuff," Sam mumbled. "I tinker with electronics. Thought maybe I could trade some of the stuff if I could get it working right?"

The operative turned the jumble over in his hands a few times, then let it fall carelessly back into the pack. "Sure. Whatever."

After they'd all been frisked and their packs rummaged through, they slung them back onto their shoulders, and the two operatives stepped to the shoulder of the road, leaving the opening in the barricades exposed.

The operative that had asked all the questions plastered on a rigid smile and swept a grandiose hand down the road. "Welcome to the Red Zone."

THREE

ADAPTATION

ANGELA SAT IN THE ASSAULT MODULE of Brinly's MATV. A windowless, tan cell, smelling of metal and heavy grease and stale body odors, crammed with hard-faced young men in Marine-digital camouflage.

And Abby.

Her daughter sat beside her in what had become Angela's mobile office of sorts—it was armored, at least, and Brinly and the squad of Marines he kept with him had become her impromptu protection detail. Every time that Angela found her eyes straying to Abby, she kept expecting to see that old, uncomfortable fear in her daughter.

But Abby looked at ease. Thoughtful, but not worried. She sat cross-legged in one of the jump seats, with a tattered paperback forgotten in her lap.

She's getting used to this, Angela thought. But it brought her no relief. Looking at how comfortable her eleven-year-old daughter sat in this Spartan, military environment, Angela realized that she didn't *want* Abby to get used to this. She wanted Abby to be…normal.

Was this the best life that Angela could provide for her daughter? Was this a new normal for her? Had she adapted to being a part of a war machine, rather than simply being an eleven year old girl and thinking about the things that eleven year old girls should think about?

And what was she thinking about right now, behind those placid blue eyes that looked so much like Angela's own?

That question was answered a moment later.

"Did he kill him?" Abby asked.

Angela blinked a few times. "I'm sorry, Honey. What?"

Abby looked at her as though she were being dense. "Lee. Did he kill that man?"

Heat crept up the back of Angela's neck. She glanced to the seat directly across from her. Brinly sat there, his hands clasped in his lap, looking relaxed, though his eyes shown sharply back at Angela. Wondering how she was going to answer that.

"Uh..." Angela shifted in her seat to face Abby a little more. "What makes you ask a question like that?"

Abby sniffed and looked away from her mother. She looked at Brinly instead. "He should."

Angela's mouth worked, but she couldn't come up with the right, motherly thing to say. All that came to her head in that moment was the cold, implacable truth of their reality. All that came to her was the thoughts of the woman she'd become. Hard. Pragmatic. Utilitarian. Focused.

Not at all what she wanted for her daughter.

Since Abby seemed to be directing this statement right at Brinly, the gray-haired Marine leaned forward onto his elbows and lifted his salt-and-pepper eyebrows. "And why is that, Abby?"

Abby swayed in her seat as the vehicle trundled across a rough patch of roadway. Her demeanor remained cool. Even-keeled. "Corporal Ryan was insubordinate. Lee gave him a chance. He put him under Sam's command when we got here, but Ryan wouldn't listen to Sam. That's insubordinate. Right?"

Brinly glanced at Angela, as though to question if he were overstepping his boundaries, but Angela was too shell-shocked—and maybe too curious—to stop him.

Back to Abby, Brinly nodded. "Yes. That's insubordinate."

"Well." Abby seemed pleased to come to a logical conclusion. "What else are you supposed to do with insubordinate people? You can't just let them get away with it. What if Corporal Ryan didn't follow orders when they were *important*? Like, in the middle of a fight? Then he might get people killed. We don't have a jail to put him in. If we just left him behind, that's the same as killing him, or worse, he might go to the other side and tell them things about us." Abby shrugged. "So what else was Lee supposed to do with Corporal Ryan except kill him?"

Brinly and Angela just stared at the girl, with her innocent blonde curls, and her not-so-innocent eyes. Brinly's expression was carefully devoid of emotion. Angela's was beginning to twist with something like ill-concealed horror.

Horror? Really?

That her daughter might see things as they are? Is the truth horrible? Or is it just the truth?

Competing emotions rammed into each other in Angela's head. She couldn't deny a sort of closeted pride—that her daughter would be so adaptable, that her daughter would so quickly learn to be strong in the face of these hardships, so quickly learn what had taken Angela years to come to terms with.

But also sadness. At the death of innocence. Guilt. Because no matter what Angela did, she couldn't protect Abby from the realities around them. Abby was a part of this world now. She was that unique generation that was coming of age outside of civility. Her memories of the world that had come before were hazy at best, and likely colored by everything she now knew about people. Things that she shouldn't have had to confront at such a young age.

That they were all animals. That civility was just a façade, always maintained through force, or the threat of force. That violence was the only currency that human beings would ever truly deal in.

Abby raised the paperback again and leafed to a dog-eared page. "Well, if Lee didn't kill him, then he should have."

A new emotion came to Angela then. Anger. At Abby. For how nonchalantly she said it.

Angela snatched the book out of Abby's hands. Abby jerked, surprised, then looked at her mother with a frown.

"Taking another human being's life is nothing to be so casual about." Angela's voice strained as she spoke. "You can't just sit here with your nose in a book and pronounce death sentences like it doesn't matter. You're not the one that has to take another person's life. You should take it more seriously."

Abby's eyes flared to match her mother's anger, but then she did something different.

Something that no normal eleven year old girl would do. Rather than react out of emotion, Abby straightened her back, took a breath, and when she breathed it out, her eyes cooled.

"Do you want me to cry about it, Mom?"

The paperback trembled in Angela's grip. She had the urge to suddenly slap Abby across the face—to slap that cold, calm look right out of her. The pages of the book crinkled as Angela's grip tightened on it.

"I don't *want* Corporal Ryan to die," Abby said softly in the face of her mother's ire. "I don't want anybody to die. But if it has to happen, then why be sad about it?"

Brinly cleared his throat, breaking into Angela's half-cocked response. "We all have our ways of coping with it, Abby. But your mother's right. It has to be taken seriously."

Abby nodded, not taking her eyes from Angela. "Was I wrong?"

Angela pressed her lips together. Was her daughter wrong? No. And Brinly was right as well. Everyone had their ways of coping with these things. Was this the best way to cope, though? Did Angela have any motherly wisdom she could impart in that moment?

She only said everything you already know. You can't even add to it.

No. Angela had nothing else to give her.

She pressed the book back into her daughter's hands. "Read your book."

Abby looked briefly disappointed, as though perhaps she wished her mother *did* have something else to give her. Some guidance. Something. She opened the book back up, straightened the pages

Angela had wrinkled, then found her place again, and began reading with a disconcerted frown.

Angela sucked in air and plastered her spine to the back of the seat, her hands gripping her thighs. "Major Brinly. How long to the rendezvous point?"

"Not long," Brinly answered, crossing one boot onto his knee. "Thirty or forty-five minutes out."

"When's the last time you heard from your scout elements?"

"Earlier this morning. All's still quiet at Triprock. Initial estimates have been confirmed. Looking at about a hundred civilians, give or take. Maybe a dozen Cornerstone, still holed up there." Brinly wiggled his boot. "That's less than Lee estimated when he was there a month ago. They must've pulled most of them back to Greeley, but left a small garrison."

Gradually, Angela's grip on her thighs relaxed. "What's the living situation like for them?"

"For the civilians? Unclear. The only folks my scouts have seen with weapons are the Cornerstone guys. Lee says that he and Abe armed the populace with a mish-mash of weapons, but whoever came in and subdued the settlement must've taken them. They might be locked up on site, or maybe taken back to Greeley. We don't know yet."

"I mean…" Angela began, trying to find a way to put it that would be acceptable to eleven-year-old ears, but then wondered if that was even necessary? And if Abby was going to be in this mobile office for the foreseeable future, then she was going to have to get used to hearing these things.

She's already used to it. That's the problem.

Brinly helped her out: “Has there been any instances of violence towards the civilians?”

“Yes.”

A shrug. “Not that we’ve seen so far. But then, my scouts have only had eyes on for twenty-four hours now.”

“What happened to the cartel that Lee reported seeing there?”

“Unknown at this time. Possible that they were disarmed too and are now in amongst the civilians. More likely, they beat feet when Lee took out Mateo Ibarra.”

Angela grimaced. “You know what Abe said when he got back from Mexico. That cartel’s not dead yet. They’re just biding their time across the border. How long before they start making problems again?”

Brinly gave her a weary smile. “One thing at a time, Madam President. One thing at a time.”

Angela grit her teeth and nodded. “Right.”

Greeley.

But before Greeley, there was every settlement along the way. Before they could accomplish their mission, there would have to be a grassroots movement from the people, a call to arms, and a willingness to join the fight.

And before there was any of that, there was Triprock.

One thing at a time.

FOUR

THE TANK

EVERY STEP THAT SAM TOOK, he expected to hear a shout behind him, and turn to find the guards at the checkpoint pursuing them, having just realized who it was that they'd let past their gates.

It didn't happen.

Which was only a partial relief to Sam.

As they neared The Tank, the smells coming from it intensified. Small gusts of wind carried alternate scents of burning wood, burning rubber, and shit. The people were visible, stacked on the shady sides of buildings, like the moss that grows on the north side of trees.

They watched the group of six walking towards them, and their looks were apathetic at best, and downright hostile at worst. Another six people to compete with. For food and water. For lodging. And for a spot in Greeley.

And that was the thing that kept Sam's mind working overtime. Not where they would sleep, or what they would eat, but how in the hell they were going to get out of this shit hole, and into Greeley.

Because Sam couldn't do a whole hell of a lot for his mission if he was stuck in The Tank. He needed intel on Greeley. And that meant seeing the troops, seeing their movements, and seeing the layout of the buildings. Where were the hard points? Where were the civilian sectors? Where were the soft entry points that could be taken advantage of?

Sam had told Lee that he was up to the task. But how was he going to accomplish it if he and his crew were stuck here? And for how long?

"Heads up," Pickell said from Sam's left side. He nodded his head a little to the left of the main street that they were taking into the small town.

There, in the middle of another street, Sam recognized the group that had gone before them. Two men and two women. Now surrounded by several others.

The newcomer's packs were on the ground, their hands in the air, and the men that had them surrounded were rifling through their belongings.

"Fan-fucking-tastic," Jones commented. "So, not only are we stuck in limbo, but we gotta deal with roving street gangs trying to steal our lunch money? Fine. I'll get down on that shit. Jackass back there got me all hot and bothered anyways."

"Just be cool," Sam reiterated. "They're distracted with someone else. Let's just saunter on through."

"Right. Yeah. Saunter. I can saunter."

Sam's elbow pinched down on the fixed blade on his right hip. They all had one. The only weapons the guards had allowed them to keep. "Anyone ever been in a knife fight?"

Silence answered him.

Sam nodded. "Yeah, me neither."

"I mean," Jones said. "They taught us some shit in basic, but that was fucking ten years ago. I've never used it."

"It's fine," Sam said, as they passed the corner of the first set of buildings, and passed out of view of the potential hard-cases. "They didn't see us. Next question: Where do we find a place to shack up?"

"My bet?" Marie spoke up. "One of the back corners, away from this main street. When Greeley's looking for people, they'll probably just come straight in here. I'd guess the closer you get to the main street the more prime the real estate is considered around here."

"Well, if being close to the main street increases your chances of getting into Greeley, isn't that where we want to be?"

"Sure. But something tells me ain't nobody gonna give up their spot for us. And we probably don't want to be starting fights. Bad way to get on the radar."

Frenchie shouldered into the midst of Sam and Marie. "We could post a lookout up here while the rest of us stay back. Holler when we see someone from Greeley coming."

Sam made a face. "As friendly as everyone looks in this place, I don't really want to split us up. Besides," he sighed. "Back corner might give us a view of Greeley. A decent view might be the best we can hope for at this point."

"Egg-fucking-scuse me," a voice cut in from the left.

Sam didn't immediately stop walking, hoping this was not directed at him. But a glance into the alley they were passing revealed the same band of idiots that had surrounded the other group of newcomers, striding out into the middle of the street to block their way.

Sam stopped. His eyes ranged over them, taking a rapid headcount.

There were seven of them. Three, small and skinny and young. Four older. Two of the older ones looked burly enough to cause problems. The biggest and burliest of them wore a snaggle-toothed grin beneath a shaved head, and Sam could only assume he'd been the one that had spoken.

Jones groaned and murmured, "You gotta be kidding me."

Sam's pulse thumped through his neck, his insides feeling tight. After counting heads, his eyes dropped to hands. A few hefty-looking pipes. Even a guy with what looked like a table leg. And yes, three of them had knives. Pretty decent ones that looked perfectly capable of splitting a man open, stem to stern.

The main guy had one of the knives. What looked like a cheap rendition of a Bowie knife, the wooden handle broken and replaced with layers of ancient and weathered duct tape. The man used this to point at Sam, and then at the ground.

"Packs on the ground, right now," he said. "Did you think we wouldn't notice you sneaking in?"

Thud-thud-thud went Sam's pulse, as his sight drew to a pinpoint. He forced his eyes to keep moving to stave off the tunnel vision.

Never again, remember? You can never be scared again.

"Well, guys," Sam said, his voice overly loud in his ears. He turned partially to look at his crew, plastering on a smile. "We got this far. Sucks that we came all this way just for this shit." He shucked off his backpack, dropped it at his feet, then turned back to the gang leader.

The man rolled his eyes. "Cry me a fucking river. Everyone pays to enter. Don't worry, we won't take everything."

Sam waved his left hand. "Go ahead, guys. Drop your packs."

"Ryder..." Jones whispered.

"No," Sam snapped, heat rising in his chest. He stoked the anger that would burn away the fear. "Go ahead. Drop your fucking packs." He thrust a hand at the bald man. "This motherfucker right here wants to take what you have. So go ahead. Drop 'em."

Sam stared at the man across from him, and instead of thinking of that big Bowie knife and what it might do to him, he pictured something else. He pictured ramming his own knife straight up through that man's chin. Straight up through the roof of his mouth, and right into his brain.

The man across from him blinked, as though he were seeing something he hadn't entirely expected. He still smiled, but a shadow passed over it.

Sam was seething now. He saw that little bit of weakness, and it bolstered him. Made him want to hurt the man even more. The fear wasn't entirely forgotten, but he was just so damned pissed that all that was left in his head was murder.

It was a quick transition, and Sam found a small voice in the back of his head reminding him, *keep control of yourself.* But he didn't know if he was going to.

The sound of five more packs hitting the ground.

The man across from him smiled, and seemed to relax. "Good."

"Yeah, it is good," Sam grunted. "Good that we don't have our packs weighing us down anymore. That'll make us lighter on our feet." Sam's right hand slipped under his sweaty, filthy shirt, and snatched out the fixed blade from his belt. He held it underhanded, as he'd been taught, instead of thrust out in front like the amateur across from him.

Sam stepped over his pack. Planted his feet.

His crew did the same.

The smile on the man's face turned brittle.

Sam lowered his stance. "You know what they say about knife fighting, Big Fuck? Winners bleed, and losers gush." He pointed to his pack. "I'm willing to gush for that bag. Are you?"

The man's smile was gone now. His posture tensed. "Listen to the mouth on this wetback."

Wetback? Sam almost laughed. But he wouldn't. He couldn't. If this guy wanted to peel back Sam's layers and see how deep the darkness went, then fuck it, let him. He felt like he was on a waterslide, plummeting downwards, and he didn't dare try to stop it now. If he tried to pull back, the fear might return.

All that was left in Sam was crazy.

His eyes widened. His mouth opened, baring his teeth. "I do got a big mouth. I really do. And it's hungry. I'm fucking starving. Let's do this, Big Fuck. Just you and me. Winner bleeds. Loser gushes. And whoever lives gets to eat the other one. That sound good to you, Big Fuck?" Sam's eyes shot down to the man's legs. "You got some nice shanks on you, Big Fuck. Me, I'm a little stringy. But a meal's a meal, right?" He took a step forward, feeling genuinely, insanely…starving. "And we're all so hungry, aren't we? Everyone's…just…so hungry."

Sam locked eyes with the man again, and what he pictured then was nothing human, and nothing that he would ever care to remember after that point in time.

A tremor passed over the man's face.

Do it, Sam willed the man. *I want you to do it.*

The man forced a smile. "You're as crazy as a shithouse rat." He straightened. The point of his blade dipped. "You know, boys, we could use a crazy motherfucker like this."

"No," Sam said, his voice almost a whisper. "No, we're not going to be friends, Big Fuck. You're gonna fucking fight me and feed me, or you're going to get the fuck out of my way. Those are the only two options here." Sam turned his wild eyes on the others. "And anyone else that wants to join in. Go ahead. Let's make it a goddamned feast."

Big Fuck clenched his jaw and glared. "You think I've never met someone like you?"

"I think you've never met me."

Big Fuck didn't move. Didn't speak. He just stared. And all across his meaty face, there was hesitation. And every man that stood with him saw it, sensed it, and drew back.

Sam straightened. Sneered. "If you were gonna jump, you'da already done it." He sheathed his knife and turned away from the man, his whole body crackling like an electrical fire. He didn't meet the gaze of any of his teammates—didn't dare let them bring his mind back to reality in that moment. He saw them out of the corner of his eyes, though, still with their knives out, standing over their packs.

Sam stooped and snatched up his pack. Threw it over his shoulders. Turned back forward.

He was almost surprised that the man was still standing there. Still vapor-locked with indecision.

Sam's throat was dry and hoarse. His heart and lungs felt like he'd just sprinted a mile. He felt a little sick, but bore down on the center of himself, pulling up every ounce of hatred and anger and insanity—all the things that curdled down in the low parts of everyone that had been through what he'd been through. Most of the time you never let it see the light of day. But this time he had.

"Come on," Sam growled over his shoulder. "We need to find a place to shack up."

Sam started walking forward.

The man with the Bowie knife took one stutter-step backwards, and then remembered himself and planted his feet. He tried that same smile again, but it had lost its wolfishness.

Every dog thinks they're a wolf until they meet something that kills for its survival.

"You ain't gonna have your friends around you all the time," the man said as Sam drew abreast of him. "Watch yourself, wetback."

Sam stopped, his shoulder just out of arm's reach of the man's knife. He stared him straight in the face, and he spoke from a place that he found was utterly and completely honest. "If you every try to jump me, it'll be the greatest goddamned day in my life."

Then Sam and his crew walked on, and the man and his crew stood back and watched them go.

They stayed on that main drag through the center of The Tank, all the while Sam feeling the eyes of the man burning into his back. The fear was a dim thing now, but his body had still geared up for a fight, and that blast of adrenaline had no outlet but to tremble through his knees as he walked, and course through his hands that he kept tight on the straps of the pack he'd been willing to kill and die for.

He would've fought for the pack. It contained the thing that he needed in order to accomplish his mission. Without the contents of his pack, the mission was dead.

After a walking in a haze of silence, straight down the road—Sam didn't want to take a turn too soon and look like they were trying to get away—he guided his crew to the left and down one of the side streets, aiming for the northwestern corner of The Tank.

A hand on his shoulder made him jerk.

He looked to his right and found Marie's sharp gaze fixed on him. "You alright?"

He smiled. "Oh, yes. I'm fine."

"Jesus, man," Jones uttered, now that they were clearly out of earshot. "Where'd all that shit come from, you crazy bastard?"

Sam shook his head and looked at Jones, trying his best to appear normal again. "Just running off at the mouth, Jones. I learned it from you."

But was that really true?

Jones gave him a weirdly perceptive gaze, like just for a flash, he could see inside of Sam. But he covered it up with a smile of his own. "I dunno if you learned that from me."

Off of the main drag, it became apparent that The Tank was not as crammed full of humanity as Sam had originally thought. The scores of disconsolate people thinned, and then disappeared. The structures around them stood in relatively good shape, compared to a lot of towns Sam had been in out east. Windows were still intact. Doors had been kicked in, probably during clearing operations some time back, but other than that most everything looked eerily "normal."

And by "normal," Sam supposed it was completely *abnormal*. Destruction and decay was the usual now. This was like some preserved diorama of a past society.

Sam guessed that any one of the buildings surrounding them now was empty, but he continued heading west and north, zig-zagging up the grid of streets. If he couldn't be right there on the main drag, he'd at least be able to see Greeley. So when they reached the edges of the town called La Salle, Sam chose a building that seemed to provide a good view straight across to the southern edge of Greeley.

A small sign on the front of the building declared it to be "Valley Packing and Catering." It had a fence around the outside of it, though the gate hung open. It struck him as a decent place to set up camp.

Looking out towards Greeley, he could see squat guard towers. They were all repurposed deer stands, he noted. The kind that stood about twenty feet off the ground, with a black polymer box seated on top, and windows all around.

The closest one to him was about three hundred yards out, sitting in the middle of another road. He could just make out the shadowy shapes of heads through the windows. Machine gun nests, ready to take out any poor bastards that might try to sneak their way into Greeley.

About a hundred yards from Sam, he could see old road constructions signs that had been painted over so that they no longer said things like ROAD WORK AHEAD or MEN WORKING. They were spaced at even intervals, and they all said, DANGER: DO NOT PASS THIS POINT.

Sam returned his attention to Valley Packing and Catering. "Seems as good a place as any, yeah?"

A resounding silence from his crew showed him a lack of objection, so they took to the structure, unsheathing their knives, and clearing it room by room, just to make sure that no one else had made their home here.

It was empty. Large. Most of the main structure was open, stainless steel tables and meat hooks and drains in the floor for processing meat and cleaning the blood off the floors. An image flashed through Sam's head of the man with the Bowie knife, hanging from one of those meat hooks, skinned and quartered…

In the northwestern corner of the building, they found a large office with a window that faced Greeley. The view barely cleared the fence that surrounded the meat processing plant, but Sam could at least finally put his eyes on the place that had, in his mind, become a mythical goal.

Greeley. Home of President Briggs. The place that had spat out Cornerstone operatives and erstwhile soldiers, and sent them after the United Eastern States to destroy everything that meant anything to Sam.

He stood at the window, his hands on the sill, staring at it with a sense of deep and abiding hatred that had soured in his guts since his bloodied and battered squad had high-tailed it out of Butler.

I'm going to burn their fucking house down.

Sam breathed heavily of that feeling, tasting it, keeping it, harboring it. He would do whatever it took to make that happen. Nothing was beyond him at this point. No task too big. Or too gristly.

He turned away from the window and looked at his team. "Well, we made it past the first hurdle, I guess. We're here. And we haven't been caught. I'll take that as a victory." He shucked his pack off and nodded to Frenchie and Johnson. "You two, get on watch. This place is ours now. No one gets close without me knowing about it."

Frenchie and Johnson nodded, then dropped their packs and headed out of the office.

Sam hefted his pack onto the cheap, Formica-topped desk that dominated the center of the office. As he unzipped the main compartment, he eyed Pickell.

"How you feeling, Kosher Dill?"

Pickell chose a rolling office chair to collapse into, setting his own pack between his feet. "If I'm being honest, Sarge…I feel a little pukey."

"I know we've got some privacy, but get out of the habit of calling me 'Sarge.'"

"Right." Pickell nodded. "Sam."

"You take your antibiotics?"

"I'll take 'em now."

"Stay on that shit. Still gotta clean your system out. Make sure you're eating and drinking." Sam stopped with his hands in his pack and regarded Pickell with a sudden welling of appreciation. "Can't believe you came with us, man."

Pickell pulled a half-empty liter of water from his pack and uncapped it with a lopsided grin. "Little thing like a gutshot can't stop me. Not gonna let you guys have all the fun." He took a sip of water and then grew serious. "Gotta do this. For Billings and Chris."

Sam nodded, feeling a familiar twist inside of him. Then he refocused himself on the pack and drew out the jumble of electronics that was tangled inside. Most of it was bullshit. Wires and random parts. Camouflage.

He separated out the useless components from the items that he actually needed. He'd done his best to dismantle the satphone to the point that it was unrecognizable. He arranged the parts on the desk—the body, the disconnected antenna, the sensitive silicon board and wires, the keypad, the battery.

"Alright," Sam breathed, staring at it all. "Now we just gotta hope that I can put this shit back together again."

FIVE

GEORGIA

IT SEEMED TO CAPTAIN PERRY GRIFFIN that Mr. Smith had come down with something.

The virus was failure, and it had led to Mr. Smith obsessing over the lines of dead bodies, sometimes inspecting a tall man's corpse for lengthy periods, as though if he wanted it bad enough, it might suddenly morph into Lee Harden.

The sickness had incubated in Mr. Smith over the course of the last week and a half as they'd finished their cleanup of Butler, and now he was downright green with it. There were no more bodies to obsess over and stare into their fly-ridden eyes. They'd all been hauled out and dumped about five miles south of Butler.

And now it was official: Mr. Smith hadn't managed to kill Lee Harden.

Interestingly enough, Griffin found himself positively sunny whenever he encountered Mr. Smith's downtrodden demeanor. A good portion of that was just that he didn't like Mr. Smith. Okay, that wasn't quite true—he fucking hated that bastard, and he sometimes wondered if he'd take the time to waste a tourniquet if he found the man bleeding out. Which is something he imagined, probably more than was healthy.

He might. Out of a sense of duty. Carry on with the mission, and all that. But he wouldn't like it.

But there was another part to Griffin's enjoyment of Mr. Smith's failure. And every time it occurred to him, he shoved it away. Wouldn't give it the time of day. Refused to admit that it was an actual thought that had come from his own brain.

Are you glad that Lee survived?

Standing in the gymnasium of the local high school, watching Mr. Smith out of the corner of his eye, Griffin again pushed the thought away. It was more complicated than that. It had to be. Because Griffin knew that if it came down to it, and Lee Harden was standing in front of him right then, he'd punch a hole right through the bridge of Lee's nose and be done with it.

He didn't view it as his job, or his calling, to kill Lee. His purpose was broader than that. It was to dismantle a machine that threatened to destroy his country. Lee was not that machine, but he was a part of it, and so Griffin would have no qualms in taking him out if the opportunity presented itself.

For Mr. Smith, it was a very different story. And President Briggs was currently making that very obvious to him. Griffin didn't know what was said over that satphone, but Mr. Smith's face went from green to white, so he could imagine.

"Yes, Mr. President," Mr. Smith said, with a deadness in his tone like the soul had been choked out of him. "We have everything in place. We'll be ready to continue our pursuit…Yes, sir. I understand, sir." Then Mr. Smith blinked, glanced sideways at the phone against his ear, and then took it away. President Briggs must have hung up on him.

Mr. Smith folded the antenna back against the phone. Straightened. Managed to summon some hardness back into his face. He placed the satphone on the bullet-chewed table that now held all of their command and control technology. He seemed to avoid Griffin's gaze, instead looking at Colonel Freeman, who stood with his arms crossed a few paces away.

"I take it the president isn't overly pleased that you didn't bag Harden," Freeman noted.

Mr. Smith's eyes narrowed. "*We* didn't bag Harden."

Freeman smiled without humor. "Sure."

"The president is putting control of the entire southeast under your command, Colonel Freeman," Mr. Smith relayed, his voice simmering with a whole soup of negative emotions. Mostly, though, it seemed like he was trying to reestablish control.

"I'm honored that he would think of me," Freeman said. "Should I continue to go through you, Mr. Smith? Or would he prefer if I contacted Greeley directly?"

A little venom rose to Mr. Smith's eyes. "I think he'd prefer that you just do your fucking job and not make a nuisance of yourself."

Freeman was unperturbed. He seemed, over the course of the last ten days, to have grown accustomed to Mr. Smith's mood swings, and had recognized what Griffin already knew: Mr. Smith was on the outs with Briggs, and really didn't have any power over them, despite what he'd like them to believe.

Mr. Smith finally steeled himself and turned his gaze to Griffin. "Captain, you're going to ready your troops for departure. We leave today."

"We aren't leaving a garrison behind?" Griffin asked, more out of professional diligence.

"We're leaving Colonel Freeman and his troops. That'll be enough."

"Roger that. Do we have a destination or are we just taking in the good ol' U-S-of-A?"

"Our orders are to push into Texas and reclaim the refinery there at all costs."

"At all costs," Griffin echoed. He hated stupid, nebulous terms like that.

Mr. Smith tilted his head. "Those were the president's words."

Griffin sighed. "And they may have been. But he didn't mean them. The troops we have with us are basically the only offensive force that Greeley has left. So, no, I don't give a fuck what the president said, we're not assaulting anything *at all costs.*"

Mr. Smith pointed to the satphone. "Would you like to call him?"

"No, I'd like to use my common sense. Someone around here has to."

Mr. Smith squared himself to Griffin, his jaw muscles bunching.

Griffin just raised an eyebrow. "And what about you, Mr. Smith? What's the president want you to do?"

Mr. Smith gave a snide smile. "Find and kill your friend."

Griffin checked his expression into neutrality. "Feels like you're implying something there."

"Don't be coy, captain," Mr. Smith growled and turned away. "You're obviously not disappointed that we didn't get Lee Harden. It makes me question your loyalties."

Griffin laughed at him. "Okay, then. Question away. I know where my loyalties lie. You want to get your panties all twisted up because I'm not sharing in your abject failure, go right ahead. I took down the United Eastern States. Now I'm going to head west and I'm going to route out the remnants. That's my job, and I'll do it well, just like I did this job well."

"Gentlemen," Colonel Freeman harrumphed. "That's probably enough of that. If you're going to mount an offensive together, you may want to bury whatever hatchets need to be buried."

Griffin held up his hands and took a step back. "No hatchets here, colonel." He gave Mr. Smith a nod, though the man was still not looking at him. "I'll ready the troops for departure."

***

Rogers had died in the night.

He'd fought like hell to stay alive, and Marlin and Wibberley had done everything they could for him, but it wasn't enough. Sepsis had taken him, making his last day on this earth a hell of fever and hallucinations and vomiting up the small amounts of water he was able to choke down.

He'd been the last surviving member of their two squads. Now it was just Marlin and Wibberley. They'd stuck with their man for ten days, huddled in an abandoned house a few miles outside of Butler, going out only at night, and only to get water from the poncho liner they'd left under the house's rain gutters.

They were both dehydrated. What little rain they'd been able to gather had mostly been given to Rogers. They kept just enough for themselves to stave off the worst effects. They hadn't eaten in a week. The emergency rations in their packs hadn't lasted long.

Marlin wasn't sweating, despite the heat of the day. Hunger came in waves, but most of the time, he didn't feel it. They were passed that point now. His stomach had given up crying out for food, and now the lack of calories had reduced itself to a sort of insane biological imperative, rather than an actual physical sensation.

He lay in the brush beside Wibberley, the two of them peering through a thicket of green leaves, to the gray pickup and the two Cornerstone operatives that stood outside of it, their quiet conversation drifting through the woods.

How far were they from Butler now? They couldn't have been too far. This was one of the outpost sentries that the Greeley invasion force had posted on the routes into Butler. Maybe a mile or two out from the town itself.

Marlin blinked away a wave of faintness that presented as a prickle of heat across his scalp, and a fluctuation in his vision—one moment, everything would get dark, and then the next it would be stark and over-bright. His heart hadn't stopped pounding all morning. His blood felt like used motor oil in his veins.

He clutched his rifle and slowly turned his head to the left, where Wibberley lay. They made eye contact with each other, but didn't speak. The time for talking was done. There was nothing more to say. Only action.

Their retreat from the fighting outside of Butler ten days ago had taken nearly every bullet they had. And every friend. Between the two of them, they had a grand total of fifteen rounds. Eight in Marlin's rifle. Seven in Wibberley's.

Wibberley gave Marlin a nod, and the two very slowly adjusted themselves and their rifles, easing the muzzles through the brush and pushing the leaves out of the way when they blocked their optics. They settled into their rifles. Marlin eased the lever on his ElCan forward, magnifying his sight picture to 4x. Wibberley did the same.

Marlin was on the left, so he took the sentry that was on the left, putting the crosshairs right on the back of the operative's skull.

Two or three miles from Butler. Close enough that the rifle reports would probably be heard. They were both aware of this. But there wasn't another option. They needed that pickup truck. They sure as shit weren't going to walk to Texas.

God, I hope they have food, Marlin thought, and it didn't even cross his mind that it might be inhuman of him to only think about food, and not the man he was about to kill to get it. Humanity was not a worthwhile consideration. This was survival.

"Ready," Wibberley whispered, just the barest susurration.

Marlin put his finger on the trigger. Tightened it until he felt the wall, past which the trigger would break and the round would fly.

He whispered back, slow and steady: "Fire. Fire. Fire."

Two rounds, perfectly synchronized into a single rifle report.

The bodies dropped.

Marlin wasted no time. He thrashed to his feet, muscles already cramping. His unwieldy legs nearly tripped as he tried to drag them through the brush and into a run. Rifle up. Shoulders burning.

They stamped out onto the roadway, pivoting around the driver's side of the truck, where the two bodies lay, fallen on top of each other and slumped against the front tire.

Marlin slapped his ElCan back to 1x, then flashed the reticle across the bodies on the pavement. Dead eyes stared at nothing. Blood fountained from their noses. "Targets down," Marlin said, immediately switching his focus to the truck. The windows were open. Marlin sidestepped, his respiration high despite the minimal effort. God, but his body was taking a shit on him.

"Clear," Wibberley said, after strafing by the open windows and checking the seats and floorboards. He moved to the bodies and began stripping them of anything useful.

Marlin lowered his rifle and checked the bed. It contained the most valuable thing they could have hoped for—and the primary reason why they'd chosen to strike these particular sentries. A large auxiliary tank, the type that looks like a truckbed toolbox, but has a gas pump sticking out of the top.

Marlin hoisted himself briefly up onto the bed, snatching a glimpse of the auxiliary tank's fuel guage. It was three quarters full. Probably in the neighborhood of sixty or seventy gallons?

For the first time in ten days, Marlin felt a tiny burst of triumph in his chest.

This was a big win for them.

In the back seat of the crew cab he found two go-packs. Marlin's mouth watered, thinking they would probably contain water and food. And yeah, maybe some extra ammunition. But mainly he thought about the water and food.

"Keys in the ignition," Marlin noted.

"Roger that. Crank her up."

Marlin slid into the driver's seat and cranked the engine. It rumbled to life with blessed ease. A half a tank of gas. Plus the auxiliary tank. It still might not be enough to get them where they wanted to go, but it was better than they could have hoped for.

Wibberly chucked two pilfered rifles and two pistols into the backseat. Then he returned and snatched one of the operative's radios from the pouch on his armor, disconnected the earpiece and stood straight, listening.

Silence. For a moment.

Then: "Sentry Five, this is command. Come back."

Wibberley traded a glance with Marlin, then brought the radio up to his mouth and keyed it. "This is Sentry Five," Wibberley said, in a decent approximation of an American accent. "Go ahead, command."

"Reports of gunshots in your area. Please advise."

"Yeah, we heard them," Wibberley said. "Sounded like they were coming from east of us."

A new voice broke in: "Command, command, *this* is Sentry Five. I don't know who the fuck that was on the radio."

Wibberley grimaced, then pocketed the radio, his voice going back to his natural accent "Guess we need to get the hell out of here."

Marlin helped him strip the armor from the bodies, piled them into the backseat with the guns, and then he and Wibberley jumped in and slammed the doors. The radio was squawking from Wibberley's pocket: "All units, switch to emergency subchannel. Comms have been compromised."

Marlin cranked the wheel to the left, then stomped on the gas. The pickup truck lurched forward and sped down the road, heading west.

***

The intersection with the two dead bodies in it remained quiet for a long moment after the last growl of the pickup's engine faded in the distance.

The birds that had been silenced by the crash of the gunshots gradually got their gumption up again and started to chirp.

And then they fell silent again.

All except a lone blue jay that squawked indignantly at something moving beneath its nest.

Shapes emerged from the edges of the trees, all along the northeastern corner of the intersection. Tanned skin of different shades. Eyes staring out intensely at the two bodies.

The Alpha waited there at the treeline, feeling its mouth filling with saliva. A rope of it began to trickle from its lower jaw as it panted quietly in the warm stillness. The Alpha was hungry. Its body needed more than the last few weeks had given it, but they had only hunted a few times. Mostly they had travelled. Fast, and hard, and for many hours.

Sleeping in the heat of the day, and the rest of the time spent moving. Ceaselessly moving.

It needed to feed. And yet it held itself back.

Some part of it that was beyond the baseline, predatory cleverness of its mind, had been hardwired by what had happened in the place where all the other alphas and their packs had congregated. The place where he had experienced The Glow, and encountered The Strange Ones.

It still did not know what The Strange Ones were. They were not like The Alpha, or even The Omegas. But they were also not like the Easy Prey. They straddled both existences. They *knew* things.

The Alpha feared them in a deep part of its brain. Because they made no sense to it. But in that fear, there was an imperative. Obedience. Somehow, someway, a part of The Alpha's instinct that could not be ignored told it to follow The Strange Ones, just as a bird knows where to fly to migrate, and a fish knows where to swim to spawn. It simply *is*.

And so The Alpha and his pack, and the other packs that had combined with his, followed The Strange Ones, and they heard the noises that they made in the darkness when they were surrounded by The Omegas—noises like the Easy Prey—and The Omegas would tell The Alpha, and all the other alphas, what to do.

And they'd been told to wait. Even as they watched two Easy Prey kill two others, and then flee in their fast-moving shell. The Alpha, cognizant enough to know that four Easy Prey would feed them more than just two, still held back. Because The Omegas had not given them permission to feed, or to hunt, not yet. And The Omegas *must be obeyed*, because The Strange Ones knew things, and told them to The Omegas.

The scent of blood tinged the air, and The Alpha's jaw began to open and close, tasting it on the sides of its tongue. Sharp. Demanding. Hungry.

A small hoot came from behind The Alpha.

And then The Alpha knew that it would feed. It had been told so. And it was grateful.

The alphas fed, while the others watched and waited, and when their bellies were full, they retreated from the bodies, and the others picked them clean. Not enough to go around. But they did not fight over what was left.

There would be more. There would be so many more.

They only needed to obey The Strange Ones.

They knew things.

SIX

LOGISTICS

468 MEN, WOMEN AND CHILDREN.

356 of which were organized into armed squads. 112 of which served as support.

45 repurposed civilian vehicles. 18 guntrucks—ten Humvees, eight MATVs. Five MATVs with the assault configuration. Eleven tanker trucks, seven thousand gallons of fuel each. Pickup beds and Humvee fastbacks and SUV cargo areas stuffed with supplies. One flat-bed semi, on which they'd loaded the Blackhawk with its rotors folded—they had to keep the bird grounded, as they needed all the aviation fuel they had for the assault on Greeley.

It seemed like a lot, but Lee knew it was barely enough. 468 people were a lot of mouths to feed, and their meager food and water stores were already down to strict rationing.

Lee stared out the windshield of the Humvee as it pulled into the rear of the convoy. The train of vehicles snaked along the roughshod access road, disappearing into the trees beyond which the Project Hometown bunker lay.

Lee had been here before. It was the bunker that lay north of Caddo, Texas. The same one where they'd launched the assault on the power plant. The same one that he'd come back to and found Deuce waiting for him.

The driver craned his neck back and glanced at Lee. "Major, would you like us to try to skirt a little closer? So you don't have to..." he trailed off, glancing at Lee's bum leg.

Lee shook his head. "It's fine. Stiff after the drive. Need to warm it up."

In truth, the hike up the road to the bunker seemed exhausting. And he hated himself for that. What was a half-mile to him? A few weeks ago it would've been a light jog through the trees, no problem at all. Now it seemed like a journey.

And all those people. Those men and women with their weapons up, setting up a perimeter around their vehicles as they'd been taught, but occasionally glancing back at the Humvee that they knew contained Major Harden. He didn't want to walk amongst them.

Limp amongst them.

He grunted against his own misgivings, and thrust his hand into the cargo pocket of his pants, drawing out the eyepatch that he only wore for the sake of others. It served no purpose other than to allow people to focus on his good eye, rather than feeling squeamish about his raw, scarred socket and the dead eye that it still held.

He slipped it on over his head, positioning the patch over his ruined eye.

"Arr, matey," Abe intoned from beside him.

Lee managed a smirk, then pushed his door open and wrangled his way out. He did his best to not let his limp slow his stride. It was painful to push the pace, but he didn't want the others to see him lagging. He couldn't hide the limp, but he could at least appear strong.

Deuce followed at his side, and Abe met him around the front of the Humvee.

Lee strode along the ranks of civilians-turned-soldiers, making eye contact with each of them, sometimes giving them a nod, sometimes a pat on the shoulder, sometimes a word of encouragement. It seemed to bolster them.

Lee wasn't sure why. It didn't make much sense to him. But if he could provide that for them, then he would.

Angela waited halfway up the column of vehicles, flanked by Brinly and his Marine guard, and surrounded by a gaggle of the civilians that served in support roles. Liaisons. Logistics. Sure, they managed to be passionate about their jobs, but Lee couldn't help but think of them as The Complaint Department.

"Madam President," Lee nodded as he hitched his way up to them. "Major Brinly."

"Bunker area is secured," Brinly said. "They're waiting on you."

"Yup. I'm coming." Lee only paused for a brief moment to cast his gaze over the support staff around them, as though wondering what they were going to ask for today. Then he moved on, Angela at his side now. Abby was with her, stealing glances of intense interest at Lee.

He pretended not to notice.

"They're wondering about the showers," Angela said, in a tone that suggested she was only saying it out of a sense of responsibility.

"Not gonna happen," Lee said. "Any water in the bunker holding tanks needs to be harvested and stored for drinking. They'll have to deal with their ass-stink for a bit longer."

"Yeah, I figured," Angela sighed. "Just passing it along."

"You should've told them it was unrealistic."

"I did."

"Well, they should've listened to you."

"They did. But I said I'd ask. It makes them feel better."

"We never promised them comfort. I think we were quite clear about what they were going to get if they stuck around."

"I'm just trying to keep everybody happy and focused. And don't be so hard on them. They're support. It's their job."

Lee didn't say anything to that. He knew the support people were necessary. They were doing the best they could. But it was the fighters that he identified with. The people that were willing and able to pick up a gun and put their life on the line for the mission.

And what about you, Lee? He accused himself. *Can you pick up a gun and put your life on the line?*

He could. And he'd probably still be more effective than most. But it was a cold comfort to him. He couldn't do what he *used* to do. He had to be useful in other ways now.

Command. That was where he was needed. That was what he could provide.

"Anything new on Triprock?" Lee asked Brinly as he made his way into the clearing where the bunker sat.

"No change."

Lee thought about that settlement as he stopped at the bunker doors and keyed the code to get in. It hadn't been changed since Mr. Daniels from Cornerstone had gotten his hands in the system and forced Tex to remove the gamut of security protocols.

He thought of the Robledos in Triprock. Sally, who had helped Abe arm himself and start the fight against the cartel. Those memories were all in shades of red. Like recalling something you'd done under the influence of some mind-altering substance.

Rage. That had been what had altered Lee's mind. And everything in those bloody days was colored by it.

Was Lee any different now? The world felt different to him. But that was just experience. He'd changed and adapted, every new iteration of him slightly morphed from what it had been before. But deep down inside, he'd always been Lee. That rage was a part of him. It was then, and it was now.

What was it that it all came from? Different fruits that came from the same seed. Something that lay at the core of who he was as a person. Something he still couldn't quite pin down.

As the doors to the bunker and the elevator inside opened, Lee turned to Brinly again. "Not sure how much is left down there, but what there is, we're taking with us. Every bullet, every gallon of water, every pack of food, and every last bandage. We won't be coming back."

"We'll take care of it." Brinly turned and began to delegate a work crew while the others piled into the elevator.

It was cool inside. Air-conditioned. It came over Lee's body like a shock.

Abby turned and looked at herself in the reflective surface of the stainless steel walls. Lee watched her as the floor moved under their feet and they began to descend. Her eyes ranged over the enclosed environment and then caught Lee in the reflection.

"You've never been in one of these bunkers before," Lee said, almost like a flinch response to her eye contact. He couldn't think of anything better to say.

She turned away from his reflection to look at him directly. She didn't seem put off by his appearance. He wondered what she would think of him without his eyepatch.

"There are lots of them?" she asked.

"There are. But most of them are empty now."

She put her hands on her hips, and for a flash, looked like a miniature of her mother. "Will there be enough guns and ammo?"

Lee traded a wry smirk with Abe. "There's never enough guns and ammo."

"But enough to do what we're planning to do?"

Lee tilted his head. When had she become so forward with him? It seemed ass-backwards. This was the little girl that had been trapped on a rooftop, so many years ago, and watched Lee kill her infected father. She'd hated him for that. Probably still did. What got to Lee was that he'd looked *normal* then. His body had been bereft of the multitude of puckered scars that it now held. His face had been whole. He liked to imagine that there might've even been a bit of idealism still glowing in his eyes.

Now look at him.

And yet Abby chose now, when he was a grizzled, hateful wreck, to suddenly start talking to him?

Kids. They made no sense.

He cleared his throat. "Well. We hope so."

They reached the bottom and filed out. The long corridor with the branching rooms to either side lay ahead, just as Lee had remembered it. And bloodstains. Those were still there. Black and old now. The blood of enemies and friends.

He gauged Abby's reaction to this, but save for an nose-curl at a large splash of it right outside the elevator, she seemed not to care. She looked down the hall. "So all these rooms have stuff in them?"

"Some stuff. A lot of it's been used up." Lee moved around the gaggle of bodies. His purpose for being in the bunker was not for the supplies—Brinly's men would take care of that. He stopped at the first door on his right and went in.

The control room. Only slightly larger than a walk-in closet. The computer terminal and bunker controls to his right. Some shelves to his left. Those were what he needed.

He quested a hand along a rank of three ring binders with enigmatic alphanumerics on them. Found what he was looking for. Pulled it out and returned to the desk where the computer terminal sat. He opened the binder and leafed to the page he needed.

Satellite photos. The US Army had seen fit to store all these images in hard-copy in the operational area of each bunker. In the beginning, Lee had considered them useless clutter, but they were a godsend now.

"Alright," Lee said, stabbing a finger down on the page. "That's Triprock."

Abe and Angela took positions on either side of him and looked down at the image. Abby seemed to know when best to butt-out and took to rolling the single office chair around on the floor.

Lee pointed to three positions around the southern and eastern edge of the small settlement, which was little more than a cluster of tiny squares in the middle of the rolling Texas countryside. "These are where Brinly's recon elements are situated. We need to figure out how to get in and out cleanly. And that all depends on whether Sergeant Ryder gives us a call anytime soon."

"Still haven't heard from him?" Angela asked.

"No, not yet. But he's only been at Greely's doorstep since this morning. No idea what type of entry procedures they might have, or how long that might take."

Abe propped himself on his hands over the image. "Recon can't stay in the bush forever. They've already been on target for over twenty-four hours."

"I know. But if we rush into this, we run the risk of someone squeaking out the back and warning Greeley that we're on the move. And that is not something we can afford at this point."

"They're going to find out we're coming eventually."

"Sure. But not yet. I'd like to get us a whole helluva lot closer to Colorado before they know we're coming."

Angela nodded. "The second they hear we're on the move, they're gonna tighten security."

"And that'll make it harder for Sam to get inside." Lee straightened his back, hiding how he favored his hip. "We can't pretend to know what they know. But it's reasonable to believe that they're not expecting what we're doing. Last they saw of us we were hightailing it west. They'll assume we wanted to hole up in our refinery and turn it into a last-stand situation."

Abe shuffled his feet in a way that Lee, even without looking at him, could tell was agitated. "You know, Lee…"

Lee looked at the ceiling. "Christ, Abe. I know. If we'd've left a rear guard to fight them on their way to the refinery we'd have extended the subterfuge."

Abe raised his hands. "So you admit that my argument had merit."

"I already fucking admitted it." A sheepish glance at Abby. "But we can't afford it. And besides, that ship has already sailed, Abe. Now you're just being…" *an asshole.* "Argumentative."

Abe faced him. "Look. I want to see these bastards taken down just as much as you do, Lee. You don't have a monopoly on wanting to see this mission succeed. I'm allowed to have opinions about how that should be done. And you're going to hear them."

Angela raised a hand between them before it could get any hotter, which it was prone to do. Like two brothers that couldn't stop bickering, Lee and Abe rarely saw eye to eye on how to get from point A to point B. But they'd still die and kill for one another in a heartbeat. It went without saying.

"Abe, you're right. We're all allowed to voice our opinions. But at this juncture there's no point. We're doing *this*. Focus on what we're doing, not on what you think we should have done."

Abe made an ornery growling noise, but relented. "Alright, alright, alright. So there's two wrenches that could get thrown into our gears, and we don't know which is going to happen first. Either the force that kicked us out of Greeley is going to show up at the refinery and realize we're nowhere to be found, at which point they'll likely intuit what our objective is, or we bungle a takedown of Greeley-loyal forces and one of them gets a communication out to their command."

Lee nodded. "We can't do anything about the force from Butler. That's a timeline we can't control. But we *can* control bungled attempts to take out Greeley forces. Or at least mitigate their ability to communicate."

"Fine." Abe returned to leaning over the map with an irritable sigh. He used his finger to carve out a swath of land all along the west and north of Triprock. "We've got an ass-ton of people—relatively speaking. We can move them into position all along this open perimeter here. Anyone gets out of Triprock alive, they can dust them."

Lee crossed his arms over his chest. "Which is a valid option. But we still need to consider the possibility of comms. They might have radios capable of reaching another outpost and outing us, or, even worse, they might have a satphone."

"Which just means we'll have to take them down fast and quiet." Abe sniffed. "Luckily, it's what I've spent the last two weeks doing."

A deep pang of regret took Lee's stomach. He barely restrained a grimace. Part of it was that he hadn't been there with Abe. He hadn't been at his side, exacting the vengeance that he so badly wanted to bring down on the heads of the cartel that had held the refinery workers' families hostage.

But another, rawer part of him hated that he would not be there with Abe when the assault on Triprock began. He saw the entire thing in his mind's eye. Moving swiftly through the night, the blackness like a cloak, his prey unaware that he was coming, his body whole, and primed, and ready. The fluid movement of death, the sort of perfectly-orchestrated eradication that allowed Lee's mind to dip down into those cold, calm waters where he was doing what he was trained to do, what he was best at.

The vision dissipated. Flew apart into fragments that swirled around him like gnats, and then settled in the dull ache of his hip, and the stiffness of his arm, and the blackness that had now taken permanent residence over half of his vision.

Useless, a shadowy, sulking voice told him. *A husk. A shell of what you were.*

"Lee?" Abe's voice, gentle now, as though it sensed the carefully-hidden turmoil inside of Lee.

"Right," Lee nearly coughed out. "Yes. That's what we need to do. And I know you can do it. But bear with me being anal about this, Abe. I'd feel a whole helluva lot better if I knew Sam was already inside before we make our move. Like I said: Risk mitigation."

Abe scratched at his beard, then rubbed it smooth again. "Okay. I accept your valid point."

"Well, hallelujah."

"Hey, when you talk logic, I listen."

"I always talk logic."

Abe made a *not-so-sure-about-that* sound. "I'll get up topside with Menendez and Breck and get our crew ready for the assault. Move into position…" he pointed to the southeastern corner of Triprock. "Right over here, where those hills will hide us."

Lee nodded. "How you fixed on batteries for the NODs?"

Abe rocked a head back towards the bunker. "Should be some hiding in here somewhere. If not, we can probably make it happen with the juice we got."

"I need to get topside too," Lee noted. "This satphone ain't gonna get a signal down here. The second I get notification from Sam that his team's inside Greeley, I'll give you the greenlight."

Abe was already moving for the door. "We'll be ready."

SEVEN

THE LONG WATCH

"I THINK IT'S WORKING," Sam said, watching the little screen on the satphone light up as he held down the power button and then released. "At least…it's got power."

Jones inclined his head to Sam from across the room where he was perched near one of the windows. "You sure you didn't cross any wires?"

Sam glanced up. "I didn't *wire* any wires. I just pieced it back together."

Jones held up a hand. "I'm just saying. You try to call Major Harden, and all the sudden some Cornerstone asshole picks up."

Marie, seated on the rolling office chair, waved Jones off. "I don't think that's how it works, Jones. Just make the call, Sam."

Sam nodded, then looked over to Pickell. "Hey, run out and check with Frenchie and Johnson. Make sure we're all clear out here."

Pickell frowned, but departed to do as asked.

Sam glanced at Marie, then at Jones. "I just want to make sure that no one's eavesdropping."

"Can't be too careful," Marie allowed.

Jones shrugged. "Won't matter if you end up calling Greeley's anti-UES Task Force tip line."

Marie looked over her shoulder at him. "Do you always talk this much bullshit? Or is it just when you're nervous?"

"Pff. I'm not nervous. And yes, I always talk this much bullshit. It keeps me centered. Otherwise I get depressed."

Sam and Marie watched him for a moment.

"I'm serious," he insisted. "It's one of my things."

"Well." Marie settled back into the office chair. "By all means. Talk away, then."

Jones looked back out the window. "Nah. I'm done."

Pickell trotted back into the office. "They say the coast is clear."

"Alright." Sam looked at the phone. He almost didn't want to dial, because once he dialed and hit the call button, and it turned out that the satphone was irreparably fucked, then what was he going to do?

He dialed anyways.

***

Abe made his way up the south side of the hill.

The top of it was crowned with a smattering of mesquite and short, scrubby live oak saplings that huddled beneath the husk of their lightning-struck granddaddy. The dark, gnarled fingers of the leafless limbs looked like a skeletal hand, warning Abe to stop and go no further.

But Abe didn't believe in omens.

They'd left their vehicle—a small pickup with a small engine that wouldn't be too loud—out in the brush, south of them about five miles. They didn't want to drive it too close and risk the sound carrying to Triprock. So they'd hoofed it in, keeping a steady marching pace across the uneven terrain.

When Abe reached the dense thicket at the top of the hill, he slowed, then stopped just outside of its shade. The sun burned the back of his neck. Sweat trickled down his forehead and into his eyes. He put a fist up to halt the others, then blinked the sweat away and peered into the gloom beyond the brightly-lit frontage of the tree line.

He couldn't see much. The forest was thick and tangled. Lots of underbrush clogging up the works between bigger trunks.

He decided to ease forward a bit more. All of those leaves reflected the sunlight, dampening his view of the shadows beyond.

He and the team behind him had all donned suppressors for this op. But that didn't make your rifle silent. It just muffled it. The zip of the full-speed 5.56 mm rounds would still create little sonic cracks in the air, and those tended to carry a good ways. Likely all the way to Triprock, which was less than a mile past the top of this hill.

He really didn't want to shoot at anything that might be hiding in the brush.

But then again, he really didn't want to get chewed on either.

The primals—teepios, as they were called around here—were not like the ones on the east coast. Whatever the hell was going on with the east coast primals, whatever their evolution had taken them to, the ones out here in the plains states still maintained a small pack order. Most of the time around five. A tight-knit little family. Sometimes as big as ten.

And they liked to lounge in the shade during the heat of the day.

Abe keyed his squad comms and whispered into them: "Y'all hold back. I'm gonna scope out this thicket. Standby."

He moved forward, sinking into a crouch and ducking beneath the first exterior branches that made up that bright wall of green. Two steps in. He stopped. Sank to a knee. Rifle up. Scanning over the top of the optic, back and forth through the thicket.

Without the sun's reflection on the leaves, he could see a lot better, and the thicket wasn't as dense throughout as it was on the edges. He could see the very top of the hill, maybe thirty yards ahead. Everything that he could currently see was clear.

But that didn't mean much.

He keyed the radio again. "Alright. You're clear to come in. Single file, right where I entered."

He made himself relatively comfortable as he waited. His stomach growled noisily. His tongue was getting dry, but at least he was still sweating, so he wasn't dehydrated just yet. Once they could clear this thicket, they'd grab a bite or two and some water, then set up for the long wait.

The sounds of the stale grasses rustling. His team moving up on his position.

He kept his focus out, all along the horizon-line of the hill above him.

An electric jolt went through his thigh, causing his whole body to jerk.

Buzz. Buzz. Buzz.

Goddamned satphone.

That would be Lee. But Abe couldn't talk right now. First, clear the thicket. Then he could talk.

He left the satphone in his cargo pocket and eventually the vibrations stopped.

Eight bodies slid into the shade with him and took up positions, creating a sort of half-moon bristling with rifle barrels pointed out. Abe finally removed his eyes from their watch on the hilltop and looked first at Menendez to his right.

"You take your fire team right, along the edge of the woods." He looked left to Breckenridge. "You take your fire team left. I'll take mine straight up the middle. We'll meet up on the woodline on the far side, get eyes on Triprock, and set up our overwatch."

No one answered. They just started moving. Stealthily through the woods, their footfalls soft in the crinkling leaves.

Abe rose up to his feet, glanced back at the two soldiers behind him, and motioned forward with his support hand. They took the rise of the hill, and Breck and Menendez disappeared to the left and right.

At the top of the slope, Abe paused for a moment, looking down and checking everything that lay before him. It looked clear. No packs of primals lurking in the shade for a noonday nap. They proceeded down the hill on the north side and met up with the other two fire teams in the center.

"Alright," Abe rubbed the gathering sweat from his eyebrows. "Spread out. Take up positions. I want a rear guard on the top of that hill behind us as well. This thicket is our home for the next twelve hours. Once you're in position, grab a bite and some water. Stay hydrated. Stay comfortable. We got a long wait ahead of us."

The soldiers slunk silently to their positions, scattered throughout the woods. Breck and Menendez stayed with Abe. This was a well-worn plan of action. They'd done this a half-dozen times in Mexico. And the bodies they'd left behind gave them confidence in its efficacy.

Menendez bore a marksman's rifle with a magnified optic affixed. Abe nodded toward the treeline dead ahead of them. "Menendez, slip up in them bushes and get eyes on Triprock. I need to call Lee back."

"Roger 'at," Menendez murmured. His short-cropped black hair glistened with dew drops of perspiration. His helmet was strapped to his small assault pack, but he wouldn't need it until it was time to start the Midnight Boogie. He dove into his cargo pocket and unfolded a tattered boonie hat which he perched on his head and shoved the rumpled brim down so that it nearly covered his eyes. He slid down the hill, just a rustle in the leaves.

Breck parked his butt on the ground and fished out a handful of jerky made from a Texas antelope last week, wrapped in an old bit of printer paper from the refinery. He bit off a chunk and chewed, looking thoughtful.

"How long you think we'll have to wait here?" he asked around the mouthful.

Abe settled back, kicking his legs out in front of him and using his assault pack as a backrest. He pulled the satphone out as he shrugged. "No idea. Lee wants to wait until Sam's securely inside Greeley. Hopefully that's what he called me about.

But we won't move from here until at least past midnight, at the earliest."

Breck nodded as Abe punched in the key to redial Lee's call. "I'll work up a quick sleep-watch schedule."

"Thanks." Abe put the satphone to his ear and waited as it rang.

Lee answered on the second ring. "Lee here."

"Sorry, Buddy. Was clearing out a section of woods when you called."

"That's alright. Y'all in position?"

"Yup. Menendez is putting eyes on Triprock right now. We're settling in on that hill."

"You made comms with the recon elements yet?"

"Negative. Called you back first."

"Roger that. Abe, I got bad news."

Abe's hope for a greenlight flopped over like a tired dog that's been out in the heat too long. "Right. When is it not bad news? What happened?"

"Sam just made contact. But he's not in Greeley yet. They got him and his team stuffed up in some sort of little holding area about a mile or two outside of Greeley. He's got eyes on Greeley, but he's not in just yet. He says that they were told the only way they get inside Greeley is if they're *needed.* Whatever the fuck that means."

Abe frowned. "Well, what *does* that mean? A few more hours? A few more days?"

"He has no clue. He says there's upwards of a hundred civilians stuck in this place. Some of 'em look like they've been there for quite a while."

"Fuck me running. What's that mean for Triprock?"

Lee let out a sigh that huffed in the microphone. "I'm still working that out. You and your team are kitted for three days."

Abe closed his eyes like a sudden pain was engulfing him. He really didn't want to be stuck in these damn woods for three days. "Can't they just sneak into Greeley at this point?"

"No. He said they got this holding area locked down tight. Said he watched a family try to make a break for it and they got gunned down."

Abe opened his eyes again. "Shit."

"Listen. Sam's motivated. He won't waste time. He'll get into Greeley at the first opportunity that presents itself. We just have to give him time."

"Lee, the recon elements only got another forty-eight hours."

"We can run resupply to them."

"We can take this place. We've done it before, we can do it again."

A pause over the line. "I know you can, Abe. But we're juggling a lot of balls right now. We let one of 'em fall, and the whole damn thing is screwed. I know this ain't what you wanna hear, but you gotta wait. Hold position. Let me figure out how best to accomplish this without fucking Sam's chances to get into Greeley."

Abe craned his neck back, feeling a smattering of kinks suddenly sharpen in the absence of forward momentum. God, he hated waiting. "Alright, Lee. We'll wait for the greenlight."

"Get on comms with the recon elements. Relay what I just told you. Tell them we'll have resupply to them in the next thirty-six hours at the latest."

"Alright. Will do."

"Stay strong, brother." A breath. "Wish I was there with you."

"I know you do."

"Stay frosty."

They hung up.

Breckenridge seemed to have lost his appetite for jerky. "Sounds like Hotel Hilltop just became an extended stay."

Abe didn't even answer. His gut was gradually tightening and tightening with every thought of the long, terrible wait ahead of them. It wasn't the wait that was the worst part. Abe was used to waiting…when he knew what the endpoint was.

But just sitting around, with no clue as to when you were going to go live—could be twelve hours, could be a goddamned week—was like having your motivation clubbed like a baby seal.

He took a breath to fight down the shaky pain of an unknown wait, and keyed his comms. "All units. Go ahead and switch to the main channel. We're going to go live with the recon elements. Stay tuned. Got some wonderful news coming your way. And by wonderful, I mean, don't get so excited about it that you shoot yourself in the head."

***

"The long and short of it, Mr. President," the new Cornerstone COO said, in that special, hesitant tone that the bearer of bad news always speaks in. "Is that we don't have enough boots on the ground."

President Briggs sat at the head of his table, his head propped up by the splayed fingertips of one hand. He stared at the figures on the paper in front of him, but didn't really read them. He didn't need to. He understood well enough.

Greeley was currently defended by a skeleton crew.

Which was to say, not really defended at all.

In the glow of his victory over the United Eastern States, it had been easy to whitewash over this particular shit stain on the otherwise perfect wall of his life. But then Briggs had received a phone call and discovered, lo and behold, no dead Lee Harden.

No dead Lee Harden.

The man was like herpes. You just couldn't get rid of him.

The COO—a likeable, but not very fierce, individual by the name of Javier—raised his hand and pointed at the papers. "If you flip over to the next page, I've gone ahead and outlined where our current manpower is dispersed."

Briggs shot his eyes up to Javier over the top of the paper. Cornerstone Military Applications was largely peopled by former warfighters. But if you wanted to run a company, you had to have number crunchers as well. Which is where Javier came along. Though he wore a gun on his hip, Briggs didn't think the man had ever fired a shot in anger, and probably couldn't hit a whale if it landed on him.

Briefly, Briggs considered not flipping to the next page out of pure petulance, but then relented and turned the leaf over.

"You'll see that we have approximately fifty operatives on rotation at the store houses," Javier narrated the contents of the page, as though Briggs were incapable of reading it for his damn self. "Another hundred assigned to various checkpoints throughout the zones, only *seventy-five* on roving patrols within our perimeter. But you'll notice, down at the very last section, that we have a *hundred-and-fifty* on rotation for securing La Salle and the checkpoints going in." Javier seemed to think this was big voodoo. "We have more people guarding La Salle than we have guarding the store houses. Which is where our flashpoint is, at the moment."

Briggs bent the paper over with his thumb so he could look at Javier again. "What the fuck's that mean?"

Javier's face did a queer little dance, as though he wasn't quite sure how to put this without insulting Briggs's intelligence. "Well. Sir. The populace is on fairly strict rationing at this point in time. The civilian-to-military ratio in Greeley is nearly thirty-to-one. If enough of the civilians get angry about the rations…well…" Another strange facial jig. "We might struggle to hold the store houses."

Briggs laid the paper flat on the table. He drummed his fingers—all but his right index, which still had not recovered from its recent degloving, courtesy of Colonel Lineberger, that ratfuck bastard.

Briggs arched his eyebrows. "And?"

Javier blinked a few times. "And what, sir?"

"What was your point about La Salle? You said I should look at it. You seemed to have a problem with it. What's your point?"

"Right. Well. If we can reduce—or better yet, even just completely nix—the manpower holding La Salle, we can push that into holding the store houses and be much more secure."

"And what about the perimeter?"

"Uh. We could borrow from the patrols."

"The patrols are already barely able to handle the shit they have on their plate. We can't take from them. What else?"

"We could reduce the manpower from the checkpoints. The Green, Yellow, and Red Zones are mostly just old monikers. It's all Greeley at this point in time."

Briggs interlaced his fingers. "Do you know what a bulkhead is?"

"Uh…"

"It's a wall. In a ship. It partitions one section from the other. It's able to be sealed. So that if one section of the ship gets damaged and starts taking on water, it doesn't flood the entire ship." Briggs leaned forward onto his elbows. "The checkpoints are our bulkheads, Javier. I don't give a shit about security in the zones—they're all secure at this point. What I do give a shit about is that if one zone goes to shit—either by civil unrest, or because of an invasion force—it doesn't sink the entire goddamn thing. Do you understand?"

Javier swallowed. "Yes. I understand."

Briggs leaned back again, feeling his chest starting to burn. "What's the current calorie count for civilians?"

Javier frowned, dove for a stack of paperwork off to the side. Rifled through it. Came up with a page. "Adult males, one thousand calories. Adult females, eight hundred."

Briggs nodded, his lips pursed. "You see, the problem isn't that we have too few soldiers, it's that we have too many useless feeders."

Javier didn't respond. Perhaps he, as a Latino, didn't appreciate Briggs's use of Third Reich terminology. But truth was truth. Even Nazi fucks had a few things right.

"We're going to lower the calorie count."

Javier's mouth blubbered for a few stuttered syllables. "But it's already at starvation level."

"We have more guns than we have hands to hold them," Briggs snapped. "If people want to eat, they need to pull their weight. I'm going to lower the calorie counts to a flat five-hundred per person, I don't give a shit about gender. Five hundred. That's what you get for sitting around on your ass and doing nothing. You wanna suckle the tit? Well guess what, the tit's running dry. No free rides anymore." Briggs had the urge to move and stood up from his chair, facing the window of his Not-So-Oval Office. "Soldiers' rations will remain the same. If anyone wants to eat a full day's calories, then we have a rifle for them to hold. And you can start with all those sad saps down in La Salle. Clear out the fucking Tank. Any able-bodied man or woman above the age of…" Briggs considered it for a moment. "Fifteen? Let's say fifteen. They're getting conscripted no matter what. If they don't like that, they can get the fuck out."

Briggs stationed himself at the window, hands on his hips, nodding to himself. In the pale reflection of the room, he could see Javier staring at him.

"Time to separate the wheat from the chaff," Briggs said, almost to himself at this point. He was brainstorming aloud, not really looking for Javier's opinion. "Once La Salle is empty, you can reduce the manpower used for guarding it and send them to the store houses. I still want checkpoints around La Salle, but from here on out, anyone that comes to

Greeley is either on our short list—doctors, engineers, etcetera—or they're taking up a rifle. All others will be turned away."

Briggs frowned and spun on Javier. "Are you getting all this?"

Javier jumped. Seized a pen. Began writing on the back of one of his papers. "Yes, sir."

"As for those already in Greeley, they have the same option. We won't kick them out—that'd cause too much of a stir. But their options are to try to survive on five hundred calories, or join up and have a full belly."

"Yes, sir."

"Oh, and Javier?"

"Yes?"

Briggs shook his head. "No military conscription from this point on, do you understand? I'm moving towards unifying our military under Cornerstone. All new recruits will be *Cornerstone.* Any of the branch faggots have a problem with that, they can take it up with me."

Javier scribbled it down. Briggs wondered if he'd written down *branch faggots.*

"Understood, sir. I'll get right on it."

"Tomorrow."

"Sir?"

"Get everything in place, but don't clear out La Salle or start the conscription until tomorrow morning." Briggs faced the window again, unable to keep a sneer from his face as he looked out at Greeley and thought of all the useless feeders down there, draining them dry like parasites. "You know how ornery everyone is at night. Better to break the news after they've slept."

EIGHT

GREENLIGHT

CORPORAL NGUYEN—AKA NUG, Nugs, or The Nug—settled into his sniper's hide for the late shift. Private Ferro, who was deemed a decent marksman, relinquished the spot, removing his DMR from the little keyhole in the edge of the brush.

"Fuckin' tired," Ferro mumbled, almost to himself.

The spot on the ground was now a worn concavity from Nug's and Ferro's bodies. The ground was still warm from four hours of Ferro's belly being pressed against it. It also smelled faintly of his body odor, but Nug didn't mind. The warmth was actually kind of nice, and they were all well accustomed to each other's stink by this time.

Nug spied a crumple of white off to his right. He grimaced and snatched the piece of paper up. It still smelled like jerky. "Goddammit, Ferro." Nug wadded it up and threw it at the other man. "Stop leaving your trash in the hide."

"Oh, yeah. Sorry." Ferro stooped and grabbed the balled up paper. "Forgot."

Ferro always forgot. Ferro was a messy fuck. Everywhere he went he reduced to shambles.

"Gonna start calling you Pigpen," Nug commented as he thrust his scoped rifle through the keyhole and settled into position.

Ferro yawned, no longer concerned. "Alright, man. Have fun."

He slipped back into the darkness, leaving Nug to his business.

Nug rested his cheek on the buttstock and tried to relax his body. It was getting harder and harder to do that, though. He'd been a latecomer to the military game, at least by Army standards, joining up when he was twenty-two, when most others in his basic class were eighteen. Now past thirty, Nug found it harder and harder to ignore the aches and pains.

He did his yoga every day upon waking. But he still had a crick in his neck, and a pinch in his lower back from spending the last two days laying in the sniper's hide. There was no amount of vinyasa that would reverse the hands of time, it seemed.

Oh well. Nothing to be done for it.

Nug rubbed the crust from his eyes, blinked them, then focused through the scope.

All was dark and quiet. His hide was directly to the east of Triprock, a little more than a quarter mile out. 1,452 yards, according to his rangefinder. Right at the edge of his comfort zone with the Mk 20 SSR.

He took a quick peek at the lay of the land. Triprock was dark—they didn't have much electricity, and it was midnight now. A few small solar panels kept some electric lanterns charged, but they'd since been extinguished.

The settlement lay there, the sides of the buildings a deep blue in the half-moon that occasionally winked at them from behind a thin layer of gauzy clouds. The shadows as black as ink. The reticle of his scope was a dimly luminous cross that scoured the scene, searching for signs of life.

There was one. Standing in the hayloft of a barn that looked like it had taken a grenade at some point in time. The sentry faced south. NODs over his eyes. Black polo shirt. Cornerstone.

Nug took note of the positions of the other Cornerstone sentries. There were four sentry positions, at all the points of the compass. And two roving sentries that conducted a constant circle of the fenceline.

Once he had everyone accounted for, Nug keyed his comms and spoke into the silence of the radiowaves. "This is Nug at Position Two. I have overwatch."

"Roger that," came a response that he thought was Sergeant Breckenridge. He'd only met the man a handful of times, but his voice on the radio was distinct—always soft and calm, with a slight Midwestern accent.

Positions One and Three—to the northeast and southeast of Triprock, respectively—checked in a few moments afterward. Midnight was shift change for everyone.

Down in Triprock, the sentries continued their watchful rounds, oblivious to the reticles that hovered over their hearts and brains.

But, according to the news they'd received earlier in the day, there would be no reckoning for the Cornerstone asshats tonight. They were free to live another day, it seemed.

Nug zoomed his optic out so that he could see the entire perimeter and keep tabs on both roving patrols. Then he settled in and started to practice his deep breathing techniques. That was about all you had to do while you were waiting around for nothing to happen. It kept him focused on something besides his physical discomfort, the constant hunger, and the thoughts of his dead family which always liked to rear their heads in the small morning hours when the night seemed big, and vast, and unending.

In for four. Hold for three. Out for eight. And so it went. On and on.

It was nearly one o'clock when the radio crackled in Nug's ear.

"Hiram at Position One. Can anyone advise on when that resupply is getting here?"

Nug's nose curled in irritation. That was an asinine question. It would get here when it got here.

Breckenridge answered. "It's not due until tomorrow morning. After daylight." A pause on the open line. "Any reason why you're asking?"

The line remained empty for a moment. "Uh…" Hiram sounded tense now. "Yeah. I'm on perimeter duty at Position One. I got shapes on the thermals, about a thousand yards directly east of Position Two."

Nug blinked. Came up out of his scope. He turned his head to look over his shoulder and saw Sergeant John "Scots" McCollum stirring from his nook against the trunk of a tree. Nug could only just make out his shock of red hair in the darkness.

"Highlander Six," Scots transmitted, using his old Hunter-Killer moniker. "I copied thermal signatures to my east? Is that right?"

"Affirmative," Hiram answered. "I'm counting five…six signatures. Moving in your direction."

"Can you identify?"

"I don't want to be an alarmist…but I think they're teepios."

***

Abe awoke with a violent start, his grip tightening on his rifle.

"Ssh." A black shape hovered over him. A patch of moonlight through the branches above illuminated Breckenridge's face. He had a hand up to calm Abe, the other hand with its index finger over his lips. "Your comms fell out."

Abe frowned, reached up, realized the acoustic tube of his earpiece was no longer in. He shoved it back in place. Silence greeted him. "What's going on?"

"Position One just ID'd six teepios moving towards Position Two."

Abe came upright from his slumped position against his pack. "Shit." He keyed his comms. "Darabie to whoever's got eyes on those teepios. How far out are they?"

It took a moment for the voice to come back. He didn't know who it was, and they didn't ID themselves. "Yes, sir. Estimating about a thousand yards. A little less now. They're not moving too fast. I don't think they've caught the scent yet. But they're definitely closing the gap with Position Two."

Abe rubbed his face rapidly with both hands. "Darabie copies. All units standby. Keep me updated if they get aggressive." He released the PTT and looked hard at Breck. "We gotta shit or get off the pot."

Breck nodded in the darkness. "Call Lee. If we have to engage those teepios, this op goes down the shitter."

***

Lee didn't sleep anymore.

Not for any length of time anyways. And not at night. The night was too dangerous. Too full of unknowns. He would lie there, as he did that night, trying his damnedest, but every time his mind began to sink below that delicate plane of consciousness, adrenaline would dump through his system, like a stew in his gut boiling over.

He'd given up around eleven. Maybe he would've slept if he was in the bunker, but he doubted it. And they'd given the bunker up to the families that had children to keep safe. Those families packed the underground fortress from the elevator all the way back to the little common area with the shower—which no one could use because they'd drained the bunker's water tanks already.

He'd chosen instead to try sleeping under one of the MATVs. At first he thought it might work out—the bulk of the vehicle over him was like a protective cage. But the world out to all of his sides, beyond the tires, was still open and endless, and his mind wouldn't let that go.

He decided that sleeping through the night was not going to happen, as it had not for several nights running now. He would nap in the early morning hours, or during the heat of the afternoon. Whenever things were calm and still and the potential for disaster was mitigated.

So, around eleven, he crawled his way out from under the MATV, agonizingly slow because his left arm and leg were uncooperative and because he wanted to stay quiet for the other two bodies that were huddled under the MATV—Brinly and his second in command.

When he'd freed himself from the confines of the undercarriage, he rubbed blood into his face, hefted his rifle, and found the nearest sentry.

It was a woman, sitting a few yards out from the line of vehicles, her back against a thin pine tree, her eyes scouring the darkness. Her sharp hearing alerted her to his approach, and she turned to face him.

She jerked when she realized who it was. "Major Harden." She started to rise.

Lee waved for her to relax. Took his time sinking down to one knee with a quiet grunt. "What's your name?" he asked her.

She seemed confused by the question. "Linn," she murmured back, her voice barely above a whisper.

"How long you been on post?"

"Three hours. I'm off at midnight."

Lee nodded. "Why don't you catch an extra hour of shut-eye?"

By the half-moon above them, he saw her eyes blink a few times. "Are you sure?"

Lee nodded. "Yeah, I can't sleep anyways. Go ahead."

She considered this for a moment, but then rose quietly to her feet. She cocked her head as she looked down at Lee's kneeling form. "You need to rest too, major."

He smiled, cognizant suddenly that he didn't have his eyepatch on, and wondered what his smile looked like in the darkness with that ruined hole in his face. Linn didn't seem to react, but Lee looked away anyways. "I'll rest. Later. Go on. I got your post, soldier."

Linn nodded. "Alright. Thank you, sir."

She disappeared into the night, to whatever vehicle had become her home, either to sleep inside of it, or under it, or maybe on top of it, if she were the type to enjoy the stars overhead while she slept.

Lee settled into her spot, the ground still warm from her body. Exhaustion and heightened awareness washed over him in alternating waves, one constantly scouring away the other in an endless cycle.

With no reason to keep his thoughts in check anymore, he allowed them to run in their random directions, allowed the worries to overtake him, allowed his mind to obsess over them. After all, how else are you supposed to occupy yourself in the middle of the night?

Would Sam get inside Greeley? How would he do it? And would he even be successful when he *did* get inside? Was Lee wrong to trust him with such a big task? Was he wrong to let Sam convince him to trust the others? Johnson and Frenchie. Sam barely knew those guys, but had vouched for them nonetheless.

Lee knew why that was. It's difficult to go into battle with someone and come out the other side, having put your life in that person's hands, and then *not* trust them.

But just because you've been to war with someone, doesn't mean they won't fuck you over in the end.

Anyone could. That was the thing. Didn't matter who they were, because everyone was an individual, with their own fears and desires and obsessions. Everyone was the hero of their own story. And that's what made them dangerous to Lee. Because no one was truly *with Lee.* They all had their own reasons for being there.

At what point would their paths diverge? And when that happened, as it inevitably did, then what would they do? You could never know. Not until it actually happened.

You could never know who to trust, and so Lee trusted no one.

Everyone had the potential to become his enemy in the end.

And, of course, this assumed they survived long enough to get to that point. Which was a whole can of worms unto itself. Because everyone had to die. Eventually. And they did it often around Lee. Sometimes he wondered if God had rendered some curse over him, that he would always survive, only to watch everyone around him die.

Who's next? He wondered. *Who's next to die? And who's next to betray me?*

Why did he even keep doing what he was doing? Was it hubris? Did he think he was some weapon of God? Or was it just violence begetting violence, an eye for an eye until the whole world was blind?

Was he a part of the problem? Was he just dragging everyone down into the depths with him?

Why so much fighting? Why so much killing? Why so much bloodshed? What was it at the core of him that guided all these things, that had brought him to this place right now?

It was in this soup of thoughts, sometime after midnight, that the satphone in his pocket vibrated.

He dragged it out and glanced at the screen before answering, his heart already accelerating, while his gut tightened with apprehension. “Abe. What’s up?”

Abe sounded like he was moving. His voice was quiet, just a murmur over the connection. “Lee. We got a problem. Pack of primals has been spotted moving towards Position Two.”

Lee’s mounting blood pressure crescendoed into a hum in his ears. He stood up, swearing. “Abe, what are you doing?”

“We have to greenlight the op, Lee. Me and my team are preparing to move into position.”

“But Sam’s not inside Greeley.”

“We don’t have an option at this point, Lee. If we wait, Position Two might have to engage those primals. And if they do, then it’ll be too late. The sentries in Triprock will hear the gunfire and know that we’re out here. We have to move *now*.”

For a flash, Lee tried to come up with a legitimate reason why this was foolhardy. But he couldn’t.

The primals were a variable that Lee could not control. No matter what he tried to do, he could not get rid of the possibility that they might close with his men on the ground, and then the shooting would start, and the op would be ruined.

Things were moving, and he couldn't stop them.

"Alright, Abe," Lee hissed, stalking back towards the line of vehicles, and then breaking into a stiff jog. "Do it quick and quiet as you possibly can. I'm gonna scramble the forces and have them moving to support you right now, and I'm gonna try to close off that northwestern corner so no one gets out."

"Roger that, Lee. We're on the move."

Lee hung up and crammed the satphone back in his pocket. He stopped along the dark bulk of the MATV that he'd tried to sleep under. He kicked the door panel. "Brinly! Wake up!"

There was a snort and a thrash from underneath the vehicle. Brinly's head appeared near Lee's boots, blinking rapidly. "What's wrong? What happened?"

"We gotta move on Triprock right-fucking-now."

Brinly was already clambering out from under the vehicle.

"Get as many squads as you can on the road within the next five minutes," Lee continued. "Have them come in from the west of Triprock and get on the main comms with the teams on the ground there. Provide support where it's needed."

Brinly hauled himself onto his feet. "Where are you going?"

Lee was already backing away from the MATV, heading for the end of the column of vehicles. "I've gotta cover that northwestern corner, make sure no one gets out of Triprock. Tell Angela and have her coordinate anyone you don't take with you."

Lee didn't wait for a response or an argument. He turned and began running as best as his raggedy hip would allow him. Vehicles flashed by on his right, the dark woods to his left. Sentries were coming alive all over the place, hearing the general stir that was spreading through the ranks like a gust of wind.

"What's going on?

"What happened?"

"Are we in danger?"

Lee didn't answer any of them. There wasn't time.

By the time he reached the back of the column, the wave of heightened tension had preceded him. At the very rear of the column was the Humvee he'd left the previous afternoon. Three figures hovered nearby, looking lost and unsure of themselves. One of them was a woman in civilian clothes, the other two were men in Army fatigues.

"You three!" Lee ordered, stabbing a finger at them. "Get in the Humvee! Now!"

Lee made for the driver's door, as the others jolted like they'd been stuck with cattle prods and jumped for the other doors. Lee had no idea who in the hell these people were, but they were his people, and now they were going to be his team, like it or not.

Lee threw himself behind the wheel, dragging his left leg in with his hands, then slamming the door, his rifle stuck between his thighs. He flipped the switch on the dash, waited two agonizing seconds for the ignition to be ready, then cranked the Humvee up.

The other doors slammed, a jumble of limbs and cursing filling the interior. Pure confusion.

Lee yanked the shifter into reverse. "One of you get in the turret, the rest of you—guns out the windows." He slammed on the gas. The engine roared, skidding dirt and gravel. The Humvee rocketed backwards, and Lee spun the wheel, ramming the backend carelessly into a stand of saplings. Shifter into forward. He cranked the wheel, hit the gas again, and then they were off, tearing down the dirt road, heading for Triprock.

NINE

INFILTRATION

NUG STAYED GLUED TO HIS SCOPE, the big objective lens soaking in enough moonlight to illuminate the scene of Triprock. Behind him, Scots held a rapid and quiet conference.

"Stetter, Jerzyck, Holmes, I need y'all to hightail it to the vehicles," Scots said.

"Shit," Holmes breathed back. "They're gonna be right on our asses."

"I know that. And I'm sorry. But you gotta do this. Get to the truck—and try to get them to follow you. This is our only chance to stave off the shooting long enough for Abe and his team to take Triprock."

"Roger that, sern't."

"I'm staying with Nug," Scots said. "Nug, you catching all this?"

Nug didn't move from his scope, but murmured, "I copy."

Down in the darkness, Nug's eyes kept creeping to the left edge of his field of view through the scope. A black stripe ran diagonally off of the border of Triprock: A shallow arroyo, cast into absolute dark by the sharp angle of the moon. That would be where Abe and his team would make their incursion.

"Alright, gents," Scots said. "Haul ass. And listen to me: If you have to shoot, then fucking shoot. I'd rather the op go to shit than lose you guys. But…"

"But try not to fuck everything up," Stetter finished for his sergeant. "We got it."

"Roll out," Scots commanded.

There was the shuffling of boots and brush, and it rapidly faded into the night.

Down in Triprock, the stationary sentries continued their endless scanning of the terrain with their night vision. The foot patrols continued their rounds. Oblivious.

Nug felt Scots settle in next to him. "Scots to Position One. Gimme a sitrep on those primals."

"They're milling around about seven hundred yards from your pos. I got eyes on your boys running. So far no response from the primals."

"Keep me updated."

Abe Darabie's voice cut in over the comms, just a whisper: "Assault element is drawing within a few hundred yards. We need the comms direct with our overwatch. If you're not on overwatch right now, switch to the secondary channel."

Scots shuffled around beside Nug, cursing under his breath as he switched the radio channel over. "You'll need to keep me in the loop about what's happening on the main channel."

"Will do," Nug murmured.

"Abe to Nug, we're about two hundred yards from the fenceline. You got us?"

Nug shifted his optic to the left a bit. He searched the dark rift of the arroyo, but saw nothing. "Negative. Y'all are still hidden. Be advised, the stationary sentries have NODs, so no IR until they're down. How copy?"

"I copy. No IR until the stationary sentries are eliminated. We're moving in. Try to get eyes on us. I'm gonna need you to guide me into that sentry on the south side. That's our point of entry."

Nug swung the scope back over to the fenceline where the sentry stood. "Roger that. I got eyes on him. Let me know when you're close to being exposed and I'll coordinate your movements."

The radio went silent.

Nug could just barely hear the murmur of the secondary channel through Scots's earpiece. "Primals have spotted our runners," Scots whispered. "But they're not pursuing yet."

Nug adjusted the magnification of his scope, focusing in on that sentry on the south side of Triprock. The mobile patrol had just passed him by, and were now striding on towards the west side. The other mobile sentry was approaching the east.

"Nug to Abe. Your south sentry is alone. Mobile patrol just moved past. You've got maybe four minutes before the next mobile patrol reaches your insertion point."

"Copy."

They didn't have four minutes.

"Primals are breaking towards our runners," Scots hissed. "Fuck, fuck, fuck. Please don't let them chomp on my guys..."

Nug's heart slammed the hard dirt beneath his chest. He never stopped his breathing exercises. It was the only thing he could control. It was the only thing that gave him a measure of calm in the chaos.

How much time until the shooting started? Because Nug was sure about one thing: His squad mates weren't gonna reach their truck before those primals reached them.

***

Abe moved like a wolf spider. Sprawled out on all fours, just his palms and toes touching the ground, the belly of his chest rig skimming the top of the dirt. His rifle was strapped tight to his back to keep it from dragging. The side wall of the arroyo stood to his right, banking sharply towards where a drainage culvert ran under the fenceline of Triprock.

Abe stopped, peered around the corner of the miniature canyon he was in. All of his muscles were locked. His core burned, but he held his position.

There. The south sentry. Maybe fifty yards away.

Abe settled himself silently into the dirt. He rolled slightly to his right, looking over his left shoulder at Menendez and the rest of the team strung out along the arroyo behind him. He raised one finger, then pointed dead ahead.

Menendez nodded, cinched closer, his rifle up.

Abe slid the fixed blade from the sheath on his chest rig. Then touched off his comms.

"Abe to Nug. In position. Going silent. Guide me in."

Nug's response was quiet, each word pronounced clearly and deliberately. "Shadowy spot on the side of a large boulder. You see it?"

Abe craned his neck around. Spotted what Nug had described—a big boulder with a deep, moon-cast shadow on the west side of it. About ten yards from him, right where the arroyo started to become too shallow for decent concealment.

He clicked his PTT twice.

"You'll have about five seconds to get there while the sentry's looking east. Standby to move."

Abe waited, muscles clenched and ready.

"Move."

Abe was a whisper of a shadow. He put absolute trust into Nug—didn't even look at the sentry. Nug had told him the sentry was looking elsewhere and that was all Abe needed to now. He skittered across the soft dirt at the bed of the arroyo, up the other side, then rolled into position behind the rock.

"Perfect," Nug whispered in his ear.

Abe glanced back to his original position. Menendez had taken it, his body pressed tight to the dirt wall of the arroyo, just one eye and his rifle barrel sticking out, trained on the sentry. Ready to take him out if Nug couldn't.

"Stand of sage on the fenceline, right at your eleven o'clock."

Two clicks of Abe's PTT.

"Standby…move."

Abe crabbed across the ground, took the sage brush, huddled on one knee. He peered through the brambles. The moon was right in his face, and he could see the silver outline of it across the sentry's head, highlighting the NODs over his eyes.

The sentry swept his gaze across the arroyo. Then right at Abe. He seemed to be staring at him.

Abe didn't move. Didn't dare breathe, for fear it might stir the branches near his face.

After a heart-stopping three seconds, the sentry looked away.

He was about ten yards from Abe. Which meant sound was becoming more and more of a factor. Abe knew how to stalk silently, but it's very difficult to get within arm's reach of someone without them hearing you.

You can do this. You've done it before.

His fingers milked the grip on his knife.

"Abe," Nug said. "You got no cover between you and the sentry. I'm gonna make a loud whistle to draw his attention east. Two clicks if you're cool with that, one click if you don't like it."

Abe gritted his teeth. A single whistle wouldn't necessarily bomb the entire op, and their options were limited. And time was running out. He clicked his PTT twice.

His pulse thrummed through his body, his lungs aching for air, everything in him focused on that sentry. There was nothing else in the world but Abe and that man, and the knife in Abe's hand, and where he planned to put it.

***

"Primals aren't taking the bait," Scots hissed. "Motherfuckers. Nug, they're still coming our way."

Nug felt his throat tighten. He had to deliberately tell himself to breathe past his locked up lungs. "When I whistle, they're gonna be on our ass."

"You stay in that fucking scope," Scots said. "Do what you gotta do. I got your back."

Nug felt his lips tremble as he pursed them and took a deep breath.

***

The whistle. Long, and low, and mournful. It could've been a nightbird. But it was too loud.

Abe watched the sentry jerk his head, looking east.

He moved, all sense of reality fading down to this finite moment in time. He slipped across the dried earth, his footfalls just whispers in the sand. Closer, closer.

The sentry keyed his comms, still staring east. "Anyone else hear that?"

Closer. Five yards. Now just six feet. The length of a man.

No breath. Abe wasn't allowed to breathe this close to his prey.

Arm's length. Just the fence between him and the sentry.

"No," the sentry griped. "I heard like a fucking loud bird or—"

Abe's boot skimmed the top of a sharp rock. The faintest little scrape.

The sentry jerked his head around.

Abe lunged, rattlesnake-quick. Left hand clamped behind the sentry's neck, yanking him forward into the fence, pinning his rifle to his body. He'd wanted the knife to sever the spine, but he was face-to-face with the sentry and the spine wasn't an option.

The sentry's mouth gaped, all the air drawing into his lungs for a shout.

Abe rammed the blade up under his chin. He felt the resistance of the roof of the man's mouth, but he'd punched the knife hard, and it cracked under the point of the blade, plunging up into sinuses and brain matter, and pinning the sentry's jaw shut.

A strange death-noise bubbled up from the sentry's throat. Abe rotated his right hand off the grip of the knife and clamped it down over the sentry's mouth, holding him with the intensity of strength that a snake constricts its prey.

The man's voice vibrated through Abe's palm. Spit. Blood. Lubricating his grip.

Abe sandwiched the man's head between his two hands as though trying to crush the skull. The ferocity of his energy made his arms tremble with the effort. The twin tubes of the sentry's NODs gazed at him emotionlessly.

Nug's voice in his ear: "Abe's got the sentry down. Move in, move in."

Abe held on. The body in his grip twitched and thrashed, but Abe knew well the sensation of a body in its death throes.

The scuff of boots behind him, rapid, stealth now giving way to urgency.

A hand on Abe's shoulder. Menendez swooped in beside him, vaulted the fence in one fluid maneuver, then grabbed the body of the still-twitching sentry under the armpits and started hauling him for the concealment of an old water trough, the liquid inside looking black as ink.

Abe swung over the fence as Breck and the other six men followed.

"Abe," Nug said. "Primals are moving into my pos. You're gonna have live fire in about twenty seconds."

"I copy. Abe to all units on overwatch, we're in. Take out the sentries. Fire at will."

Abe slid into cover behind the water trough, the dead sentry between him and Menendez. He sheathed his knife, then swung his rifle off his back and posted, bringing the reticle up on the dark figure of the patrolling sentry as he approached.

The others in Abe's team were still scattering like cockroaches.

The approaching sentry spotted them. Stiffened. Rifle coming up.

Pink mist erupted from the back of his head, cast in neon by the backlighting of the moon. The mobile patrol toppled forward, and as he fell the sound of Nug's suppressed shot reached Abe's ears: The scrape of the supersonic round splitting the air, followed by the muffled thump of the report.

This sound was immediately followed by several others, so rapid that they sounded like one long crackle of electricity.

"IR's on!" Abe spat out, snatching the chemlight on his shoulder and cracking it. He reached up and lowered the NODs on his helmet over his eyes. The world became bright and green and clear, the shadows dispelled. Around him, one by one, the IR chemlights were activated, invisible to the naked eye, but shining like beacons for he and his team as they all activated their nightvision.

"On me," Abe said, moving around the trough towards the side of the main barn that dominated this section of Triprock. "Main building. Weapons free. We're moving."

Out to the east, a burp of unsuppressed gunfire told Abe that stealth was out the window.

***

"You got me?" Nug couldn't help it from seething past his lips as he forced himself to stay in his scope, even as he felt Scots's hot brass skitter across his neck and shoulders, and heard the movement of primals tearing through the woods.

"I got you!" Scots shouted back, pivoting rapidly and firing into the darkness.

Nug's perception of reality kept trying to widen out to encompass what was happening behind him, but he forced it back to the magnified image in front of his right eye. The reticle. The target. That was his world.

The sentry on the western side of Triprock had called the alarm, shouldered his rifle, and began firing at the corner of the destroyed barn where Abe and his team were stacking up. Nug fitted the reticle snugly over his chest and squeezed.

The blat of his suppressed rifle.

Flight time.

Snap. The sentry staggered, then crumpled around the hole in his chest.

The comms in Nug's ear: "Overwatch!" Abe called out. "We're taking a lot of heat from that main building! Give us some breathing room!"

Nug grit his teeth. Beside him, Scots accidentally nudged his foot into Nug's side, skewing his aim for a fraction of a second. A long string of rifle fire over Nug's head.

"Reloading!" Scots gasped.

Nug got his sights on the main building. A big rectangle right in the middle of Triprock. Nug keyed his comms. "The side of the building facing south, Abe! It's got no windows! Go for it when I put 'em down!"

The stamp of rapid footfalls, coming in from Nug's left.

Oh, Jesus…

"Up!" Scots screamed, and immediately fired on full-auto.

Nug felt something tumble to the ground, just a few feet to his left. Heard the wheezing, inhuman gurgle. He stayed in his sights. Put that reticle on the window of the main building that was sprouting a rosette of yellow fire, tracer rounds punching at Abe's position.

Nug couldn't see the target. He let fly with three rounds, evenly spaced, right on top of that muzzle flash. The chatter of machinegun fire ceased. Nug didn't look to see if Abe and his team was moving—they would be. He shifted his sights to the next window, waiting for any sign of life to appear.

A shadow of movement. No positive ID, though. It could be anyone through that window.

"Nug!" Scots yelled. "Help!"

Nug had no choice. He rolled onto his back, his big rifle coming up. A massive shape loomed through the darkness. He couldn't use the scope. He pointed the barrel, point-blank, and let it rip. The big round blasted the center of the primal's chest out, causing it to stumble in its charge.

Scots pivoted, firing a burst that stitched the primal through its sternum, neck, and face, and pitched it to the ground beside Nug.

Nug let the rifle go. Swept down and yanked his pistol from its holster, coming up onto his knees. The shadows surrounded them like swirling shapes in a storm. They were eerily silent as they moved, only the huff of breath, and Nug could hardly tell whose breath he was hearing—his, or Scots', or the primals'.

He fired at shapes as they came at him, aware that they were surrounded, aware that even as the one he was pumping 9mm rounds into directly ahead stumbled, there was another looping around to his back, and another to his side.

Nug and Scots scrunched tighter and tighter as the noose tightened around them. Shoulder to shoulder, back to back, they fired. Slides and bolts fell on empty chambers. Hands grasped at spare magazines. They did not speak anymore, did not call their reloads. They both knew what was about to happen to them.

The shadows closed in, and enveloped them.

***

Target identification. That was Abe's entire world.

The rest of reality bled away in the half-light glow of his night vision. He mounted the steps to the main ranch house, the sides of it still pocked with the hundreds of rounds that had been shot through it months ago when he and Lee had taken over this very same settlement from the cartel.

He could hear the boots on the deck boards behind him—Menendez and his team falling in, ready to take the building.

Windows empty of glass. A shape in the one to the right of the main door, which hung open on its hinges. Abe snapped his rifle up, his infrared laser aiming device blooming on the chest of someone wearing a black polo and armor plates. Abe twitched his aim up and sent three rounds into the neck and head, spilling the man back into the house.

Abe sidestepped the open front door as the shell casings clattered to the deck. "Frag it," he snapped over his shoulder. Menendez was one step ahead of him, his rifle tucked under his arm while his support hand chucked a grenade through the broken window.

Abe hunched against the coming blast, cinching his shoulder up to cover his exposed ear.

The explosion rocked the house, billowing tattered curtains out of the open windows and slamming the front door shut. With the sound of shrapnel and detritus still peppering the walls, Abe took a single sideways step and mule kicked the front door open.

Menendez flowed past him, straight into the smoky breach, and Abe rolled off of his shoulder. Menendez went left. Abe went right. Straight into the room that had just been fragged. Three bodies in a circle around where the grenade had detonated. One of them was still moving. Abe could not see a weapon, but he saw body armor, and that was identification enough. He put two rounds into the head as he stepped into the room, then scanned the rest of it.

A couch in the center of the room. He couldn't see behind it.

Gunshots from elsewhere in the house. No verbal commands—no shouts to show hands or surrender. That's not what they were here for.

Abe was aware of Breckenridge, to his left. Abe pointed to the couch, then took two big strides towards it and front-kicked the left armrest, sending the entire furniture piece skidding backwards. It thumped against something behind it.

A body shot up, hands in the air. "Don't shoot!"

Black polo. In the green of nightvision, the red Delta symbol of Cornerstone looked like a neon sign.

Abe and Breck both shot the man twice. He crumpled back behind the couch.

Abe stepped around the couch, muzzle following the path of where the man had fallen. He lay, curled on his side behind the couch. Still writhing. Abe put him out of his misery.

Abe saw no other places where a body could hide in this room. "Clear."

The sound of a door slamming.

Shouted curses. A smattering of gunfire.

The comms in Abe's ear clicked: "We got a runner!"

***

Lee tore through the night, heading north. He was close enough now that the radio in the Humvee's center console was picking up the squad chatter.

"We got a runner!"

Shit, shit, shit!

The road ahead was long and straight and dusty. To his right, Lee could see the valley in the Texas hill country where Triprock huddled in the darkness. He knew the death and destruction that was descending on that place, but he couldn't see it. No muzzle flashes. No fires burning.

Lee pressed his thumb to the PTT on the radio handset and shouted, "Lee here! I'm on the western side of Triprock—where's the runner?"

Pedal to the floor, the engine roared. Lee strained to see through the midnight distance between him and the moonlit shapes of the settlement in the center of the valley—less than a mile from him now.

He couldn't see anything. No bodies running.

The radio chirped. Menendez's voice: "He just squirted out the back! I lost sight of him. Running northwest."

"Hold on!" Lee called to his passengers and then yanked the wheel to the right, sending the Humvee careening over the shallow shoulder. It slammed its way across the uneven terrain, jostling the occupants.

Lee pointed the grill of the Humvee towards the empty space northwest of Triprock. The headlights flashed across low, scrubby hills and stands of brush that slashed the sides and undercarriage of the vehicle. He still couldn't see a runner.

"Overwatch," Lee transmitted. "Can anybody get eyes on that runner?"

There was a pause over the line. No one responded.

The Humvee hit a berm and vaulted, going airborne for a sphincter-puckering second before crashing down, the wheel jerking around in Lee's hands.

Abe's voice now, urgent: "Check the arroyo! There's one that runs north out of Triprock!"

Yes. That made sense. A runner with half a brain wouldn't run across the open landscape, exposed. He'd take the landscape feature that offered him some cover.

The headlights slashed over a dark schism in the landscape—the arroyo. Lee jerked the wheel to the left to keep the Humvee from crashing into the dry streambed. A flash of movement, far ahead.

The soldier that had taken the turret shouted down: "I got him!"

"Take him out!"

The M2 thundered overhead, the tracers arcing through the blackness. They went every which way, a haphazard pattern of uncontrolled automatic fire. The Humvee was moving too much for the gunner to control his muzzle.

Lee lost sight of the target as he roared along the left side of the arroyo. But not for long.

The gunner spat rounds at a more even pace but they were still flying without accuracy.

"I can't aim!" the soldier shouted.

But Lee wasn't going to stop the Humvee.

Another flash of movement. The headlights struck the pale flesh of a man running—his clothes were as black as the night around him, but Lee could see his arms pumping, and the back of his neck. Lee accelerated again, feeling the grip of the Humvee's tires loosen as he pushed the vehicle to its off-roading limit.

Distance estimation…

Seventy-five yards? Maybe a hundred?

Another berm of dirt sent the Humvee up. Lee felt his ass leave his seat, his head crunching into the ceiling. The steering wheel got squirrelly in his grip and he barely kept the Humvee from pitching over the side of the arroyo.

He got control. Accelerated again.

Fifty yards. Twenty.

Another burst from the M2—no joy.

Lee swore, knowing he had to stop. He was close enough now—wasn't he? A sudden wave of doubt slammed him as he stamped down on the brakes and sent the Humvee skidding through a cloud of its own dust.

Can you make that shot?

Lee was out the door. Rifle in hand. Left leg screaming in pain at the misuse, but Lee gave it no quarter. He heard the shouts of the Humvee's occupants behind him, confused, wondering if they were supposed to follow him, and then simply doing it.

Lee posted on the painfully-hot hood. It seared his exposed elbow. He forced himself to relax. His ruined eye made it hard to estimate distance, but he only needed one eye to shoot his rifle.

The shape of the man, still running, approaching a bend in the arroyo.

Lee's red dot was overbright in the darkness—still set for daytime. Rookie mistake. Another tidal wave of doubts clenched his stomach, a sensation he was wholly unaccustomed to. He didn't bother adjusting the optic's brightness. He had no time, and the runner was well within reasonable range for a quick shot.

A shot that would've taken Lee less than a second before his injuries.

Red dot, square on the back.

The turret thundered, its rounds more controlled now, but still striking wide.

Lee pulled his trigger. One shot.

He saw the body jerk, then fall out of sight.

Lee came out of his sights, already moving for the arroyo. "On me!" he shouted to the others. The lip of the arroyo was only four feet tall. Normally, Lee would have just lept into it without thinking. Now he hesitated for a split second, then went down clumsily onto his right hip so he could slide gracelessly to the bottom.

Dust and pebbles filled his boots. His mind told him *Run!* but his body was only half able. He heard the others clattering down into the arroyo with him. He hitched his way along, and only as he approached the bend in the arroyo did he realize that getting *into* the stupid ditch had been a bad choice.

The cavalcade of doubts and hesitation had clouded his usually-clear thinking.

He was reactive, not proactive. He fucking hated it. Cursed himself for an idiot.

Rifle up. He slowed as he reached the bend. He knew that he'd landed that shot, but the body wasn't there. Maybe the hit hadn't been as damaging as he'd thought, or maybe the man was wearing armor.

Scuff marks in the loose soil. It looked like someone had scrambled through it on all fours.

"We're with you," one of the soldiers said from behind him.

Lee tracked the disturbed dirt to where it disappeared around the bend. Best to take the corner hard. Right? Or was he about to make another stupid decision? Why wasn't he able to just trust himself like he used to?

He took the bend in the arroyo as aggressively as he could.

A straightaway. An alley with dirt walls on both sides.

A shape, thrashing along, fifteen yards ahead. Farther than Lee would have thought that someone could crawl. But crawling he was—on all fours.

A weaponlight speared the gloom. Not Lee's. The soldier to his right shouted, "Lemme see your hands!"

Lee had no such compunctions. He fired on the shape, three rapid rounds, right up the ass. The figure pitched forward, face-planting in the dirt, his backend still up in the air.

There was a gasp of shock from behind him. It sounded like the civilian woman. That tiny noise seeped into Lee's consciousness as he pushed himself into a jog, keeping his muzzle as controlled as possible.

Why had she gasped? Did she think they were taking prisoners?

The man in the dirt, still alive. Still moving. Lee heard a noise of agony as he ran up. The man's legs moved like they thought they could still run, even though his upper body seemed limp. He only managed to pitch himself over into a fetal position.

Lee's mind was on fire. The doubts at his own abilities, the moral accusation of that woman's gasp, the fury that coursed through him as he thought about someone getting away and destroying his carefully laid plans—they all clashed in his brain.

Lee reached the body. Heard the ragged breathing. Still alive. Hands now curled up into his chest. Lee activated his own weaponlight. What was in the man's hands? What was he clutching to his chest? A weapon? A grenade?

Wide, terrified eyes looked back at him, bone-white in the glow of his weaponlight.

Doubts. Recrimination. Rage. Fear.

Lee put a single round between those eyes.

"What the fuck!" the woman shouted.

The sound of it was like claws on a chalkboard. It shivered through some primordial substance in Lee's spine, causing his entire body to tense up.

"Enemy combatant," was all Lee said.

He wanted to kick the body over onto its back, but he could neither kick with his bum leg, nor could he balance on it to kick with the other. Instead, he bent down—painfully—and shoved the man's shoulder hard enough to get the body to roll.

It was limp now. The limbs melted, fell to the side.

A satphone clattered to the dust.

"Goddammit," Lee growled.

In the distance another burst of automatic gunfire.

Lee had no comms—the only radio was back in the Humvee. He didn't know what was going on in Triprock and suddenly felt miles away. Removed. Like he was on the dark side of the moon.

He snatched up the satphone. The casing of it was coated in dust. "Search the body," Lee commanded, taking a step back while the two soldiers swept in, one posting over the body as though it might suddenly come alive again, while the other began rummaging through pockets and gear.

"Why'd you kill him?" the woman's voice scraped at Lee again.

The satphone trembled in his hands. He tried to activate it, but his thumb kept missing the button.

"Did he have a weapon?" she was right at Lee's shoulder.

Lee spun on her, the words rising to his mouth: *Shut the fuck up!* He managed to bite down on them before they left his lips. His eye hit the woman's, and everything that he didn't say in that moment came through in his gaze like a transmission burst.

She took a step back from him, the indignation in her face giving way to the fear that someone feels when a mean dog with no leash bares its teeth.

Lee tried to swallow, but his tongue was desert-dry. "Enemy combatant," Lee husked.

She is not your enemy. She is one of your people.

The fear in her eyes added a note of shame to the toxic mix boiling up in Lee's brain.

Lee held up the satphone. "It turned out to be a satphone. Could have been a gun, or a grenade." Breathe in. Breathe out. "I would kill a hundred of him before I let one of you get taken out. This is war. This is what it looks like."

The woman's lips trembled. She knew it was true. But truth, and what we wish was the truth, often collide and leave a mess of gore in their wake.

The woman managed a nod.

Lee wanted to ask her name. Wanted to shift down, take himself out of the red, appeal to her reason, *connect* with her somehow. But there wasn't time for that.

His hands had stilled enough. He thumbed the satphone on. Looked at the call log.

The last phone call was made approximately two minutes prior.

TEN

GRASSROOTS

THEY TOOK NO PRISONERS.

The assault on Triprock lasted nine minutes, from start to finish. The majority of the Cornerstone operatives still in residence were holed up in the main ranch house. Abe left them where they lay. There was no point in cleaning anything up.

Structure-to-structure, the three fire teams cleared the entire settlement, pulling the civilians out that had taken cover during the brief and violent raid. They amassed the civilians in the center of Triprock, telling them only one thing: "We're friendly. We're here with Abe Darabie and Lee Harden."

Abe stepped out of the last cleared structure, one of the bunkhouses that had harbored mostly civilians, and one man that the civilians had identified as Cornerstone, despite the fact that he was not in uniform. Abe waited until the civilians had left before putting the man down.

He didn't beg for mercy. He seemed resigned to his fate.

Abe touched off his comms, spinning in a slow circle, his eyes finally shooting out to the surrounding overwatch positions. "Abe to all elements, Triprock is secured. Positions One, Two, and Three, check in."

Position One checked in, and told Abe they were moving into Triprock.

Then Position Three checked in.

Abe turned and looked towards the distant copse of trees that stood out black against the navy sky. "Position Two, you copy me? Abe to Nugs or Scots, or anyone from the Highlanders."

The line remained empty. Dead.

A crackle.

Abe's sinking heart gave one last hopeful twitch.

It didn't last long.

"This is Corporal Turner to Major Darabie." The young man's voice was haunted. Strained. "We lost Scots and Nugs. The…the primals got them."

Abe clenched his teeth, air hissing through them. "I copy, corporal. Did you take those fuckers out?"

"Affirmative. We got them…we got them when they were trying to haul the bodies away."

Shit.

"Abe copies," he transmitted, his chest feeling hollow. "Meet up with us down here."

***

His adrenaline subsiding, Lee's aches nagged at him for attention. But he had work to do.

He drove the Humvee into the front gates of Triprock, his lips tight and turned down at the corners.

He should be glad. The mission was a success. At least partially. Triprock had been liberated. They'd only lost two soldiers. He should be counting his blessings. But the reality of that one man that had escaped and made a phone call was like a meat hook that caught his guts and dragged them down low.

There were no lights on in Triprock, save for the weaponlights of the fire teams, scouring through the darkness, illuminating in bare flashes the gathering of civilians in the center of the ranch.

How many were there now? A hundred? Maybe less? Had anyone died in the crossfire? Had anyone that he'd known in Triprock been killed by Cornerstone in the intervening months since he…

Abandoned them?

He pulled the Humvee straight up to the crowd, the headlights illuminating faces—some of them familiar to Lee, others not. He searched the crowd for the Robledos, and Sally Sigman. He put the Humvee in neutral, activated the emergency brake, and cut the engine.

He tried his best to not look too lame as he struggled his way out of the vehicle. As his feet hit the dusty ground, he remembered his eye, and the patch in his pocket. He let his rifle hang, and stood behind the door of the Humvee, almost furtively, while he dove into his pocket and strapped the eyepatch over his head.

There. At least he didn't *look* like a monster now.

The two soldiers and one civilian woman emerged from the Humvee. Lee closed his own door and looked back. The woman had sat directly behind Lee, and was on his side of the vehicle, now facing him. Her eyes glanced off of his, avoiding contact.

"What's your name?" Lee asked, trying to sound human.

She hesitated. Swallowed. "Darcy."

Lee dipped his head. "Hey. You did good, Darcy."

Darcy finally met his eyes, her own narrowed. "I didn't do anything."

Lee managed a smile. "But you didn't do anything wrong, either."

Her shoulders straightened a bit at that. "I'm sorry about earlier. I didn't…"

Lee waved it off. "Nothing to apologize for. These things are hard on everyone."

Darcy nodded. "You were right to shoot him."

Lee's smile left his face like a bit of tumbleweed caught in the wind. He turned away from her without answering. Yes. He was right. The man he killed wouldn't haunt his dreams. Already, Lee had forgotten what his face looked like. Just another *enemy combatant.*

But he wouldn't forget the sound of Darcy's voice. That would stick with him. A little clarion call of humanity from some long lost part of him. A reminder that his brutality was a means to an end, and not the real him.

It *wasn't* the real him.

He did what he did so that one day, he wouldn't have to anymore.

Was that logic flawed?

"Lee."

He turned and found Abe standing before him, his NODs pushed up from his eyes.

Abe jerked a thumb back. "Settlement's clear. No more Cornerstone. These are all the civilians. I got eighty-four by my last count."

Lee nodded and moved away from the Humvee, towards the crowd of onlooking civilians. Abe fell into step with him. "Angela and Brinly are ten minutes out with the rest of us. Have you made contact with the Robledos?"

Abe shook his head. "Haven't seen them."

Lee stopped before he reached the edges of the crowd and lowered his voice. "The runner got a call out on a satphone."

"Goddammit."

"Nothing to be done for it." Lee turned back to the crowd. Raised his voice. "Eric or Catalina Robledo?"

The crowd shifted. Uncomfortable. Eyes glanced around—not looking for the Robledos, but instead avoiding a nasty truth.

Lee knew the truth just from looking at them.

A slim, dark-haired young woman pushed her way to the front of the crowd. "They were killed."

Lee had the urge to smile at the sight of Sally, but her words prevented that. Her eyes connected to Lee's, and he saw in them—or imagined that he did—a note of accusation. He opened himself up to it, knowing what was coming. "When?"

Sally's hands clenched and unclenched. "Last month. After…"

After I abandoned them.

Lee nodded in understanding, and Sally let him off the hook. Thank God.

"But you're here now," Sally declared. She turned to the others that surrounded her. "He came back."

A murmur of assent went through those gathered. It was mild. Shock at the sudden changing of their fortunes, and probably a good bit of confusion. They'd all been ripped from their beds by the sound of gunfire. They were still piecing together what the hell had happened, and how their entire reality had been overturned. But at least they weren't hostile.

Sometimes that was the best you could hope for.

Lee had learned one valuable lesson with people: You couldn't trust them, but you sure as shit could rely on them to act like people. And people were selfish, panicky, and generally stupid. It was a breath of fresh air that Lee didn't find himself suddenly put on the defensive with a bunch of accusations about how none of this would have happened if he hadn't abandoned them in the first place.

Lee took a deep breath. "Alright, everybody listen up. I'm gonna keep this short and to-the-point. The last time me and Abe were here, we took out the cartel that was holding you down. And before we left, we advised you all to leave."

Another murmur. This one less friendly. A little more defensive.

Lee held up a hand. "We're here again, and this time you don't have an option. One of the Cornerstone operatives got a call out before we were able to stop him. I don't know who he called, but we should assume that someone in the Cornerstone command structure now knows that Triprock is not theirs anymore."

Sally took another step forward. “We’re in the same damn situation as last time, Lee. Where the hell do you want us to go?”

Lee met her eyes. “I want you to come with me. All of you. We’re not staying here. Me and my people are on the move. And we’re heading for a fight.”

A man that Lee didn’t know stepped forward. “All due respect, sir. But there’s only, like, what? Twenty of you? Who exactly are you talking about fighting?”

Lee shook his head. “There’s more than twenty of us. President Angela Houston and Major Brinly of the Marine Corps will be here momentarily with nearly five hundred others. And, as for who we’re fighting? We’re fighting the people that did this to you.”

“Cornerstone?” the man asked.

“Greeley.”

No one spoke for a moment. Not even a whisper. Everyone chewed on it in the silence of their shocked and sleep-fogged minds.

“There’s a war going on,” Lee said, scanning the crowd, looking for those eyes that would shine back at him and show him a person that believed, a person who was willing to fight to the death for that belief. “We’re beyond just trying to make do and outlive the plague. We’re past that. This is a war for our home, for our country, against people hell-bent on subjugating you at your most vulnerable. But you’re not as vulnerable as they think you are. You’ve got teeth. You can bite back.”

Sally spoke up again. Practical as ever. “They took all our weapons.”

Lee nodded. "Don't worry about the weapons. We can provide you with weapons. All you need to do is pick them up and be willing to use them."

A third person stepped forward, an older man. "And what if we don't?" he asked, his voice weary. "What if we just want to be left alone?"

Lee made eye contact with the man. His weathered face. The age in his eyes, far greater than what was obvious from his body. He might be in his fifties. But his eyes looked ancient. Lee understood that exhaustion. He lived it, every day.

The problem was, Lee couldn't trust them. If he let any of the people in Triprock simply wander out on their own, then it would only be a matter of time before they talked, spread the word, outed Lee, and crippled the mission.

The truth was cold and bitter: Lee couldn't let any of them walk away from him. But that was not a truth he was willing to reveal at this point. It would do more harm than good.

"Being left alone isn't an option anymore," Lee answered, evenly. "The truth is..." *How to put this?* "...If you want to live, then your only option is to join us."

***

Brinly had unplugged his earpiece from his radio, allowing Angela to listen to the traffic as they approached Triprock. Her heart had downshifted out of its palpitations that had taken her straight from the moment of waking to the moment she heard Abe transmit the "all clear."

And only two dead.

She hated herself for that. For the fact that *only* losing Scots and Nug felt like a victory. But compared to what her imagination had conjured when the operation had been forced, it *was* a victory. She'd imagined a lot more of her people dead.

Abe. Menendez. Breckenridge.

Lee.

Goddamn him for running out there like that.

She swore, one of these days she was going to chain him to a seat in the command MATV.

Close beside her, taking it all in with a complete lack of emotion—or at least emotion that could be seen—sat Abby. As they pulled into the gates of Triprock, followed by a long line of vehicles crammed with their rag-tag army, Angela stole a few glances at her daughter, trying to suss out what was going on behind those eyes that looked so much like her own.

Abby had grown up. Sure, she'd gotten longer and leaner and didn't look so much like a kid anymore as she approached her tweens. But the real changes were happening on the inside. And Angela wasn't sure she liked what she was seeing.

Abby used to have a deliberate policy of mental avoidance, acting like everything was fine, finding other kids to play with, complaining about the lean meals they ate, and otherwise being a shining example of a person unwilling to admit the gory changes in the world that was falling apart around them.

Now she'd become a sponge. Taking it all in. Like she was opening her eyes to the reality of their world for the first time. And rather than recoil in horror, she seemed to find it fascinating. Like a logic problem that needed to be solved.

She both envied her daughter, and yearned to see her be more…

Emotional?

Wasn't it a good thing that she was like this? Wasn't this a better way to live? Did she really want her daughter to spend the rest of her life with a knot in her gut? Wasn't it better that she adapt to these challenges?

Abby was, in truth, a tiny microcosm of what was happening to all of the people that had evacuated from Butler. They had left their pretensions of stability, and thrown themselves wholesale into something completely alien. They'd thrown themselves into Lee's world. A world where the right to be alive was guaranteed only by the muzzle of the gun in your hand, how many rounds you had left, and how willing you were to put down anybody that threatened it.

As Angela and Abby exited the back of the MATV, she found herself looking for a place to deposit Abby, to get her out of the way of the adult conversations about to take place. But there was no place to put a child in Triprock. There were only bullet-chewed buildings, and the dark, slumped figures of bodies on the ground.

So Abby stayed with her. As had become the norm.

Angela rounded the back end of the MATV with Brinly, and spotted Lee, doing his best to walk without showing his limp.

Angela's mind filled with discordant thoughts, but Abby apparently had no such problem. She stepped out in front of her mother, showing that strange development that still surprised both Angela and Lee: She didn't shrink away from Lee like she used to.

"Did you get them all?" Abby asked, as though asking if all the garbage had been bagged up.

Lee's one eye flitted down to Abby. A frown dipped his brow for a fleeting second. A consideration of what to say. And then a decision. "Yes. We got them all." He returned his eye to Angela. "One of them made it out. We stopped him but he had a satphone, and he did manage to make a call out."

Angela looked over Lee's shoulder to the center of Triprock, where the survivors of this little settlement were moving about. Some of them going to the places where they lived, others carrying their minimal belongings out, and still others standing with those belongings, as though waiting for a train to whisk them away.

"Is Triprock on board?" Angela asked.

Lee nodded. "Didn't take much convincing. After last time, I guess they can see the writing on the wall."

"No dissenters?"

"Not really. Nobody with any real convictions."

"What's the temperature like?"

Lee turned so that he was shoulder to shoulder with Angela, looking at the gathered people. "I think they're ready. Cornerstone did one good thing: They pissed them off."

"Should we move out?"

Lee shook his head. "No, I think we should camp here until morning. Let everyone get a few more hours of sleep. If they can. And Triprock is safer than being exposed out in the middle of nowhere."

"But the satphone call. Aren't you worried about a response?"

Lee lifted a finger and scratched under his eyepatch. "It's a crap cake no matter how you slice it. But it's only four hours to dawn. Cornerstone won't mobilize a response in that amount of time. Triprock just isn't that strategically valuable. And we have a lot of logistics to cover before we hit the road."

Angela breathed out a sigh. "Well. I won't be sleeping again."

Lee shook his head. "No, me neither."

ELEVEN

CONSCRIPTION

SAM WAS ALREADY AWAKE by the time Frenchie whispered to him, “Hey, yo! Something’s goin’ on!”

Sam was upright and on his feet with the speed that only a young man’s body can accomplish. He hadn’t been sleeping that deeply anyways, and the murmured alerts between Johnson and Frenchie had peeled back the last layers of dozing.

Instinctively, Sam found his eyes swooping around for his rifle. But, of course, it wasn’t there. He was unarmed in enemy territory.

He righted his gaze to Frenchie, rubbing crust out of his eyes. “What?”

Frenchie shrugged, then pointed. “Saw a few people moving down the main street with a purpose. I think there might be someone looking for workers.”

“Shit!” Sam spun, his eyes hitting the open door to the outside and seeing the dim gray light of dawn. He hadn’t expected Greeley to come calling so early. But he couldn’t waste the opportunity. “Frenchie, get everyone up and packed and meet me down there. I’m gonna run ahead and see what’s up.”

Marie, who had been sleeping—or pretending to—nearby, was getting to her feet noticeably slower than Sam had, but no less awake.

"I'll roll with you," she husked in a dry morning voice.

Frenchie was already off to rouse the others. He stopped and shot back over his shoulder, "Don't forget about that asshole. You might want more backup."

Marie seemed miffed. "What? I'm not enough?"

Frenchie didn't seem to know how to respond, and used his orders as an excuse to retreat.

Sam moved for the doorway out, checking to make sure the knife was still on his hip. "Come on, Marie. I know you got my back."

"Damn right I do," Marie grouched, falling in step with him as he exited the dark building, out into the dawn light. Everything was flat and gray, save for the sky to the east which shown a deep red.

What was that they said? Red sky in the morning, take warning?

Sam wasn't a fan of the omen. He decided not to be superstitious today.

As he and Marie hit the street outside, an amplified voice lilted over a cool morning breeze that scoured away any lingering sleepiness. He couldn't tell what the voice was saying, but his eyes caught movement on the main street: A few people were running now.

"Dammit. You good to run?"

Marie started running.

Two, four, then ten people flitted by on the main street.

They became enemies in Sam's mind. He had to beat them to the punch. It didn't matter if they were poor, starving families trying to feed their little chaps—it was more important that Sam get inside

Greeley, and if Greeley was only taking a few people, Sam wasn't above barging through and trampling other people's hopes for the sake of his mission.

He broke the corner of the main street, and what he saw did nothing to ease his sense of urgency.

Straight down, at the very beginning of the main street, a single pickup truck sat with a man in the bed, speaking through a megaphone. He was surrounded by no less than a hundred people.

"I don't give a fuck who we have to trample," Sam shot at Marie. "We're getting into Greeley today."

The voice of the soldier—or rather, the Cornerstone operative—with the megaphone began to clarify into words: "Pack it in tight, people! I don't want to repeat myself! Come on! Hustle up!"

Sam hustled, spying another group on the opposite side of the street, and perceiving the competition of a footrace burgeoning between them. Everyone in The Tank shared Sam's decision: Everyone else was their enemy.

Sam and Marie staggered to a stop at the back of the crowd. It was already packed shoulder to shoulder. He had every intention of barging through their midst, but those present had every intention of not allowing him.

He tried to worm his way between bodies but they closed ranks on him. An old man shot an elbow at Sam's face, which he managed to avoid by a bare inch.

He saw the old man's other hand drop to a knife sticking out of his pocket. His rheumy eyes glared at Sam. "You stay in the fucking back! Shove me and I'll fucking gut you!"

Sam drew back a single step, his own hand touching the handle of his knife, more than willing to respond to the old man with violence. The tiny space that he'd given up was immediately filled by another three desperate refugees. The old man smirked viciously at him.

"Everyone's pretty motivated," Marie observed.

Off to the left, a scuffle broke out.

Sam couldn't see over the heads of the people gathered, but he could hear the savage sounds. His eyes shot to the operative in the back of the truck. The scuffle hadn't escaped his notice, but he watched it with a bemused smile for a few beats before raising the megaphone to his mouth again.

"Alright, hey! Hey!"

The scuffling downgraded a few notches.

"Chill the fuck out! There's no need to fight! We got an opportunity for everyone in The Tank." The operative had a thick Boston accent. "Cool your jets, you buncha fucks. Christ."

The rumble of big diesel engines caught Sam's ears over the worried yammering of the crowd. He stood on tiptoes, and caught the tops of three city buses, nosing their way into The Tank.

"Alright!" Boston cleared his throat. "Everyone quiet down and listen up! I'm only gonna say this one time and there's no question and answer session afterwards, so pay the fuck attention."

Boston pulled a piece of paper from a cargo pocket and unfolded it as the crowd stilled and a strange silence fell over those gathered. Every man, woman, and child present was desperate, and in their desperation, they were easy to control.

The operative raised the paper with one hand, the other holding the megaphone to his lips as he read aloud: "By order of the President of the United States of America, all refugees currently being held in the town of La Salle—that's The Tank to you—that are over the age of fifteen, are now eligible for conscription."

A wave of excitement and shock roiled over the crowd. The operative looked briefly annoyed as he waited for silence again. "Can I fucking continue?"

He got his silence again. The crowd stood with an unnatural stillness.

Boston smacked his lips and returned to reading the paper. "Furthermore, and also by order of President Briggs, the town of La Salle is to be closed as a refugee encampment." He stopped there, crumpled the paper, and shoved it back in his pocket. "Now let me put all that in plain speak for you. Everyone in The Tank has until noon today to make a decision. Option Number One: you agree to pick up a rifle and be conscripted as a Cornerstone soldier, to be put on guard duty, or latrine duty, whatever the fuck we say. Option Number Two: you pack up your shit and find somewhere else to live."

Boston held up his hand against another wave of murmurs. "Shut up. Shut up, please. I'm not done."

Everyone shut up.

"All of you who choose Option Number One will be afforded daily rations of food and water for you, as well as any children in your care under the age of fifteen. No, you are not allowed to be a stay-at-home mommy or daddy. If you're over the age of fifteen, you *will* have a rifle, and you *will* do what you're told. You'll also be provided housing. Further details will be given upon your conscription.

"If you choose Option Number Two, then you have until sundown today to leave La Salle. Any and all persons still inside La Salle after sundown will be shot on sight. And by the way, sundown means twenty-hundred—eight o'clock, P.M."

Boston pointed behind him to the three city buses as they pulled to a stop at the edge of the crowd. "If you choose Option Number One, you will form three, orderly, single-file lines, evenly distributed between these three buses. No pushing, no jostling, no shouting—none of your bullshit. If you can't follow these simple orders that I'm giving you right now, then we will take that as a sign that you're not the type of person we want holding a rifle and you *will not* get inside Greeley. If anyone gets out of hand, you will be shot. This is going to go off nice and civilized. If you make this difficult for me and my men, you will be shot. I hope that I'm abundantly clear on that point."

Boston lowered the megaphone a few inches, revealing a wan smile. He eyed the crowd, which had become very still in the light of his threats. No one knew what exactly rose to the occasion of being "difficult," and so everyone simply froze in place.

"That's good," Boston noted. "Good start. Alright. Three, orderly, evenly-distributed lines."

The crowd began moving. One big blob of humanity, inching towards the promise of a better life, scared to death to shoulder each other too hard, lest it be seen as disorderly. Sam had never seen so many people so suddenly fall in line.

Sam started moving too, but Marie tugged on his elbow. "We should wait for the others."

He met her eyes and felt a note of urgency. "What if they fill up?"

Marie shook her head and lowered her voice. "They're as desperate as these people are, they're just hiding it better. They're going to take everyone they can get. And we don't want to get split up. We need to stay together."

Sam grit his teeth, feeling the mass of people flow around him. She was right. He knew she was right. But it was difficult to simply stand there.

Boston scanned the crowd and his gaze eventually alighted upon Sam. A frown creased his brow. He pointed. "You. You choosing Option Number Two or some shit?"

Sam swallowed hard, feeling the attention of everyone around him. He stood up straight. "No, sir. I'm waiting on the rest of my team."

Boston's eyebrows arched. "Your team?"

"I came with four others. They're my team."

The operative hopped down out of the pickup bed and stalked towards Sam. As he moved, his eyes flitted back and forth through the crowd that parted before him—very orderly—and his jaw was set.

Sam's body geared up for a fight, but his mind pressed down on that. He had a mission. He *had* to get inside Greeley. This was his chance, and he wasn't going to fuck it up by bumping chests with this douchebag.

Just tell him what he wants to hear.

Boston stopped in front of Sam. Eyed him up. "Name," he demanded.

"Sam. Sameer. Balawi."

Boston looked pained. "Sam Sameer Balawi?"

"First name, Sameer. Last name, Balawi. I go by Sam. Sir."

"Alright, Sam Balawi. You got prior military experience?"

"No, sir."

"You sure about that? Because you sound like you do."

"I've learned some things along the way."

"Yeah? From who?"

"Other soldiers." Sam felt his face flush, feeling like the operative was a shovel scraping away at his thin layer of deception.

"Boy, you better start using some plain speak to me. Because I get the sense you're not telling me something."

Sam's pulse hummed in his ears. Everything in his chest and gut seemed to have welded itself into one molten-hot lump of panic. "There was a soldier I met in Oklahoma, where we're from. He told me to always keep my team together, to not get split up. He called it 'unit cohesion.'" Sam swallowed on a dry tongue. "He died later on. Killed by…infected."

Sam barely kept the word *primal* from coming out of his mouth.

Boston looked over Sam's shoulder. "This them?"

Sam turned and found Jones, Pickell, Johnson, and Frenchie jogging up the street to them. Jones was fixated on Sam, worry gouged across his usually playful expression. He didn't like Sam facing down a Cornerstone operative.

"Yes, sir. That's them."

"Alright, Sam Balawi." Boston reached into another one of his cargo pockets and drew out a plastic nametag with clip. He stuck it unceremoniously onto Sam's collar.

Sam looked down at it. Read the words upside down: SQUAD LEADER.

Boston tapped the plastic tag. "You're a squad leader now. When you get off the bus, the receiving team will pull you into a separate group of people that have half a brain. Congrats."

The operative turned without saying anything else and edged back through the crowd.

Jones and the rest of the team stamped to a halt beside Sam.

"What was that about?" Jones demanded, breathing hard. "Everything okay?"

Sam gripped the little plastic tag in bloodless fingers and let out a shaky breath. "Everything's good. He just appointed me a squad leader."

Jones relaxed. "Oh. Okay, good. Congratulations. You're already making friends." He heaved a deep breath, then spat off to the side. "What's next on your career path?"

Sam raised his eyes to the lines forming at the buses. He pointed to the middle line, which looked slightly shorter than the others. "We're getting on that bus." Sam started moving towards it. "Eyes open, mouths shut. Do *not* get into it with anyone. They said if there's any disorderliness, they'll just start shooting."

"Great," Jones commented, his voice slightly lower. "Fantastic."

Marie touched Sam's shoulder as they positioned themselves in line at the middle bus. "You did good, Sam."

Sam stopped in the line, about twenty people back from the open bus doors where what looked like a US Army soldier stood with a clipboard, taking names as he allowed the people on board.

Sam looked behind him, worry cinching knots around his heart again. He found Jones and looked at him meaningfully. "Did you grab it?"

Jones looked put-out. "No. I left it behind. I forgot the most integral piece of equipment. Whoops."

"Sorry. Just checking."

"Actually, that was a lie. I didn't forget it. I dropped it and it shattered into a billion pieces." Jones held up his hands. "Butterfingers Jones. That's what they used to call me."

"Alright. I get it."

"Christ. You should give me that squad leader tag. How dare you question me."

Marie reached out and squeezed Jones's forearm. The soldier on the bus was eyeing them—the only people in the line that were murmuring amongst themselves. Dangerously close to being disorderly.

Jones took the hint and shut his mouth.

The soldier grimaced at them, but didn't call them out, and continued taking names.

They shuffled forward in silence. Sam kept scanning around him, looking at the other lines as they boarded the buses. God, but everyone was so quiet.

Sam reached the steps of the bus. The soldier nodded at his name tag with a smirk. "Already, huh? That what you ladies were giggling about back there?"

Sam chose not to answer that.

The soldier got his name and jotted it down. "All the way back. Right side of the bus."

Sam did as instructed. The right side of the bus was already half-filled. Sam scrunched in beside a middle-aged man and woman. He couldn't tell if they knew each other or just happened to be sitting in the same spot. They didn't speak. Didn't even make eye contact with Sam.

Marie, Jones, and Pickell filled in the seat directly ahead of Sam. Then Johnson and Frenchie the next one up, followed by a stranger to take the aisle seat.

The bus grew stifling. The sun was barely up and hadn't had time to cook the air, but the quiet breaths of the people crammed on board made the atmosphere dank and heavy. It smelled foul. The breath and body odors and filthy clothes of a hundred unwashed people, shoulder to shoulder with each other.

The right side of the bus filled up. Then the left side began to fill, starting at the back.

Sam watched the people as they came on board. Young. Old. Men. Women. Hungry, hopefully eyes. Excitement and fear in equal measures. A palpable sense that Sam could pluck right out of the air—the anxiety of what was happening to them. Being crammed into buses.

Sure, they'd been told they were being offered conscription. But what if it was a lie? What if this was something else? What if they were being taken to a mass grave to be disposed of?

Well, maybe that was just Sam's worries.

But Marie had been right. Greeley was hurting for manpower. This move made sense from that perspective. And it revealed a weakness. Something that was very much worth reporting back to Lee: Greeley was about to be secured by a bunch of untrained civilians.

People who had no real loyalty to Greeley.

People who might be swayed.

Sam began to look about him with a fresh perspective, eyeing the faces, and wondering who among them could be turned? And then wondering how he could accomplish that. How was he going to open a dialogue with these people? If he did it too soon, he would shoot himself in the foot. Everyone was so scared right now—scared that this dream might be shattered—that no one would be willing to listen. Not so soon after being given this opportunity.

When was the right time to start talking to them?

You are in over your head, Sam realized. And suddenly felt enormously guilty for telling Lee that he could do this. He was going to fuck it up somehow. What the hell had he been thinking, promising Lee that he could accomplish this mission?

Lee's trust was hard to come by these days. And Sam stood on the precipice of betraying that trust with his abject lack of abilities. It had all seemed possible when it was theoretical. Now, being faced with the prospect of it as a reality, Sam's stomach was sinking further and further into his pelvis.

Sam was so lost in his thoughts in that moment, that he didn't notice the man that sat directly across from him, until that man spoke.

"Well, well." A harsh whisper. "Look who it is."

Sam jerked, looked over the aisle.

It was the asshole. The one that Sam had threatened to cannibalize—*Jesus, did I really say that shit?*

The asshole leaned forward in his seat, his haughty eyes drifting down to the tag clipped to Sam's collar. An expression of chagrin passed over the asshole's face.

"Huh. Guess they hand those out to anyone."

As the asshole said it, he fingered something hanging from his own collar.

An identical tag: SQUAD LEADER.

The soldier leaned back into the bus. "Hey. Lock it up back there."

The asshole grinned at Sam, then settled back into his seat.

TWELVE

NORTHWARD

BY THE TIME DAWN BROKE over Triprock, Lee's brain was operating on its last reserves. He knew he needed sleep, but there was too much to do.

All through the waning hours of the night he'd moved restlessly through Triprock, his brain slugging through the arithmetic of war. Beans, bullets, and bandages, as they used to say.

The people of Triprock were committed, which gave Lee hope for his ultimate plan. But some of the leaders of Triprock had their own ideas, which irritated him. Who were they to suddenly begin deciding on strategy? They'd sat under the thumb of a squad of Cornerstone operatives that they could've overthrown if they'd nutted up about it. Now that the threat had been dealt with, all of the sudden they wanted to leverage their opinion on how to proceed?

Which led Lee to this point, right now, rubbing his dirty palms across his face, trying to massage some life back into his head.

"It's impressive what you've done so far," one of the Triprock leaders was saying. His name was Aaron. And he was a think-for-yourselfer. "But you're still talking about trying to invade an entire city with…what? Four hundred people?"

Lee blinked to clear his vision, trying to wrap his head around being diplomatic when all he really wanted to do was point a gun and tell people to get on board or else.

That was just the exhaustion talking. The well of his patience was a tad dry.

Abe responded on Lee's behalf: "With everyone from Triprock, it will be about five hundred. And as we continue to move north, we'll garner more support from other settlements."

"But we're not soldiers," Aaron pressed. "Most of the people you have aren't soldiers either. They're just civilians with guns."

Lee frowned at him, finding his eyes taking longer than normal to focus. "Civilians with guns created the United States of America. And they beat one of the most formidable world powers of the time."

"I'm not arguing against fighting," Aaron returned. "I'm arguing that one big massive horde of us trying to knock down the gates of Greeley isn't the way to do it."

Lee couldn't help himself. "Oh? Is that what your vast experience in military strategy tells you?"

Aaron bristled, but Sally cut him off with a hand to his shoulder. "Aaron, you should listen. Lee knows what he's talking about."

"I have been listening," Aaron snapped. "And I disagree. If I'm putting my life and the life of everyone in Triprock on the line, then I believe I should have the opportunity to speak my mind."

Sally gave him a withering smile. "But you don't know what the fuck you're talking about."

Aaron rounded on her, glaring. "And you do?"

Angela cleared her throat loudly. "Alright. Thank you, Sally. And thank you, Aaron. Your perspective is valuable and appreciated. However, it doesn't change the situation. We've built a certain strategy, and there's a lot riding on things going a certain way. The fact of the matter is, an insurgency is not the way to get things done."

Aaron shook his head. "Every war in recent memory says differently."

"And how long did those insurgencies last?" Lee demanded, cutting to the core of the issue. "Decades. An insurgency is designed to *slowly* undermine a more powerful force. Death by a thousand cuts." Lee stabbed a finger at the ground. "We don't have that kind of time."

"Why not?" Aaron demanded.

"Because Greeley is weak *now*. They've overextended themselves. The majority of their fighting force is on the east coast. They've left their heart unprotected and vulnerable. Now's the time for a decisive blow. Not a slow insurgency that will give them time to bolster their defenses. If we give them too much time, we'll lose momentum. We'll lose everything."

"An insurgency is safer!" Aaron insisted. "Small operations. Small, surprise attacks and raids. And then we melt back into the populace. It's worked before against world powers."

Abe shook his head. "It's worked against world powers that are concerned about human rights violations. That's not what we're dealing with here, Aaron, and you know it. Think through what you're suggesting here: You and your people stay in Triprock and mount small raids, always returning to your home base. Well, what do you think happens when Greeley figures it out? Back in the day, we would know that there were insurgents in a village, and we'd have to try to route them out. President Briggs has no such restraints. When he learns about a settlement that might be harboring insurgents, he'll just send in his troops and wipe everyone out wholesale. He doesn't give a fuck about human rights, and you know it."

Lee nodded along with Abe, and saw some of the logic getting through to Aaron. Sensing that they had their last detractor on the ropes, Lee pressed forward for the knockout. "The army that Briggs dispatched to the east coast? They're not going to stay there forever, Aaron. They're going to come this way, if they haven't started already. And when they do, they won't be pulling any punches. How confident are you that you're going to be able to convince them that you're not aligned with us? How are you going to explain the missing Cornerstone operatives?" Lee thrust his hand out. "One of them got a message out last night, Aaron. You know this. How long do you think you have before Cornerstone shows up again? Do you think they're going to ask questions? Or do you think they're just going to roll in and wipe everyone out?"

Aaron put his hands on his hips and avoided eye contact for a protracted moment. Staring out at the collection of buildings that surrounded them. This was his home. He didn't want to leave it.

"Here's the cold, harsh truth, Aaron," Lee pressed his advantage. "Triprock isn't valuable enough to Greeley. You and your people have survived here through pure, blind luck. The second Greeley learns about what happened last night—if they haven't already—they're not going to come back to ask questions and investigate. They're going to come back and level this fucking place, and everyone in it."

Angela slipped in to land the final punches. "What we're doing is the only way to win. A grassroots movement. A wave of people that are willing to leave behind their current false sense of security, in order to secure their future survival. The window of opportunity is open to us. The time for an insurgency to be effective has passed us by. The only way to win now is open warfare. One massive blow while Greeley is unprotected. And every day—every *minute*—that we spend arguing and not moving towards our objective, is more time for Greeley to figure out what we're doing and shore up their defenses." Angela gave Aaron a sympathetic smile. "I know you don't want to leave your home. I didn't want to leave mine either. But if you want to survive, if you want to have a home sometime in the future, a normal life, then you have to be a part of what we're doing. It's the only way, Stephen. I wish it wasn't, and I wouldn't be standing here in front of you if there *was* another way. But there isn't. This is it."

Sally had the emotional intelligence not to be aggressive in that moment. She chose instead to lay a gentle hand on Aaron's shoulder. "You're already willing to fight. We're *all* willing to fight. It's just the 'how' that we need to agree on. And Lee is right. Lee and Abe were right when they freed us from the cartel and told us to leave. We didn't take their advice then, and look what happened. Think of the people that we've lost by staying here. Eric and Catalina and so many others. For what? This isn't our home anymore, Aaron. It's got too much death in it.

We're all willing to fight, so let's fight. Let's be a part of the solution. Let's end this now."

Aaron stood there, jaw muscles bunching as he continued to avoid eye contact with everyone in the circle. He was alone, and he knew it. He was the last holdout. There were others that shared Aaron's opinion, but they would listen to him. If he changed, they would change with him.

Aaron let out an exhausted sigh. In that exhalation, Lee sensed victory. He still didn't meet their gazes. He looked around him as Sally's words settled on his soul, turning it.

"It's ugly," Aaron murmured. A strained smile flitted across his lips. "I want to see it as home, but all I see is all we've lost. It's just…ugly." He dipped his head and regarded his feet. "We'll go. We'll be a part of this movement. You're right. There's not another way."

The tension in Lee's chest abated. But the irritation somehow remained. God, but would he have to have this conversation every damn time? People. They were just so fucking blind. Scrubbing the scales of their own denial from their eyes was a constant battle. For once, Lee would love to just say something, and not have to argue a ten-point thesis to get what he wanted.

Lee turned away from Aaron, not trusting himself to keep the irritation from his voice. He traded a glance with Abe and gave a small nod.

"Sally," Abe said. "Aaron. We need to get on the road. Go get your people loaded up and ready to roll. We'd like to be on the move in thirty minutes."

Aaron nodded and turned away from them. Sally hung back just long enough to give them a fierce smile. Then she spun and followed.

The second that they were out of earshot, Lee, Angela, and Abe all let out a pent up breath sewn with a few expletives.

"Every damn time," Lee muttered, turning to the others. "Thanks for the backup."

Angela gave him a sardonic eyebrow. "You seemed tired."

Abe smirked at Lee. "What she means to say, is that she was concerned your filter might be a tad porous this morning."

Lee grouched out an irritable noise. "I can only speak the truth. Can't make these fuckers believe it."

Angela eyed him. "You might start by not thinking of them as 'fuckers.'"

"When they stop acting like fuckers, I'll stop seeing them that way. It's like herding cats. Always has been." Lee lifted a finger. "This is why I don't trust anyone."

"Except us," Abe put in.

Lee allowed it with a nod. "Except you guys." He settled himself, smoothing the raised hackles of his brain. "Abe, you got everything you need? Your people ready to roll?"

"We are. Got the route west to New Mexico planned out. We'll check in via satphone at regular intervals, and when we make contact with settlements out there."

Angela stood between Lee and Abe, and didn't look at either of them. Lee watched her for a moment, and realized she was holding back. Probably in an effort not to irritate him further. Which meant she had yet another dissenting opinion.

Lee briefly considered letting her just hang onto whatever she had to say. But that wouldn't do them any good. They needed to be a united front. And he didn't mind dissenting opinions from the people he actually trusted. Angela had been around the block a few times. Her perspective was valuable.

"Go ahead, Angela. Spit it out."

Angela grimaced. "Nothing to spit out. I've already said my piece about it."

"We're only splitting our forces for a short time," Lee said. "Oklahoma and New Mexico are ripe for the picking, but we can't be two places at once. Fastest way to a grassroots movement is to hit them both at the same time and link up in Colorado."

Angela nodded. "I know. Your logic is sound. I just have concerns."

Lee shrugged. "Don't we all? Wish there was a guarantee I could give you, but that's not how these things work. Yes, it's a risk to split up. But it's a risk we have to take. Even moreso now that Greeley might've caught word that we're on the move. We still don't know how much that has shrunk our timeline."

Angela gave him a weary smile. "I know. You've got us this far. I trust you."

***

Thirty minutes later, the long convoy of vehicles snaked their way out of Triprock. What they left behind was only dust and bullet-riddled buildings and bodies. The convoy stayed whole until they met the highway.

Lee, Angela, Brinly and his Marines, and the vast majority of their guerilla fighters, headed north. The people of Triprock went with them.

Abe, along with Breck and Menendez and all of the old soldiers that had served under Terrance "Tex" Lehy, turned west, heading for New Mexico.

THIRTEEN

PURSUIT

"WHY IN THE FUCK did you wait until now to tell me this shit?" Briggs clutched the mug of coffee in his hands so hard he thought he might shatter the porcelain. The contents were now forgotten. The news from Javier was doing a better job of getting his heart pumping than caffeine ever could.

Javier managed to keep his cool, though his dark complexion seemed to have paled. "I was notified of it very early this morning. I decided to pursue as much information as possible prior to bothering you with it. The communication we received was vague."

"Vague? What the fuck do you mean by 'vague'?"

Javier lifted yet another one of his pieces of paper. This guy was obsessed with papers and notes and facts and figures. That was his little accountant's brain at work. It pissed Briggs off to no end. Why exactly had he chosen this beady eyed mole to be his COO?

Javier read aloud: " 'We've been hit. I repeat, we've been hit. Unknown hostiles. Unknown numbers. Requesting immediate QRF.' " Javier cleared his throat and looked up from the page.

"Then there were some expletives, a lot of heavy breathing, and a series of gunshots."

Briggs slapped the coffee mug down. Brown liquid sloshed out onto the table top.

Well, Javier hadn't been exaggerating. That was vague.

Briggs took a long, steadying breath, bulldozing his anger so he could speak and think levelly. "And what else were you able to find out?"

Javier placed the paper on the table. He blinked a few times. "Nothing, sir."

Briggs stuffed his hands into the pockets of his bathrobe. He still hadn't had time to dress, for chrissake. He pressed down on those pockets until he heard the terrycloth begin to strain, threads snapping. "Nothing, huh?"

"Which is why I came to you."

"It took you three hours to come to me with nothing?"

Javier didn't answer.

"Did you dispatch the QRF?"

"I did, but the nearest element we have was three hours away. They should be at Triprock shortly and be able to provide a report about what has happened." Javier swallowed. Reached up and scratched at his temple. "It's possible that it was the people of Triprock. They may have risen up—"

"It wasn't them," Briggs snapped. "Bunch of fucking sheeple. If they had the balls to do that, they wouldn't have waited until now. Someone came in and took out a full squad of our operatives, and they did it fast enough that only one of them was able to make a half-assed report. That's not civilians with farm implements. That's military precision."

"It could have also been a pack of infected, sir."

Briggs briefly considered hurling the coffee cup at Javier. "It wasn't a pack of infected, Javier. Think before you speak next time. Our boys would have handled a pack of infected, and even if they *did* get overrun, they would have specified that in the transmission." Briggs thrust his hand in the direction of the paper on the table. "He said 'unknown hostiles'! Not 'infected'! And then there were *gunshots*, Javier. Gunshots!" Briggs planted his hands on the table and leaned in, the veins in his neck distending. "Does that sound like fucking infected to you?"

Javier dropped his gaze. "No, sir. It doesn't."

"No, it fucking doesn't! It sounds like a military force."

"Yes, sir. I agree with that assessment. I simply wanted to explore all the possibilities."

"I don't want all the possibilities, Javier. It's *possible* that fucking space aliens came down and invaded last night! Don't give me fucking possibilities, give me *probabilities*!"

For once, Javier let a flash of annoyance cross his features. This only served to anger Briggs even more. He preferred that Javier remain supplicant. There's nothing worse than someone who randomly decides to grow a spine in the middle of a conversation.

"Probabilities?" Javier returned. "It's probable that it could be the remainders of Terrence Lehy's militia from Texas. It's also probable that it could have been *Nuevas Fronteras*, trying to make a comeback and send a message. It's also probable that it could be any number of former military from New

Mexico and Oklahoma that were loyal to the two rogue Coordinators that we killed during the operation at the power plant several weeks ago. Those are the probabilities."

Briggs stared at his COO, his mouth a thin line gradually and inexorably turning down at the corners. "No."

Javier's left eye twitched. "No?"

Briggs smashed his palm across his mouth, feeling the stubble that he had yet to shave. "I'll tell you who the fuck it was."

"Yes, sir?" Javier spoke tightly.

Briggs nodded, his eyes widening as that probability in his mind suddenly bloomed like black mold, morphing into the inevitable truth. "It's Lee Harden. That's who it is."

Javier glanced about like he thought this was a joke. "Mister President…No one has caught wind of Lee Harden or any of his compatriots since we toppled the United Eastern States."

Briggs's roiling ire suddenly stilled, like being in the eye of a storm. He straightened. Drew his shoulders back. "You think I'm being paranoid?"

Javier dodged that question. "You asked for probabilities, sir. I believe that Lee Harden still being alive, and furthermore mounting an assault on one of our outposts is…less probable."

Briggs growled low in his throat, shaking his head. "You see, Javier, I disagree with you. You don't know this man like I do. I've been dealing with his fuckery for years. *Years*. I'm not jumping at shadows. This is…" Briggs gave a savage smile. "This is just like him. It stinks of him."

Javier chose his words carefully. "What could Lee Harden possibly have to gain by assaulting Triprock?"

"He's a madman," Briggs snapped. "You can't put logic to his motivations. He's obsessed with me. He's obsessed with undermining everything that I've tried to build here." Briggs began tapping a finger rapidly on the table top, the rhythm of it a metronome to his wild thoughts. "He tried to build a nation to fight me, and I beat him at that. He knows that he can't win in a straight fight. So he's trying to bleed me dry. He doesn't even care if he wins or not—as long as I lose."

"We're not even sure that he's still alive, sir."

"No. I'm not making that mistake again. I've made it before and it's bitten me in the ass. Until I have confirmation that he's dead—by which I mean his fucking head with a bullet hole between the eyes—then I'm going to assume that he's still alive."

Javier shifted his weight from foot to foot. Clasped his hands behind his back. "Well, sir…if that is the assumption that we're operating on, then what should we anticipate as Lee Harden's next move?"

Briggs snatched the chair out from the head of the table and flopped into it, staring into the middle distance, his mind conjuring a hellish image of the madman that was so obsessed with destroying everything Briggs had created.

But what would Lee Harden do? What was his next move? What did Briggs know about this man?

"Insane or not," Briggs said, his voice lower, pensive. "Lee Harden is good at one thing: manipulating people. It's his training. He was trained to go into a populace and get them all to work together for a common goal." Briggs looked thoughtfully at the ceiling, a finger on his lips. "He goes in, convinces people that I'm the devil, and arms them. Convinces them to rebel against me."

Javier appeared unperturbed by this possibility. "If he chooses to harry a few outposts, it's really quite inconsequential to us. Greeley is still relatively secure, and now that we've begun our conscriptions, we'll be well defended against any outward attack that he could mount."

Briggs shook his head. "It won't be an outward attack. He's not stupid. Insane, yes, but not stupid. He would never try to just barge in and invade Greeley." Briggs lapsed into a silence for a long moment, his mind gradually connecting dots according to the "facts" as he believed them.

As he connected those dots, a deep frown settled over his brow.

"Sabotage," Briggs grunted. His eyes snapped back into focus, peering at Javier. "You've already begun the conscription from The Tank?"

"Yes, sir. That began at first light this morning."

"I want you to stop it."

Javier blinked rapidly. "Stop it, sir?"

"I don't want any of those people to be given a gun. Yet. I want you to gather our best interrogators, and I want them to question every motherfucker that we've taken in within the past two weeks—including everyone from The Tank."

"You believe Lee Harden is going to try to infiltrate Greeley?"

Briggs snorted. "No, not himself. But some of his true believers. I can buy that for a dollar." Briggs nodded to himself, becoming surer by the second. "He'll have sent someone here to try to start an uprising. And I want to find out who the fuck that is, and I want to put them in the goddamn ground."

***

Griffin's army had driven through the night and arrived in Texas by dawn. But it wasn't until almost noon that Griffin had his growing fears confirmed.

As the sun had arced into the sky and gave Griffin a reminder that the Texas sun was not to be fucked with, he'd retreated into the refinery—the last known location of the rebels.

Right around the time Griffin had been setting up outside of Fort Bragg, preparing to invade North Carolina, this particular refinery had been wrested out of the hands of the *Nuevas Fronteras* cartel, and taken over by elements from the United Eastern States.

Griffin was aware of this—he'd received the intelligence reports after they'd lost two birds and a squad of Cornerstone operatives to whatever the hell had gone down between Lee Harden and Mateo Ibarra, the head of the cartel.

But the place was a ghost town now.

He'd approached with due caution, sending in several assault teams to clear the massive collection of structures. It had taken them a while. They'd gone slow and deliberate, initially fearing an ambush from people, and then, as the reality that the place was abandoned became clear to them, they began to inch along slowly, checking for booby traps.

There were neither rebels nor booby traps in the refinery.

There was, however, still electricity running to it. And electricity provided air conditioning. Which Griffin was extracting as much pleasure from as he could manage, with his gut sinking and his concerns mounting in his deadlocked, puzzled brain.

But, hey…air conditioning.

He stood in a small office that must've been the foreman's back when the refinery had things like that. His armor lay, inside out, draped across a desk, drying out. His helmet lay next to it, the pads inside still dark from Griffin's sweat.

Were you here, Lee? Griffin wondered as he looked around the room and drank from a water bottle to try to replace what he'd lost. *Did you come here after Butler? Or did you just run?*

Running didn't sound like Lee.

Someone had been here, though. Griffin was positive about that. He could smell their habitation in the nooks and crannies of small rooms like this. He could smell their fading body odors, and the smells of their sweat-and-salt stained clothes, even though the clothes were no longer there.

And whoever had been here had left recently. Which seemed an awful big coincidence to Griffin for it not to be Lee Harden.

Lee had been here. And then he'd left.

But why? Why give up your one resource? Why throw away the one ace in your pocket?

He heard the footsteps coming down the grated walkway outside the office. He didn't move as he perceived them, just kept staring at the room around him, mulling over the possibilities. Wondering what he was missing.

The footsteps stopped at the open door to the foreman's office.

"Captain Griffin, sir."

"What." Griffin didn't bother to turn. He knew who it was.

Lieutenant Ron Paige stepped up to Griffin's side. Even without looking at him, Griffin could see unwelcome news on the horizon. He could tell by the tone of Paige's voice, just in the three words he'd spoken.

Paige didn't mince his words. He laid it out plain and simple. "Holding tanks are bone dry. There's not a fucking gallon of any refined fuel left in this place. Even the crude oil's been drained off." A discomfited sigh. "And the system's been sabotaged."

Griffin had no strong reaction to this. He'd been expecting it. He planted his hands on his hips and turned to look at Paige. "What do you mean by 'sabotaged'?"

"Honestly, I don't even know. Pulowski's from the Engineering Corps and he said the word 'sabotaged' so I just repeated that to you."

Griffin gave Paige a flat smirk. "That's very helpful."

Paige shrugged. "What do you want from me? I shoot things. I don't do engineering."

"What about the offshore rigs? Are they still viable?"

"Well," Paige shifted his weight. "I'd love to be able to have info on that, except for there's no way to get to the rigs. There's a dock out back that looks like it had some boats, but…no boats."

"Well, I guess that figures, now doesn't it?"

Paige nodded. Swiped a bead of sweat from his brow. "I may be just a humble ground pounder, and know nothing about high level strategy, but from my layman's perspective it appears we've been denied resources."

Griffin gave a more genuine smile this time. Because what the hell else were you going to do in these situations? Get pissed and yell? Sometimes you just had to see the humor in these things. Sometimes it was hard to find, but Griffin and Paige were quite practiced in finding it amongst all the bullshit. They were like humor cactuses.

"Well, that's a very astute observation for a ground pounder."

"I know. They should give me your job."

Another set of footfalls became clear, and Griffin and Paige both waited expectantly, until Mr. Smith came stomping into the room. He did not look like he was capable of seeing the humor in the situation. He looked quite angry.

"There you are!" Mr. Smith spat. "I've been looking for you."

Griffin's sense of humor dried up under the arid suck of Mr. Smith's presence. "Well. You found me."

"There's no fuel. The tanks or completely fucking empty."

"I'm aware."

Mr. Smith arched his eyebrows. "And the system's been shut down, and our guys don't know how to get it back up and running again. Did you know that?"

"Yes."

"Well?"

"Well what?"

"You just gonna stand there?"

Griffin slowly turned himself to Mr. Smith. "As opposed to what? Running around and getting pissed about circumstances beyond our control? Getting all flabbergasted because our opponent had half a brain? You seem to be doing a good job of that."

Mr. Smith's face reddened. Not so much at the jibe, Griffin detected, but the fact that it had been done in front of an "underling." Mr. Smith's eyes jagged to Paige, and it didn't seem to help the situation that Paige was smiling at him.

Griffin watched the Cornerstone man with a sort of clinical curiosity. Mr. Smith was somewhat volatile, but he wasn't an idiot. He did seem to be easy to fluster, but he also knew when his chain was being yanked, and he knew how to shut it down.

Mr. Smith relaxed himself with a deep breath. "Alright. Glad we're all up to speed then. Have you uncovered any evidence as to who was here?"

Griffin shook his head. "Whoever it was didn't leave much behind. Certainly nothing we could use to identify them with. But I think we can reasonably assume it was an element loyal to the United Eastern States. And if I were to place a bet, I'd say that it was Lee."

"Why?"

"Why would I bet it was Lee?" Griffin swept his gaze around the room. "Oh, I don't know. I suppose you had to have known the man. He's fucking stubborn as a mule. One of those fight-to-the-death types. Assuming he did make it out of Butler, he would have come here. And it makes sense that he wouldn't want to stay. He'd know this refinery would be our next objective. He'd know he couldn't hold it."

"So, instead," Mr. Smith offered. "He chooses to deny the enemy resources. Takes whatever he can, sabotages the rest."

"Right." Griffin leaned back and sat on the edge of the desk next to his armor. "Question is, what's next? What does he do after that?"

"Takes the money and runs," Paige put in. "So to speak."

"Where?" Griffin asked. "Can't go back east. South is Mexico, and a cartel that wants to skin him alive."

"West?" Mr. Smith suggested.

Griffin shrugged. "Possible. But he's gotta know at this point that the west coast didn't fare any better than the east coast. LA to Seattle is a fucking dead zone. Too many massive cities, just like the northeastern population centers that wiped out everything north of the Carolinas. I don't think he would go west. Too much risk, not enough potential gain."

"Which leaves two options," Mr. Smith reasoned. "Either he's in hiding somewhere in Texas…or he's heading north."

Griffin frowned. Looked at his dirty boots as his thoughts meandered through the possibilities. Mr. Smith was correct. As Griffin saw it, those were the only two realistic possibilities. But which one was it? A hit and run guerilla insurgency in Texas? Or something more aggressive?

"You say you know the man," Mr. Smith prodded. "Where do you think his head's at right now?"

Griffin grimaced. "I said I *knew* the man. But a lot has happened. And I don't know what affect the loss of the UES has had on him. I don't even know if he has people backing him at this point."

"The number of civilians left in Butler was nowhere near where it should've been. A good chunk of them got out before we got in."

"That doesn't necessarily mean they're with Lee. They could've just scattered."

Paige crossed his arms over his armor. "Something like that? The fall of Butler? It either breaks your will…or it pisses you off even more."

Mr. Smith's face screwed up. "What could he possibly do with a handful of civilians on the run? Except mount an insurgency. Try to hassle us and mount raids and generally make our lives difficult."

Griffin looked at his Cornerstone counterpart. "That does seem pretty weak, doesn't it?"

"That's not what I was getting at."

"No, but it's true nonetheless. The very fact that he came here and fucked up the refinery and took all the fuel…he's not running scared. He's pissed. He wants revenge. That'd be my bet."

Mr. Smith let out an unstable-sounding titter. "What could he possibly hope to accomplish besides hit-and-runs?"

"Well, that depends on how much he knows about Greeley."

"About Greeley? How would he know shit about Greeley?"

"They knew our invasion force was coming," Griffin answered. "They were prepared for it. More than they would have been if they'd just spotted us coming. Someone told them ahead of time that an invasion was happening, or we wouldn't have received half the resistance we did."

Mr. Smith's eyes narrowed. "The fucking Canadians."

Griffin nodded. "We know they had an envoy from Canada and the UK embedded with them. And yet, we never came up with any Canadians or Brits. Whoever was with Lee in Butler would have been in contact with the envoy in Greeley. And they would have known the invasion force was coming."

Paige scratched at his stubbled face. "Okay, I can buy that. But what's that got to do with Lee's current strategy?"

Griffin looked at Paige. "If the Canadians told them about the incoming invasion force, doesn't it stand to reason that Lee would know that Greeley shoved all of its resources into that invasion?"

Paige and Mr. Smith were silent for a moment, chewing on it.

But the more the silence stretched, the more confident Griffin became in his ultimate conclusion. And it was very strange, because at the same moment that he felt a certain dread for Greeley, he also felt a thrill work through him. And he couldn't quite pinpoint why he felt that way. A hundred shadowy possibilities lay deep within his psyche and he had neither the time nor the inclination to dive that deep into himself at the moment.

Mr. Smith finally cleared his throat. "He'd be mad to try to invade Greeley."

"Would he?" Griffin shrugged. "I don't know. Depends on how many people he has with him. But let's assume my theory is right. Put yourself in Lee's shoes. You come off of a big loss in Butler. You're pissed, and you're stubborn as fuck. You know Greeley is virtually undefended. You got a bunch of pissed of civilians and a collection of

Marines and Texas militia—mostly former military, mind you—that want to hit back. What would you do?"

"Well, I'll tell you what I'd do," Paige inserted himself. "I'd grab all the fuel I could from this refinery, take it off-line, and head for Greeley."

Mr. Smith was vehemently shaking his head. "He doesn't have the manpower for that. Even if *everyone* that was missing from Butler is still with him and willing to fight for him, that's still not enough people to invade Greeley. So he's either completely insane, or we're missing his real objective."

Griffin wasn't so sure. "Mr. Smith, how many settlements through Oklahoma and New Mexico and Colorado have your goons pissed off?"

"Fucking excuse me?"

Griffin wasn't trying to bump chests. He was just being honest. "Come on, Mr. Smith. It's no secret that your Cornerstone operatives have a history of being a little heavy handed. Let's not argue the obvious here. Just accept it as fact and see where it takes you."

Mr. Smith's jaw muscles bunched as he stared Griffin down. But he didn't bother denying it any further. "You think he's going to try to get support from the settlements that…shall we say…are a little peeved at Cornerstone."

"That's typically how rebellions are born, Mr. Smith. Some faction of people, feeling marginalized and abused by another faction. That's what pisses people off to the point they're willing to take up arms and fight."

Mr. Smith's expression gradually changed. From defensive, to accepting, to thoughtful.

After a few moments of silence, he reached into his back pocket and drew out the satphone that would connect him directly to President Briggs. "Well," Mr. Smith said, airily. "Assuming you're correct, that's an easy enough situation to fix."

FOURTEEN

AN INTERVIEW

SAM WAS DRENCHED in sweat by the time they called him off the bus.

The heat only made his confusion more frustrating. They'd shut the buses off—presumably to preserve fuel—and allowed the occupants to open the windows, but it was still a hotbox, baking in the noon sun, and no one knew why they were being held on the buses.

One by one, agonizingly slow, a Cornerstone operative would lean into the bus and shout "Next!" They'd started at the very front, working their way from left to right, from the first aisle back.

Sam's concern about what was happening was overshadowed by his enormous discomfort from stewing in his own juices for five hours. He knew when it was his turn—had been counting the minutes as they oozed by. So when the operative yelled "Next!" Sam came out of his seat with gusto, even though he didn't know what he was walking into.

His biggest concern was that he was the last person in his team. Everyone else had already been called off the bus. Sometimes the split between calls for *next* was only a few minutes. Sometimes it was as long as ten. But the clincher was the fact that no one got *back* on the bus.

Wiping sweat from his face and pulling his sodden shirt from where it stuck to his flesh, Sam stamped down the stairs of the bus to be met by the same soldier with the clipboard that had greeted him when he got on.

"Sameer Balawi?" the soldier said, reading from his clipboard.

"Yes, sir."

The solder keyed his radio, bored and indifferent. "Sending Sameer Balawi." The soldier released his PTT and then pointed.

The buses had stopped just inside the south end of Greeley. They now sat in a large, dirt parking area. All along one side were shipping containers that reminded him fleetingly of Camp Ryder. Each of these shipping containers had a number written on a piece of cardboard and taped to the top of the opening. Inside the gloom of each Sam made out two chairs. In each shipping container, one of the chairs was occupied by an individual wearing the black polo shirt of a Cornerstone operative, but no combat gear.

"Number five," the soldier said.

Sam pointed himself to the shipping container with the number five on it, and started walking. A frown creased his brow as his eyes shot down the line of shipping containers. There were ten of them in a row. Each one numbered.

The facts began to align in his head, and they only deepened his concerns. Ten shipping containers, each with two chairs and a Cornerstone operative. They were being interviewed for something, Sam guessed. But if there were ten shipping containers, and ten interviewers, then that meant that each of these interviews were lasting much longer than five to ten minutes, as he'd assumed.

How many questions did they really need to ask a bunch of conscripts? How much of an interview could you give a person who was slated to carry a rifle and guard a perimeter or clean a latrine?

This isn't a job interview, Sam realized as he stepped up to Shipping Container #5. *This is an interrogation.*

He stepped up onto the metal deck of the container. A small, rechargeable camp fan sat next to the Cornerstone operative, blowing its meager breeze across the operative only. The operative was a woman. Sam hadn't seen many of those in black Cornerstone polos. In fact, this was his first.

The woman also had a clipboard perched upon one thigh of her crossed legs. She looked up from this. "Sameer Balawi?"

"Yes, ma'am."

"Yes, *sir*."

"Excuse me?"

"Call me sir, not ma'am. Do I look like a ma'am to you?"

Well, actually, you do. But Sam didn't push his already faltering luck. "Sorry, sir."

The woman flashed him a bright smile. "I'm just hassling you. But do call me sir. I deal with enough misogyny. Please, sit."

It was the first time any of the Cornerstone people had bothered to be genuine, or to speak to him like he was anything more than an annoyance. Sam stepped forward and took the chair directly across from the woman, feeling dumbly eager to converse with someone that didn't treat him like ten pounds of shit in a five pound bag.

And he had to guard against that. It was a natural human instinct—you get treated like dirt, and then someone treats you nice, all the sudden the little social animal inside of you blossoms and you want to be that person's best friend.

But it was all lies. Manipulation. This woman didn't actually give a shit about him.

He sat stiffly in the seat, as though he was afraid to touch the backrest.

"My name is Gabriella Franks. But let's just stick with 'sir' for now." She had nice eyes. Not the eyes of a mercenary. Had she always been Cornerstone? Or was she a recent recruit?

She looked down at the clipboard. "And you are Sameer Balawi. Am I saying that right?"

"Yes, sir."

"What is that?"

"I'm sorry?"

"Where's that name come from? What's your ethnicity?"

"My family is from Afghanistan, but I was born in the United States."

"Good. So you're a citizen of the United States."

"Yes, sir."

She scribbled something. Then tapped her pen. "You're young. Where's your family?"

"Dead."

Gabriella gave no reaction to this. It was probably a common enough story. "When did they die?"

"During the outbreak."

"Were they infected?"

"No. They were killed by other people."

She met his eyes. Sympathy in hers. It seemed real, but then, so did she. Sam might be young, but he'd learned a lot about people. Lee Harden was right: You can't trust anyone.

"I'm sorry to hear that," Gabriella said. "Where did your family live before the outbreak?"

Sam restrained himself from swallowing. His fake backstory didn't go back that far. He couldn't tell her that they'd lived in North Carolina—that would set off too many warning bells. The best he could do was go with his already-constructed story.

"We lived in Oklahoma."

"So which FEMA camp did your family evacuate to in Oklahoma?"

Trick question, and Sam knew it. He dodged it. "We never made it to a FEMA camp. My family got killed before we could start the evacuation. There were people who believed the bacteria was a terrorist attack. And I guess me and my family looked like terrorists."

It was partially true. And partially true is always the best lie.

Gabriella's expression shaded a bit. Not quite as compassionate as it had been a second before. "Yes, but which FEMA camp were you *intending* to go to?"

"I don't know. I was eleven at the time. If my parents had discussed going to a FEMA camp, they never told me about it."

Gabriella appeared to let go of that line of questioning. Sam felt his gut tightening, wondering how much untruth he could get away with. If he kept dodging questions, it was only going to make her more suspicious.

And he realized, in that instant, what this was all about.

They're trying to figure out if I'm from the UES.

It was only by a monumental effort of tricking his brain—forcing himself to actually visualize and believe in his lies—that he managed to keep his pulse from skyrocketing. He was already pouring sweat, as was every other person that got off the bus, so he supposed he was free to perspire. But he didn't want his pulse throbbing in his neck.

"Do you go by Sameer?" Gabriella asked, folding her hands over the clipboard as though it no longer mattered. Just a conversation among friends.

"My friends call me Sam."

"Okay, Sam. You seem like a good dude, and you've already been pinned for squad leader." She gestured to the tag still clipped to his collar. "I'm gonna shoot straight with you."

I doubt it.

He nodded along, playing the rube.

"You're aware of the conflict between our President Briggs and the rebels on the east coast?"

Sam briefly considered denial, if for nothing else than to avoid this line of questioning. But he and his team—thanks to Jones's big mouth—had already admitted to knowledge of the UES during their questioning to get into The Tank. Sam needed to assume that Gabriella was aware of this.

"Yes, sir. I've heard about what's going on."

Gabriella smiled again. "Well, it's not going on anymore. We sent an invasion force out just a week or so ago and wiped the floor with them."

She let the words hang there, and Sam could see she was gauging his reaction to this.

Well, it wasn't news to Sam. He remained motionless in his seat, his expression carefully neutral. "Oh. I hadn't heard about that. Good."

Gabriella didn't immediately respond to that. Her eyes searched Sam's face, and for a brief moment, he thought she was still looking for some sign of emotion in him. But as he held eye contact with her, he saw something else lurking below the surface.

A hesitation. A reticence. A hope.

What am I looking at right now?

Gabriella let out a low sigh. "Yeah. Good."

Her words rang hollow in Sam's ears. And everything went tilt-a-whirl in Sam's head. Something new sprouted into his consciousness, something about the woman sitting across from him. A new and disruptive possibility.

She doesn't like that the UES got wiped out.

"Anyways," Gabriella refocused herself. "All of the bullshit that went into that invasion is neither here nor there." She seemed to be staring at her clipboard, but not seeing it. She tapped her pen a few more times. "I suppose there's been bullshit going on since the conception of the United States of America. That's something you'll learn firsthand. Doesn't matter where you go, there's always bullshit. There's always things you don't agree with." She looked at him. "It's important that, if you're going to be a soldier in Greeley, you understand that there's always going to be things you don't like going on behind closed doors. Just because you don't agree with it—just because I don't agree with the treatment of the United Eastern States and the wholesale killing of civilians that happened during the invasion—doesn't mean that the government I work for is 'bad.'

You need to understand that shit like that was going on long before the plague hit, and will continue to go on. That's just the way it is. Do you understand that, Sam?"

Sam found himself in vapor lock. His mission here in Greeley suddenly came crashing to the forefront of his brain, obliterating the wonderful acting job he'd done by forcing himself to believe his own fictitious background.

His mission was to find detractors. To convince people to take up arms when they didn't agree with how things were being done. And here was Gabriella, a Cornerstone operative, that didn't agree with how things were done.

Too easy, a warning klaxon blared in Sam's mind. *Don't trust anyone.*

But that was the problem. The very nature of his mission was predicated on the fact that, eventually, he was going to have to trust *someone*. He couldn't recruit people to fight for a cause if he never revealed that he was a part of it himself.

You haven't even made it inside, Sam told himself. *This is too early.*

But weren't they on a short schedule? Wasn't time slipping out of his hands faster than he had expected when he set out? Lee was on the move towards Greeley. Sam's mission was on a timeline. He needed to act fast.

"Sam?" Gabriella broke into his thoughts, frowning. "I asked you a question."

"I'm sorry," Sam said with a twitch. "I was just..." *Go gently, cautiously.* "...I was surprised to hear you say that."

Gabriella straightened, a whiff of something like worry flying across her face. "Well, I—"

Sam managed an earnest smile. “No, it’s fine, sir. I appreciate your honesty.”

Gabriella’s expression flashed hopeful, and then immediately went stony. “It’s neither here nor there. My entire point being, as a soldier here, you may see things you don’t agree with. And when you see those things, you’re not going to raise a stink and cause trouble. You’re going to put your head down and do what you’re told. Is that understood?”

“Yes. I understand.”

Gabriella seemed to relax a bit. “Good. We’re all going out on a limb right now. President Briggs is giving you all an opportunity for a better life. We’re trusting you all to do your duty. And you need to trust us, no matter what you see, that we’re trying to do the right thing. We’re trying to preserve the better life that we’re offering you. Unfortunately, in this world, you have to crack a few eggs to make omelets.”

Sam swallowed, feeling the dangerous opportunity being pulled away from him. “I’m sorry if I’m not supposed to ask this kind of question. But what kind of stuff are you talking about?”

Gabriella regarded him with a tilted head. “Sam, have you ever killed someone?”

Sam’s mind went to the ambushes during the assault on Butler. The images, the sensations, the sounds—pulling the trigger, hearing the bang, seeing the body of a soldier jerk and fall.

“Yes.”

“And did you want to do it, Sam? Are you a killer at heart?”

“No.”

“No. You did what you had to do.” She sniffed. “Sometimes survival is ugly.”

"What did they do to those people on the east coast?"

Gabriella sat in silence for a moment. Gradually, she looked down at her clipboard and scribbled something. When she spoke, it was with a dismissive tone. "War. That's what they did. And any time there's war, there's civilian casualties. That's just par for the course. The sooner you make your peace with that, the better off you'll be here in Greeley."

She finished scrawling whatever note she was writing, then uncrossed her legs. "I'm confirming your recommendation for squad leader, Sam. Don't make me regret it. Remember what I said." She folded her hands over the clipboard. "Do you have any questions for me?"

"Were you always a part of Cornerstone?"

She frowned. "Interesting that you know the name."

Sam felt heat rising up his neck. "I've just heard, that's all. The black polo shirts. The red triangle. Everyone knows about Cornerstone."

"Hm." Gabriella stared at him with narrowed eyes. "No. I was in the Air Force. But President Briggs is consolidating all military forces into Cornerstone. Yet another thing that, even if you don't like it, you go along to get along. Do you understand?"

Sam nodded, feeling a little ray of hope shine down on him. "Yes, sir."

Gabriella stood up. "Myself or another operative from Cornerstone will be checking in with you periodically." She paused, her mouth working as though trying to find the right way to say something. "I'm considered your official case officer. So if you have any questions for me…" hesitation, as though she were extending something to him that went beyond professionalism. "I work in logistics, located inside the old Wal-Mart building downtown."

Sam rose from his seat. "Thank you, sir."

Gabriella avoided any further eye contact. "You're dismissed."

FIFTEEN

SCORCHED EARTH

ABE STOOD JUST OUTSIDE the passenger side of the MATV, a pair of binoculars up to his eyes, his elbows braced in the V created by the door and the frame of the vehicle. Through the binoculars he observed an eerily quiet setting.

Buildings. One big one, like a hangar of some sort. Probably to house big farming implements. A small school. A collection of houses. They all sat, somewhat gray in the thinly overcast skies. A strong wind was kicking up, and the only movement Abe could see were little dust devils that sprouted up and dissipated shortly after, and the hectic waving of a few acres of immature corn.

The crinkled map on the dash called this tiny dot MOSQUERO. From all the intel that Abe had received through the grapevine—mainly from Breck and Menendez and a few others from Tex's old crew—this was supposed to be a settlement, and it was supposed to be loyal to the New Mexico Coordinator, Captain Tully, though he was MIA—captured or killed by Cornerstone, Abe wasn't sure which.

Abe sucked his teeth and lowered the binoculars, peering over the top of them. "I got nothing."

Menendez shuffled forward from the door just behind Abe and looked over his shoulder. "What do you mean you got nothing?"

"I mean I don't see any movement."

"It's hot out and it's noon. They could be taking shelter, waiting for it to cool down a bit."

Abe didn't immediately reject this idea, but it didn't feel right. He raised the binoculars again and surveyed the outskirts of Mosquero. "I got big old garden plots on the east side. Don't see a damn person working them. No one sitting in the shade. No guards posted."

Menendez let out a disconsolate grunt. "Well, what power are those things?"

"Six."

"Aight," Menendez growled. "Hang on." He keyed the squad comms. "Pervy, get up here with that fancy gun of yours."

Pervy—whose real name was lost on Abe, but who kept a tattered stack of "Barely Legal" magazines and had been caught more than half a dozen times jacking off while on guard duty to "stay awake"—was one of their two snipers. And he did indeed have a fancy gun, with a fancy optic.

A vehicle door slammed somewhere down the column of vehicles, and Abe heard the footsteps jogging up. He kept his eyes in his binocs, but now scanned the horizon, wondering if there was anything more telling out beyond the surrounding flatness of the New Mexico countryside.

He found nothing of note. Just a few low hills, lined with scrubby growth.

Pervy trundled up behind them. “Sergeant?”

“What’s the power on that thing?” Menendez demanded, referencing the optic on Pervy’s Barret .300 Win-Mag.

“Goes up to twenty times.”

“Get eyes on this town up there. Find me some people.”

“Roger that.”

Not finding anything worth looking at, and with his binocs offically out-powered, Abe let them hang and stepped back from his perch. Pervy went around to the back of the MATV, lugging his big rifle with him, and clambered up onto the top of the vehicle where he had a better view of the town a mile in the distance.

Abe shook his head slowly as he looked out at the low huddle of buildings. “Not a fan, Menendez.”

“Me neither.”

“When’s the last contact you remember from this settlement?”

Menendez considered it for a moment. “Hell, I don’t know. Last I know for sure was back before Tex even found you and Lee. So it’s been a bit.”

“You think they would’ve left this place? Maybe decided to try their luck in Greeley?”

Menendez shook his head. “I don’t think so. They fucking hated Greeley.” He nodded towards the crops on the east side of town. “And if they did go anywhere, it was recently. Those crops have been tended to.”

“Alright,” Pervy sighed as he settled into position. “Let’s see what we got.”

Menendez smirked and hiked a thumb up at Pervy, speaking loud enough for him to hear. “Ol’

Pervy's just excited to peep through people's windows."

Pervy snickered, but otherwise didn't respond.

Abe's brain didn't correctly process the next sound he heard. He thought someone had slammed another vehicle door somewhere down the convoy, but then realized it didn't sound quite right.

The zip-crack of a supersonic round hit his ears at the same moment that pink mist wafted over his face.

Abe jerked, snapped his head up. He couldn't see Pervy—only a snake of brain matter clinging to the top of the MATV.

"Shit! Sniper!" Abe slammed his door shut, grabbing Menendez in the same movement, and hauling the two of them into cover behind the engine block and the front axle. The violence of his movement sent Menendez crashing into the dirt, scrambling up to his hands and knees, grappling for his slung rifle.

Abe hit the squad comms: "Cover! Cover! We're taking fire! Get on the right side of the vehicles!"

Menendez's eyes swam into reality as he righted himself and shouldered his rifle, scrunched in close to Abe by the front tire. "Pervy!" he yelled. "Pervy, you alright?"

Glass spewed from the passenger side window where Abe had just been standing.

Zip-CRACK

Menendez saw it. Saw the blood painting the inside of the MATV's window. "Willis!" he yelled at their driver. Started to rise, but Abe yanked him back down.

"They're fucking dead!" Abe snapped. "Don't be stupid!"

All along the convoy of a dozen vehicles, doors ripped open and nobody bothered to slam them shut. There was the scramble of feet across the dusty ground, a few shouts, but mostly silence. Everyone was saving their air for sprinting.

Abe snatched his gaze down the column of vehicles, seeing his troops sliding into cover behind engine blocks and axles.

Menendez hunkered down into a low squat, swearing up a storm. "Did you see where it came from?"

"I didn't see shit."

But that wasn't entirely true. Abe might not have seen the shooter, but he'd perceived a few things that all rammed together in his head at the same instant. The nearest hill—the obvious choice for a sniper—was at least a half-mile distant, maybe more. The shots had struck true—he didn't know where Willis had been hit, but he knew without having to look that Pervy had been pegged in the head.

Long distance, precision rifle. And a good shooter.

No boom of the rifle report, just the sound of the bullet splitting the air. Which meant it was suppressed. Which made it even harder to pinpoint where it was coming from.

Somewhere to the west, based on the direction of the blood spatter.

What now? Abe's brain kicked into gear.

"Casualty report," he transmitted, forcing his voice down to a more normal volume.

No one responded immediately. Then, Breckenridge, from a few vehicles back: "We're all good here, major. Only casualties I can see were Pervy and Willis."

Two shots. Two dead bodies.

Not for the first time, Abe wished he was back in a war zone overseas, where he would have a JTAC or at the very least some artillery support. How much easier life would be if he could just paint the surrounding hillsides with high-explosives munitions and be done with it.

If wishes were fishes…

"Alright," Abe said over the radio. "Everyone take it down a few notches. Watch your tidbits. Greenman," Abe called to their second sniper. "You with us?"

"Two vehicles behind you," Greenman came back, leaning out just a hair to give Abe a quick wave.

Abe nodded. "Shot came from the west, almost directly broadside to us. See if you can't deploy your rifle and get a bead on this fucker."

Hesitation. Then: "Roger that."

Three vehicles down, a soldier's ankle exploded.

A slurry of screams and curses.

"Goddammit, I said watch your fucking tidbits!" Abe yelled, not bothering to transmit.

The wounded soldier was grabbed by his comrades and hauled further into the cover behind the knobby back tire of a pickup truck. Abe stared down, a mix of anger, frustration, and concern flooding his chest.

The soldiers around the wounded man worked their angles, but their cover was small. Five men squashed behind two tires. The wounded man let out a strangled yelp as they worked to isolate his leg and get a tourniquet on him, all in the narrow space of a less than three feet.

Two vehicles back, Greenman squirmed onto his side, his squad mates trying to make room for him and not expose themselves at the same time. His big rifle—an M2010—snugged tight to his chest as he eased the bipod out.

Abe had no illusions that Greenman was safe. His life was on the line the second he showed a sliver of himself. They had no idea where the gunman was positioned, but he wasn't about to let their last sniper get pegged.

"Greenman," Abe transmitted. "Let me know when you're ready to deploy. We'll give you all the suppressive fire we got. All units, on my mark, I want you to hit those hills to the west."

Menendez fidgeted, tucking a wayward knee in tight to his body. "We need to get into Mosquero. We can't stay out on this fucking road."

"You wanna hop in the driver's seat?" Abe snapped. "I know we need to get off this fucking road. One thing at a time."

"Roger 'at, just making observations."

Abe fixed his gaze back on Greenman. The sniper had his bipod extended. He flipped the scope covers up. Eyed the turrets on his optic. "Can I get a range estimation? Even a ballpark would help."

"Best guess is that hill directly west," Abe answered. "Estimating about a thousand meters."

Greenman torqued the elevation turret on his optic. "Alright. On you, major."

Abe knew an ugly truth in that moment: They weren't going to kill the sniper with suppressive fire.

And one of them was about to die. Every single man in that column, huddling behind their cover, knew it. No one wished ill for their comrades, but everyone hoped it wouldn't be them.

"On me," Abe reiterated. "Send everything you got." He took a deep breath. "Mark!"

Menendez went high, over the hood of the MATV. Abe rolled right, sighting beneath the engine. The entire column erupted in fire. Abe had no target—just a hillside. Dust began to pock and sprout across the hillside, the dry vegetation crumpling and wilting under the onslaught of projectiles. He tried to focus his fire on whatever spot on that hill didn't seem to be getting enough attention.

One by one, rifles began to die out, running out of ammunition. Calls of "Reloading!" and "Down!" began to sprout up along the line of soldiers, and then, all at once, it went silent.

Abe rolled back into cover, dropping his mag and seating a fresh one in place. "Sitrep! Anyone hit?"

"Negative!"

"No!"

"All good!"

Abe looked incredulously down the line. He expected to see at least one body, splayed out of line with the others, bleeding and thrashing, or perhaps already dead with a hole in his brain. But all he saw was a bunch of worried soldiers hugging their rifles and looking back at him.

Greenman was still in his scope. He looked stressed—well aware that he was the only one out of cover at the moment. Finally, he called out, "Shit! I got nothing!"

"Did you take a shot?" Abe hollered.

"No, I got nothing."

Abe mumbled a curse under his breath, then shouted, "Get back into cover before you lose your head."

Greenman gratefully rolled back into the cover of the tire, his back up against the shins of two of his comrades. He met Abe's eyes. "What the fuck do we do now?"

Abe didn't immediately answer. He was still busy strangling his thoughts back into order, trying to figure out how to come at this problem from another angle.

"You think he ran?" Menendez suggested.

"Well, I don't know," Abe growled. "Maybe he's just a cool customer."

Abe needed to do something more. Maybe their suppressive fire had been too aggressive, if there could be such a thing. Maybe the sniper *wasn't* a cool customer and had taken cover while the hillside was blistered with fire.

Maybe Abe needed to give him a better target.

Abe shuffled, squirming up so that his back was against the tire hub. He wasn't wearing his lid, and didn't have it on him, but Menendez wore an old OCP floppy hat—a boonie hat, as it was sometimes called.

"Menendez, let's give him the old hat trick."

Menendez looked dubious, but pulled his sweat-soaked hat from his head. "Might as well." He stuck the hat on the barrel of his rifle, fluffed it so it looked like it might contain a head, and slowly began to inch it upward.

Abe stared at it, but called out: "Greenman, get ready to spot a shot."

Greenman swore, but got ready to roll out of cover again.

Menendez pressed the hat a little higher. Inch by inch. It cleared the top of the MATV's hood.

Greenman eased out of cover, already sighting through his optic.

They waited for the zip of an incoming round.

Abe's breath was locked in his chest.

Was the sniper going to fall for it? Or had he already dismissed it as a trick and targeted the sliver of Greenman that was exposed?

Nothing happened. The silence was vast and uncomfortable.

Menendez glanced at Abe. "He's not falling for it."

"I still got nothing," Greenman seethed out, the angst in his voice obvious.

Time stretched to its breaking point. Abe couldn't wait any more—couldn't leave Greenman exposed. "Alright, fuck it! Back into cover!" He reached up and grabbed Menendez's arm, forcing the hat and rifle back down.

"He's gone," Menendez asserted. "Hit and run, Abe."

"Maybe." Abe squirmed to turn himself around and get his knees under him. He looked to his left, to the town of Mosquero. It'd looked suspicious at first. Now it looked inviting. Anything would be better than being stuck on this long, flat road. "We need to get into the town."

"What a genius idea," Menendez retorted. "How you wanna do it?"

"Only way we can." Abe transmitted. "Alright, folks. We're gonna make a break for Mosquero. Squad leaders, lay down covering fire and get someone behind the wheel of the vehicles. Then everyone pile in or grab a handhold and haul ass for the town. Everybody got that?"

Acknowledgements were hollered down the line, rather than transmitted.

Shuffling about occurred. Breck and the other squad leaders appointed their drivers, who Abe was sure were not thrilled with the assignement. But everyone knew they couldn't just stay out here, and no one wanted to run a mile in open terrain. Driving was the only way.

"Menendez, I'll cover you."

Menendez sighed, but didn't balk. "Fuck it. Alright."

"Squad leaders, on my mark," Abe said, suddenly growing exhausted. "Mark!"

He popped up again as a dozen rifles started spitting hate and discontent at the hillside. Menendez broke around the rear of the MATV and hauled for the driver's seat along with the other appointed drivers.

The fusillade was slower this time—not just an ammo dump.

Between steadily spaced shots, Abe heard doors slamming and tires skidding. The others that had been in his MATV with him simply grabbed a hold of what they could and stood on the running boards on the passenger's side of the vehicle. Abe heard the MATV's transmission shift, and with it, he grabbed a hold of the sideview mirror and pulled himself onto the running board with the others.

The MATV lurched forward, all the men clinging to their handholds desperately as it accelerated towards Mosquero, and the entire column of vehicles fell in behind it, all of them adorned with soldiers holding onto the passenger's sides.

Their covering fire ceased as the vehicles got up to speed.

Whoever the sniper was, he didn't fire another shot.

***

Everything became clear to them as the convoy skidded to a halt in a wash of dust.

It had taken a lot of energy to stabilize himself and keep from falling off the side of the MATV as it hurtled towards Mosquero at sixty miles an hour. So when Abe stepped down, his muscles shook and his knees trembled.

Boots onto the ground. They were behind the cover of the massive hangar-like building that dominated the town of Mosquero. As the vehicles shifted into idle, and all the soldiers stepped down from their precarious perches, no one spoke.

The evidence lay before them, stark and ugly.

One by one, the vehicles' engines died. The drivers stepped out, their movements unrushed. Doors slammed. And then nothing. Nothing but the wind in the plains.

And the buzzing of flies.

Abe stood there, staring at it, his eyes squinted against the bright sunshine, his lips tight. He let his rifle hang from its sling. Planted his shaking hands on his hips.

In the center of Mosquero, perhaps twenty yards from their current position, lay bodies.

No pit had been dug for them. No grave bothered with. Abe's eyes coursed over them, and saw how it had happened, saw how the bodies had fallen. Three individual ranks, each one about a dozen bodies long, had fallen atop each other. They'd lined up a dozen and then mowed them down, and then lined up the next dozen, and the next.

Men, women, and children. Young and old.

Abe spat off to the side and shook his head.

How did people die like this? He'd always wondered that. He remembered watching videos of Nazi soldiers exterminating Jews. Setting them up, just like this, and then walking down the line and shooting them in the back of the head. Abe had never understood how the last guy in line just sat there. Did he think he would be granted mercy at the last minute? Or were their spirits just broken? If you knew you were about to die, why not fight back, even if you knew it was hopeless? Why not at least run? Why not at least make it harder on the fuckers that were trying to murder you?

He'd never understood it. But that's what had happened here.

Three dozen people. Each dozen had watched the previous dozen get murdered, and still they'd allowed themselves to be pushed into position over the bodies of their family and friends, and they'd met their fate with wide, disbelieving eyes.

Menendez and Breck met Abe where he stood.

"Christ," Breck breathed.

Abe tore his eyes from the pile of bodies and the cloud of flies that swarmed over them, and took in the houses around them, the silent, empty buildings, the quiet stillness of the countryside around them.

"Whoever was here knew we were coming," Abe said.

No one responded. They knew it was true.

"That sniper wasn't there to take us out. He was there to report when we arrived and give us something to think about. Fucker probably ran after those first three shots."

"Cornerstone?" Breck suggested.

Abe nodded. "That'd be my guess."

"How'd they know we were coming?"

"I don't know. But not only did they know we were coming, they know we're here right now."

Menendez looked soul-sick. His face pained. "Why would they fucking do this? Why not stand and fight us? Why kill the civilians?"

Abe frowned, allowing his gaze to be drawn back to the bodies. "Because they know what we're trying to do. They know we're trying to recruit the settlements."

Breck swore under his breath. "Easier for them to just gun down the civilians than to stand and fight us over them."

Abe nodded. "We have a serious fucking problem, gentlemen."

SIXTEEN

THE BELLY OF THE BEAST

SAM WAS IN.

That was the most important thing. There were a million other tendrils of worry and doubt that pervaded the background of his thoughts, but that was the central emotion that he felt: Victory. He'd got into Greeley, he'd fooled the interrogators, and been given a squad leader position, and a tiny flat in the southwestern corner of what was referred to as the "Yellow Zone."

After his entire team had been vetted, they'd been shoved back on the bus and then driven about the city, the people on the bus with them unceremoniously dropped at various locations where there was room to house them. Each group, including Sam and his squad, were given verbal instructions before they were kicked off the bus and into their new living arrangements.

"Orientation is at Aims Community College, located off of 20th Street. The Ed Beaty Hall," the soldier at the door to the bus rattled off, the words coming out of him by rote, the same as he'd instructed every other group. "Orientation begins at sixteen hundred. Be there fifteen minutes early."

That had been about one in the afternoon, so they had a few hours to spare.

There was electricity in Greeley, but air-conditioning was prohibited. The flat was on the top floor of a three-floor building, exposed to the sun and uncomfortably hot. The windows of the place had been left open for air flow, but when Sam shut the door to the flat behind his team, he immediately went to the windows and closed them.

They didn't need air flow right now. They needed privacy.

There was no furniture in the flat. They gathered, standing at a counter that separated the small living area from the tiny kitchen.

"Alright, let's keep our voices down," Sam murmured. "We need to just assume that someone's got their ear to the wall, listening to us at all times."

The others nodded their assent to that.

Sam fixed onto Jones. "You said you got the satphone?"

Jones nodded, slung his pack off and placed in on the counter. "Lucky they didn't search my shit again." He unzipped the main compartment, dove in, and pulled out the satphone, which he'd buried at the bottom.

Sam left it on the counter for now. "Jonesy, what was your interview like?"

Jones curled his nose. "Frankly, it was insulting. There were a lot of implications that I might be allied with those bastards from the United Eastern States." Jones huffed dramatically, then smiled. "I convinced them of my loyalty."

Johnson shuffled in place. "I think they hit me with the same questions." His face screwed up. "It's like they know something's up, Sam."

Sam nodded. "That's the impression I got as well. Like they knew that there might be elements trying to infiltrate them. Which is concerning."

Frenchie kept wiping his sweaty palms across the counter in an odd self-soothing motion. "Man, I don't know about this. They're on high alert right now. It is *not* a good time to be running around out there trying to talk to people out rebelling."

"Hey." Sam frowned at Frenchie. "You knew what you signed up for. You all knew what this was going to be. Lee didn't promise it was going to be easy. We're going to have to be smart about this. We're gonna have to be slick as shit. But we *are* going to do what we came to do."

"I don't see how," Frenchie snapped. "The second you open your mouth to anybody, they're gonna be so worried about saving their own skins they'll turn you in at the drop of a hat."

Jones blew a raspberry. "Frenchie, when'd you turn into such a pussy? When we left Texas you were all rarin' to go for the resistance. The second you realize it's not gonna come easy, you get cold feet? Grow a fucking sack, bro."

Marie, who had watched the others in silence, finally interjected. "Neither of you are wrong, and neither of you are right."

The others looked at her.

"There is gonna be extra scrutiny. I don't know what information they have, but I think we all had a similar interrogation, and it sure as hell seems like they suspect that Lee sent someone here to infiltrate them. *But*...they don't know it's us. Or they would've already locked us up. Or flat out killed us. Which means that we still have a chance to slide in under the radar and do what we need to do. It'll be challenging, but like Sam already said, you knew it was going to be challenging when you agreed to come."

"I knew it would be challenging to secretly convince people to rebel," Frenchie retorted. "I didn't think we were going to be getting this much attention while we tried to do it. It's borderline impossible at this point."

Sam felt a flush of heat rising up his neck and into his face. He turned to Frenchie and glared at the man so hard that Frenchie looked away and his worrying hands fell still.

"Frenchie, I swear to God, you better not fuck this up. I vouched for you, do you understand that? You too, Johnson. Lee didn't know either of you, and he didn't want to send you with me because he doesn't trust you guys." Sam stabbed a finger down on the countertop. "I vouched for both of you." Sam shook his head, his eyes flashing intensely between Frenchie and Johnson. "Don't make me regret that."

After an awkward silence, Pickell cleared his throat. "Alright. So it's been established that there's more scrutiny than we thought. How do we move forward?"

Sam hiked his elbows onto the counter and raised his fingers, ticking off his points. "First off, the scrutiny has practically no bearing on one aspect of our mission: we can still observe and report. We can still identify the soft targets, the entry points, and we can still provide up-to-the-minute intel for Lee. That's huge in and of itself.

"Secondly, we don't know what that scrutiny is going to entail. It could just be tough talk, designed to scare us, and make the others be on the lookout for anyone talking treason. What we need to do right now is figure out how hard that scrutiny is, and whether we're being treated any different than anyone else."

"What difference does that make?" Johnson asked.

Sam felt disappointed by the question, because the answer was damn obvious. Did he have to spell everything out for these two new guys? He'd vouched for them, but he was already regretting it. "Because if they're scrutinizing us and not everybody else then that's a bad fucking sign. You get it?"

Johnson looked enlightened. "Right. Gotcha."

"So we need to take extra care to stay off the radar and not get any extra attention. At the same time we need to *discreetly*—again, *discreetly*—monitor how much attention we're getting. Are there going to be people following us? Watching us? Dropping in and questioning us at random times?"

"They mentioned something like that," Jones put in. "My interviewer told me that someone would be 'checking in on me.'"

Sam nodded. "I got the same warning. Which leads me to point number three."

He hesitated here, wondering how to sum up what amounted to little more than a gut feeling. The others watched him carefully as he tried to form a concise morsel of knowledge that they could digest.

"It's possible—I'm not positive, but it's the vibe I got—that my interviewer might be a weak link."

"Weak link?" Pickell asked. "Like, you might be able to turn him?"

"Her," Sam corrected. "And yes."

Jones's eyes lit up. "Oh. 'Her,' huh? Was she hot?"

Sam just closed his eyes for a moment. He'd come to understand why Billings had always seemed like a harried father looking after a bunch of wild children.

"I'm just sayin'," Jones raised his hands in defense. "If she's hot, and maybe she thinks *you're* hot, or even better, maybe she'll think *I'm* hot…Maybe we can turn her by, you know, layin' that good pipe."

Sam looked heavenward. "I should've left you behind."

"Everything's on the table," Jones replied, sagely.

Sam finally returned his eyes to Jones. "You're right. Everything's on the table. Jonesy, if your dick is so magical that you can turn people with it, then you go right ahead. Do what needs to be done."

Jones seemed pleased by that. "Gonna fuck my way to freedom and democracy."

Bridling a smirk, Marie met Sam's gaze. "Bringing us back around to the original point: What makes you think you can turn her?"

"She said some things that made it seem like she didn't agree with how Greeley was being run." Sam mulled it over as he spoke. "Like she might have a moral problem with the treatment of civilians. Particularly after Greeley took Butler."

Marie kept her eyes on Sam. "Is it possible she was trying to bait a response from you?"

Sam considered this. Then nodded. "Yes."

Marie's lips tightened. "Be careful with that, Sam."

"We all need to be careful with everything," Sam returned. He straightened up, passing a look around his team. "We don't have a lot of time before Lee's knocking at the door. So we're going to have to be smart. Keep your ears open. Prompt people to talk, and then just listen. Let's figure out who says what. Who seems like they're a true believer in Greeley, and who seems like they're just toeing the party line. And in the meantime, keep your eyes open. We need troop counts, locations, response times. Anything that bears on Greeley's ability to withstand an assault. Try to find weak points in the structure. Things that can be taken advantage of, either by an assaulting force, or through sabotage."

Sam gestured to them all in a sweep of his hand. "At the end of the day, Lee might come knocking, and it might just be us inside Greeley. And if that's the case, we'll work with what we have. Because even just five of us, working smart and discreet? We can do a helluva lot of damage."

***

The Alpha knew it would feed.

But it also knew that what came next was not about food.

It could smell it in the cold implacability that radiated off of the Omegas. It could see it in the stillness of their sinews, in the focus of their eyes, as they crept through the woods in the place outside where the Easy Prey had gathered.

To the Alpha, this was confusing, because it was something it had not experienced before. Much of what had occurred had been new to the Alpha. When all the Others gathered in one place, and yet did not kill each other. When the Strange Ones began to lead them, through the Omegas. When the pack that had been his, became theirs, and became one with many other packs of Others, and the scents of the Others started as strange and feral in the Alpha's nose, but now had become simply the scent of the pack.

All of this was new to the Alpha. And yet it was right. It had to be right, because something inside of the Alpha followed it and conformed to it. It simply was, and what is must be right, because that is where the tide had taken them.

The Alpha was animated by something that lurked in a place beyond thought. It was simply a flow, and the Alpha knew that it was right and should not be challenged, because the flow swept the Alpha up. What is must be right.

Like the moon. Like the flow of wind. Like the rise and fall of the sun and stars. Like the air that grew hot, and then cold, and then hot again. It moved, and the Alpha moved with it, in it, and all of this was right.

The Strange Ones wanted something. They yearned for it day and night. The Alpha could smell their hunger for it permeating the many Others that had become the one pack. The Alpha did not know what they hungered for, but he knew that it was not something to be consumed, not something that could satiate the belly.

Their hunger was the hunger that takes a bird and causes it to fly to the place where it knows that it will be warm instead of cold. It was the hunger that causes a female to flow into estrus, and the hunger that causes the male to flow into her. It was the hunger of knowing without knowing that the flow takes you in its tide, and where it goes is the right place to go.

It was, and what is must be right.

And so the Alpha knew that it would feed. It would feed, but it would not rut. Not with the Omegas, whose time to Glow had gone with the changing of the moon. And it would not rut with the females of the Easy Prey either, for that time had changed as well. The Alpha would hunt, and it would kill, and it would feed, but the tide that had taken the pack was not for the purposes of feeding. The killing tide was for only one thing: Killing.

First the killing, and then the feeding.

And so the pack that had once been Others, but was now just the pack, waited. The Omegas led them to the place that the killing tide pushed them, and the Alphas and the rest of their packmates followed.

The scent of the Easy Prey was strong and heavy, mixed with the rot of the forest floor; the verdancy of all the living green; the warm tinge of scat; the heady rush of the killing tide. When all was still and silent, the Alpha could hear the Easy Prey. It could hear the rumble of their hard-skinned shells that rolled faster than the Alpha could run. It could hear the strange calls that the Easy Prey made to each other with their mouths.

By scent, and by sight, and by hearing, the Alpha knew that the Easy Prey were relaxed. They thought themselves secure. The screaming had not begun. The fear could not yet be smelled. But it would come soon.

Closer and closer they crept. First the Omegas, and then the Alphas, and then the pack.

The killing tide surged the Alpha's pulse, and it sharpened the Alpha's eyes. Hunger fled. The hunger to feed, and the hunger to rut. The killing tide swept all of that away, and all that was left was the hunger for killing.

The sun beat down in hot shafts that leaked through the trees above them.

The call of the insects filled the air.

When the time came, the Omegas did not call out. They simply moved.

And the tide swept the Alpha up.

Running. Surging. Through the woods. Trees flashing. Brush thrashing.

Into the open. The sun hot and loud. The scents heady and all-consuming.

Across the hard black rivers that the Easy Prey had built, towards the massive doors where they came and went, the doors that rattled and squeaked so loudly when they were opened and closed.

This was the place, the Alpha had learned, where there were no humming threads that killed with their hot lightning. Here the doors were covered with tangles of steel brambles that would cut and slice, but not kill.

A scream went up from the Easy Prey.

Movement, straight through those doors.

The thunderous crash, the flash and billow of stinking smoke. The buzz of the fast stones that the Easy Prey hurled at them—they whisked past the Alpha's ears, found the flesh of a packmate, thudding sharply and spewing blood.

The Omegas split in many different directions, opening the way to the doors ahead of the pack, and the pack did not shy from the flow of the killing tide, but let it carry them on.

The Alpha launched itself at the doors. Its clawed hands and feet latched onto any handhold it could manage, and began to writhe upwards. The steel brambles cut and slashed, but the Alpha paid them no mind. Blood brought blood. That was the way of things.

Packmate after packmate slammed into the doors, dozens, then hundreds, and the doors creaked and groaned and began to fold on themselves, unable to bear the weight. The Easy Prey kept up their mindless screaming, and their tools of death continued to bark and spew and slam the life out of the Alpha's packmates, but the pack was many, and the Easy Prey could not withstand it.

Over the door, even as it fell.

The Alpha tumbled to the ground, the world in its vision rolling over on itself. The Alpha's claws clenched the hard black ground and righted itself. Blood poured from flaps of flash torn by the steel brambles, and scraped off by the hard ground.

Movement. Prey.

Screaming. Running.

Two of them, side by side, their tool of death peeling like thunder, emitting a hail of stones that threatened to chew through the Alpha's packmates. They did not see the Alpha. Their fear was too great, and they only saw what was in front of them.

The Alpha launched itself into their sides, tackling both of them with the weight of its body. The fell, thrashing and screaming. A black claw in the hand of one of them, slashing the air. The Alpha snatched the arm in its mouth and clenched its jaw with everything in it. Blood gushed. Bones cracked.

The Easy Prey beat at the Alpha with its fists. The Alpha plunged its claws into the prey's jugular and ripped out that river of life so that it spilled over. The other prey tried to draw a black thing that the Alpha knew would spit killing stones, so the Alpha slashed, and the object went flying from the prey's ragged hand.

Blood dripped from the Alpha's mouth. It seized the prey by its face and plunged its claws through the frightened eyes and into the brain, then smashed the skull against the hard ground.

No time to feed.

Only killing.

***

How had it come to this?

Colonel Freeman had no place to run, and barely even a place to hide. He had found a janitorial closet in the Butler High School and had run into it without thinking, while the screams and gunshots rose to a crescendo behind him, and then petered out into silence.

He was scared. Of course he was. He was crammed into the dark backend of a closet, hiding behind a wooden bin of something that Lee and Angela's folks had left behind—not janitorial supplies, that was for sure.

But Colonel Freeman was an intelligent man, and not prone to full-on panic. He was able to think, even as his heart thudded along at an alarming rate and his breathing increased to the point that he could no longer fully oxygenate through his nose and had to pant like a tired dog.

They would smell him. He knew that. And because he knew that, he knew that he was going to be found, and that when he was found, he was going to die. He'd emptied his sidearm during his retreat from the gymnasium—the very same command center that Lee Harden had used—and he had no other weapons on his person.

He began to fumble around in the darkness, trying to be quiet, but also trying to find something sharp, or with enough heft to brain one of the creatures when they finally came for him. Oh, it wouldn't save his ass, he knew that. But he wasn't going to lay down and just let them kill him. No, he'd take at least one of those bastards with him.

It was right at that moment of thought, the world beyond the darkness of his hiding place now filling with grunts and growls and the skitter of claws on tile floors, that he stopped. His hands were frozen on an empty rack.

He was going to take one of those bastards out with him?

Really?

For what? So he could be pleased with himself in the afterlife? To prove a point? To who? The creatures?

Dimly, his own words lilted through the background of his memories, mocking him: *You've always been a grunt, you always will be a grunt, and it doesn't matter what promotion Angela's seen fit to give you, you'll shirk the very obvious responsibility that she was trying to bestow upon you, and run out into the wilderness to lug a rifle and try to justify your fucking existence.*

He'd said those words to Lee, feeling hot and self-righteous as he did.

But Lee had survived. *Because* he was a fucking grunt.

Maybe if Colonel Freeman knew as much about fighting as he did about commanding troops, he wouldn't be in this position right now.

Oh, the fucking irony.

And the irony didn't stop there. No, the hits just kept on coming.

He'd barged in through Lee's perimeter and attacked him at his most vulnerable, and then he'd set up shop in the gymnasium, right where Lee had stationed his own TOC. And now he, Colonel Freeman, was being overrun, forced to abandon that very same cursed gymnasium, and run for his life, because the primals had come through the very same perimeter that he had.

Because they hadn't been able to shore up the defenses yet. They hadn't been able to find enough wiring to get the high voltage lines on again.

In a sort of horrified haze—horrified at the cosmic, not-so-funny-humor of the universe—he turned into the darkness and staggered towards the back of the closet, towards that bin filled with things he hadn't been able to identify.

He almost wanted to be wrong, because that would take some of the sting out of it. But as his groping hands touched the top of the bin, he grew more and more certain of what it was.

The top of the bin was round. Wooden. About chest-height.

Freeman fumbled beneath the top, and found that it wasn't a bin at all. What he'd thought was a lid, was just the top of it. And as his fingers touched what lay beneath that wooden top, he found a dark little laugh bubbling up in his chest. It came out of him as a wheezing cough.

You can't be fucking serious.

Not a bin at all. A spool, wound full of heavy-gauge wiring. More than enough to resurrect the high voltage lines on that battered eastern perimeter.

But they'd searched! They'd searched for ten fucking days, trying to find supplies to get the defenses running again!

Had no one checked this fucking closet?

A clatter of claws.

Freeman spun, staring at the sliver of light beneath the door.

A huffing noise. The shadow of something beyond. It was smelling him from under the door.

The door. Did you lock the door?

Freeman stood there dumbly, not able to believe his own shortcomings. Here, this whole time, he'd considered himself an intelligent military man. A goddamned colonel. A colonel who had run into a place that had no retreat, and forgot to lock the door behind him.

The door flew open.

Dark shapes beyond.

Light bloomed into the closet.

Illuminating a long-handled torque wrench that sat, just to the side of the door.

Freeman laughed again, unable to control himself.

The primals lunged in at him, silent save for their haggard breaths.

This whole time, Freeman thought—his last thought. *This closet had everything you needed...*

SEVENTEEN

VICI

LEE DISCONNECTED THE SATPHONE, Abe's words ringing a low, hollow note through him.

He was in the back of the command MATV, with Angela and Brinly.

And Abby. Because where else would she be besides with her mother? He felt the eyes of Angela and Brinly on him, but Lee found himself looking at Abby instead.

She jostled about with the movement of the vehicle over the potholed roads. She held her crumpled paperback, her brow furrowed in concentration, and Lee thought that maybe she was just concentrating on looking like she hadn't heard the exchange between Lee and Abe.

"So," Angela prompted, softly. "Mosquero."

Lee stirred. Folded the satphone antenna. "Wiped out. Recently."

Abby glanced up from her book, then back down again, her frown deepening.

Neither Angela nor Brinly gave any immediate reaction. They had expected as much based on the one-sided conversation that they'd heard.

"No survivors?" Brinly asked, though it sounded like he already knew the answer.

Lee shook his head. "Abe was engaged by a sniper. Lost two soldiers. Wounded a third. Sniper beat feet after that. They think it was Cornerstone. Most recent intel that we had put Cornerstone in Mosquero."

"Why would they do that?" Angela said, her voice harsh and bitter.

"To deny us," Lee answered. "That's the most logical conclusion. Which means that they know we're out here, and they know what we're trying to do."

"They're pulling back," Brinly said. "Consolidating in Greeley and scorching the earth behind them. It's a viable tactic for a desperate defense. Harsh, but effective."

Lee leaned forward onto his elbows. "We can't let this out."

"What do you mean?" Angela asked.

"I mean if other settlements find out that this is going on, they're not going to risk joining us."

"We can't just lie to them. They need to know what they're up against."

"Angela, we *have* to keep it from them. Fear isn't the way to get them to join up with us—they need to have a sense that we can actually pull this off. If they're terrified to leave their families, they won't join us. And then we're dead in the water. All of what we've done will be for nothing."

"I wouldn't join," Abby piped up, her eyes still focused on the pages of her book. "Not if I heard what happened to Mosquero."

Angela tensed. "Abby. Honey. Read your book."

Abby raised defiant eyes. "I *am* reading my book."

"No, you're sticking your nose where it doesn't belong."

"I can't help hearing you talk."

"But you can keep your opinions to yourself," Angela snapped.

Abby rolled her eyes and then settled them back on her book. "Just saying."

Angela brought her hands up to her face, her fingertips mashing her eyebrows. "It doesn't feel right not to tell them the risks."

"It doesn't matter if it doesn't feel right to you," Lee said, keeping his voice neutral. "Strategically, it's the better decision. If we want this movement to actually gain traction."

The radio in the front of the MATV cracked, receiving a transmission: "Recon One to command. We got a bit of a situation."

Lee straightened, looking to Brinly.

The Marine nearest the radio snatched the handset and passed it back to Brinly. The old Marine put it to his ear. "Command to Recon One, what's going on?"

"Sir…uh…we're about two miles out from Vici. We got a buncha people with guns here, and they don't really want us to continue on to Vici. They're demanding to speak to someone in charge."

Brinly's brow furrowed. "Are they from Vici? And has there been any shots fired?"

"Negative on the shots fired. And they won't answer any of our questions."

Lee sidled forward in his seat. "We're still twenty minutes out."

Brinly nodded. "Recon One, explain to them that we'll be there in twenty minutes."

"Uh, yes, sir. I've explained that to them. They seem real hinked up by the concept of a convoy rolling into Vici. I, uh…well, one of them is right here. He wants to speak with you directly. Permission to put him on?"

Brinly eyed Lee.

Lee considered it for a brief moment, then nodded.

"Go ahead, Recon One. Put them on."

A pause over the airwaves, followed by a very irritable sounding voice with a southern accent so thick that the words were almost unintelligible: "Who'm I speakin to?"

Brinly blinked a few times, translating in his head before he responded. "My name is Major Brinly. I'm in charge of those men you have at gunpoint. I'd urge you to lower your weapons and discontinue hostilities."

"Fuck that, man, I dunno you."

"I assure you, we don't mean any harm. All we want to do is talk."

"We talkin now."

"Sir," Brinly growled. "We will be there in twenty minutes. I'd much prefer to do this face to face."

"Nah, you can shove at right up yer ass. Cain't be rollin in with all your guns and shit. You wanna talk, you gonna talk one-on-one, yahear?"

Lee cut a hand across his neck. "Stop the convoy," he snapped. "We'll roll in by ourselves."

Brinly lowered the handset. "They don't sound overly friendly."

"Would you be overly friendly to an unknown military force when you've had Greeley breathing down your neck for five years?"

Brinly's lips thinned out. He brought the headset back to his ear. "I didn't catch your name, sir."

"Cuz I din give it. You comin or what?"

Lee nodded. Brinly turned his head and hollered up to the front of the MATV. "Stop the convoy. We're going in solo." Then he transmitted with the handdset. "Yes, sir, we're coming."

***

It was Lee in the center of the road. Brinly stood to his right, Angela to his left.

The command MATV sat rumbling at idle behind them.

Ahead of them, Recon One's single pickup truck—a dusty, silver F-250—was parked right on the faded center line of this long and lonesome stretch of highway that headed north towards the little cluster of buildings on the horizon that Lee assumed was Vici, their objective.

The four Marines of Recon One stood at the back of the F-250, and surrounding them were no less than a dozen men and women with rifles held in various poses of general hostility. The Marines themselves had their rifles hanging and their hands clear of their weapons, but weren't in any deliberate positions of surrender.

"You sure we should be bringing the president into the middle of this?" Brinly murmured as his squinted eyes surveyed the scene.

Lee didn't look, but he could feel Angela bristling.

"You're dreaming a dream if you think I'm waiting in the command truck, Brinly," she said.

Lee cast a sardonic look at Brinly. "Well, there you have it."

"Alright, fuck it," Brinly steeled himself and began striding forward. "Let's get it over with, then."

Half of the dozen armed strangers were focused on the Marines of Recon One, while the other half had become fixated on the three approaching figures. Lee scanned across the faces looking back at him, still about fifty yards distant. He wasn't sure which one had done the talking over the radio, but he spotted a lean, surly-faced man that seemed itching to talk. He was out front and center from the others.

Lee let his gaze travel out to the flatlands around them, and didn't miss the poorly disguised lumps, perhaps a hundred yards out from the road. Two on the east side of the road, and two on the west. Snipers, though their haphazard attempts at ghillie weren't quite cutting it. They were dark, forest green shapes amid the pale green and tan grasses of the plains.

"You see the snipers?" Lee murmured.

Brinly nodded. "Two on the right, two on the left."

Angela seemed to have spotted them as well. "That's actually a good sign," she observed. "At least we know that Vici isn't populated by a bunch of pacifists."

"Yeah," Lee grunted. "Provided this doesn't end in gunfire, it's super great."

"If it does, it'll be mutual destruction," Brinly noted. "Our gunner behind us will fuck them up, but I don't see us getting back to the truck."

"Well," Lee sighed. "We'll just have to make sure it doesn't end in gunfire."

The lean man with the sour face stepped forward and raised his hand when they were about twenty yards off. "That's far enough!" he hollered at them. "I'll come to you. Don't try nothing stupid or I'll fuck your shit up."

Lee stopped, unable to contain a cold smirk. He decided that, should it come to a gunfight, the sour-faced man would be his meat shield.

Then, poisonous doubt: *Are you strong enough to restrain him now, you crippled old fuck?*

Two others accompanied the sour-faced man as he strode up to them. A man and a woman. They hung back a few paces, their rifles shouldered, but their muzzles held at a low ready. The man had an AK variant. The woman a scoped bolt-action. The sour-faced man had a run-of-the-mill AR with what looked like a ridiculously overpowered scope on it. Probably used to use it for blowing the heads off gophers. He seemed like the type of guy that would get a kick out of that.

The sour-faced man stopped a few paces from Lee, his two companions behind him. His lips were pursed, like a draw-string bag all shut up tight. He had dark, beady eyes, just slits in the bright afternoon sun. He looked at Lee, then at Brinly, then at Angela.

"Y'all the ones in charga them fucks in the pickup?"

"Those 'fucks'," Brinly said. "Are United States Marines."

The man spat off to the side. “Ain’t no Yoo-nited States no more, so you can stow all that bullshit. Whadya want and why’re you here?”

“We came to talk.”

“We’re talkin. Whadya want?”

Brinly exchanged a sidelong glance with Lee.

But it was Angela who stepped up. “Sir, my name is Angela Houston.” She thrust her hand out to him.

The man had what seemed to be a moment of panic. Here, a pretty lady had just put her hand out to be shaken. Old habits die hard. He reached for her hand at the same moment that he realized it went against his whole gruff demeanor.

Too late. Angela grasped it and pumped. She smiled. “And you are?”

“Dave,” the man said, and a smile cracked his visage. Then disappeared, almost self-consciously. He withdrew his hand. “Waitaminit. Back up…”

Angela seemed to already know what question had popped into his head. “Yes, I’m Angela Houston. From what was formerly known as the United Eastern States.”

Lee’s entire body tensed. Jaw locked. He became utterly aware of the distance from his right hand to the pistol on his hip. *You shouldn’t have said that, dammit…*

Dave just stared at her. That tiny smile was nowhere to be found, completely buried under more doubtful scrutiny. “Right.”

Angela charged ahead, wielding trust like a weapon. She gestured to the men standing to her right. “This is Lee Harden. And this is Major Brinly, a Marine, formerly of Camp Lejeune in North Carolina.”

Dave's two companions looked at each other. Then at Dave. Then at the three people they'd just been introduced to. Then back to each other.

Dave took a deliberate step back, as though pulling away from the truth. Which he obviously did not consider to be truthful at all. "You ain't Angela Houston."

Angela quirked an eyebrow. "Oh?"

Dave made a bitter raspberry noise. "Angela's a scrappy bitch. She got bigger balls than any man I've ever met. You? Naw. You just…you just look like you done dropped the kids off at soccer practice. You ain't no fighter." Dave turned his gaze on Lee. "And you're not Lee Harden." This, Dave actually managed to laugh at. "Lee Harden's killed men with his bare fuckin hands. You look like you're struggling to stand up straight. You ain't even gotta eye. You got a bum leg and a bum arm. You're gotdamn beat to fuck. You spect me to believe you're Lee Harden?" Another scoffing laugh. "You're scrawny, half-starved, and you look like you need a gotdamn walker to get around." He looked at Brinly. "You? I never even hearda you."

Brinly sighed. "Figures."

Angela's smile became amused. And dark. "This man that you think needs a walker? He'd never use one. He's too damn stubborn. And yes, he's killed men with his hands before. I've seen him do it. And with his teeth. And with knives. And with bullets. He tore the *Nuevas Fronteras* cartel to pieces, just him and another man, and they were called *Nadie y Ninguno*. He rebelled against Greeley because they wanted to abandon the east coast, and he was the one that kept us alive, who beat back a horde of millions of infected." Angela looked at Lee, and Lee had to look away, because her eyes had too much in them. Too many things for Lee to deal with in that moment. "The bum arm he got from chasing down an infected and killing it with a knife—it ripped his arm to shreds. The leg and the eye?" A shadow fell across Angela's features. "Those he got protecting me, when Greeley invaded."

Dave shuffled uncomfortably. "So they did invade? They wiped out the United Eastern States?"

Angela shook her head. "They invaded. But they didn't wipe us out. They didn't win. They only pissed us off. And now we're here. And we want to talk."

Dave seemed on the cusp of believing, but then his dubious nature got the better of him, and his face hardened again, like magma cooling to volcanic rock. "Aight. You make a lot of claims, lady. But I gotta way to pull out the truth. I got people who'll know whether you're lyin or not."

"Take us to them," Angela said.

"Angela…" Lee growled.

She turned to look at him. "This is why we're here. You wanted to talk to the people of Vici? This is how we do it."

Lee spoke low, though he knew that Dave could hear him anyways. "You wanna just waltz into a bunch of people with questionable loyalties?"

Dave took umbrage and spat again. "Questionable loyalties my ass. Fuck Greeley and fuck President Briggs. And fuck his Cornerstone goons to boot. But fuck you too, because I still think you're full of shit. But we gon see."

Angela held eye contact with Lee. "You want them to trust you, Lee? You gotta show them trust first."

Lee flashed his teeth in irritation. Then forced his eyes to Dave. "Alright. Fine. I'll go with you. Just me."

"Lee..." Angela warned.

Lee spun on her, holding up a finger. "Just me. Don't argue."

Angela's face was stiff with irritation. But she had to see the logic in it. There was no sense in all of them walking into the lion's den. One beat-to-fuck Lee Harden was better than the whole of their leadership. The resistance could move on without Lee. But they couldn't survive without all three of them.

She turned away from him, but did not object any further.

Lee stepped forward. "Who are these people that you think can confirm who I am?"

Dave merely smirked at him. "You'll see."

EIGHTEEN

MYTHS AND LEGENDS

LEE'S EYES COURSED over the settlement as they approached it. He knelt in the back of a pickup truck—a little white Toyota that had come rocketing out of Vici after Dave had called in on a little two-way radio.

So far, what he saw was good.

Vici was clearly organized. Clearly not a friend of Greeley—at least if Dave was to be believed. And they were clearly aggressive about protecting themselves from outsiders. Those were all things that Lee could work with. Provided that he could convince them of who he was.

Being fairly confident in his identity, Lee was willing to take some risks he might not have taken in other circumstances. But he got the vibe from Dave that, if he could prove he was Lee, Vici would be an instant ally.

Who was it that they had that could identify him? Someone he knew? Someone who simply *claimed* to know him? What if they didn't really? What if they called him a liar?

Well, they hadn't taken Lee's pistol from him, so that was always an option.

Dave and his two companions were in the bed of the pickup with Lee, their rifles trained on him because he had refused to give up his sidearm. In a way, Lee thought it was a good sign that they hadn't argued harder to disarm him. Maybe they *wanted* to believe him.

The first thing that Lee noted as the pickup pulled into the southern edge of Vici, was the fact that they had no fences. No walls. Nothing to keep out the primals—or whatever they called them around here.

Tex had been a proponent of a similar strategy. All the little settlements that made up his coalition of Texans had simply had a vested interest in killing all the "teepios" they could.

"Your defenses," Lee said, speaking loudly to be heard over the growl of the truck. "You don't have a problem with the infected?"

"You mean the teepios?" Dave asked.

Interesting. The colloquialism from Texas had spread.

Lee nodded.

"Define 'problem'," Dave grunted. "They're smart puppies. They know not to fuck with us. Every time they do we leave their pack scattered out on the field. I think they've learned at this point."

Lee pursed his lips thoughtfully. "Never more than ten or so?"

Dave eyed him. "Why do you ask?"

"Because in Georgia we ran into hordes of hundreds. And they weren't shy about fucking our shit up."

Dave frowned, a look of disbelief passing over his face, but he didn't respond. "How bout you just quiet down for now, m'kay? You'll have your chance to talk."

The people of the settlement were already hanging around, watching with curiosity as the pickup truck pulled into their midst. Their gazes crossed over Dave and his people and settled on Lee. His first instinct was to grow uncomfortable under their scrutiny. But his second instinct was to hold up under it. To not only be who he was, but to embody the myth that he had become.

A myth was a powerful thing. Dave clearly thought that the real Lee Harden should be some muscle-bound killer, so good at fighting that he didn't have any scars. That was fine. Lee could harness that unrealistic expectation and use it to his advantage.

And who are you, really?

Just a man of violence, always seeking an outlet for his anger? Was he wrath? Was he vengeance?

Yes, I'm all of those things. I am a violent man. I have sought out the evil and executed violence on it. I have been wrathful. I have been vengeful. And perhaps I am a little off in the head.

But was that all that lay at the center of him? Was his core just a vicious animal, trained to go for the throat, looking for opportunities to be let off the leash? Or was he, perhaps, something a little bit more than that?

The pickup truck stopped in the middle of the street, towards the center of Vici. Dave stood up in the truck bed and moved to the tailgate. "Make sure he doesn't move from this spot," he growled to his companions, then hopped down.

Lee looked at the woman to his right, and slightly behind him. She glared back with no trust in her face, the muzzle of her rifle held steady on him.

"Don't even fuckin look at me," she snapped.

Lee smirked, but looked away.

In the reflection of the back glass of the pickup truck, he could see her and her male comrade exchange a worried glance. So, all the bluster was to mask a genuine fear. Perhaps fear of who he really was. Because if he *was* Lee Harden, if he was the myth that they believed about the man, then the very fact that he still had a pistol strapped to his hip might be quite worrisome.

After all, Lee Harden could apparently kill a platoon of men with a toothpick. Give him a gun and he might wipe out this whole settlement if they incurred his wrath.

Dave walked around the front of the pickup and met several others that appeared to be waiting for him. There were five of them. What looked to Lee like an entourage, with a woman in the center who appeared to be in charge.

Dave dipped his head and spoke in tones that Lee couldn't hear.

The woman, a stubby little thing with short-cropped brown hair, looked over Dave's shoulder and met Lee's gaze. She held it, defiant.

In his kneeling position, his left hip and leg began to slowly tighten into a cramp. Lee tried to keep the burgeoning pain off his face, but there's something very insistent about an incoming cramp.

"I'm going to pull my leg up," Lee said to the woman on his right.

"Don't move."

Lee ignored her and drew his left leg up. "I'm keeping my right knee on the ground."

"I said don't move."

Lee looked over his shoulder at her, his expression mild, but undeterred. "I took a bullet to the hip about a week ago. You ever been shot?"

She didn't answer. She seemed to really want him to obey her, but she also knew that she wasn't going to force the issue. Because she was afraid of who he might really be.

"I've been shot a good bit," Lee sighed, stretching his left leg as best he could and massaging the cramp out of his upper thigh. "Muscles around the wound like to bind up. They never quite feel the same after something's gone through them."

"If you're such a fuckin badass, why'd you get shot so much?"

Lee smiled without looking at her. "Honestly, I'm surprised I'm even alive. Died one time, after getting shot in the chest. I was lucky to have a good doc—" *Julia* "—to bring me back to life."

The man on his left scoffed out a snort. "So the great Lee Harden gets his shit pushed in on a regular basis. That's disappointing."

Lee shrugged. "Not a fan of it myself."

The quiet conference at the front of the truck ended. The stocky woman that appeared to be in charge departed with her entourage, and Dave circled back to the truck bed. He looked up at Lee, his eyes still full of suspicion.

"They're goin to get em now. We'll have this sorted out real quick."

"Am I supposed to know these people?" Lee asked.

"You'll see."

"Right." Lee shook his head. "I'll see."

A few minutes passed in relative silence. Lee looked around him, meeting the eyes of the people of Vici. Some of them stared back. Others shied away and found their shoes or the sky much more interesting.

Lee imagined that word traveled pretty fast in a settlement like this. He could hear the subtle murmurs around him, like the trickle of a stream, carried from mouth to ear, coursing through the people gathered at the edges of the street. The rumor of who he claimed to be making the rounds. Who knew what elaboration was being added to each iteration of the rumor?

People. They never change.

A stir brought Lee's attention front and center. Over the cab of the pickup, he saw the stocky woman approaching again. Two men had been added to her entourage, trailing behind her. They wore civilian clothes. One was black. One was white. Lee had never seen them before in his life.

"Hey, Dave," Lee said, tilting his head to the man on the ground. "I hate to break it to you, but if those two are the ones that claim to know me, you're about to be disappointed. I don't recognize either of them."

Dave was unimpressed. He spat off to the side again. "Dudn't mean they don't know you."

Fantastic. So now Lee was being put on trial based on two fuckheads who claimed to know him, and were likely lying through their teeth. Possibly to ingratiate themselves with the populace.

How was he going to handle this?

The woman in charge hung back a few paces from the front of the pickup truck. The two strangers continued forward and stopped beside Dave, looking up into the truck bed at Lee. He made eye contact with them, his expression calm. Neutral.

The white guy put his hand on the side of the bed. "Who are you?"

"Lee Harden."

A quirk of an eyebrow. "No rank?"

"Well…I've been a captain and a major, and God knows what I am now."

This was apparently strike one against Lee. The man exchanged a knowing glance with his companion. Then back to Lee. "Alright, hot shot. Tell me something only Lee Harden would know."

"Considering the fact that I don't know either of you from Adam, I can't see how you're going to verify anything I say."

"Try me."

Lee smiled. "I once had a girlfriend named Deanna who kept a betta fish in her office."

Silence.

"What?" Lee squinted at them. "Was that too personal? Hm. Guess you don't know as much about me as you thought. Should I try for some shit that two random dudes who claim to know me can verify? Okay. I was a Coordinator for Project Hometown. I left my bunker early. That pissed off President Briggs, who saw Project Hometown as his personal honeypot. He's had it out for me ever since. Labeled me a 'non-viable asset'. Sent a bunch of people to kill me, but I killed them first. Sent one of my good friends to kill me, a man named Abe Darabie, but Abe rebelled and now we work together. A little more than a month ago, me and Abe spent some time in Texas, killing all the cartel we could find. Then I got called back to the east coast just in time to get invaded by Greeley. And now we're here." Lee tilted his head, challenging them. "How's that for starters?"

"Common knowledge," the man replied without missing a beat.

"Of course." Lee looked skyward. "Well, why don't you just ask me some questions then. You want proof of who I am, you're gonna need to be specific about what you consider to be proof."

The man was ready. He held up two fingers. "You met two men. One was from Canada. The other was from the United Kingdom. What were their names?"

Lee reared back, taken off guard.

The man's expression became vindicated, like he'd finally caught the imposter in a lie.

Lee's heart slammed a few times in his chest. Who the hell were these guys and how the hell did they know about that? Should Lee even tell them anything? Had he completely misread the situation? Was Vici as anti-Greeley as they had appeared, or had he let himself get lured into a trap?

The silence hung. The man shook his head, his nose curling as though Lee disgusted him. He began to turn away, and Lee could already see, in the span of just a few seconds, what was about to happen next.

He was about to be labeled a liar. And then everything would go tits up.

Lee pulled the bottom out of his hesitation. Plunged forward. "Marlin and Wibberley," he spat out.

The man froze, his mouth still open in preparation to tell Dave that the man in the pickup bed was full of shit. He turned back to Lee, his eyes widening.

"Marlin was from Canada," Lee said. "Wibberley was from the UK."

"Holy fuck," the man murmured.

Dave fidgeted, his head pivoting rapidly between Lee and his questioner. "What? What's going on? Is that right?"

A shocked smile crept onto the stranger's face as he stared at Lee. And something like awe. "I can't believe you're still alive."

Lee frowned. "Yeah, we were just talking about that. Now who the hell are *you*?"

The man immediately thrust his hand out. "My name is Worley, Canadian Armed Forces. This is Guidry, British Army."

***

"What's going on out there?" Frenchie worried, hovering over Sam's shoulder as he leaned out the window, trying to put eyes on the cause of all the bustling about that he heard.

Straight down the road that their apartment flat sat on, Sam could see the next three intersections. Through the farthest intersection, coming straight out of the compound known colloquially as "FOB Hampton," a series of guntrucks roared by, heading south.

Following the guntrucks, a motorcade of dark-colored SUVs flew by, bumper-to-bumper in their urgency.

Sam shook his head. "Well, I don't know what the hell's going on, but someone fucking kicked the hornets' nest."

He drew his head back out of the window and frowned at Frenchie's complete disregard for personal space. He gained some distance by putting a hand on Frenchie and pressing him back.

Something had happened. What that something was, Sam could only guess. But in the last five minutes, the relatively quiet streets of Greeley had suddenly become inundated with the refrains of big engines roaring to points unknown.

Sam looked back across the cramped confines of the flat. Marie and Jones hung out the window on the back side of the apartment. Pickell and Johnson huddled near the kitchen counter, the satphone sitting there between them.

Jones pulled out of the window. "Something's got 'em all hot and bothered. Bet you don't need twenty questions to guess why."

Sam met Jones's eyes, which were serious for once. "You think they caught wind of Lee?"

Jones raised his hands in a shrug. "Yes? Why else would they be sprinting for the perimeter?"

Sam shook his head, approaching the kitchen counter. "We don't know that. We don't know shit. This could be normal for around here."

Marie negotiated herself out of the window frame. "All the civilians out there rubbernecking tells me this isn't normal."

Pickell looked grimly thoughtful. "It was bound to happen at some point, Sam. Lee's got an army heading this way. He couldn't go unnoticed forever."

Sam grimaced. "This soon, though? Hell, we just left them a few days ago. The army couldn't have gotten that far north."

Marie and Jones took positions on either side of Pickell. Marie seemed confident in her assessment of the situation, and it appeared she agreed with Pickell. "There's no telling, Sam. Greeley could have agents in the settlements that Lee is trying to talk to. It would only take one to sound the alarm."

"It could be primals," Johnson offered. "Like when they tried to rush Butler."

Sam shook his head. "It's not the same out here. Intel says the primals out here don't horde up. They're just packs. That's why Greeley and every other settlement around here doesn't have walls or fences."

Johnson looked put out. "Well. It *could* happen. First time for everything."

Marie tapped a finger on the satphone. "Sam, you might want to make the call to Lee and tell him what you can. There's no telling when you're going to get another opportunity if shit breaks bad around here. We're already under scrutiny. With this shit coming down the pipe, things are only going to get worse."

Sam nodded and stepped up to the kitchen counter. He'd hoped to have some actionable intelligence to give Lee when he called, but at this point Marie was right. Lee didn't even know that Sam had gotten inside Greeley yet. He reached for the satphone.

"Yo!" Frenchie called from the front, where he had taken Sam's position in the window. "Sam! Incoming!"

Sam's whole body flushed with adrenaline at that little word: *incoming*. He snatched the satphone from the counter and bounded to the window.

Frenchie retracted himself, thrusting a hand out and pointing down onto the street.

A convoy of pickups laden with armed men had split off from the main intersection and now approached at high speed. Sam's eyes snatched from vehicle to vehicle. Men in the beds. Men hanging onto the running boards. Some of them wore black polos. Others wore fatigues. All of them wore white armbands—with a red Delta symbol on them.

Cornerstone.

The satphone became a lead weight in Sam's hand. His palms and the small of his back began to sweat. But still he watched. Perhaps because he didn't want to believe it. He wanted to believe that all these troopers were speeding their way to some perimeter…

They weren't.

Tires locked up. Men clung to handholds, as pickup after pickup curbed itself in front of buildings. The very same sets of buildings where the newly-minted conscripts had been housed only hours before.

And yes. One pickup, right below them.

A man in a black polo hopped off a running board, rifle in hand, and looked up. Right at Sam.

He pointed. "You!"

Shit.

Sam snatched himself out of the window. Spun around. Frenchie looked terrified. The others were confused, not sure what it was that Sam and Frenchie had just witnessed.

The satphone. In his hands.

The sound of boots on the ground. A door slamming.

Footfalls on the stairwell leading up.

"They're coming," Sam breathed.

Frenchie and Johnson were paralyzed.

Marie, Jones, and Pickell sprung into action. For a moment their movements seemed nonsensical: They raced about the kitchen, ripping open the small set of cabinets and drawers, as though they were trying to prepare refreshments for their imminent guests.

It only made sense to Sam when Jones looked at him, clapped his hands together, and held them up in a catching position. "The phone!" Jones hissed.

Even as Sam realized what they were doing, he tossed the satphone in an arc. Jones snatched it out of the air, then spun, looking for a place to hide it.

Pickell yanked a kitchen drawer out, bent low to look into the cavity, then straightened. "Jones! In here!"

Jones twisted, looked into the space where the drawer had been removed.

Footfalls pounded closer and closer.

Jones made a face, and Sam knew in an instant what it meant: The hiding place wasn't great, but they didn't have time to find better.

The footfalls reached the landing, right outside their door.

Jones chucked the satphone into the cavity. Pickell tried to get the drawer back in, but it was caught on something.

A fist slammed into the door, three times. A harsh voice: "Cornerstone! We're coming in! Hands up!"

Pickell's teeth were bared, his eyes wild with panic as he tried to negotiate the stubborn drawer back onto its tracks. Sam and Marie flashed onto the same idea at once and moved quickly to stand between the door and Pickell, blocking him from view.

A hand on the doorknob. Sam heard it rattle. Saw the brass knob twist.

The door flung open.

The sound of a drawer closing.

Bodies poured into the flat, rifles shouldered, muzzles directed at faces and chests.

Sam and his entire crew jolted their hands into the air.

Sam watched their entry with the authority of someone who'd done them countless times: Point came in, splitting towards the group, shouting, "On your knees!" The second man entered and took position near the window, scanning the corners of the room. Then three more barged in, filling in the gaps and angling their rifles to avoid friendly fire and keep Sam's crew in a crossing arc.

It was a well-executed entry, Sam thought as he hit his knees with the others.

The point and two others held coverage on Sam and his team, while the last two operatives skirted around and cleared the kitchen. The flat had no rooms. They were just checking nooks and crannies.

Sam looked over his shoulder at the two operatives in the kitchen, fearing that they would take interest in the drawer that Pickell now knelt in front of, his figure blocked by the kitchen counter. A hand grabbed the top of Sam's head and mushed it down.

"Look at the floor," a voice growled.

Sam kept his head facing the ground, but peered upwards from under his brow.

As several calls of "Clear!" were announced, the last operative entered the room, clearly the one in charge. You can always tell the one in charge from the foot soldiers. He wore no armor or helmet. Just the black polo and a pistol on his hip.

His gaze circumvented the room and came to rest on Sam.

"Sameer Balawi?" the man asked.

Sam nodded, still keeping his head down. "That's me, sir."

"Squad leader?"

"Yes, sir."

A single moment's thought. Then: "Bag him and the woman. And this one right here. What's your name, kid?"

"Trudeau, sir," Sam heard Frenchie murmur, his voice shaken.

Out of the corner of his eye, Sam saw a black sack produced from one of the operative's cargo pockets. While his comrades kept cover on the group, the operative fluffed it open, then slapped it down over Sam's head.

It wasn't until everything went dark that Sam started to truly panic.

NINETEEN

LOYALTY

This was bad. Really bad.

Sam saw, again and again, those last few moments of daylight. The thought had grown like an aggressive tumor in his brain: *Should I have done something?*

What if this was it? What if he never saw the light again? What if the end of this was a bullet in the back of the head, and they were just transporting him to the hole they had dug in the ground so that when they killed him, he'd topple conveniently into his grave?

I should have done something.

Run. Fought. Shouted. Jumped out the window. Tried to disarm one of the operatives. Anything. Anything would be better than simply raising your hands, going to your knees, and getting snatched into the darkness.

His hands had been cuffed behind his back. Traditional metal handcuffs. He was in the cargo area of the SUV they'd driven up outside of the flat. Frenchie and Marie were there with him.

None of them dared speak. One of the operatives was crouched in the back with them, and he'd already told them, "Don't say a fucking word, don't grab each other's asses, or try to communicate in any way. I promise you that you're not slick enough to get away with it."

And so none of them tried a damn thing.

Squashed together with Marie and Frenchie, Sam could feel their chests heaving with the same rapid, fear-drowned breaths that filled his own lungs.

They were going to kill him. And his team.

But then why take just the three of them? If they were going to kill everyone, then why not just merc them all when they were kneeling in the flat with their hands over their head?

God, I can't believe you knelt!

It had just…happened. He'd been so worried about the damn satphone not being found that he'd completely whiffed the obvious signs that he was about to get black bagged. The secret police had come to round him up, and it wasn't for a tea party in his honor.

He could drum up all the excuses he wanted to try to assuage the horrific guilt of his own inadequacy, but in the background of it all, he could see Lee's stern features, glaring at him, filled with disappointment.

You let yourself get caught. You let yourself get taken. You stopped thinking like a predator, and you started thinking like prey.

And you know what happens to prey? They get eaten alive.

You think an 800-lb zebra couldn't stomp the fuck out of a 300-lb lioness? That's less than half the zebra's body weight. Would you be afraid of someone that was half your body weight? No, you'd just kick their ass.

But a zebra is hardwired to be prey. It doesn't even think about killing. It just thinks about getting away.

Sam had been a prey animal there. He'd been perfectly capable of fighting back, but he hadn't even thought of it. He'd just thought about how to get away with having the satphone.

Once the lion dragged you down to the ground, well then you were just meat.

So, what now, little boy? What now, Sameer Balawi who became the rough-tough Sam Ryder, who then regressed back into Sameer Balawi? Did you think it was all an act? Your regression, so that you could get your foot in the door in Greeley?

Or maybe you got it all wrong. Maybe you got it all flipped around and reversed. Maybe Sam Ryder was the act. Maybe, when you put on the mantle of Sameer Balawi, you were just returning to your true self: Scared.

Terrified. Run away. Prey animal.

Everyone dies because of your fear.

He'd promised himself *never again*, but now here he was…again. And he hated himself for it. He loathed every fiber of his being for how he didn't see it coming, how he blanked in the moment, and how that moment just flitted away like a little bit of dandelion fluff, never to be seen again. He had one shot to make things go right, and he'd hesitated. He'd let the fear grip him, and he'd missed it.

He hadn't changed at all. He was still the same old Sameer Balawi, out there pissing his pants because danger lurked around every corner. Out there, hiding in the dark, while everyone he loved got ripped to shreds and shot dead.

What a hero.

His skin prickled all over. Hot, then cold. Sweat broke out on his palms and across his back and face.

The vehicle skidded to a halt.

Sam's self-recrimination wasn't helping the situation. Savagely, he acknowledged that he'd fucked up. Okay, move on. He couldn't go back and change it. The worst thing he could do now was become so wrapped up in his own self-loathing that he missed another opportunity.

What are you gonna do? You're no Lee Harden. You can't get out of this.

He was ripped from the vehicle first. His head smacked the bumper as his body was dropped like a bag of trash. With his ears still ringing from the blow, he felt hands wedge themselves under his armpits, hoisting him upright.

Feet on the ground.

A hand on his chest.

"You move, you die. Can't make it any simpler."

The sounds of Marie and Frenchie being hauled out of the vehicle. A quiet whimper—it sounded like Frenchie.

What is this? What's going on?

His brain conjured all kinds of images in an attempt to read the future. That is what brains are designed to do when they're in danger. But he couldn't seem to move past the one where he was lined up and shot in the back of the head, tumbling bonelessly into a mass grave.

A hand slapped down on his head. Grabbed the sack—and some hair with it—and yanked it off.

Air. Cool against his sweat, though the day was still hot.

His eyes blinded by sunlight.

He blinked. Figures came into focus. Marie and Frenchie, across from him—the three of them formed into a small circle—their hoods removed. Marie had her head back, her hair sticking to her face, her eyes taking on that intentionally dead caste, when you don't want to let any emotions show through.

Frenchie wasn't as tough. His eyes were wide, and fearful, and red. His lips quivered, though he seemed to be trying hard to keep it under control.

The operatives surrounded them, rifles up.

Sam looked around. He half-expected a blow to the face and a harsh command not to look around. But it didn't come. All around them was nothing. Just plains. Some of it green. Some of it tan. The blue peaks of the Rockies, just a jagged disruption to the horizon.

The lead operative parked himself between Sam and Frenchie. He was young. Short cropped hair. A goatee that he was clearly proud of. He looked between them. "Time's short. I don't enjoy this. I'm going to get right down to it." He grimaced, shaking his head. "Sameer Balawi, during our investigations, it became apparent that this guy, Trudeau, is a spy for Lee Harden."

Frenchie's eyes peeled even wider. "Wait! What?"

The operative spun and held up a finger, his face suddenly going dark. "I swear to fuck that I'll kill you flat out if you say another word."

Frenchie's mouth worked.

The operative rested his hand on his pistol, his lips pursed, ready to hear a single word issue from Frenchie's mouth and make good on his threat.

Sam gave his comrade the slightest of head shakes.

Frenchie snapped his mouth shut. Averted his eyes.

The operative huffed. "Sameer, you have a traitor in your midst. And, as harsh as it is, there is only one way that we deal with traitors. Do you understand me?"

Sam stared at him, his heart thudding, feeling the possibility of hope that this wasn't just an execution, that maybe there was a way out of this.

The operative squared himself to Sam. "You're the squad leader. These are tough decisions. But that's the world we live in, my man. You gotta roll with the punches."

"I don't understand," Sam husked out.

The man gave him a quirk of a smile. "Yeah, you do."

"He's not a traitor."

"No, he is. Our investigation has *proved* it, Sameer."

Sam's tongue was drying up as fast as his hopes. "He can't be. We've been in Oklahoma the whole time." His eyes jagged to Frenchie, saw tears spilling out of the man's eyes. "He's never even been to North Carolina."

"Maybe," the man said, nodding sympathetically. "But maybe someone from North Carolina got to him."

Was this some sort of a trick? Was Sam being bated into admitting something? He had no idea if Frenchie really was being targeted here, or if Frenchie was simply being used as a pawn, and the real target was Sam.

His eyes moved to Marie. He asked the question before he really thought about it—it was just the first thing that came to him: "What's she doing here?"

He instantly regretted it.

Marie did not emote anything. Not really. But Sam knew her well enough at this point, that he could see the tiny micro expressions that no one else could. The slightest cinching at the corners of her eyes. The barest flattening of her lips.

I'm sorry! He tried to transmit the apology through his eyes. He was caught on his heels, and he'd simply gone with the first thing he could think of.

The operative looked over his shoulder at Marie. "She's a witness. That's just how these things have to work. Otherwise someone might claim that things didn't go like they actually went. You know what I'm talking about."

A shudder worked its way through Sam. The feeling of something dangerous on his heels. He was still thinking like prey. He needed to think like a predator. Think of how to get them out of here. Not just how to survive, but how to triumph.

"I don't know what the fuck you're talking about," Sam spat. "Trudeau's not a traitor. I'd put my life on that. Is that what you want me to say?"

The operative leaned back, his eyebrows furrowing, a look of intense interest in his eyes. "Well, let's have you put your money where your mouth is."

The operative grabbed his pistol from the holster on his side. Sam's eyes tracked with it, boring into it, and he'd never seen a weapon that he'd been so afraid of. The operative dropped the mag. Presschecked the chamber. Then held the pistol out to Sam.

"Go on," he said. "Take it."

Sam couldn't rip his eyes off of it. Distantly, he recognized that it was a Glock. It would fire without the magazine in it. And it had one round in the chamber. Sam knew what that round was for.

The other Cornerstone men tensed as Sam reached out and took the pistol.

The lead man didn't need to explain the situation. It was obvious enough: One round in the chamber. Sure, Sam could do something stupid with it. But he'd be shot to shit by the four men with rifles immediately after using that one little round.

Unless he used it in the way that they wanted.

The pistol hung loose in Sam's grip. His pulse had reached an uncomfortable level now, the arteries in his neck feeling distended and stretched. His chest felt raw.

"Sameer Balawi," the operative stepped around to Sam's side, a devil on his shoulder. "You got one round in that thing. You know what to do with it. Our investigation has proven—*proven*—that this guy Trudeau is aligned with Lee Harden. You have a traitor in your squad, Sameer. And you're the squad leader." The operative's voice was harsh in Sam's ear. "This is *your* responsibility. *You* have to take care of this."

"You can't fucking be serious," Sam seethed, glancing sideways at the operative. "You're asking me to…to…What evidence do you even have?"

The operative's expression went brittle. "Evidence? You think this is some sort of congressional fucking hearing?" The man frowned deeply, as though confused by something. And then, an affectation of enlightenment. "Unless...unless you're a traitor too."

This is just one big trap, Sam realized. *They don't have evidence against Frenchie, or me, or anyone. They're just fishing. Applying pressure and waiting to see what comes out.*

Sam dipped into a well of strength that was running dry and muddy by now. "This is bullshit and you know it. You're asking me to execute a close personal friend of mine—someone I *know* is not aligned with Lee Harden—someone who's been through all kinds of shit with me, just because you *claim* that he's a traitor?"

Sam let the loosely-held pistol in his hands sink down. "This is ridiculous. You can't honestly expect me to kill him. You can't even tell me what he did wrong."

The operative put his hands on his hips and tilted his head at Sam. "Alright. I suppose it doesn't matter. I'll shoot straight with you. I have multiple witness statements from folks in The Tank that all corroborate that Trudeau tried to convince each of them to commit treason against President Briggs."

Frenchie made a sound, but choked it off before it became words. That didn't save him from a muzzle-thump from the operative behind him.

"That's bullshit," Sam said, realizing even as he said it, that it didn't matter. This was a game being played, and logic and truth were not a part of the rules. A willingness to kill to prove your loyalty—even kill a friend—was the only way to win the game. "He was with me from the time that we entered The Tank to the time we got here."

"Oh." The operative looked intrigued. "So, maybe you're in on it, then. Maybe I should give this pistol to the lady—what's your name again, lady?"

Marie didn't seem inclined to answer until the man behind her kneed her in the back, causing her to stumble forward. She regained her balance, then looked up with her carefully-deadened expression. "Marie."

"Right. Marie. Maybe I should give the gun to her. Unless she's in on it too. Jesus Christ. Are all of you traitors? Are you all aligned with Lee Harden?"

Sam's grip tightened on the pistol, though he still pointed it at the ground. "No. None of us are. Whoever gave you these statements is a liar." But Sam knew better. There never had been witness statements. This whole thing was a lie.

"Squad Leader Balawi, I'm starting to lose faith in you."

"You can't just ask me to kill someone based on hearsay."

"Things move fast these days. There's not always time for a full investigation. You either get on board the train, or you get left behind, my friend. Which one are you going to do? Are you going to get on the train? Or are we going to have to leave you behind out here?"

Objections, arguments…logic. They all came swirling up to Sam's brain, and even as they did, he knew that it was hopeless. None of that was the point. The real truth was as plain as day: This was a loyalty test, and Sam was at a fork in the road. Kill, or be killed. There was no other option. And no amount of talking would get him out of it, because the truth was immaterial.

This operative only wanted to see one thing: He wanted to see if Sam was loyal enough that he would kill his own man to stay in Greeley.

And was he? Was Sam loyal enough—not to President Briggs, but to the mission—to do something like that? No. He couldn't. He wasn't that type of person. He wasn't like Lee. He couldn't make terrible calls like this. He couldn't just kill someone—*one of his squad!*—just to keep the mission afloat.

This couldn't actually be happening.

"Hey!" The operative snapped his fingers. "You need to make a fucking decision here. What's it gonna be?"

Sam struggled to find some point of reference to put this situation in. Something that would help to clarify what he was supposed to do. But it was all so alien to him, so surreal, that he found his thoughts bouncing around in a vacuum.

Why was it so hard to think right now?

He was prey. And he was running.

"And if I refuse to kill him?" Sam asked, his gaze going to Frenchie and finding him with his eyes shuttered hard, tears streaming out of them. Unable to face the situation.

"My God, kid," the operative growled. "You gotta know what that looks like. A known traitor, and you refuse to take him out? No, you gotta do this. Or…well…you know what *I'm* gonna have to do."

It was all a trick. It had to be. There wasn't really a round in the chamber. Yes, that was it. They were just trying to see if Sam would actually pull the trigger. When it clicked on an empty chamber, the operative would laugh, and this whole fucked up situation would be thrown into the light.

It was obvious. This was all a ruse.

Maybe because it was the only thing that made any sense to him in that moment, or maybe because he knew, deep down inside, that he had no other option, Sam raised the pistol and pointed it at Frenchie.

"Sam," Marie warned.

"Shut the fuck up!" one of the men snapped, grabbing Marie by the shoulder and putting the muzzle of his rifle close to her head.

Sam stayed focused on Frenchie. He needed Frenchie to look at him. He needed him to understand. Because when that striker clicked home on an empty chamber, Frenchie needed to know that Sam had *known* it was empty—Frenchie needed to know that Sam wouldn't murder him.

A hiss of breath near his face: "You gotta take him out, Sameer!"

"Frenchie," Sam called.

Frenchie's eyes popped open. Saw the pistol aimed at him. His flushed face blanched a terrible white and he nearly fell over.

"Hey! Hey! Frenchie, look at me, you motherfucker!" Sam took a step towards him, the pistol steady in his grip. "Look at me."

Frenchie looked at him. Really *looked.* Saw what was in his eyes.

"You know why I have to do this," Sam said, each word running over with unsaid meanings. "It's all going to be okay, Frenchie. Now, nod if you understand me."

Frenchie nodded, a violent, shaky gesture.

"Quit wasting time," the operative urged. "Take the traitor out. Prove yourself."

The gun's not loaded. It's not loaded. It can't be.

But it could. That was the ugly reality. And Sam knew it, even as his finger tightened on the trigger. But it wasn't something he could dwell on. What good did that do him? It was much better to convince himself that this was all a cruel trick. It was much better that way, because Sam didn't see a way out of this, he didn't see how he could walk away from this, how the mission could still be viable, if he didn't pull that trigger.

God, I hope I can convince Frenchie that I knew it wasn't loaded.

God, I hope he's not so mad at me that he runs off or some shit.

God, I hope this thing really isn't loaded.

The trigger broke.

And the gun bucked.

The flash, the boom, the flinch that went all the way through Sam.

And Frenchie fell.

TWENTY

NO PUNCHES PULLED

LEE STOOD FRONT AND CENTER before what appeared to be the vast majority of the people in Vici. He scowled out at them with his one good eye, the other covered by the patch. He didn't bother hiding his attitude. He was over playing politics. All that had ever gotten him was grief.

This was war. Lee Harden was its harbinger. He didn't need to smile and convince. He only needed to speak the truth. Some would listen. Others wouldn't. Those that wouldn't would die. That was their problem, not his.

The meeting space was in a church in the center of the settlement. It didn't look like a church anymore. Lee could see the places where the pews used to be, but they'd long since been removed, perhaps to be hacked up for firewood. Now it was just one giant open space, with a dais a few steps up from the floor.

It was close, and crowded, and it stank.

It reminded Lee of the Camp Ryder Building, and brought back a flood of unpleasant memories that deepened his frown, and his resolution not to play games with these people.

He stood upon the dais, like some sort of guest speaker. With him was the stocky woman who was apparently in charge of Vici. She'd introduced herself as Cassandra—"Call me Cass." Along with her stood the men that had identified themselves as Worley and Guidry.

Down off the dais and to the side, stood Angela, her arms draped protectively over Abby, and Brinly, accompanied by a few of his Marines. They'd chosen—at Lee's insistence—not to show their force just yet. The rest of their convoy of soldiers and guerillas waited in relative safety, a few miles away.

The murmur of the crowd had grown to a dull roar when Cass cupped her hands around her mouth and hollered, "Yo! Quiet down and listen up!"

The people responded immediately. Which Lee thought was a good sign. They were used to listening to someone and not arguing. That was better than most.

Lee scanned the faces in the crowd, gauging the expressions. The people that were focused in. The people that looked geared up and ready. The people that looked doubtful and reserved. Others that looked downright hostile.

Tellingly, the hostile ones seemed to stick to the back of the crowd.

Lee snorted quietly to himself when he saw them back there. You just couldn't escape human nature. If you gathered five people together, you'd have two that were determined to be assholes. In this crowd of about a hundred and some change, Lee speculated that the handful that he could spot as the hard cases were just the tip of the iceberg.

"I'm sure there's been a lot of talk going on," Cass continued, projecting a surprisingly powerful voice out of her small frame. "Let's put aside all the bullshit you might have heard and get it straight from the horse's mouth." She turned and looked at Lee. "This here is the horse. He's been positively identified as *the* Lee Harden, one of the founders of the United Eastern States, which has, unfortunately..." She trailed off, then gave a grim smirk. "Well, I'll just let him tell it."

She gestured with one hand, giving Lee the floor.

Old habits, ingrained into him despite his natural inclinations: Lee had the urge to ease fears, to explain away defeats, and try to bolster support. But sometimes old habits withered and dried up. Sometimes your true nature reasserts itself when the situation demands it.

Lee wouldn't pull his punches anymore. "The United Eastern States is dead." Lee endured the disconsolate murmurs with a blank expression. When they died down to silence again, he continued. "Hence, why I'm here, and not there. Due to infighting and a massive horde of what we call *primals*, and you call *teepios*, we initially lost Fort Bragg. We regrouped in another Safe Zone in Georgia, called Butler. Before we could re-secure Fort Bragg, the teepios moved out and Greeley moved in. They used it as a staging point to assault Butler. And they won. Or, at least, they took Butler. But they didn't beat us."

Someone near the front of the crowd raised their hand like a kid in class and started to speak, but Cass immediately cut the man off. "Let's hold our questions until the end," she commanded. "Let the man finish, and then we'll open the floor."

Lee gave Cass a minor nod of appreciation. Back to the crowd. "They didn't beat us. Many of us got out. We're still alive, still armed, and we're mighty pissed off. In addition to that, it's come to our attention that the so-called President Briggs over-extended himself by invading the United Eastern States. His fuel reserves are essentially nil, and Greeley itself is currently guarded by a skeleton crew, because all of his trained fighters are in North Carolina and Georgia. Or, at least, they were as of ten days ago. Which brings me to another point.

"That invasion force will be on the move, if they're not already. They want me dead, and they want to crush any resistance, once and for all. It won't be long before Briggs realizes that I'm coming for him, and he'll seek to send that force after me, as well as hardening his defenses in Greeley. I aim to be on his doorstep before he can really get his feet under him. I aim to take advantage of his shitty strategy and make him pay. And to do that, I need fighters."

Lee stopped there. Frowned deeper. Considered saying something else. He cast a glance at Angela and Brinly, who looked like they expected him to continue, but…he didn't have much else to say. He shrugged. "And that's why I'm here."

Like Angela and Brinly, the crowd of people seemed to wait expectantly for something else. Something inspiring. Something that would get them all hot and bothered and ready to take up arms.

Lee had nothing to give them. Nothing that they wanted to hear anyways.

Cass arched her eyebrows. "Okay. Is that it?"

Lee nodded. "Yeah. That's it."

She blinked a few times, as though perplexed. Then shook it off and looked at the crowd. "Alright then. I guess…we'll open the floor to questions."

The same person who had jumped the gun on questions earlier stepped forward again. "What's your strategy? You say you want to take Greeley. I want to know how you think that's possible."

A ripple of assent went through the crowd. Good question, they all thought.

Lee arched his eyebrow at the questioner. "My strategy at the moment would be to not share my strategy with people who haven't agreed to fight alongside me."

The man looked taken aback. "You can't honestly expect us to agree to fight without knowing what we're getting into."

Lee nodded. "Fair enough. You want to know what you're getting into? I can tell you that. You're getting into a war. Whether you like it or not. Whether you agree to fight with me, or you turn your back on me, it's coming for you all the same. There aren't any neutral parties anymore. If you knew me, you'd know I don't like ultimatums, but I'm not here to blow sunshine up your ass. I'm here to speak the truth. It's war. Briggs's version of America, versus the people's. And anyone that thinks they're going to sit pretty on the fence is gonna get swept up and forced to pick a side."

A woman in the middle of the crowd raised her voice. "We heard a rumor about some small settlements that used to have Cornerstone outposts in them getting wiped out. Is that because of you?"

Lee pulled his head back. "Is it because of me? I guess you could choose to see it that way if you want. Maybe that wouldn't have happened if I'd been sitting on my ass doing nothing. But I'm choosing to fight. Our enemies will probably do worse things before all this is over."

"So you don't care about those people that got murdered?"

"I don't accept responsibility for the actions of a tyrant," Lee growled. "One way or another, he's getting taken down. And he'll probably scorch the earth to try to stop it from happening. I can't control what he does. I can only work to make sure he's never able to do something like that again."

A new face, towards the back: "So Briggs knows that you're coming. You don't even have the advantage of surprise."

Lee clenched his jaw. "I don't know what Briggs knows or doesn't know."

"You seem awful fucking *laissez-faire* about this."

"Do I?" Lee grunted. His eyes strayed to the far back, just a few people behind the current speaker. A small group moved for the exit, their movements surreptitious, their glances veiled. Lee's eyes narrowed at them. The way that they looked…Lee had seen it so many times.

He cleared his throat. Refocused, though his peripheral attention was on those half-dozen people now slipping out the back door. "You want me to be something I'm not. You want me to come in here and give you a back massage and tell you everything's going to be alright. Well, it's not. I won't apologize for leveling the uncomfortable truth at you. Consider me a messenger. My message has been delivered. You know what needs to happen, and you know the consequences of doing nothing. There's really nothing else that I need to say about it."

His eyes went to Angela and Brinly again. And Abby.

Angela looked mortified. Brinly was stone-faced.

Strangely, Abby was smiling. Like she knew exactly what Lee was saying. Like she got it.

Lee's next words caught in his throat as he stared at the girl. He let out a low cough to clear the blockage. Waved an unsteady hand at the crowd. "I have nothing else to say. I'll be camped out three miles south of you. I'll give you until dawn tomorrow to decide what you want to do."

In the shell-shocked silence, Lee hitched his way down off the dais, striding past Angela and Brinly without looking at them. "Let's go," he murmured. "Trust me on this."

***

Sam staggered back into the flat. There was no other word for it. He couldn't feel his feet.

Honestly, he couldn't feel much. He was stuck in a nightmare.

The Cornerstone operatives that had escorted he and Marie back up the stairs to the flat simply turned and left without another word.

What the hell had he been thinking?

His eyes ranged over the flat, saw the shapes of his team moving towards him, heard their voices distantly, as though his head was stuck underwater. He couldn't see their faces. For a moment a splinter of panic nipped at him—was he crying? Was that what made their faces so blurry?

But no. He blinked and his eyes were dry. It just took a moment to get his eyes to focus.

What would Lee do?

Gradually, the tumult of voices honed into to actual words. They were asking about Frenchie. Where's Frenchie? What happened to him? Did they take him? Where did he go?

Marie's voice, cold as frosted metal: "Cornerstone took him."

Sam jerked at the statement. He felt Marie's hand on his shoulder. It was as hot as her voice was cold. He pulled away from it. "No."

Marie gave him a warning look, but Sam was not to be deterred. He shook his head violently. "No they didn't."

Jones, Pickell, and Johnson—their heads swiveled back and forth in unison.

It would have been comical if Sam had any inkling of humor left in him.

"Sam…" Marie murmured, her voice matching her expression.

Sam held up a hand. "I killed him. Alright? I'm not gonna fucking lie about it."

"You killed him?" Johnson breathed. Johnson, who was Frenchie's friend. The two new guys on the squad. Bonded together by their rookie status.

Jones raised both hands, patting the air. "Sam, I know you like to take responsibility for everything, but if Cornerstone killed him, that's not your fault. That's—"

"Would you shut the fuck up?" Sam said, but the words had no heat behind them. Only tired desperation. He locked eyes with Jones. "You weren't there. I was. And Marie is just trying to cover for me. I shot him. In the head. I *executed him*." Sam looked away from Jones. From everyone. Found a spot on the wall. He waved dismissively at Marie. "Go ahead and tell them the truth."

"Alright fine," Marie spat. "It was a loyalty test. They put a gun in Sam's hand, and they forced him to do it. They claimed they knew Frenchie was allied with Lee Harden. Said that Sam had to take him out or they'd kill us all. Sam didn't have another option."

The words *I didn't think the gun was loaded* came to Sam's mouth, but he stopped them there, right behind his clenched teeth.

What an infantile thing to say.

The silence of the others became a hollow ringing in Sam's ears. It began to hum, and it took on the tones of revilement, of accusation, of hatred.

A loud blubbering noise snapped the humming quiet. Sam dragged his eyes to the one he knew had made the sound: Johnson. His shoulders stooped. His eyes spilling over. His lips quivering. God, but he looked like a fucking child.

He looks like you, hiding under a stump, crying for your dead family.

Never again.

Sam had promised himself that he'd never be afraid again, that his fear would never again cause the death of the people that he cared about. But what happens when your fear kills one to save the others?

"You killed him?" Johnson retched out. "You fucking shot Frenchie?"

Pickell stepped forward quickly, hands raised as though to stop a fight from happening. "Let's all take a minute before we get overly emotional about this."

"Overly emotional?" Johnson nearly shrieked. "He was my friend! I know you don't give a fuck about him but—"

Jones turned and popped him in the mouth. One quick jab that rocked Johnson's head and caused him to stumble backwards a step. "Quiet down before you say something dumb, you half-boot fuck. You think we're at home in footie pajamas watching cartoons and eating animal crackers? We're in fucking…" Jones stopped, lowered his own voice to a harsh whisper. "We're in fucking enemy territory. We are fucking surrounded by people that don't trust us and will kill us the second they have an excuse. You wanna cry for your dead buddy, you go right ahead. None of us are going to judge you. But put shit into perspective, Johnson. One dead is better than all dead."

Johnson held his mouth, glaring over the top of his hand at Jones, and then over Jones's shoulder at Sam.

Pickell shuffled between Jones and Johnson, hooking Jones under the arm and pushing him back. "Alright. That's good. We're all good."

Johnson didn't reply. He removed his hand from his mouth. There wasn't even any blood. His lip looked a little swollen, but that was all. Jones hadn't hit him that hard. His teeth were bared in a savage grimace, though. Hatred. Rage.

He spun towards the door and managed to take two steps toward it before Marie blocked his way, a single finger pointed at Johnson. "Where the fuck you think you're going?"

"Marie," Johnson growled. His fists balled at his sides.

The motion—the implication of those fists—was like a single red spark landing on a bed of gunpowder. Sam lurched forward, snatched up Johnson's wrist, intending to pull him away from the door. But the second Johnson felt the contact, he spun, eyes flashing.

It went downhill fast. Jones pushed into the middle of them, snatching up fistfuls of Johnson's shirt. Marie grabbed the arm that Johnson was rearing back to punch Jones with. Pickell shouted something, then grabbed onto them, maybe trying to pry them apart, but the next thing Sam knew, they were all on the ground.

There were no more words after that. Just grunts and snarls. Fingernails gouged across skin. Elbows mushed across faces. Knees landed on ribs.

Johnson was fighting like a wild animal. Sam had the single errant thought: *Where was this much piss and vinegar before?*

Pickell ended with Johnson in a rear-naked choke, but he wasn't sinking it hard, just trying to control him. Jones had the man's arms—he was kneeling on one, and had both hands on the other. Marie had straddled his thighs, keeping his legs from thrashing.

Sam realized he had his knife in his hand.

And that was when someone finally spoke.

It was Sam.

He got Johnson's attention with the tip of the knife blade, held just under his nose. "Johnson. Hey. Johnson." Sam was panting. Heart exploding. "I don't want to do this. I had to kill Frenchie. You hear me? I had to do it. I didn't want to. And I don't want to hurt you either. But you listen to me real fucking good, okay, you sonofabitch? I've got a fucking mission. Lee trusted me, and I promised him that I would get it done. And I'm telling you this right now, Johnson, I hope you're fucking listening because I can't be any goddamn clearer: If you endanger my mission, I will fucking slit your throat."

Something in those words must've made it through to Johnson. Or maybe he'd simply burned himself out. Maybe reason had reasserted itself. Sometimes the exhaustion that hits you in the middle of a fight can do that. You start to wonder what the hell you were fighting about in the first place.

Whatever it was, Johnson stilled. Stopped thrashing.

They existed in a little cloud of hot, stinking breath. Body odors. The humidity of sweat. So close. So intimate. Ready to kill each other at a moment's notice. God, how had they gotten to this point? Who the hell were they?

Sam had to grip the knife harder to disguise a sudden tremor. "Are you gonna be cool, Johnson? Can you be cool with me?"

Despite Pickell's choke hold, Johnson managed a nod. His eyes weren't even taking in the knife under his nose. He was locked into Sam. Defiant. It made the nod of agreement seem like a lie.

But what are you gonna do? If someone says they're going to be cool…

Don't trust anyone.

Sam started shaking his head, feeling like it was falling to pieces, tiny chunks of his skull just breaking away, and taking his brain with them. He swallowed hard, found his mouth dry. "Johnson. This isn't a fucking joke. I'm not fucking around. You need to promise me. Promise me right now that you're not going to do anything to endanger my mission."

Johnson started to nod again.

Sam cut him off with a snarl: "Say it! Goddammit! I need to hear you say it out of your mouth!"

Pickell eased up on the choke, so that Johnson could work his jaw easier.

Johnson sucked in a big breath. The hardness and anger fled from his eyes. He looked like a man on the brink of crumbling. He looked like he had when he'd first learned that Frenchie was dead. Before he'd learned that Sam had killed him.

Sam didn't know if that was a good thing or not.

"I promise," Johnson croaked out. Sam couldn't tell if it was emotion, or strain from the choke. "I promise not to endanger your mission, Sam."

Everything suddenly hit Sam, like standing under a waterfall and feeling it beat you down. It was the strangest sensation he'd ever felt in his life. As though his brain suddenly lost its ability to filter out the extraneous, and let everything in all at once. He saw himself, huddled there over a man he considered his friend, holding a knife under his nose. He saw their little flat, in a place fully surrounded by the enemy.

The enemy? What was the enemy? And why?

What was he fighting for?

Why was he here? What was he even doing? And why was he threatening to kill this man that he would also die for?

He loved Johnson, and he hated him. He wanted desperately to save his life—would in fact kill himself to save Johnson—and yet in the same moment, he would thoughtlessly slaughter Johnson to save the mission. He felt guilt and righteous anger, and indignation at himself, and rage at the world for thrusting all of this on him, and pride that he was here in the first place, and loathing that it was necessary at all.

Everything all at once.

He gasped. Realized that he had tears in his eyes. And he didn't care.

Realized that his throat was blocked up, and didn't care about that either.

He reversed the grip of the knife in his hand, and that simple motion seemed to kickstart his brain into doing its job: filtering information and allowing him to focus on the most pertinent.

With the knife blade now snugged against his wrist, Sam's hands crept up and took ahold of Johnson's face, gently, but firmly. His hands shook as he did. He could feel the warmth of Johnson's skin, the moisture of his sweat. The life within him.

"Don't make me do it, Johnson," Sam whispered past the strangling blockage in his throat. "Please. Don't force me to be something I'm not."

In that moment, Johnson, more than anything, looked worried for Sam.

Sam's tunnel vision expanded just enough that he was able to perceive, peripherally, that Pickell and Jones were staring at him too. He could only imagine that Marie was watching him as well. But none of that mattered. All pretenses had been stripped away.

Sam was not a murderer. And yet he would murder. He knew it of himself. He knew he was capable. And he knew he was closer to it now than he'd ever been before. He did not like it, but he was far past self-deception. He'd ripped himself open.

Johnson nodded again. "Okay, Sam. I won't. I'm…I'm sorry."

Sam almost choked. Had to turn his head and cough. He squeezed his eyes shut for a moment, clearing the tears from them. Shame was a distant memory. He looked back. "I'm sorry too."

TWENTY-ONE

IMPASSE

IN THE DARKNESS on the side of a midnight road, Lee waited like a spider in a web.

He lay on the top of the MATV, staring up at the sky. He had watched the moon rise, and now saw it, blood red on the horizon. Mars had risen and stood above him, glowering down at him, a mocking god. The Milky Way stretched vast and implacable, uncaring, so far beyond the pitiful human struggles that occupied the lives of those trapped on this dust speck.

Meteors occasionally streaked the sky. In the absence of light, Lee could see the movement of satellites every once in a while. They were still up there, their orbits degrading. Perhaps some of the meteors he saw were those pieces of former technology, plummeting through the atmosphere, no one left on earth to care about the utility they'd once supplied.

Here on earth, all that remained was survival of the fittest. That fertile, hot-blooded concept that civilization fought to bridle. But civilization was gone. Survival was king again, its usurpers dead and gone.

Lee had explained himself to Brinly and Angela. Neither of them had called him paranoid. Such accusations were baseless in this reality. Paranoia was the spirit of survival. Paranoia, and aggression. Kill or be killed.

Beneath him, Angela was sequestered in the armored confines of the vehicle, Abby with her, along with a few Marines to guard her. Brinly was out there, somewhere, in the scrubby flatness. Silently waiting with several squads of trained killers.

Lee's armor was heavy on his chest. His hands rested on his rifle. He breathed steadily against the downward pressure. In through the nose, hold, out through the mouth, hold. Box breathing to suppress the humanity of his stress.

His legs ached to find a new position, but he kept still. He thought perhaps that Abby was asleep beneath him, and he did not want to shuffle about on the roof and stir her awake. He had no doubt that Angela was just as wakeful as he.

His earpiece crackled softly. Brinly's whisper: "You called it, Boss. Got a visual on a crew of ten to fifteen, moving towards your poz."

Lee didn't stir. Somehow he managed to be disappointed. How did that work exactly? He didn't trust anyone, and he usually assumed the worst. And yet when he was proven right, he didn't feel satisfaction. He felt disgust.

He keyed his comms. "I copy. Any chance it's Cass coming to talk?"

A pause. "I don't think so, Lee. Positive count on fourteen. Moving overland, off the road. Armed. Not looking like they're in it for a talk."

"How far out?"

"About a mile from you."

Lee took a heavy breath. How was this going to play out? Well, he supposed it would play out however they chose. He would respond accordingly. "I copy. Keep on them. Let's give them a chance to do the right thing. The second they present a threat, take them out. I trust your judgement."

And so he waited. As the stars continued to wheel silently and slowly overhead. And the distance between him and a dozen strangers dwindled.

He never moved. A part of him was curious, and there was enough starlight for him to see by. If he rotated onto his stomach, he could probably see them approaching. But he'd seen it all before. No need to watch it again.

Brinly didn't narrate anything further, and Lee didn't allow himself to hope. That was simply unrealistic at this juncture.

There was silence for a time, and then there was gunfire.

It ripped the stillness of the night to shreds, and yet Lee still didn't move.

It didn't take long. A rolling peel of thunder, maybe a quarter mile from where the MATV sat. And then silence again.

Lee leaned up into a sitting position. Underneath him, he heard Angela standing, preparing to exit the vehicle. Staring north, Lee saw shapes in the darkness, like ghosts coalescing out of nothing, bleeding into this reality from the landscape where they'd hidden.

The image of unearthliness was broken by the stab of weaponlights. Several bright white beams surrounding a spot to the right of the road. Distance?

Maybe three hundred yards? The darkness made his depth perception even worse.

A muzzle flash, followed by the crack of a gunshot. Then two more. The weaponlights winked out, one by one, until only two remained.

"Alright," Brinly sighed over the comms, his voice no longer lowered. "Confirming fourteen threats eliminated. You're clear to come in. You see our location?"

One of the weaponlights waggled in the darkness.

"Yeah, I got you," Lee answered. "We're on the move."

Getting down off the roof was harder than going up. Lee mumbled curses at his broken body and gingerly set himself down on the concrete as Angela opened the back hatch and emerged.

"No, you stay here," she said to Abby. The two Marines inside seemed unsure whether they were supposed to accompany Angela, or babysit the kid.

"I want to go out there," Abby said, flatly.

Lee tilted his head at her, regarding the girl's placid expression. She never whined anymore, Lee had noted. That hadn't always been the case. In the beginning, Lee remembered thinking that the high-pitched whine was just Abby's default voice.

Not anymore.

Angela was in the process of loading yet more motherly retorts, but Abby calmly slid down out of the vehicle, completely ignoring her mother. "I might as well go with you, Mom. That way the guards can stay with you."

"But the…" Angela trailed off.

"Bodies?" Abby asked. "I'll see them eventually anyways." Now she turned and looked at Lee. "Weren't you planning to bring them back to Vici as proof?"

Damn, she got sharp.

Lee detected Angela staring at him, though it wasn't with a question. She knew that was the plan. She was looking for an out. But Lee didn't have one to give her. He simply shrugged and nodded. Yes, Abby was going to see the bodies regardless.

The five of them strode out into the darkness.

Lee scanned through all that black, wondering what might be out there lurking, but he knew that Brinly's men would have 360 outward coverage. The land was flat as a griddle. With their NODs, they'd see any primals coming.

"Why you wanna see the bodies anyway?" he asked Abby, glancing down at her. He'd considered saying nothing at all, but it seemed that Abby appreciated bald-faced honesty these days, and that was one thing Lee could provide.

"Curious," was Abby's single-word answer.

Lee considered that for a few paces. "It's not good to be fascinated by death."

By dim starlight he saw her look at him. "I'm not fascinated by it. I'm curious if they're the people that left the meeting early."

"Huh. You noticed that too, then?"

Abby's silence was answer enough.

They neared the glow created by the two weaponlights. A cluster of Marines stood alongside Brinly. Lee knew that there were many more out in the darkness, unseen. They created a sort of ring around a scattering of bodies.

They'd bunched up, Lee noted. Lack of discipline. Bad tactics. They should have scattered when they started getting shot. They should have tried to assault through the ambush. Instead, they went static and jumbled up together in a panic. That just made them easier to shoot.

Lee stepped into the center of the light, where the greater majority of the bodies lay. A few were on the outskirts. Maybe they'd had half a brain and tried to move and shoot instead of becoming rooted to the ground in an indefensible position.

Many of them were curled up, face down in the dirt. A few were on their backs. That was enough to identify them by. Lee recognized at least two faces from the meeting earlier. He'd been right—as had Abby. These were the people that had left the meeting early.

Brinly stepped up to Lee's side. "One of them had this."

Lee looked at the object in Brinly's hand. He knew it well. The only form of viable long-distance communication that existed anymore: a satellite phone. They were used extensively because all of the Project Hometown bunkers had come equipped with a rack of them.

The United Eastern States had used them. And so did Greeley.

This particular one had received a bullet, straight to the center of it. The shattered exit hole was speckled with bright, arterial blood. They wouldn't be able to turn it on and see the numbers called, but Lee could make a reasonable assumption.

"You think Cass and the rest of Vici is in on it?" Brinly asked.

Lee shrugged. "It's possible. Also possible that these were outliers. Maybe Cornerstone got to them somehow. We won't know until we see what Cass thinks about this. Either they'll be shocked, or they'll be disappointed. And that'll tell me everything I need to know."

Angela stepped up to them. "Should we call in the rest of our people?"

Lee nodded. "I'm not rolling back into Vici without every gun we have. Just in case."

"They might take it as a threat."

"Maybe. But we outnumber them."

Angela stared at him for a long moment. Lee met her gaze and expected recrimination, but that's not what he found. Her expression was tired. Humanity worn to thin threads by practicality.

If Vici wanted a fight, they'd get one. And Angela held no illusions about how Lee would conduct that fight. Either they were with Lee, or they were a liability. And Lee was not in the habit of leaving liabilities alive.

Lee found Abby off to the side. One of Angela's guards stood close by her. She didn't seem overly concerned with the bodies. She had her hands stuffed into her pants pockets, and no longer looked at the bodies, but instead out into the darkness. Her face held a mild twist of disgust.

That's a good sign, at least.

At least she wasn't riveted by the gore.

"Come on," Lee ordered. "Pack up the bodies. Angela, call in the rest of our people. If we're going to do this with Vici, I'd rather it be on our terms, and that means getting there before dawn."

***

Lee rolled up to the outskirts of Vici, this time not kneeling in the back of a pickup, but standing in it. The rest of the bed was filled with bodies. Another pickup trailed behind, that one also filled with bodies. And all of their convoy followed with him.

Lee looked over the top of the cab as the pickup slowed to a stop in the road, the headlights splashing across the sentries bustling out to meet them, alarmed by this unscheduled visit.

He leaned over to the open driver's window. "Go ahead and start unloading these bodies. I don't want them in my trucks. Let Vici figure out what they want to do with them." He hoisted his bum leg out of the bed first, then squirmed down until his boots touched hardtop.

He strode out to the meet the sentries, the headlights casting his shadow ahead of him, long and black.

An artificial dawn came upon that section of road. Numerous pairs of headlights spreading the glow out, as Humvees and MATVs and all their cobbled-together technicals spread out in a line.

This was no friendly meeting. Not anymore.

"Stop right there!" the sentry ordered, brandishing his rifle.

Lee stopped, but only because he didn't need to walk any farther. He held up a hand to the sentry, as two more fell in line behind the first. "I'm in no mood to take any orders from you, son," Lee grunted at the man. Another stranger that he didn't recognize.

The sentry looked off-balance. His eyes strayed over Lee's shoulder, and Lee heard the arrhythmic thud of bodies hitting pavement.

"What's this?" the sentry uttered, trying to sound demanding, but failing miserably. He might not be able to see all the guns trained on them behind those dozens of pairs of headlights, but Lee was pretty sure he got the gist.

"Those?" Lee cast a casual glance over his shoulder. "Those are fourteen dead bodies. Some of your people that came in to try to take me out. Now I want you to listen very carefully before you do anything stupid. I've got enough firepower trained on you and your crew to turn them to ground chuck, and enough people to burn Vici to the ground if you so much as twitch in a way that makes me feel hinky."

The man balked, but Lee held up a hand before he could protest. "Yes, that's a threat. But it's conditional: If you don't do anything stupid, then there won't be any more bloodshed. I just want you to understand the situation. I won't be taking any orders from you, or anyone else in Vici. Right now, Vici needs to explain itself. So do whatever you need to do to get Cass out here, and we'll figure out how we're going to proceed. Got it?"

Less than ten minutes later, a pair of headlights bloomed in the squat cluster of buildings that was Vici, and came roaring down the road towards them.

Lee keyed his comms. "Brinly, give me a sitrep on Vici. What're you seeing?"

Brinly's response came quick: "Just the one vehicle coming out. My spotters have eyes on a few armed civilians gathering near the front of the main street, but that's it. No overt aggression at this time."

"Roger that. Thank you."

The incoming vehicle skidded to a stop about twenty yards from Lee. He squinted against the wash of dust and the blazing headlights. Doors slammed. Silhouettes appeared, hurrying forward. One that he recognized as Cass. Followed by three others, and the three sentries.

Cass's features coalesced in the glow of the competing headlights. She looked tired, stricken, scared, furious. Lee simply watched, not feeling a damn thing.

"What is this?" she nearly shouted. "I thought I had until dawn. And my guy says you killed some people?"

Lee nodded. "We did. But they were trying to kill us. Or, more likely, me."

He reached into his cargo pocket, drew out the ruined satphone, and handed it to Cass as she came near enough to him. She snatched it from him after a brief hesitation, and Lee watched her carefully. No semblance of recognition.

"The fuck's this?" she turned it over in her hand. "I mean, obviously some sort of phone. Why are you giving me this? Is that blood on it?" She looked briefly horrified.

"That was on your man's body," Lee stated. "It's a satphone. Same model that's used extensively by my people, and Greeley. They're from the Project Hometown bunkers. They just…" A humorless grin slashed his face. "Keep turning up."

Cass did some mental computations. She held his gaze the whole time. "Are you accusing me of being in league with Greeley?"

Lee shrugged. "Are you?"

Cass spat off to the side. "Fuck that. And fuck you for asking."

"Well." Lee took a breath. "Come with me, then."

Cass didn't move. "I'm starting not to trust you."

"Good. That means you have a brain. You shouldn't trust anyone. But if I wanted you dead, I'd give a signal and have my people mow you down right here and now. And then we go into your town and…well, you get the picture. Right now we're just talking."

"Fine. Then let's talk."

"You don't want to see the bodies?"

"Who are they?"

"Beats me. I recognized a couple from the meeting earlier. I don't know their names."

"You fucking callous asshole."

Lee pointed a finger at her. "And you're either plain-old-ignorant, or you knew these people were going to try something, just like I did. So which one is it, Cass? You fucking got your head in the clouds or did you know and not do anything about it?"

It was a cruel question to which there was no good answer. Lee knew it, and so did Cass. Rather than respond, she nodded towards the bodies that were now heaped on the shoulder of the road. "Show me the bodies."

Lee turned to escort her. Her sentries made to follow, and Lee halted. A brief and silent interchange occurred: Lee shook his head at the sentries, causing them to stop; Cass turned and looked at them; they looked worriedly at their leader; she waved them off.

Lee and Cass walked back along the roadway, neither saying anything.

In the steeply angled glare of headlights, in the warm thrum of the engines, and the speckles of dust that floated through the air, Cass stood there with her hands on her hips and stared down at the bodies.

"Sonofabitch," she murmured.

Lee stood next to her. It was odd, he thought. Standing so close to someone whose people you just killed, and who you've just threatened to wipe off the map if they looked at you wrong. To stand there, almost shoulder to shoulder and look down at the crumpled human forms with their slack mouths and dead eyes, as though it was all nothing more than the aftermath of an unfortunate accident.

Like a shelving unit that's collapsed, or a vehicle that's blown a tire.

Lee waited for Cass to say something.

She eventually straightened, and gestured to one of the bodies in the middle. "Fucking Denny. I should've..." She looked away. "I should've known."

Lee thought, *Yeah, you should have*, but hadn't he made that same mistake?

He chose to stick to more practical matters. "Who was he talking to on that satphone, Cass?"

Cass whirled, glaring. "How the hell am I supposed to know?"

Lee gauged her face, her reaction. It's earnestness. Maybe she was, maybe she wasn't. People liked to think of themselves as good at reading other people. But what Lee had come to realize was that it didn't matter if you were good at reading people. Because other people were just as good at lying. Humanity lived in a constant arm's race of deception.

"Have you had any contact with anyone from Greeley?" Lee asked.

Cass hesitated, and Lee knew the truth, even before she nodded. "Some of Briggs's goons—the guys with the red triangle—"

"Cornerstone."

"Right. They came through. But that was a long time ago."

"How long?"

"Months." She considered. "It was cold. It had to've been January or February."

"What did they want?"

"They wanted to set up an outpost. We told them no."

"You got lucky. That must've been before Briggs started to let them off the leash."

"Yeah, well." Cass rubbed her forehead. "Obviously Denny had a private meeting with them. That's the only time I can think of that he would've come into contact with anyone from Greeley."

"Did he ever speak out in favor of Greeley?"

More hesitation. Cass seemed to know where Lee was going with this.

He pressed. "If there are more people in your community that might dime us out, I need to know about it."

Cass straightened. Crossed her arms over her chest. "If you think I'm going to let you come into my town and...do whatever it is you think you're going to do...you're mistaken."

Lee sighed, hooking his hands together on the butt of his slung rifle. He looked off into the east, where the first light of dawn was turning the horizon gray. What a shitty crossroads to find himself at. But he had known it was eventually going to happen.

Still, standing in that moment, facing that choice, he realized he'd never quite made up his mind about what he was going to do.

Cold practicality said that Vici could not be trusted. And if they could not be trusted, Lee could neither let them join him, nor could he leave them behind. So…cold practicality said that the only real solution was to wipe them out.

The people in his convoy, loyal or not, would not do that. If Vici had turned into a threat, Lee knew that his people would engage and win. But that was hot-blooded. Easy to rationalize. That was combat.

This would be murder.

Lee couldn't let them go, and he couldn't take them with him.

But he had to do one of those two things.

"You're not making this easy on me," Lee grunted.

"You think this is easy for me?" Cass snapped back. "You have no idea the clusterfuck you've put me into."

"Oh, I know. We're actually both in a similar dilemma, Cass. I can't trust your people. And yet I can't remove them as a potential threat. I'm a lot of things, and maybe I am a callous asshole, but I'm not a mass murderer. Yet."

"That's hardly comforting."

"It wasn't trying to comfort you." He took another deep breath and faced her. "We're at an impasse, you and me. So maybe it's time we sat down and figured out how to extricate ourselves from this shitty position."

TWENTY-TWO

HOSTAGES

THE LAST TWELVE HOURS had passed in a haze.

Sam still doubted his senses as he swung out of the flatbed truck that was making the dawn rounds, dropping off the overnight guard shift that were packed into the back like migrant laborers.

He still doubted that this was real. There were moments when he would settle into this new and strange version of things, and for a few brief seconds of respite, he would relax. But then he would remember shooting Frenchie, and having to threaten to kill Johnson to keep him in line, and how he had spent the entire night making the rounds in an unfamiliar section of perimeter in the middle of enemy territory.

Then everything would swirl and he would become certain again that this was a nightmare from which he fervently looked forward to the sensation of relief he would experience when he awoke and realized that none of the past twelve hours had actually happened.

He stopped on the sidewalk as the flatbed trundled away, carrying two other teams of guards with sleepy, drawn faces.

Head count, Sam told himself. *Make sure you got everyone.*

Was that really necessary if this was a dream?

He decided to do it anyways.

He turned in a bleary circle. One, two, three, four…five?

Oh, yeah. Frenchie was dead.

Only four now, not counting himself.

No one spoke. Not even Jones. The scuffle in the flat, only minutes before they'd had to go to their "orientation" where they received their shitty overnight guard duty assignments, had created a wall between everyone. A strange, invisible, and yet sound-proof barrier.

They trudged up the stairs to their flat. The thud of their feet on the treads bore a sloppy, exhausted rhythm. The heavy footfalls of people ready to crash.

They had only the blankets they'd brought with them, no bed rolls, and no beds provided. And yet, Sam thought about pulling that blanket around him and snugging himself into a corner of the room with his back against the wall, and he thought that he would never sleep so comfortably.

Unless you keep thinking.

Ah, but wasn't that always the problem. The body wanted sleep, but the mind was high-strung. Unable to release its fearful death grip on reality.

Was it strange that he pictured Johnson standing over him while he slept, putting a knife to his temple and slamming it through?

If you'd have asked Sam a single day ago, that would have seemed like a macabre fantasy. Now it seemed like a real possibility.

This is why Lee doesn't trust anyone.

They entered their flat, Sam coming in last and closing the door behind them.

His eyes went to his pack, to the corner of the room that he'd staked out to be his bed. But he shook his head and forced his heavy eyes wide.

"We can sleep in a few," Sam said, his voice ragged with grogginess. "Right now, we need to debrief and call in a report."

His team of four gathered at the kitchen counter, leaning slackly on it, like their legs might melt away at any moment.

"Come on, guys," Jones grunted. "Not like we haven't done an overnight shift before."

It was true. But this overnight shift had come on the tails of several less-than-restful nights, and a day full of mental trauma. Everyone was on their last dregs of can-do.

Sam forced himself to remain upright at the counter, though all he wanted to do was ooze down onto it. "Alright. Debrief. What did you see?"

"Buildings," Jones yawned. "The same fucking fifteen buildings, over and over again. That's what I saw."

"Very helpful, Jones," Sam sighed. "Be serious. I don't have the energy for jokes."

"I wasn't joking."

"Roughly a quarter-mile stretch," Marie said. "That's what I paced off. One squad, roving, over a quarter-mile stretch. And those squads are untrained. Watching their weapons familiarity when they passed out the rifles?" Marie shook her head. "They're newbies. If they have any experience with fighting, it's whatever they gathered while surviving the last five years."

Pickell nodded, rubbing his face vigorously. "Realistically, the makes Greeley's perimeter weak as shit. Five inexperienced fighters per quarter mile of perimeter. And there's probably some gaps."

Sam frowned, tried to do the math, tried to figure how many people he'd seen loaded onto buses, and how that might factor out along Greeley's entire perimeter. "That's just guesswork, though," he concluded. "We're making assumptions. There's no telling if other sections of the perimeter are stronger, and there's no telling how many civilians from Greeley have also been pressed into service."

Pickell shrugged. "Does it even matter? We know that our section is weak. And our section is run by *us*. Should…" Pickell lowered his voice. "…Should Lee make an incursion, it'd be best if he came in on our perimeter so we could just turn it over to him."

"That's true," Sam admitted. "Except we were posted on the southwestern perimeter. That's the opposite end of where Lee wants to enter."

Johnson shifted and spoke for the first time since Sam had a knife to his throat. "We also don't know if we'll be assigned the same section of perimeter every night. They might rotate the squads around."

Jones propped his face up on his hand, mushing his features. "Lee wants to hit close to the airfield, right?"

"Ideally," Sam nodded.

"Did anyone notice if any of the other untrained squads were assigned to a section near the airfield?"

No one answered.

"My assumption would be no," Sam said. "Greeley's got to know that's prime real estate. I don't think they'd assign untrained squads to that area. They'd want it covered by Cornerstone. Better trained, and better equipped."

"That's a reasonable assumption," Marie agreed. "But still just an assumption. And you know what they say about assuming."

"Right."

Pickell crossed his arms. "Any reason why Lee can't hit two places at once? That's a classic feint move. He could run an assault on our section, draw Cornerstone into the fight, then hit the perimeter near the airfield with a secondary attack."

Sam shook his head. "You're right, but I'm not going to develop strategies for Lee. He'll do what he sees best. Our job is just to report."

"And to see if we can turn some people to our side," Marie noted.

Sam grimaced. "That's seeming less and less likely. They have the new squads on a fucking stranglehold. We're not even allowed in certain areas of Greeley. They don't trust us, and my sense is that they're going to keep watching all of us very closely."

Marie gestured to the drawer where they'd hidden the satphone earlier. "No point in speculating. Report the situation and let Lee do with the information as he sees fit."

Sam sighed. "Not much to report. Anyone else see anything that could be useful?"

"Yeah," Jones said with a frown. "They gave us two mags. One for the rifle, one for a spare. As far as I could see, that's what they gave everyone. That's not much. An untrained rifleman is gonna burn through that within one minute of being attacked."

Sam considered this. "Question is, did they only give us two mags because they don't trust us? Or because that's all they have to give?"

"It'd be awesome if that's all they have to give," Jones replied. "But we can't operate on that without knowing it. At this point, all we can say is that big sections of unimportant perimeter are being guarded by untrained and under-equipped riflemen. They'll fold fast if they get hit with even moderate pressure. Sixty seconds, they burn through their ammo? They're not true believers. They're not going to keep fighting. They'll turn and run or straight up surrender."

"It seems too easy," Pickell observed.

"Well, it's not," Jones replied. "Lee busts through on one of these shitty perimeters, that means he's got miles of urban fighting to get through before he reaches anything important. Which is probably why he wants to hit closer to the airfield. The weak perimeter might be more trouble than it's worth as an entry point."

Sam opened the drawer, finagled the satphone out. "Marie's right. No point in trying to plan the strategy for him." He drew out the satphone. "Jones, Pickell, gimme some eyes on the outside and at the door. Gimme ten minutes and then we'll catch some sleep."

***

Dawn broke over a long, straight section of road directly to the south of Vici, Oklahoma.

Sprawling across this road, a belt of vehicles and people—mostly vehicles on the south side, and mostly people on the Vici side.

Directly in the center of this ring of intense scrutiny, like two prize fighters in a cage-less match, stood Lee and Cass.

Brinly and Angela stood close behind Lee, and the same gaggle of strangers from yesterday backed up Cass.

Cass was currently in furious discussion with what Lee assumed were her advisors. Perhaps co-leaders. He didn't really know how they'd worked it all out, only that Cass seemed to have the ultimate say-so.

Lee waited patiently, his armor and rifle doffed, for the time being. Even without the extra weight, he was tired of standing. Everything ached, and a night without sleep had left him impatient.

A gentle touch at his elbow.

Lee turned and looked at Angela, who looked just as wrung out as he was.

Angela leaned in close enough that he could smell her. "What's the backup plan here?"

"I don't even know," Lee admitted.

Angela's gaze strayed past him to the people across from them. She was not bewildered or angry. Just resigned. "How's it always come down to shit versus shit?"

"Guess we're lucky like that." Lee sighed. "If you've got any ideas on how to exit with the least amount of shit, I'm all ears."

Angela's eyes finally found their way back to Lee's. They held no guile. No attempts to sway him one way or the other. When she spoke, it was just plain old, ungilded truth: "Well, I guess a big part of that's up to you. Either you murder a whole settlement, or you decide to trust them."

"Both shit."

Angela nodded. "But you're going to decide which shit sandwich you can stomach."

"And what if I decide to wipe them out?"

Angela didn't have the reaction that he thought she would have. In another place and time, she'd have become shocked, perhaps irate at the suggestion. Now she simply gave him a facial shrug. "I've known you for a long time, Lee. We both know what you're capable of."

She said nothing more. She didn't need to.

It was plain to both of them: Lee was capable of many things, but wholesale slaughter of innocents wasn't one of them. He'd lost a lot of himself in the void that the world had become. But he hadn't lost his sense of right and wrong. He'd ridden the ragged edge of it, lived in the gray areas of morality. But he'd never truly crossed that line.

The truth was, he *couldn't*. Oh, he could entertain the thoughts. He could bitterly think about wrath and vengeance and the throwing away of human life. He could think about it. Maybe even imagine himself doing it.

But he couldn't. It was anathema to him. If he did it, then what was he even fighting against? If he massacred the people he didn't trust, then this entire war was just a pissing match between him and Briggs. Nothing more than two despots slugging it out.

"Well." Lee sniffed, smudging his nose with a finger. "I guess we know which shit sandwich we'll be dining on."

Angela gave him a single nod. "But *they* don't know that."

"No, they don't. And I intend to use that element of doubt to come out with the best deal I possibly can." He managed a careworn smile. "Maybe I can get a little mayo on my shit sandwich."

She smiled back at him, and for a brief moment, they were just two tired people at the end of their ropes, smiling against the pain, each taking a bit of strength from the other. Just enough to keep hanging on.

A Marine trotted up and whispered rapidly to Brinly.

The major nodded, then turned to Lee. "We got a call." An arched eyebrow. "From your boy."

Lee understood. Nodded to release Brinly, who immediately stepped away to take the call.

Good. At least there was *some* forward motion. He didn't know what Sam was going to report. He could only assume it would be yet another conundrum to overcome. But at least Sam was still alive, still in Greeley. He hadn't been found out. The worst hadn't happened. And that was a good thing.

"Alright," a voice snapped from behind him.

Lee turned, and found Cass approaching again, her advisors trailing her.

Lee struck all humanity from his face. Became the callous asshole again. We all have to play our roles. "Have you come to a decision?"

Cass's eyes were squinted, though the dawn light wasn't strong. Squinting as though trying to peer through a fog. Trying to determine the truth in all the subterfuge. "First off, you need to know that Vici had nothing to do with what happened last night. I can't control the actions of every single person. If I could, I would have stopped it from happening. Me and my people are not allied with Greeley, or Cornerstone. And…" she swallowed. "I apologize. On behalf of my people."

Lee waved it away. "That's a wonderful sentiment, but pointless."

"It's not pointless," she said with an ill-concealed snarl. "I say it not to beg or plead. I say it because it's true. A handful of people that represent me did something stupid last night. They paid for it with their lives, but it is still important that you understand that me and every person behind me condemns that action."

"Cass," Lee sighed. "You can't possibly speak for every damn person in Vici. If you knew what they all were thinking, then you would've known what was going down last night. So don't try to present the facts as though all the people behind you are of one mind."

"No, maybe they're not. And frankly, staring at your goddamned horde, ready to rip us to shreds, there's probably a lot of people behind me that don't view you in the most friendly light right now."

Lee shrugged. "I don't really care how they view me. I only care what actions they're going to take. I only care what actions *you're* going to take that'll make me feel warm and fuzzy enough inside that I can stand to turn my back on you."

Cass shifted her feet. "Let's get a few things straight. Number one: You're not coming into my town. I get it—you have the numbers, you have the firepower, and you could wipe the floor with us. I hope that you won't. But I'm not giving you carte blanche to stride in and search or interrogate my people to the point that you might feel comfortable, which probably wouldn't happen anyways, as you seem determined to be mistrustful."

Lee arched an eyebrow. "That right?"

Cass raised her chin. "Yeah, that's right."

"Okay. What's number two?"

Cass seemed momentarily surprised that her defiance wasn't met with a stronger reaction. She looked unsure of herself for a moment, but recovered quickly. "Number two: As a show of goodwill, we will commit one hundred fighters to your cause."

Lee made a face. "One hundred fighters that I can't fully trust."

"Maybe not. Do you know how warring kingdoms used to do this in the past?"

"Enlighten me."

"They'd exchange hostages. One side would send someone important to live in the other kingdom. The understanding being, that if the trust between them was ever broken, the hostage would pay the price."

"So if Vici ever pulls some shady shit on me, you're giving me the go ahead to execute the hundred people."

Cass blanched. "No. No, that's not what I'm saying. The fighters are a show of goodwill." She swallowed again. "The hostage is me."

Perhaps Cass expected there to be more haggling. She seemed surprised when Lee considered it for the span of two or three seconds, then nodded and stuck out his hand.

"Deal," he said.

Cass frowned at him. Then looked at the outstretched hand.

"Should I demand more from you?" Lee asked.

Cass quickly took his hand and gave it a firm pump. "No. That's the deal. We have a deal."

"Good," Lee said, as she released his hand. "Because we need to get mobile again. I'll give you one hour to do what you need to do. Do your hundred fighters have transportation?"

Cass blinked rapidly. "We only have a few working trucks. They're needed here in Vici."

"Fine," Lee waved a dismissive hand. "We'll make room for them. We'll remain right here. We're mobile in sixty minutes."

Without waiting for any further conversation, Lee turned away from her and began striding back to the waiting line of vehicles. Angela fell into step with him.

"Well, look at that," she commented wryly. "You got mayo *and* ketchup. Lucky you."

Lee smirked. "It's the best outcome we could've hoped for. Minimal concessions on our part."

"God, is every settlement going to be like this?"

"Only if they try to kill us in the middle of the night."

"Well, you just never know. You're such a popular guy."

"I know. People can hardly contain themselves."

They walked in a companionable silence back towards the command MATV. For a moment, despite the exhaustion and the anxiety and the ever-present undercurrent of anger, Lee felt peaceful.

He looked to Angela, as though she'd said something surprising. She didn't seem to notice him looking. She walked along with a half-smirk on her face, still darkly amused by the brief banter between them.

He shared her subtle expression and looked forward again, the moment fading quickly in the rush of things to be done.

Brinly had already disconnected the satphone by the time they reached him. His expression was serious, but not to the level that Lee felt any worry. Brinly handed the satphone off to a Marine lieutenant and turned to face Lee and Angela.

"Sam and his crew are…" there was a hesitation before the next word. "Safe."

Lee frowned.

Brinly shook his head. "I'll bring you up to speed once we're rolling. There's nothing that requires our urgent attention." He nodded towards Vici. "What are we doing with them?"

Lee leaned an elbow on the grill of the MATV. "We've got a hundred volunteer fighters, plus Cass, as—" he put up air quotes "—a hostage. Presumably to keep Vici from pulling any shady shit behind our back."

Brinly quirked an eyebrow. "Sounds good. Not sure how it'll play out in practice."

Lee allowed it with a nod. "It's the best we can hope for."

Angela put her hands in her pockets. "How are we going to integrate them?"

Lee let his gaze wander over to Vici, the conglomeration of people milling back towards their homes. Some of those people, Lee was sure, would be the volunteers. "I don't want them separated. I want them in existing squads. Pull a hundred of our people out and have them form a new set of squads. The space they create will be filled by the new volunteers. Give the new people grunt work—drivers, or whatever. Something that limits their opportunity to fuck up." Lee glanced at Angela. "Cass should stay with us, as interim command. I'd like her people to see her as in charge, even though she won't be. That'll make it easier to control them if a dispute arises."

Brinly considered his orders with pursed lips, then nodded. "Sounds good to me. I'll get it working."

"So," Angela sighed. "Who do we visit next?"

"I'd like to hear Cass on some recommendations," Lee said. "She probably won't like it at first, but she might be a valuable tool in getting us in the door with others, if she knows them."

Angela made a face. "Yeah, I don't think she'll like it."

Lee shrugged. "She doesn't have to. But time is short, and we're moving on Greeley."

TWENTY-THREE

A MIDNIGHT CHAT

IT WAS A COLLECTION OF SETTLEMENTS, scattered along the Arkansas River. The information that Abe had on them was minimal, but the one he was looking at through a high-powered scope was La Junta.

Menendez and Breckenridge, having been the closest to Tex, and Tex having been in contact with Coordinators from other states, had given Abe what they knew about active settlements. The intelligence, unfortunately, didn't extend much into Colorado, where they currently were.

Colorado, Abe thought, blinking and pulling out of the scope for a moment to stretch his neck. It was weird to be here. A place that should feel like the belly of the beast, like infiltrating Germany circa 1945. Instead, it just felt like every place else they'd been.

Their luck after Mosquero hadn't improved. The few settlements along their route into Colorado had been ghost towns. Whether or not Cornerstone came through those towns, or if the people had simply given up, or if they'd all fled to Greeley, Abe didn't know.

All he knew was that he was now staring at the town where he was supposed to meet up with Lee in the next few days, and he didn't have single extra fighter to show for his journey.

On the plus side, because he hadn't had to deal with convincing any settlements to back their invasion of Greeley, they'd made good time.

Since they were ahead of schedule, Abe felt comfortable doing a little extra recon on La Junta to determine if it was a place they should even go into. So far, the signs were hopeful.

"No sign of Cornerstone," Abe commented, noting that his tongue was dry. He fished for the bottle of water in his day pack that lay at his side. "I am seeing civilian activity. Nominal amount of people with guns. None of them look like military."

Menendez, stationed at his side in the baking morning sun, squeegeed sweat from his brow with a hand and nodded. "Doesn't mean they're not loyal to Briggs."

Abe undid the cap on the water bottle and took a slow sip, letting the liquid linger on his tongue. He swallowed. "No, it doesn't." He shoved the water bottle under his pack so the sun wouldn't heat it up. Propped himself on his elbows. "We're three days ahead of schedule. I don't want to waste time that we don't have, but there's also no need to rush into anything."

Menendez shifted his position in the dusty top of the tiny hill they occupied. It was the only position in all this flatness that gave them any sort of overwatch on La Junta, but it placed them nearly a mile out. The distance made gathering details hazy.

"You think we'll get anything more by sitting out here for another day?" Menendez asked.

Abe shrugged, settled back over the scoped rifle and rested his chin on the stock. "Maybe not.

The intel Tex had on La Junta was minimal. The Colorado Coordinator is with Briggs, as far as we know, which is a mark against them. But if we sit around and wait for evidence of them working with Greeley we might just be wasting our time."

"Any reason to believe Cornerstone might've passed them over?" Menendez asked. "They haven't exactly pulled their punches on any other settlement."

Abe felt his stomach tighten at those words. He was not one to relive the past—it remained behind where it belonged. But the abject cruelty bothered him. The images from Mosquero drifted through his brain, making his spit taste sour.

"Could be the size of the settlement," Abe noted. "La Junta is pretty big. Mosquero was tiny. Tiny towns can't defend themselves. It'd be hard to wipe out a settlement like La Junta."

"If they'd told Cornerstone to go fuck themselves, don't you think Cornerstone would've come back with a few choppers at least?"

"The way I hear it, they put every last drop of aviation fuel into taking down the UES. I don't think they can field aircraft at this point."

"Still leaves us at square one. We don't know whether La Junta is still here because Greeley doesn't have the manpower to pacify a settlement of that size, or because they're allied with Briggs."

"The leader here—the Reeves guy…"

"Jonathan Reeves."

"Right. Did Tex ever talk about his political leanings?"

Menendez shook his head. "All the information we had on Colorado settlements was third hand. Tex heard it from Cheech, who heard it from people passing through. And La Junta in particular was never really mentioned outside of the fact that it's here, and it's run by a guy named Jonathan Reeves."

"Reeves." Abe consulted a scrawl of penwork on a scrap of paper taped to the rifle stock. "Black male, tall, skinny, bald." He shook his head. "That could describe a dozen people down there. And there's no telling if Reeves is even still in charge of this settlement. Tex's information might be out of date by now."

"If you watch long enough, I think he'll make himself known." Menendez smirked. "He'll be the one doing all the delegating."

"Be real hard to make a positive ID. And besides, we can't just waltz in and start chatting him up, even if we could ID him properly."

"Maybe not. But, correct me if I'm wrong, I see a very porous perimeter."

Abe considered that with a frown. "You're not wrong."

"Settlement like La Junta, they're comfortable because of their size. They've got their attention on large actions and teepio incursions."

Abe squinted sideways at Menendez. "But not necessarily small, stealthy incursions."

Menendez smiled. "And that's something we're good at."

Abe looked back at the town over top of the scope. "Lot of ways that could go wrong."

"Lot of ways for it to go wrong every other way, too. Small scale infiltration mitigates the risk to our entire team. Gives us the best chance of getting some honest answers."

"We wouldn't even know where to begin looking for Reeves."

"Maybe so. But I bet we could find out."

Abe chuffed softly, then settled back into the scope. The heat mirage made the image of La Junta shimmer and waver in disorienting patterns. "Yeah, I bet we could."

***

They waited until dark.

Sitting cross-legged at the base of a scrubby bush, ensconced by the dark foliage, Abe sank into a version of himself he kept locked away, only to be released when absolutely necessary.

You couldn't live your life like an animal. Human life required humanity. At different times, logic, forward thinking, mercy, compassion.

None of those things were useful at the moment. And so Abe let the savage, half-starved, blood-hungry animal out of the depths where he languished during the daylight. But it was night now. It was time for the animal.

So Abe let it come, but kept a tether to his humanity, like a lifeline, like a ripcord to be pulled the second things got too out of hand. Because, ultimately, his mission was not destruction.

An odd line to walk, but Abe was capable. He'd done it before.

He leaned forward from his meditative pose, peering through the foliage. The leaves tickled his face. He did not do what humans did and brush them away. He remained cold and steady, eyes wide to let in the starlight, fixated on the settlement below.

A few electric lights burned still, but the settlement did not seem to have electricity to burn. What light there was seemed to be from dim solar lanterns. Some candles that stood out mournfully in the blackness. Even those steadily winked away, the people below settling down for the night. A primitive existence—down with the sun, and up with it as well.

It was time.

Abe filled his lungs, let it out silently through flared nostrils. He sidled quietly out of the bush that had hidden him in the waning hours of twilight. His body was taut where it needed to be, loose where it didn't. He flowed like a shadow.

Dim shapes huddled in the darkness next to him.

He knelt beside them, catalogued his loadout. Armor, rifle, suppressed pistol, fixed blade, NODs—put away in their case for now—and comms. He pressed the acoustic tube into his ear canal, making sure it was secure. His connection to the world of humans.

He did not speak to the forms he knelt beside. They were far enough away from La Junta not to be overheard, but in this place, language was only for when necessary. Instead, he touched the first form.

Menendez. Face blacked out. The whites of his eyes in the starlight all that was visible. Menendez nodded, reached across, and touched Breckenridge, then slipped quietly to his feet. The touch was passed down the line. Only five of them. No need for more. More was just extra noise.

When all five were on their feet, Abe touched his comms off and spoke sparingly: "Overwatch, we're ready."

Not far away, Greenman lay with his rifle. Abe couldn't see him, and only heard his quiet response in his ear: "On target. Move."

The five left the squat ridge, a single-file line that picked its way silently down to the flatness below.

Twelve hours of reconnaissance had led Abe to believe that the sentries that held the perimeter—precious few of them—were ill equipped. No NODs. Likely no thermals. He hadn't seen radios either.

Still, Abe snaked his way closer and closer to the settlement, keeping low and choosing his path according to the minimal concealment provided him. It was always best to assume that someone was scanning with some sort of night vision. Best to maintain cover as long as possible.

He had already picked out his staging point—a clump of low brush, about two hundred yards from the perimeter of La Junta.

The five figures slipped into the brush, and there they doffed their heavy equipment. Armor and rifles. The NODS. Abe kept only his suppressed pistol, his fixed blade, and the radio. From around his neck he pulled off a tattered old shemagh. He rarely used it, but it was one of those items that had so many applications, he always kept one if possible.

Tonight's application was as a garrote. He swept it into a tight roll, then snugged a single knot in the center. Then replaced it around his neck, tucking the ends into his shirt to keep it secure.

Then he waited. After a moment, the others had finished as well, eliminating as much noise-making equipment as possible.

Slicked down to their most quiet, Abe led them out again, this time straight towards the perimeter.

Night insects created a steady thrum in the cool air. A rise and fall of noise, different species overlapping one another. A light breeze gusted occasionally out of the south, chilling the sweat on the back of Abe's neck, and heralding a storm on the southern horizon that occasionally let out a distant rumble.

Close and closer to the perimeter he crept. Lower and lower, until he scuttled softly through the sandy soil on hands and feet. Angling a little to the right, now. Stopping. Eyes up. Scanning.

A few structures sat in the darkness, not incorporated into the perimeter, but abandoned because they were too far out from the rest of the settlement. Too unsafe to be populated when the lights went out.

Abe used these as cover when possible.

At the edge of one of these, he sidled up to the corner and peered through a gap between a clump of dry weeds and a rusted downspout. A tiny keyhole through which he could see the perimeter ahead of him, perhaps another fifty yards.

Two sentries. Walking beat. They passed each other with a murmured greeting. Tired and bored. Another long night watching the stars pass overhead.

Abe watched their path. They seemed to share the same route. As would the other sentries that circled the perimeter. It seemed that La Junta preferred roving sentries to stationary ones. Which let them cover more perimeter with fewer people, but also exposed the sentries to more danger.

Along the path the sentries walked, Abe spotted another bush, similar in size and shape to the ones he'd hidden in while waiting for night to fall. He stared at it for a time, judging how close it was to the path the sentries walked. Sometimes distances could be deceiving when calculated from a ground-level.

He decided the bush was close enough.

He pushed back from the corner of the building. Rolled onto his side, and looked behind him, catching Menendez's feral gaze. Abe motioned with his fingers, and Menendez slid forward, shoulder-to-shoulder with him.

Abe didn't speak. He rested his arm on Menendez's shoulder and pointed to the copse of brush. Menendez followed his gesture, then nodded. He understood.

They waited another minute, until the two sentries had walked a good distance away. Off to the left, Abe could see a third sentry approaching. He stared at the figure for a moment, fixating on it.

That was their target.

Abe rolled onto his side again, made eye-contact with Breck and the other two soldiers. He held up a palm to them, motioning for them to stay put. He got thumbs-up in response.

Their target was a hundred yards away from the copse of bush.

It was now or never.

Crawling on their bellies, Abe and Menendez snaked through sand and rock towards the bush. Abe's belt buckle scooped the sand up, letting it slip into his pants, gritty against his thighs and crotch.

Seventy-five yards until the sentry neared the bush.

Abe's focus flashed back and forth between his destination and the sentry. He stilled his movements when the sentry's head seemed to be facing their direction, then squirmed forward when the sentry looked away.

Fifty yards now. Abe and Menendez reached the bush. Went low under the foliage. He had minimal time to prepare himself. The sentry was already within hearing range. The occasional distant thunder and the racket of the insects was Abe's only cover.

As the distance dwindled, Abe eased himself up until his feet were under him. Buried in the bush in a tight squat. Menendez followed suit, close enough that Abe could feel his body heat.

Twenty-five yards.

Abe pressed himself steadily forward through the bush, until his body was just inside, the branches ringing his frame. If someone were to look directly at the bush, they'd see him, an odd shape amid the foliage, a pair of eyes amid a blacked-out face.

He could hear the sentry's footfalls now. Soft. Scuffing. Careless.

Abe's movements were the slow machinations of a spring-loaded trap being set. Tense, ready, he grasped the ends of his knotted shemagh and eased it from around his neck. Abe's focus remained completely on his prey. Menendez served as his peripheral vision.

Menendez eased his hand right over Abe's shoulder, so that it was just inside his field of view, and held a thumbs up. Abe knew that Menendez was watching everything else all around them, making sure that no one appeared and bungled the whole attempt. If at any point in time Menendez saw a threat to their stealth, he would put his thumb down, and Abe would know to stay put.

His thumb remained up.

Abe watched the sentry approach. Nearly abreast of him…

Menendez's thumb went down.

Abe's heart squirmed into his throat, but he didn't take his eyes off the sentry.

From somewhere off to Abe's right, just inside the settlement, he heard the slam of a door. The sentry that took up all of his vision didn't seem to notice. A distant voice called out, but it wasn't to the sentry—he paid it no mind.

Abe felt his pulse nearly choking him.

The sentry was *right there*. If he turned to look, he would see Abe, half exposed in the brush, ready to pounce, little more than an arm's length away. Abe could smell the sentry—body odor and woodsmoke.

Another distant slam of a door.

The sentry was two paces away. Almost too far…

The thumb went up.

Abe made a split-second decision: Fortune favors the bold.

His acceleration was controlled, until he felt the foliage of the brush release him, and then he exploded forward.

The sentry jerked at the sound of Abe's feet, started to turn. Abe got the flash of widened eyes, scared by something moving in the darkness.

Abe swept the knotted cloth down around the sentry's head in one swift motion and yanked back, cinching the knot under his chin while he simultaneously jumped and wrapped his legs around the man's waist, locking his slung rifle to his abdomen.

They fell backward.

Abe held his core tight as his back slammed the ground. The sentry's hands grappled with the sudden choke—that was instinctive, and Abe had been counting on it. There was only a bare few seconds of opportunity before the sentry realized what was happening and tried to go for his rifle. Even with Abe's legs pinning it down, he might still get to the trigger…

Menendez swept up, pinning the man's legs and seizing the rifle. Abe let his legs slacken just enough for Menendez to twist the rifle like a windlass, causing the two-point sling to tighten around the sentry's neck and shoulders, adding pressure to the choke Abe was already applying.

Abe and Menendez were two parts of an anaconda. Every motion that the sentry writhed through, they just tightened a little more, until he could no longer move. The sentry's desperation became herky-jerky—the signal of oncoming unconsciousness. He tried with fumbling fingers to get to the rifle, but Menendez had his whole body pressed down on it, his hands covering the trigger so no accidental shots would give them away.

Abe counted the seconds in that strange embrace. Hot air huffed from him and Menendez. Their lock on the sentry was absolute—there was not even the sound of scuffling feet.

At thirteen seconds, the sentry went limp, not enough blood flowing to his brain.

Abe held it until a count of twenty, when he was sure the man was fully unconscious, and then immediately released the choke. They only had a few short moments before the sentry regained consciousness.

A glance in either direction showed that there were no sentries coming.

They grabbed up the body, with Abe keeping the shemagh around the sentry's neck in case he needed to be silenced again. Menendez took the feet, and they hauled as fast as they could for the building where the others hid.

By the time they scurried into cover behind the building, the sentry's head was swimming back into reality, his eyes glassy but open.

Their three teammates swept up beside them, two of them lending aide in carrying the body, and Breck keeping his attention on the settlement.

"Go," Breck whispered. "We're clear."

They sprinted for the copse of brush where their equipment still lay.

They were halfway there when the sentry began to thrash again.

Abe halted, cinching the shemagh tight just in time to cut off a tiny mewl of terror.

Breck, who was hands-free at that moment, immediately brandished his fixed blade and pressed it to the bottom of the sentry's eye socket. "You make one goddamned sound and I'll murder you and everyone you care about."

The sentry went still. His brain was in vaporlock, just barely conscious as it was, and extremely pliable.

Abe let him have air and blood through his neck.

They reached the copse of brush without further incident and disappeared inside, like goblins dragging a victim into their lair.

They stopped there, concealed in the hollow created by the overhanging foliage.

The two soldiers took positions on the captured sentry, one keeping control of the cloth around the man's neck, while the other held his blade to him. They didn't need to speak. Breck had already spoken for them.

Rapidly, Abe, Menendez, and Breck, suited up.

"Overwatch," Abe husked into his comms. "We have the initial target secured. Sitrep on that perimeter."

"All's quiet," Greenman replied. "No one seems to be missing the sentry yet."

"Roger. Stay on it. We're infiltrating in one minute."

Abe snugged his armor down, slung into his rifle. Helmet on. NODs attached. He slid up to the terrified sentry, grabbed him by the face to make eye contact. "La Junta," Abe whispered. "Is it allied with Greeley? Nod yes or shake your head no."

There was some hesitation. Abe allowed it—the man was in a panic.

A shake of the head.

"Good," Abe said. "If that's true, then no one is going to die tonight, do you understand me?" He flashed a smile that probably wasn't as warm as he had intended. "We're friends, but just very cautious friends. Now, I need you to answer a few questions verbally. You will speak in a whisper. Is Jonathan Reeves still in charge of La Junta?"

"Yes," the man husked.

"I need you to tell me where to find him. Again, we are not here to hurt anyone. If La Junta is not allied with Greeley, then you have nothing to be afraid of, and neither does Jonathan Reeves. But I need to speak to him on my own terms. So tell me where to find him."

"Who are you people?" the man whimpered.

The soldier holding the knife to him jerked. "You motherfucker!" he hissed, pressing the knife hard against the man's cheekbone so that the point dug into his flesh. "Whispers only! Don't make us ask again!"

Abe patted the man's chest. "Look, buddy, we're either your best friends, or your worst nightmare. That depends on how truthful you're being. Now don't fuck around with me. Where's Jonathan Reeves?"

The man appeared to be doing some serious mathematical feats in his head. Self-preservation, competing with his duty as a sentry, competing with his fear for his friends in La Junta.

Eventually, with a pained expression, the man said, "He stays in a little cream-colored house on the corner of Edison and East Fourteenth."

Abe felt relief that they had cooperation. He nodded. "Where is that in relation to the perimeter?"

"It's right in the middle of the settlement."

Abe's sense of relief dried up like a tumbleweed and blew away. He grunted. "Fine. Who's in the house with him?"

"He has a wife and kids. Jesus, don't hurt them!"

"Hey, I already told you we're not going to hurt anyone. That's not what we're here for."

"Why are you doing this?"

"Because I need to make sure you're not lying about being allied with Greeley. Do the kids sleep in the same room and how old are they?"

"I don't know. I don't know how old they are or where they sleep."

"Does he have any animals in the house?"

"No, I don't think so. Oh, God…"

"Stay with me. Is Jonathan armed?"

"All the time."

"Will he be asleep, or is he a night owl?"

The man shook his head. "I'm not sure. But he's always up before everyone else. I just assume he goes to bed early."

Abe patted the man's chest again. "Alright. Hey. You did good. And if you're telling me the truth, then this is all going to work out great." Abe rose to a crouch, nodded to Menendez and Breck who were kneeling, ready. Abe keyed his comms. "Overwatch, we're heading out. We're looking for a cream-colored house on the corner of Edison and Fourteenth. Get your spotter on the map and guide us in."

"Roger that," Greenman replied. "Start making your way in, and we'll find the location. Good luck."

***

Jonathan Reeves awoke firmly believing he was having a nightmare.

There were faceless men in his room, and they were pointing rifles at him and his wife. They didn't seem overly aggressive, as they only stood on either side of the bed, and hadn't touched him or his wife.

"If you yell, we will have to kill you," one of them said.

Jonathan just blinked, frowning. He could feel his heartrate ramping up, but in the same moment, he was fairly sure he was still dreaming, so he wasn't overly worried about it. In fact, he'd had this nightmare hundreds of times—waking up to find that some hostile forces, or perhaps even the crazies, had infiltrated his settlement and were in his bedroom with him.

Even while his fight-or-flight response geared up, the more rational part of him said, *this is just one of those dreams again. No need to get yourself in a tizzy.*

Generally when he was having a dream like this, his solution was to holler as loudly as possible, which, in reality, would come out as a strangled groan from his still-sleeping mouth, but it would be enough to wake Tammy up, and then she would shake him awake, he would thank her and apologize, and they'd both roll over and go back to sleep.

"We're not here to hurt you," one of the men was saying. "We just need to talk, but we need to do it quietly and without raising a ruckus."

Tammy sat up on her elbows, her hands grappling across the covers and seizing his elbow. "Jon?"

Jonathan started at the touch to his elbow. Like a lightning rod grounding a bolt of electricity, the touch brought it all home to him in an instant: This was not a dream.

The one that had already spoken—the one with a thick black beard—held a finger to his lips, his rifle still trained on them with one hand. "Ssh. Easy now. Remember, we want to do this quietly. Quiet means no one gets hurt. Loud means people have to die."

While Jonathan was still wrestling with his new flash of insight, Tammy was the first to actually kick her brain into gear.

"My kids!" she hissed—but kept her voice down. "Where are my kids?"

The other man in the room with them, who stood on Tammy's side of the bed, patted a hand in the air. "They're fine. We didn't touch them. They're still sleeping. And that's how this should stay. No need to trouble them. We're just here to talk."

Tammy, who slept only in a T-shirt and still managed to maintain some semblance of old-world propriety, gathered the covers up around her chest. The move was just so Tammy, Jonathan noted, in a strange, distracted fashion—always worried that someone might see her without a bra on. Such an inane concern.

But the defensive motion lit off a spark of protective instincts in Jonathan, and he sat up sharply, his head nearly striking the muzzle of the rifle pointed at him. He glanced to the left as anger and indignation flashed through him.

"No," the man next to his bedside said sternly. "If you're looking for your shotgun, I already moved it. We don't need to get crazy."

Jonathan's fists clenched. "Who the fuck are you?" he demanded, his voice rough from sleep.

"We're from North Carolina. Lee Harden sent us. And we have questions for you."

North Carolina. Lee Harden. Questions.

A hundred thoughts began T-boning each other in his mind. One in particular managed to survive the carnage and come out of Jonathan's mouth: "Lee Harden?"

"When you hear that name, what do you think?"

It was such an odd question. Like a survey from a pollster. It seemed so out of place coming from a face-painted man holding a rifle to him. A rifle, and a night-vision device, propped up on his helmet, Jonathan thought. And body armor.

Professionals.

Cornerstone?

What was the right answer?

Well, they'd said that Lee Harden had sent them, so that made him think that they weren't Cornerstone. Unless they were, and this was a trap. Some sort of loyalty test.

Jonathan wasn't a big fan of lies, or loyalty tests, or any of that horseshit. He was a plain-spoken man who expected everyone around him to be plain-spoken as well, as anything else was just a waste of time and breath.

"I think a couple of things when I hear 'Lee Harden,'" Jonathan snapped. "I think enemy of Greeley, and I also think, how fucking dare he send a guy into my goddamned bedroom in the middle of the night."

The man standing beside Jonathan smiled. Just a flash of white teeth in the darkness of the room. "Don't blame him for that. He sent me to talk, and this is how I decided to do it. Tell me about 'enemy of Greeley.'"

Jonathan felt like his brain was seizing up. These questions were surreal. "Tell you about…? What the fuck is this, an interview? You break into my home in the middle of the night to sit down and interview me?"

"I need to know where your loyalty stands," the man said, calmly. "I'm sure you understand the position I'm in. I have to approach these talks with caution."

"My loyalty stands with La Junta," Jonathan growled, unable to do anything in that moment except speak his mind. "Greeley can go fuck itself, and so can Lee Harden, if this is how he chooses to go about things."

That flash of a smile again. The man turned and looked at his companion, on Tammy's side. "Menendez, step back and keep coverage." As the other man stepped back to the foot of the bed, the man beside Jonathan pulled the muzzle of the rifle up. "How about some light?"

"Some light would be nice." Jonathan couldn't help the hostility in his voice. "I don't prefer whispering in the shadows. I like to see the face of the man threatening my family."

The man took his rifle, unclipped it from his sling, then turned on the weaponlight. A harsh white glow filled the room, but the man upended the rifle and propped it against the foot of the bed so it cast its light on the ceiling, giving the entire bedroom a muted, bluish glow.

Then the man did something very strange. He sat on the edge of the bed, as though he were a doctor dealing with a terminally ill patient. In the dim glow, Jonathan could see the man's face better. The big, black beard. The dark face paint covering his features.

The man extended his hand to Jonathan, and Jonathan, completely flummoxed, found himself taking that hand and giving it a firm shake.

"Abe Darabie," the man said. "Now. Let's talk."

TWENTY-FOUR

AN INVITATION

MACLEAN LOOPED BACK around the charred remains of the buildings, and almost snapped his stolen rifle up when he saw the figure standing there. Everything looked strange in the monochromatic grayness of dawn.

Wibberly jerked his head up and looked at him. "Did I scare you?

Maclean stepped towards his companion, looking out at the washed out landscape around them. "Little jumpy, as usual."

Wibberley stood looking down at a water trough in the center of what had clearly been a ranch. Recently occupied. Now everything was char and ashes. The buildings were nothing more than blackened skeletons. Most of them had burned so hotly that all that remained were a few black studs poking up from the rubble, like rib cages.

The air stank of smoke. It coated the inside Maclean's nostrils, and he could taste it, sharp and acrid, on the back of his tongue. One of the only surviving structures—likely because it wasn't a shelter—was the big frame over the gate. From it, the brand of the ranch creaked steadily, hanging on rusted chains.

Three rockers. Which would make this Triple Rocker Ranch.

Nothing remained of it.

The garden patches had been trampled through, anything edible taken from them and the rest ruined. The fields of immature corn had been run down and crushed by what looked like multiple vehicles. An acre of what had likely been some type of grain had been set ablaze and was now just a barren scape of ash. The small silos where that grain would have been stored were emptied, and the only reason they still stood, Maclean assumed, was because they were made of metal.

"I don't know if we want to drink this," Wibberley noted, still staring at the dark water in the trough.

Maclean leaned forward. The surface of the water had a thick skim of ash and charcoal on it. The windmill that had kept the trough pumped and full of fresh groundwater now lay collapsed, burned chunks of it floating in the water.

"Well," Maclean sighed, his throat dry, aching for water. "We could just consider it charcoal filtered."

Wibberley coughed out a laugh.

There are strange moments that come upon you sometimes, when everything is just so dead set against you that you have to laugh at it. That's what Maclean felt like in that moment, as laughter bubbled up from his chest: Like he was some bumbling actor in some slapstick comedy where his job was to be the butt of the joke.

The two men stood there looking at the water and laughing, their voices dry, hoarse.

Maclean wiped a precious tear from the corner of his eyes, stifled the rest of the ridiculous laughter. "Wasn't even funny."

"I know. You drink it and tell me what you think."

Maclean drew out the empty plastic water bottle from his cargo pocket. It was crumpled down to fit better. He popped the lid, puffed a breath into it to inflate it again, then dipped it into the trough. Grainy flecks of wood char coated his hand as he pushed it below the blackened skim.

He brought it up. Held it to the little light he had out of the east. He could see through it, at least, though it did look a tad cloudy. On the one hand, the appearance of the water was not appetizing. On the other hand, he was dehydrated and desperate. So he drank.

And drank.

Until the bottle collapsed again.

Then he pulled it away, coughed once, licked his lips. "It definitely tastes like the inside of a grill."

"Fuck it," Wibberley grunted, then produced his own water bottle and filled it.

They drank what they could, then topped off their bottles, all the while one or both of them peering out into the dawn to see if any threatening shapes emerged. But it was like the infected knew this place held no sustenance for them. There hadn't been a whisper of activity in the vicinity.

"Was this Lee or Cornerstone?" Wibberley asked.

"Had to've been that force that came out of Butler. Lee would've already passed through this area, and I don't see him scorching the earth like this."

"So they're on Lee's ass, then."

"Probably. If I were to take a gander, I'd say Lee came through and gathered up whoever lived here. If he left anyone behind, that Greeley army disposed of their bodies somewhere else, or maybe took them prisoner. I didn't see a single corpse. You?"

Wibberley shook his head. "This shit is getting brutal."

They stood in silence for a moment, Maclean wishing there was some food in this place.

"Every time you think civilization has evolved beyond this kind of shit," Wibberley said, his voice quiet, disappointed. "Something happens and we go right back to it."

"Can't do anything about human nature."

Wibberley turned himself in the general direction of north. "Greeley army is out there somewhere. I don't want to run into their rear lines. We need to get around them if we ever hope to catch up to Lee."

"No telling where the hell Lee is."

"If we can get ahead of the army, find a settlement that hasn't been burned to the ground, we might get some idea of where Lee's gone."

"Well, ultimately, I think we know where he's going."

Wibberley nodded. "We could just go straight for Greeley. Eventually Lee is going to show up on their doorstep."

Maclean considered this for a long moment. Smacked his tongue, which still tasted faintly of woodsmoke, from the air or the water, he wasn't sure. "We don't have a lot of fuel left."

"We have enough to get into Colorado. Probably."

"Maybe."

"Nothing risked, nothing gained."

"But I'd like to be as close as possible when we run out of gas."

"Of course. But there's nothing we can do except put the miles down and hope for the best. Hedge our bets on the most likely place for Lee to be and head there."

Maclean knew that his friend was right. They could theorize all they wanted, but ultimately, their limiting factor was the fuel. It would likely run out before they were able to track Lee down. Their best possible option was to make a straight line between themselves and Greeley, and hope that they got stranded close enough to Lee's path that they would stumble across him.

Maclean chose not to think about what would happen if they failed.

They were in the plains states. A lot of massive, flat areas. A lot of high desert. Not a lot of food or water. If they got their asses stranded out there, their survival would be a ticking clock, and they were already hungry and dehydrated.

But sometimes you just had to throw the dice.

"Alright," Maclean finally said. "We cut a straight line northwest, towards Greeley. And we hope for the best."

Wibberley nodded. "That's about all we can do at this point."

***

The killing was complete.

And the pack had fed. They had gorged themselves, and the scent of blood and meat was still thick in the air. The Easy Prey were plentiful here, though they had not saved any of them. The pack would feed on them for a time, until their meat grew too sour.

Giant black birds circled overhead in numbers that the Alpha had never seen before. It stared up at them, its belly distended, its movements slow as it groomed the filth from its face and neck and chest. The birds would often come down and pick at what was left of the Easy Prey. None of the pack stopped them—there was enough to go around, and the bodies they chose were ones where there was little left to feed on.

The killing tide had released the Alpha from its pull, but it was still there, in the background, ready to sweep the pack up again.

It was a strange time for the Alpha. A calm had come over the pack, a scent that came from the Strange Ones and the Omegas, something that stilled their desire to fight amongst themselves.

The Strange Ones had created a den, and disappeared into it. A large place, much like the place where the Glow had come upon them, but that was not going to happen this time, the Alpha could sense that. The Omegas surrounded the den, and sometimes they would go in and out, but mostly they lay there, guarding the Strange Ones.

Others were arriving all the time. The Alpha watched them slink in, unsure of themselves, baring their teeth at the many members of the Alpha's pack, but none of them fought. The scent of the Strange Ones stifled the Alpha's aggression, and that of his packmates, and that of the Others that came in.

The scent was like the Glow, but not. It was the Stillness.

The Strange Ones wanted the Others to be there. They wanted the Others to become the Pack. The Alpha did not comprehend why. It simply knew. That was the purpose of the Stillness. To bring them together. To make one from many. To bind the Others into the Pack.

The hunger that the Strange Ones had, the urge that soaked their bones, had not left. The Stillness was a part of that, but only a small part. The hunger was for someplace else.

And their time to go to that place was coming. But they would not go until the many became the one. Until the Others became the Pack. And when the Others had become the Pack, then the Pack would go to the place where the Strange Ones' hunger led them. They would move as one pack, as a tide unto themselves.

But for now, the Stillness kept them here.

The Alpha relaxed into it.

One of the Others approached a kill that the Alpha had gorged itself on, and the Alpha did not move to stop it. The Other sniffed the remains of the Easy Prey, and then began to feed. Its belly was sunken in. Its body was fatless and in need of nourishment.

The Alpha let it feed. The Other was now the Pack. And the Pack would grow strong.

It was, and what is must be right.

***

It was the last round of patrols.

Sam felt wrung out and high from not sleeping. His body wasn't used to sleeping during the day and patrolling all night. And sleep had been hard to come by. He would lie awake all day long in the stuffy flat, no amount of blankets over the windows enough to block out the daylight, and no amount of steady breathing enough to block out his thoughts.

Every time he laid down to sleep, it seemed like he couldn't stay awake a second longer. But then in the stillness, his mind would begin to run wild. His body desperately wanted rest, but his mind was too overwrought, too on edge to fully release its stranglehold of paranoia.

Every sound, no matter how inane, would send a bolt of adrenaline through his system, setting his heart racing and his palms sweating. Was that footfall the sound of Cornerstone operatives coming up the stairs to raid them? Was that slamming car door the sound of a troop transport disgorging soldiers to black bag his team again?

What was happening in Johnson's head? Was he percolating on what had happened, coming up with a plan of his own? Had Sam been a fool to trust him?

Maybe I should just kill him right now. Maybe I should just nip this in the bud before anything bad comes of it.

But the time for that had passed. If he was going to murder another teammate, he would have had to do it in the heat of the moment when he was holding that knife to Johnson's throat. He couldn't just do it in cold blood. Now he was trapped by that decision. Forced to wait and see what might come.

It was more or less those thoughts, playing on a loop, that had kept him awake. They became stale. Over-trodden.

Like this patrol route.

Sam took a heavy breath and realized that he'd walked nearly two city blocks without seeing a damn thing. He'd been too lost in his own thoughts—the very same ones that plagued him while he tried to sleep.

He frowned, glancing behind him, wondering if he'd wondered off course. But no. His squad was right there behind him. Their faces gray in the light of dawn. Washed out. Their expressions exhausted.

Around them, Greeley was waking up. Vehicle patrols—about the only thing that Greeley seemed to allow fuel for—were beginning to rumble along the streets. Workers were exiting the places where they lived and slept, heading in clusters of hunched, mumbling humanity, to whatever job kept them safe and fed.

Sam had no comms with whoever was running the show. He had no way to tell exactly the time, so he judged it by the rising sun, and waited for their relief to arrive.

It wasn't the most efficient way of guarding a perimeter, Sam thought. Even if he was of a mind to protect Greeley, if they came under attack, he would have no way to report it to command. Greeley likely didn't have enough radios to go around to the hundreds of squads they now had on foot patrol.

Sam stopped, letting his issued rifle hang, and rubbed his face. "Alright," he called out, his voice cracking and brittle. "One more round. Relief squad should be here soon."

The one benefit of being on the nightshift was that the streets were so empty it was easy for Sam to spot anyone monitoring them. Over the course of the last eight hours, he hadn't seen a single suspicious vehicle or group of operatives that might be keeping tabs on him and his squad.

Did they trust them now? Or was Sam just overlooking it?

They couldn't possibly keep tabs on *all* the patrols. And he and his team had done a good job of mitigating suspicion. They hadn't given them any reason *not* to trust them. So perhaps they weren't being watched anymore.

As they finished trudging along their last round—what was it? The fifteenth time they'd walked this specific section of sidewalk?—he spotted a lone figure approaching him.

It took a moment for his sleep-deprived brain to realize that the figure was going against the flow of all the other civilians, and that he recognized who it was, with a slow, dim recollection.

What had her name been?

Gabriella. That's right. The lady that wanted to be called "sir."

He halted his patrol as he realized she was indeed walking right for him.

He waited there in silence, a vague sense of misgivings coming over him, but almost too tired to care, or really parse through what this could mean.

As she drew closer to him, he saw that her pleasant face had a stern caste to it.

Great. She's pissed about something.

Had he done something wrong?

"Sir," Sam ventured as she stopped in front of him.

Gabriella's eyes passed over him and his team, as though assessing them. "Good morning, Squad Leader Balawi."

Squad Leader Balawi. So formal.

"Morning," he grunted back.

"Anything to report?"

Sam wondered if he *should* have something to report. Was this another test? Had he missed something? But no. There had been absolutely nothing of note. Just another eight, dreary hours of mindless walking.

He shook his head. "No, sir. Everything was quiet and normal. I guess."

"You guess?"

"I don't really know what normal is for Greeley," Sam sighed. "Nothing stood out to me. Why?"

Gabriella fixed him with that stern look. "It's my job to ask, that's why. And it's your job to notice things."

"Did I miss something?"

"Did you?"

Sam stared at her for a long moment. It was like his adrenaline wanted to spike, but couldn't quite find the energy for it. Maybe it was saving itself for later when he was trying to sleep.

"Look. Sir." *Don't be rude. Try to play it cool.* "I don't know if you're trying to get at something or what. But I didn't see anything out of the ordinary. The streets were empty. Everything was quiet."

She nodded as though mollified. "How's your squad holding up?"

"Fine." It was a canned answer.

She looked briefly uncomfortable. The shadow of a grimace overtaking her mouth. "I heard about what happened."

Sam didn't reply.

Gabriella let out a long, slow sigh. "I'd like to have a conversation with you."

"Isn't that what we're having?"

She shook her head. "Not here. And with some other people." She looked at him pointedly. "Other people you might want to talk to."

Now his body found a little reserve of energy to give him a jolt. His whole body tingled. He was suddenly very awake. This could be more Cornerstone bullshit…or it could be the break that he'd been looking for.

"Okay," he said cautiously. "When?"

"As soon as you finish your shift. Your replacements should be here in a few minutes." Gabriella looked around, and it didn't escape Sam that her movements were furtive, as though she were concerned about someone watching her. She pulled something out of her pocket and slipped it discreetly into his hand.

Sam felt paper. Didn't look at it just yet.

"The place is written on that paper. Be there as soon as your shift ends." Her eyes never connected to his again. They remained focused outward. "We'll wait up for you. Come alone."

Then she turned and marched away.

Marie, who had been close enough to overhear the conversation, slid up to Sam's side. "What the hell was that?"

Sam shook his head. "I don't know."

"She said to come alone. I don't like that."

"I don't like it either. But…" *But I have to go.*

How could he not? How could he pass on a potential opportunity?

"Besides," Sam continued, as though Marie had been privy to his thoughts. "If it's a legitimate order I can't just say 'no.'"

Marie made a quiet noise of stress. A hiss through her teeth. "Goddamn this place." She grabbed Sam firmly, his shirt bunched in her fist as though she were about to fight him. "You be fucking careful, Sam. Don't give them rope to hang you with. Or us."

"I know. I won't."

But even as he said it he realized that might not be an option.

***

Weaponless now, Sam walked the morning streets of Greeley with his hands stuffed in his pockets. The paper Gabriella had given him was sweaty and crumpled in his right palm.

The rifles they were given for patrol were on loan. They stayed with the patrol route, so that when one shift arrived to relieve the other, they simply turned the rifles over. During their "orientation" the Cornerstone man that had briefed them stated that operatives would do surprise inspections of the rifles, to make sure that things weren't going missing, particularly ammo.

So far, that hadn't happened yet, but Sam had only been on the job for a few days. He figured it was coming.

Which was a minor concern in the grand scheme of things. Sam hadn't messed with the rifles or the ammo—too risky. And he had other things on his mind at the moment.

Like who else was going to be at this "meeting."

And whether or not this was an official meeting at all…or something else.

Gabriella's tone, her words, her expressions, kept coming back to Sam's memory in finer and finer detail. Every twitch of her mouth, every slash of her gaze, every nuance of her word choice, was subject to interpretation.

Or maybe he was reading too much into it. Maybe this was just a meet for the squad leaders.

But then why would she have looked so strange? Why would she have been glancing over her shoulder? Why would she have given him the paper with the directions on it in such a secretive way?

Sam was well aware of his faltering cognition. His brain was running on willpower and adrenaline at this point, his body simply dragged along like an unwilling dog on a leash. Knowing that he wasn't in the clearest headspace only increased his paranoia.

He'd already committed the scrap of paper to memory, because he didn't want to be seen referencing it. In case he was being followed. Which he kept checking for, but didn't see anyone surveilling him. They were either too good, not there in the first place, or Sam was just too tired to spot them.

Gabriella hadn't told him to make sure he wasn't followed. If this were some sort of secret meeting, as he hoped for the sake of his mission, then wouldn't she have said something like that?

Maybe. Maybe not. If she had, it would have been a giveaway that this was not official, and she might be trying to play her cards close to her chest.

Sam jogged a left at an intersection, heading north now, away from the taller buildings of the more commercial area where he was usually posted. After about a mile, he found himself in a residential area. Neighborhoods. Cookie-cutter houses. Big swaths of these neighborhoods were demolished. Some of them looked intentional, the houses bulldozed into scrap heaps. Other sections looked like they'd been burned, or shot to pieces, but hadn't yet been knocked down.

And in the midst of all of this typical destruction that had become, over the years, somewhat humdrum for Sam, he found himself in something much stranger. Like little islands, there were other sections of these neighborhoods that looked…normal.

All the little houses still standing in a row. Windows intact. Lawns not exactly manicured, but not overgrown with chest-high weeds either. Sidewalks where an occasional pedestrian passed by. Sam felt like an interloper, but they paid him no mind.

When he found the correct street, he began looking at the numbers on all the identical mailboxes. He had the urge to double check the note in his pocket, but he trusted his memory of it. He eventually stopped at the driveway of a house. A little sable-colored affair.

The number matched.

Was this where Gabriella lived?

Sam had a brief moment, standing there, where he felt something like vertigo. An odd, spinning sensation that left him feeling as though this little house in front of him couldn't possibly be real, this must've been a waking daydream, or a memory from times passed.

He swallowed, shook his head slightly, and moved for the door.

His heart kicked out a steady rhythm of tension in his chest. He stood there, staring at the numbers posted on the door for a long moment, listening, but not hearing anything from inside the house.

He raised his hand to knock, but before his knuckles could strike the door, it opened.

Gabriella stood there, looking just as cautious and stern as she had before. Her gaze flitted over him, making only the barest moment of eye contact before scouring the street beyond. She nodded to him, and held the door open.

"Come on," she murmured, jerking her head.

Sam stepped through the doorway.

There, standing in a barren living space, stood about a dozen other individuals.

Sam's eyes shot across each of them, searching for signs of who they were. But they were all dressed in civilian garb. Except for Gabriella, who still wore her black Cornerstone polo. Those gathered were just as interested in Sam as he was with them, and yet no one spoke.

Sam's gaze passed over one of them—and then snapped back.

The man watched him. Smiling.

And Sam recognized him.

"You again, huh?" It was the man from The Tank. The asshole with his little gang that had tried to rough Sam up when they'd come in.

Sam's jaw locked down and he looked to Gabriella.

"Sameer, I see you've met Nolan," Gabriella said.

"Sameer, is it?" The man named Nolan remarked. "So I guess you're not Mexican after all."

"Wetback. Hadji." Sam didn't bother looking at him. "You call me whatever you want, Nolan. I've heard it all before."

An awkward silence descended. There was a nervousness in the air that made it feel stretched and thin. Sam got the distinct impression that no one really had a good idea of whether or not Sam and Nolan were kidding with each other or serious. It was also obvious that no one knew why they had all been gathered.

Sam, for one, had no intention of making more of an enemy of Nolan than necessary. So he was an asshole. Big deal. Assholes were a dime a dozen. Sam could work around that.

Gabriella closed the door behind her. It didn't escape Sam the sound of the deadbolt being thrown.

"That's everyone," Gabriella said, stepping up to Sam's side.

No one responded. Everyone's expression was withheld. Cautious.

Sam blinked a few times in the ripe stillness. Then cleared his throat: "May I ask what we're doing here?"

Gabriella stepped around him and stood at a point in the room where the rest of them formed a loose semi-circle around her. They watched her carefully. She folded her arms across her chest, then seemed to decide that was an unwelcoming posture, and relaxed, holding her hands at her waist.

"Right now? We're here to talk."

Another woman, middle-aged and severe looking, like a harried school teacher, put her hands on her hips. "About what? And also…" she swept a finger across the room. "I don't know any of these people."

Gabriella nodded. "None of you know each other—except for maybe Sam and Nolan. But you all know me. I was your intake specialist. I talked to each of you when you came into Greeley. And the reason that I asked each of you here today, was because it sounded like you…" Gabriella paused, appearing to struggle with how to state what she wanted. "…Maybe shared my reservations. About things."

So, this *wasn't* an official meeting.

Sam's heart skipped a few beats, then redoubled its efforts. He could see the effect Gabriella's words had on the others. Their eyes moved rapidly over everyone else. Scared. Maybe a little excited.

He looked at Nolan, relieved to find the man's attention now on Gabriella.

So, Nolan-The-Asshole might be an ally?

Sam didn't like the guy one bit, and trusted him even less. But he was…interested.

"Does command know that we're having this meeting?" A man asked, his voice low, hesitant.

Gabriella forced a smile that was entirely unconvincing. "I'm not required to notify command just because I want to talk to some people. And that's all we're doing here. I need to make that clear. We're just talking. I'm just…taking your temperature, so to speak."

"You're seeing if we're loyal to Greeley," Sam suggested, in a tone that didn't give away whether he was or wasn't.

Gabriella shook her head, but Sam could see the dishonesty in that motion. "No. Again, I'm just talking. Seeing where everyone's head is at."

"Okay," the School Teacher said. "Why don't you lead us off then, sir?"

Gabriella took a stiff breath. "Alright. Let's start this way. If anyone is happy and satisfied with everything going on in Greeley, then you don't really need to be here. If you're happy and satisfied, you're free to go." Gabriella pointed for the door. "No hard feelings."

No one moved. Not even a shuffle.

Gabriella nodded. "So, if you're still standing here, then you have some concerns."

Again, nothing. No reaction at all. No one wanted to be the first to show their cards, and it didn't seem like Gabriella wanted to either. But someone was going to have to make the leap of faith. Someone was going to have to extend a modicum of trust to the others, or they'd all just sit in silence, too terrified to speak their minds for fear of reprisal.

Don't trust anyone.

That's what Lee had told him.

But occasionally, you have to take the risk.

No one wins in a poker game full of too-cautious players. At some point, someone has to make a serious gamble.

"Yeah," Sam said, his head humming with worries as he heard his mouth speak. "I have reservations."

Gabriella cast an appreciative look in his direction. It seemed earnest. Encouraging. "Well, that's a start, Sam."

And it was. Because Sam's words were the hole in the dam, and after that, it became apparent that everyone in the room had reservations. And more than that, they were fucking pissed.

TWENTY-FIVE

MOMENTUM

LEE SPUN AWAKE in what had become a normal fashion for him.

Complete and utter disorientation.

He was used to it at this point in time, and while his threadbare brain tried to piece together where he was and when he was and what was going on in that instant, a small, logical part of him told him to wait it out. It would pass.

Bulkhead. Steel and bolts. Daylight. An annoying chiming noise.

Someone touched his leg.

He sat up.

It was Angela. Her hand on his leg. She sat on a jump seat in the back of…

Where?

The chiming noise went on.

"Lee?" Angela said gently. She was, perhaps, just as accustomed to his disorientation upon waking as he was. "You with me?"

Lee realized his hands were gripping the rifle that lay on his chest.

He was in the MATV. Laying in the center of it, between the two rows of jump seats. The doors were open. It was broad daylight outside.

"I'm getting there," Lee mumbled.

"Your satphone is going off."

Satphone. Yes. That was the chiming noise.

Lee released the grip on his rifle. Looked blearily about for the satphone, then realized it was in his pocket. The where and when of his current existence started to leak back through and supplant a hazy skein of strange dreams. Violent dreams. Dreams where he stood in firelit darkness and let everything and everyone around him burn.

Right. That wasn't real. *This* was real.

Their convoy was positioned nearby to the settlement of Lakin, Kansas. He had been awake all night and had chosen to get some sleep while Cass went on ahead. She said she had good rapport with Lakin. They'd done some trading in the past.

Lee felt misgivings take him—had he really allowed Cass to leave on her own? Had he really decided to trust her that much? But then he recalled that it wasn't that much trust—she'd gone in alone, and he still had a hundred of her people, distributed through their ranks.

Something of a judgement call, but Lee didn't think she was going to pull anything.

Snippets of conversation drifted back to his mind as he leaned over and fished the satphone from his pocket. Things that Cass had said. Things that made him more comfortable with her as an ally.

She was not a fan of Lee's tactics, but she was less a fan of Greeley. In their conversations in the back of the MATV as they had travelled into Kansas, she'd made it clear that she was willing to look past the way that Lee had handled the situation in her settlement, in order to support the overall objective—defeating Briggs.

That was good, Lee thought, as he extended the satphone's antenna, taking a moment to clear his head before answering. He could see the number calling. He had hoped it would be Sam—Sam had been in his dreams, and he felt a residual fear caking the inside of his mind.

But it wasn't Sam's number. It was Abe's.

"Abe, that you?" Lee answered, somewhat cautiously, like he wasn't quite sure what to expect on the other line. The weirdness of his dreams still made him expect the worst. Or perhaps that was just smart to do.

"It's me," Abe's voice came over, strong and clear.

Lee relaxed. "Good deal. Sorry, just waking up."

"Sounds like it. You awake enough to talk?"

Lee rubbed his face with his awkward left hand. "Yeah. Yeah, I'm here."

"Well, this oughta perk you up a bit. I got some good news."

"God help me, that'll be refreshing."

"So, we infiltrated La Junta last night—"

"Infiltrated?" Lee frowned.

"Right. Try to stay with me. It's a big settlement and we weren't sure about their loyalties, so we played it very cautiously. And we may have had to rough a few people up. Some feelings got hurt."

This doesn't sound like good news, Lee thought, but restrained himself from saying.

"All's well that ends well," Abe concluded. "We had a nice, long, midnight chat with the guy running shit here in La Junta—Jonathan Reeves. Long story short, after we explained why we had to ninja our way into his house in the middle of the night, he understood, and he's on board."

"Onboard? Like…?"

"Like he's an ally. La Junta is open for business. I've got my whole team settling into some temporary quarters. The entire settlement is one-hundred-percent anti-Greeley. In fact, Cornerstone came through only a few days ago and tried to bully them into supporting Briggs, but they weren't having it and they told that handful of Cornerstone operatives to go fuck themselves. Now, I've got a solid contingent of people from La Junta that are ready and raring to go for a push on Greeley. It's not everybody, but it's a solid number, and it's got some solid fighters. Some former military personnel, and they've been doing some training with the civilians. Right now, we got about two hundred people ready to mount up and ride on Greeley."

"That's fantastic," Lee said, even as he frowned, rubbing his eyebrows. Of course, this was the plan. And it was always wonderful when the plan worked out—which it so rarely did. But now there were myriad other concerns. "How're they fixed on weapons and ammo?"

Abe made a noncommittal noise. "Could be better. We'll need to supplement, but we won't have to provide everything."

Lee considered their stores and how much they actually had to hand out. While they'd taken what they could from Butler, and they'd emptied out every bunker in Texas, a lot of that had already been used, and a good chunk of what was left had gone to arming the people from Butler and a few from Triprock.

Luckily, Cass's people had come prepared and well-equipped enough that Lee didn't have to dip into their mobile armory. That wouldn't necessarily be the case with Lakin. That remained to be seen.

"Alright," Lee nodded to himself. "You've done an amazing job, as usual. Give me some numbers? You said two hundred. How many of those are well equipped?"

"Well, most of them have rifles. But a lot of them don't have much ammunition to go along with it. I'm still gathering the specifics."

"Roger that. I'll wait and we'll hash it out when I get there."

"Where are you currently?"

"Just outside of Lakin, Kansas, making contact with a settlement there. After this, we're heading your way."

"Any leads on Lakin?"

Lee grimaced. "Not sure on that yet. I've got a lady that has a relationship with them working on it right now."

"Any word from Sam?"

"Not in the last twenty-four hours."

"Gotcha. Well, that's all I got for you, Supreme Leader."

Lee rolled his eyes. "We'll aim to be there by tomorrow at the latest."

"We'll be ready for you." Abe sounded like he was smiling as he spoke. "Things are looking up. Stay strong and watch your back."

"Same to you."

Lee hung up the satphone and stared at it for a time.

Abe was right. Things were looking up. But Lee had learned not to trust blue skies. They only made him wonder when the next storm would blow in.

***

It wasn't really a question of when Sam had slept last. It was more a question of how many hours he'd slept in the past several days.

He knew he needed sleep. He figured he'd had about ten hours total, in the entire week since leaving Texas. But he didn't think he was going to get much today. His brain was sparking and his body jittery as he climbed the steps to his flat.

When he reached the door, he gave the requisite knock so that no one would attack him when he came through—three knocks, pause, one more knock. "It's Sam," he hissed at the door. "I'm coming in."

He pushed the door open to find all four of his squadmates sitting in various poses on the floor, staring at him eagerly. He caught how their eyes flitted over his shoulder, as though wondering if he had brought any unwanted guests with him.

He closed the door behind him, then turned, his hands kneading at each other.

Jones leaned up and crossed his legs under him like a kid. "What's the word, Boss?"

Sam stepped into the middle of the room and then lowered himself to the floor in the same position as Jones. He grabbed eye contact with each of his team—Marie, looking tense; Jones, looking eager; Pickell, curious; Johnson, reticent. He motioned for them to huddle up closer.

His team tightened up around him, a little circle, like a slumber party, and Sam was going to tell them ghost stories with a flashlight under his chin.

He spoke in a whisper: "The meeting was…interesting."

Jones rolled his eyes. "Jesus, man. We don't give a fuck about the preamble. What the hell happened?"

"Gabriella, the Cornerstone woman that came to talk to me while we were on patrol? She got a group of squad leaders together. People she'd given the entrance interviews to and felt they all had concerns about how Greeley was being run."

"How many?" Marie asked.

"Eleven. Plus me."

"What about this Gabriella chick?" Jones demanded. "Where's she stand? Is she just milking you? This isn't like…" he gave Sam a suspicious look. "…another *Charlie* situation, is it?"

Sam scratched his eyebrow irritably. "If you're asking whether we're fucking, then no."

"Well, I mean, I'd be curious about that too," Jones admitted. "But no, I was wondering what she said. Did she come out and say anything legitimately seditious? Or was she just trying to pump you guys to see where your loyalties lie?"

Sam shook his head, unsure. "I dunno, man. I'd love to tell you that I had a perfect fix on her, but I'm not a mind reader. Y'all know I've been screwed before, and I'm not gonna act like I'm immune to it." Sam made a pained face. "I'm so fucking tired right now, I'm having a hard time trusting my perception of anything at this point. All I've got to go on is what she said."

Pickell peddled his hands over each other. "Which was?"

"She wants to know who would stand up to Briggs if it came down to it."

"Ooh. Shit." Jones bared his teeth. "That is risky as fuck. What did you say?"

"I tried to keep it downplayed," Sam admitted. "But the conversation took on a life of its own."

"So," Marie lowered her head. "What you're saying is that now Gabriella knows we're not loyal to Greeley."

Sam's heart thudded in his chest, all the hopefulness turning to doubts at the way that Marie phrased her question. "I don't think there's any way around that at this point. Yes, she knows."

"Shit." Marie shook her head.

"What the hell was I supposed to do?" Sam hissed, getting defensive.

Marie held up a hand. "There's nothing you could have done."

"No, there's not," Sam confirmed, still heated. "Our mission was to sow sedition and get intel. We've got the intel, and now this is a chance to reach out and make contact with others that might be willing to fight for Lee when he gets here. I had to take a risk."

"I know." Marie folded her fingers at her chin. "I'm just worried about this Gabriella lady."

"I'm worried too," Sam said. "I had to take a leap of faith, and I'm still in midair. I'd love to tell you guys that I'm gonna land on both feet and everything in that meeting was just what it was represented as. But none of us are that stupid." He pointed to Marie. "You're right. Gabriella could be playing us. That's why we need to keep our head on a swivel."

"Oh, cool." Jones rolled his eyes. "Because we've been totally relaxed up to this point. This has been a fucking vacation."

"Well, there's no other way to put it, Jones," Sam snapped. "Our asses are in the wind. We've got a chance to capitalize and actually accomplish the other half of our mission. But we need to all admit that there's a strong chance I just got played. Cornerstone might be rooting out dissenters."

Johnson spoke up, his voice distant, almost childlike. "So what do we do if they come for us?"

Sam stabbed a finger down on the ground. "We got in. We're behind enemy lines. That's a position we had to work for, and I'm not giving that up, no matter what happens. Even if all we can do is be eyes for Lee's invasion force—well, that's better than nothing."

He paused, took a deep breath, wondered if his command of these others was as solid and logical as he hoped it was, or if he would wake up after a solid sleep one of these days and discover that, in hindsight, he'd been delirious.

"If they come for us," Sam continued. "We scatter. But we don't give up our position behind enemy lines. That is not an option."

"Where the fuck we gonna go if something goes down?" Jones asked.

Sam nodded. "Western edge of the Red Zone—you remember when we patrolled around that area?"

Jones nodded. "Yeah, it's mostly abandoned."

"You guys remember that three-story building that looked like it'd been fire-gutted?"

Another round of nods.

"If we have to run, we'll try to meet up there. It's not being used, and the entire area around it is abandoned. We should be able to get in and out without attracting attention. That'll be our fallback point if shit goes south."

"Okay," Marie said. "So what if shit doesn't go south? What if Gabriella is telling the truth?"

"Then we use her to help us," Sam replied. "And we try to get as many dissenting squad leaders to bone up and be ready to cause trouble the second Lee arrives."

"Elgops," Pickell interjected with a knowing glint.

Sam frowned. "What are you talking about, Kosher Dill?"

"It's an acronym," Pickell explained. "L-G-O-P. Little Groups Of Paratroopers. During the invasion of Normandy in World War Two, the allies dropped shit tons of paratroopers into occupied territory. They were scattered all over the place, but they they'd meet up in little groups, and run around the countryside wreaking havoc."

Sam shook his head. "How do you know all of this shit?"

"History major," Pickell replied, as though that explained everything.

"LGOPs," Sam said thoughtfully. "Yes. That's it exactly. If we can get enough small squads on board, we can run around and tear shit up during the invasion. Start fires, blow things up, ambush Cornerstone, steal supplies. Anything to undermine their defenses. We don't need any specific strategy—just find places to apply pain."

Marie looked troubled. "Sam…does Gabriella know that Lee is coming?"

Sam shook his head. "No. I didn't want to give that information up."

"Are you planning to?"

Sam hissed air through clenched teeth. "I don't know. I'm not sure I should trust her with that."

"What about the others?" Pickell suggested. "The other squad leaders? You're not sure about Gabriella's motivations, but what about them? What reason could they have had to lie?"

Sam nodded thoughtfully. "You're right. I should start reaching out to them. Talking to them privately."

No one spoke for a moment.

Marie leaned back, her eyes suddenly heavy-lidded. "You gonna get any sleep?"

Sam laughed without humor. "I'll close my eyes for a bit and hope for the best."

TWENTY-SIX

THE WILL TO FIGHT

LEE WATCHED the approaching vehicles from Lakin.

The day had turned uncomfortably warm. Lee had his sleeves rolled up as high as they could go. The scars on his left arm were bright pink and raw. He drank the last of the water from a bottle. It tasted faintly of plastic. Sleep had overtaken his need for water, but he was on the verge of getting dehydrated. Not fully there yet, as he was still pouring sweat in the midday sun, but he had yet to piss today, so that wasn't a good sign.

The vehicles in the distance were just a shimmer in the mirage coming off the road, but he could see that there were two of them. One he recognized as the pickup they'd loaned to Cass. The other must be from Lakin.

"So," Angela said, leaning in the minimal shade of the MATV. "She's got someone following her. I guess that's a good sign?"

Lee shrugged, stuffing the empty water bottle into his cargo pocket to be refilled later. "Maybe they just wanted to come tell me to fuck off in person."

"Boy," Angela sighed. "There you go again, being nauseatingly positive."

Lee smiled at her. Sopped a bit of sweat from his sodden eyepatch. When it got soaked, it smarted against his ruined eye. But one more pain was nothing to balk at. "You're right. It's probably a good sign."

The watery shapes of the vehicles gradually became more solid. The sound of their engines lifted over the light breeze and the murmur of general conversation at his back. He turned and looked behind him. The convoy stretched out on this long, flat section of road until the back ends of it shimmered, just as liquid as those two approaching vehicles had.

All throughout the convoy, people stood outside of the vehicles, where the air was marginally cooler than the baking interiors. Soldiers, Marines, guerilla fighters. Men, women, children. Boys and girls that looked too young to be toting the rifles on their backs or strapped to their chests.

Their conversations were subdued to the point that Lee couldn't pick out any single words, just the low trickle of it all. Many of them faced forward, watching the road to Lakin and the two approaching vehicles. Many more seemed to be looking at Lee. Or Angela. Or both of them.

"How many of them are ready for what's about to happen?" Lee wondered, quietly.

Angela hesitated for a moment, then said, "All of them. You were clear with them, Lee. You told them what to expect, out on that road when we evac'd from Butler. If they're still here, they're ready."

"And afterwards?" Lee asked. "When half of them are dead?"

Angela let out a long, uncomfortable sigh. "One thing at a time, Lee."

Lee faced back forward. The two vehicles' engines lowered from the roar of acceleration to a downshifted idle, then rolled to a stop. He could see Cass in the cab of the pickup, about fifteen yards from them. The other vehicle was an older, blue sedan. It looked like an unmarked police vehicle. Interesting choice.

Cass stepped out. Closed her door behind her. Looked to Lee and nodded once.

A nod was a good thing, right?

The front doors of the sedan opened, and two men emerged, one from behind the wheel, the other from the front passenger's side. Both with dark, short-cropped hair. They wore gunbelts with pistols, but no rifles. Just looking at the belts, and the holsters, and the pistols inside those holsters, Lee had a pretty good bet what they'd been in their past life.

Cass fell in beside them and approached.

Lee and Angela met them halfway.

"Major Harden," Cass announced, gesturing to him, then Angela. "President Houston of the former United Eastern States. Lee, Angela, this is Paul and Stephen Eller."

Lee extended his right hand, his eye coursing over the two men and noting the resemblance. "Brothers?"

The first one smiled as he shook Lee's hand. "I'm Paul. That's Stephen. Yeah, we're brothers."

Lee shook Stephen's hand. "And cops."

"Well, we *were*," Paul admitted. "Back in the day. Now we just try to keep the good people of Lakin from bickering too much with each other."

"Very Mayberry," Stephen said

Lee laughed.

Stephen and Paul traded a glance, still smiling. "That's funny?"

Lee shook his head. "Well, it is. But I've just…" He gathered himself and nodded. "It's kind of refreshing to hear that, to be honest. Makes me think everything's been normal in your little corner of the world."

Paul chuckled. "Yeah. Normal-*ized.* People adapt. First year or two it was pandemonium. But then it just becomes life. We don't have to worry much about Jim-Bob getting drunk, but we do have to worry about infected eating our cattle. But then it gradually just becomes Same Shit Different Day."

"So, gentlemen." Lee put his hands on his hips. "I assume Cass has told you what we're here for."

"Yeah," Paul nodded. He seemed to be the older brother—the one slightly more in charge than the other. "We're in."

Lee arched his eyebrows. "Just like that, huh?"

Paul nodded, still smiling.

Lee tilted his head, a slight frown coming to his brow. "What exactly did Cass tell you we were here for?"

Paul and Stephen exchanged another glance. "Taking down Greeley. Right?"

Lee didn't immediately answer. He had the urge to hold back on confirming that. Like their friendliness might be a trap. Was that too much paranoia? Did he honestly think that's what was happening?

Stephen shifted his wait. "That is what we're talking about, right?"

"And who's in?" Lee asked. "Just you two?"

"Oh," Paul laughed. "Hell no." He hiked a thumb over his shoulder at Lakin. "I got about a hundred and fifty people that are hot to trot in there."

"Why?"

"Why?" Paul echoed, looking a little confused.

Lee nodded. "Why do they want to fight?"

Paul appeared to silently hand the reins to Stephen.

"Lakin? Used to be an outpost for Greeley. Some soldiers—mostly those dicks in black polos—"

"Cornerstone."

"Right. They barged in here about a year back, set up shop without asking and basically told us if we had a problem with it we could take it up with their flight of gunships." Stephen frowned. "Obviously that wasn't popular with our people, but no one wanted to get mowed down by an Apache. So we went along with it. I'm not sure what changed, but earlier this past month, they pulled a good bit of their shit out and sent it back to Greeley. Left a little garrison of maybe ten guys—all of them Cornerstone this time. Complete fucking assholes, pardon my French. Then, about two weeks ago, the garrison up and leaves." Stephen's features darkened. "But not before they 'requisitioned'—as they called it—about twenty head of cattle, a metric ton of corn, and a good portion of our weapons and ammunition. Said they needed it in Greeley."

Lee looked over Stephen's shoulder to the settlement, barely visible in the distance. "Are there any more still in Lakin?"

"Hell no," Paul spat. "Took all that shit, packed in in a convoy of trucks, and took off. Haven't seen them since. All they left behind was about three hundred very pissed people."

"And now half of those people want to fight?" Lee questioned.

Paul frowned at him. "Look. I was told you were asking for help. But you seem to have a lot of questions. Are we not on the same page?"

It was Angela that answered. "Gentlemen, Major Harden is a cautious individual, and he has every right to be so. I'm sure you can understand—it takes a lot of trust, and a lot of circumspection. That's Major Harden's job."

"Right," Paul bobbed his head. "I get that."

"And do you understand what we're asking for?" Angela pressed.

"Yeah. You're asking for fighters."

"Great. And do those people that want to fight, do they understand what that means?"

Paul relaxed a bit, a knowing expression coming over his face, as though he had finally decoded the thread of conflict between them. "Ma'am. Sir. Let me explain something to you. This ain't about some missing cattle and grain. Sure, that's what it's about on the surface. But there's history behind why that hit us so hard."

Paul wiped sweat from his hairline. Wiped his fingers on his pants. "What we have? We worked hard for. Those cattle we lost? That's years' worth of work. All that grain they took? That's more years. And do you know what happened in those years? People starved. We had an outbreak of something—still don't know what the fuck it was—but a lot of people got sick, and we didn't have enough food to keep them strong. We lost a lot of people two winters ago." He paused, a thin scribble of emotion going across his face. "Lot of kids."

He took a deep breath and centered himself. "What we had? The stuff that they took? That was our lifeline. That was what we worked hard for to make sure we didn't have another bad year. To make sure we didn't have to bury two dozen kids out back of the town and stack up piles of rocks over their graves so the infected couldn't dig them up and eat them."

The smiles were gone now. Paul and Stephen looked at Lee, and the hardness in their eyes was something that Lee knew intimately. It was a connection between them. Something only people who had lived through the end of the world and paid for their survival in blood and tears could understand.

"So if you're wondering why a hundred and fifty people are willing to fight over some cows and some grain? You're right. They're not fighting for that. They're fighting for the fact that our chance at survival was taken away from us. That we have to face another bad year now, with not enough to go around, and, frankly, everyone's terrified. Because they remember the last time. That security that everyone in Lakin worked so hard to establish? It got stolen from them by some two-bit dictator that calls himself the president.

"So, if what you're really asking me is 'are those hundred and fifty people willing to die to take down Greeley?'" Paul's eyes flashed hot. "Then my answer is yes. Yes, they are. And so am I. And so is Stephen. If it's a fight you're offering, one with even just a hint of a possibility of success? Then you got yourself some people to fight it."

Lee made eye contact with Paul, and then Stephen, and finally, a nod of respect to Cass, who had a slightly smug look on her face. "That's all I needed to hear, gentlemen." Lee glanced skyward. "Daylight's burning. And we have places to be."

Paul looked confused. "Wait. You're not staying?"

Lee shook his head. "No. And neither are you. If you want in on this, then get your people mobile. We're going to move in one hour. We got a town in Colorado where we're meeting some more friends."

Stephen looked uncomfortable. "Sir, I know you got your own timeline to keep, but a lot of the folks that are coming have families they'd like to say goodbye to. And we haven't exactly worked out the kinks of who we're leaving in charge."

"Two hours then?" Lee offered.

Angela touched his arm, giving him a quick, stern look. "Lee. It's just after twelve. We can make it to Abe in a few hours. Dusk isn't until almost nine."

Lee made a disgruntled face, but didn't object.

Angela looked to Paul and Stephen. "We're mobile by six o'clock. Your people have until then to get ready."

Paul nodded, though he still looked unsure. "Okay. I guess we can work with that." He jerked his head at the convoy stretching out behind Lee. "Your people coming in? We don't have much to spare, but—"

"No," Lee cut him off. "We have our own shit to handle."

"Gotcha." Paul looked around awkwardly, like he wasn't sure what was next. "Well, I guess we'll head back."

"Six o'clock," Lee stated.

"Right. Six o'clock."

Paul and Stephen retreated to their sedan. Lee, Angela and Cass watched them until the doors closed, at which point Cass turned on Lee with a glower.

"Christ, Lee. These people are doing you a favor. You can't give them the night?"

Lee pulled his head back like Cass had said something truly outrageous. "They're not doing me a favor, I'm giving them an opportunity. They want to keep being Greeley's bitch, they're welcome to do so."

Cass folded her arms over her chest. "You are one salty asshole, you know that?"

"He knows," Angela griped, turning Lee towards the convoy with a gentle hand on his shoulder. "Alright, two doses of good news. Now for the bad."

"But of course."

They started walking back down the line of vehicles, their pace unhurried. Cass walked with them. Lee didn't mind. She might as well hear what they were up against. It might make it easier for her to understand the choices Lee would have to make.

"Food and water," Angela said. "Those are the problems."

"Weapons, ammo, and ordnance?"

"No, we're good on that. If you consider a rifle and two mags good. And some folks only have pistols. Ordnance is spread thin—pretty much just the soldiers and Marines."

Lee nodded. It was best to leave the explosives in the hands of people that didn't require additional training to use them. The soldiers and Marines were Lee's heavy hitters. He'd planned for that. As for the rest of his fighters…

"A rifle or pistol with a spare mag." Lee clucked his tongue. "It ain't much, but I can work around it. What's the situation with the water and food?"

"The situation is…there's not enough."

"Put it in terms of time for me."

"Two days."

"Really?" Lee grimaced. That was less than he'd thought, but he wasn't truly surprised. These issues were to be expected.

"When we left the refinery, we had stores that might've held up for a few weeks. But after Triprock and Vici, that got stretched pretty thin by the newcomers."

That was the price you paid to have an army at your back, Lee supposed. Even one so ad hoc as this.

"In two days, we'll be completely tapped," Angela continued. "The squads will still have whatever reserves they've got in their packs, but that won't be much. It might buy them another day at best."

Lee stopped in the middle of the dusty road, between the MATV and the rest of the convoy. "The squads need to keep what they have for the assault. Which means we need to be hitting Greeley in two days' time."

An army runs on its stomach. It was an old adage, but a true one. Something that Western militaries hadn't really had to worry about for a long time. But they'd been kicked back to the 1800s now. If they hit Greeley with several hundred half-trained and half-starved fighters, Lee could only imagine how that would go down. The soldiers and Marines would likely stay on task. The less disciplined guerillas would get distracted by looting opportunities. The more time they spent trying to find food, the less time they'd spend reaching Lee's strategic objectives.

Angela looked pensively out at the hundreds of people standing outside of their vehicles, cluttering the roadway. "Do you think they know they'll be fighting for their lives in forty-eight hours?"

It was a strange thought, Lee supposed. For them, at least. It was easy to agree to a fight when it was in some nebulous future. But when the clock ticked down and it was go-time, the pucker factor would turn their guts to water.

"These are hard people," Lee said. "Let's not forget that. They've been through the wringer and come out swinging on the other side."

"Who you trying to convince?" Angela murmured. "Me, or you?"

Lee sighed. "Me, I guess."

"And are you convinced?"

He pursed his lips. "I don't have much of a choice, do I?"

No one spoke for a long moment.

Lee simmered over the logistics. Beans and bullets. By all reports, Greeley wasn't much better off. But they still held the advantage. They still held the fixed position, and even with Lee's numbers swelled from the last few settlements, they were now likely on par with each other, as far as fighters.

But Greeley had more food, and more bullets. Time was on their side, whereas Lee was up against the clock. The longer it took him to make headway into Greeley, the hungrier, and more dehydrated his people would become. Not to mention the vast majority of them would be out of ammunition in the first ten minutes of fighting.

If he had any other option, he might've taken it. Might have called a halt to the whole plan in favor of getting his army better fed, and better equipped. But where would they find it? They'd already emptied out as many Project Hometown bunkers as they had access to.

No, there wasn't another option.

Angela seemed to have shared his train of thoughts. "I guess it's like you always say, Lee."

He glanced at her. "What's that?"

Angela nodded grimly at their cobbled-together army. "It's do or die time."

TWENTY-SEVEN

LIBERATORS

THE RATION LINES IN GREELEY didn't give a shit if you were third shift. They were open from 10:00 to 15:00, and if you weren't there, then oh well.

Sam got in line just after two, which he hoped would give him just enough time to make it through the line before they closed promptly at three. The people running the ration line would close it down right in front of you, like they had urgent business elsewhere.

As hungry as he was, it was a sick, unappetizing sort of hollowness, rather than the type of hunger that makes you want to stuff your face. More the type of hunger where you plod into it, choking the food down because you know you need it.

And food wasn't what he was really here for.

Gabriella had called the previous meeting. And maybe she meant what she said, or maybe she was full of shit. There was no way for Sam to know. But he was relatively certain that the squad leaders he'd talked to at that meeting had no ulterior motives, and were genuine in their grievances with Greeley.

And Sam could work with that.

A ration line was a good place to foment revolt. No one liked having to wait for hours with their hat in hand. It made you start to think about inequities. Made you start to think about what you might be willing to do to correct them.

Sam's squad were distributed around the ration line, but not in it. They hung around street corners, and walked innocently around blocks, all the while keeping their eye on Sam, while he kept his eye on the crowd, and identified the people he was looking for.

Of the ten squad leaders at the meeting with Gabriella, Sam had noted that eight of them were third-shifters, just like himself. He'd reasonably intuited that they'd try to get in line for rations as late as possible to afford themselves the most sleep. And he'd been correct.

In fact, he'd already spotted all of the third-shifters. Except Nolan. Sam searched the line several times to see if he'd only missed the man, but no, Nolan wasn't there.

Well. That was fine by Sam.

As the line gradually shuffled forward, Sam waited for those squad leaders to make it to the distribution table, receive their box of rations—as squad leaders, they were permitted to receive the rations for their entire squad—and begin to walk away.

As the first of those squad leaders made it to the distribution table, Sam scanned the edges of the crowded parking lot and made eye contact with Jones. He gave Jones a single nod, and jerked his eyes meaningfully at the squad leader at the front of the line.

As the squad leader hefted a cardboard crate and turned away, Jones stepped out from the sidewalk where he'd stationed himself, and casually approached them.

Jones fell into step with the man. He was middle-aged, and had an early head of gray hair, and careful, watchful eyes. He saw Jones coming and stiffened up, but kept walking.

"What do you want, man?" the squad leader asked, a little defensively, perhaps wondering if Jones was going to try to beg rations off of his meager stash.

"I'm with Sam Balawi," Jones said, his tone calm and even. Not too secretive, not to loud. "I believe you met him last night."

A slight stutter in the man's steps. A cautious sidelong look. A slight tremor worked its way through the man's features.

"I don't know what you're talking about," the man stammered.

Jones ignored that—he'd figured it was coming. "You know the burned out three story office building over on the western perimeter?"

A swallow. "Maybe."

"Sam wants to meet. Tonight. Twenty-one hundred."

The man looked confused.

"That's nine o'clock," Jones clarified with a sigh.

"Look man, I don't know you, and I'm not going to meet anyone anywhere."

"Stop." Jones held out a hand like a crossing arm, forcing the squad leader to halt. Jones nodded in the direction of Sam. "Take a look."

The man blinked a few times, then turned slowly and cast his gaze down the ration line. Sam stood there, looking back at the squad leader. When their eyes connected, Sam gave a minimal nod, then faced forward.

"You can trust us," Jones said. "Something big is coming down the pipe. If you want to be a part of it, be at the burned out building at nine o'clock."

And with that, Jones disengaged with the man and walked back to his post.

By the time Sam made it to the front of the line, his squad had individually made contact with all nine of the dissidents he'd identified. Every time it happened, his heart had jumped into his throat, wondering if any one of them might cause a scene, but none of them did.

Were they willing to meet? How many would actually show up at nine o'clock? Would Sam and his squad be there by themselves? Or would they be met with a welcoming party of Cornerstone operatives?

Fortune favors the bold, Sam reminded himself, as a battered plastic crate half filled with mystery packages was pushed into his hands. *Gotta risk big to win big.*

He hefted the crate. It was light. Was this really enough food for an entire squad?

He smiled at the woman in the distribution line. "Thanks."

She barely glanced at him. "Yeah, sure. Move along."

***

In the waning hours of daylight, Captain Perry Griffin stood outside of the Tahoe in which he'd driven across half of America, and looked out into the distance north of him.

As it turned out, it wasn't hard to track Lee Harden's movements. On these dusty, abandoned roads, the passage of hundreds of vehicles was obvious. They left a wake of evidence behind them—tire tracks being the most evident, but he could see where they'd stopped, too. Wherever they'd stopped, there were footprints all over the place, criss-crossing and trampling over each other and through the brush on the sides of the road where piles of human shit could be found, swarmed by flies.

You couldn't hide the movement of an army.

And the more that Griffin had observed, the more certain he was that Lee had an army.

They had stopped here, Griffin could see. And smell.

Beside him, Mr. Smith pointed up the road. "It keeps going." The trampled brush to either side of the road—evidence of Lee Harden's convoy having stopped here—extended for quite a ways. "Fuck me. That's a long ass convoy."

"There's your missing people from Butler," Griffin noted, frowning into the distance. "And I think we can safely assume what happened to the people from Triple Rocker Ranch."

"How many do you think he has?"

"I don't know. Enough to cause trouble for Greeley, if that's where he's heading." Griffin waved a hand at the tire tracks. "And if his goal was to mount a decentralized insurgency, they wouldn't be in one big jumble." Griffin spat off to the side. "He's doing exactly what we did to him. This is his invasion force."

"Mostly civilians."

Griffin gave Mr. Smith a contemptuous glare. "So's the majority of Greeley's defenses at this point. The active troops that know their ass from a hole in the ground are right behind us. Briggs shoved them all into the UES and left himself open. We both know it, and so does Lee."

Mr. Smith ignored Griffin's look and put his hands on his hips. "President Briggs is aware of the situation. And he still has a large contingent of Cornerstone in Greeley." Mr. Smith nodded to the roadway. "Why'd they stop here?"

"Vici," Griffin said. "I've got it highlighted on the map. It's another settlement, a few miles ahead."

Mr. Smith's face darkened. "You think they joined up with him like Triple Rocker Ranch?"

"We won't know until we ask," Griffin said, turning back towards the convoy of military vehicles and technicals behind him. He stepped to the side of the Tahoe where Lieutenant Paige sat in the back, his arm out the open window. "Ron, get everyone mobile again. We're going to head right into Vici. Show of force. Guns out. Don't take any shit from anyone." Griffin held up a hand. "But no stupidity. Standard ROE—don't start shooting unless there's a threat."

"Roger that," Paige replied, settling back into his seat and grabbing the command-channel radio.

As Griffin piled into the front passenger seat and Mr. Smith went around to sit behind the driver, he could hear Paige disseminating the orders.

All down the line, the idling vehicles shifted into drive and started rolling north.

It was time to see where Vici's loyalties lay.

***

It was just after nine o'clock when Lee and the massive convoy behind him rolled into La Junta.

Lee stared out the open back doors of the MATV, his jaw slack with shock.

The road into La Junta was unguarded and open, but all along the streets, people had gathered to see the newcomers. As they caught sight of the giant snake of vehicles that stretched into the dusty horizon, Lee watched the faces of the people on the street come alive.

A handful of them started to clap. To holler. They caught sight of Lee looking at them and raised fists into the air, shouting things at him that he couldn't hear, but could only interpret by the fierce joy on their faces.

"These people think we're fucking liberators," Lee griped, only able to frown back at the crowds. His expression didn't seem to deter them. They simply turned their attention to the next vehicle in line—a Humvee that was following just behind the MATV—and started to wave to the bewildered Marines inside.

The one in the turret raised a hand to them and gave a demur little wave, like he wasn't quite sure whether to be friendly or hardassed.

"Aren't we?" Brinly asked, sitting beside Lee at the last set of jump seats next to the open doors.

Lee shot the old Marine a look. "We're not anything until we take Greeley."

Brinly smiled at him, despite Lee's sour disposition. "Just enjoy it, Lee. Might be the last time you get a pleasant reception from anyone."

Lee grunted irritably. "They can clap and cheer all they want. We'll see how many of them actually follow through on their promise to fight."

The MATV and the convoy behind it threaded their way through the city streets, towards where Abe had instructed them to set up camp. Unbridled by the constraints of a perimeter of high-voltage wires, La Junta seemed a massive sprawl for a settlement. They had numbers on their side, and used that as their defense against the small packs of primals that roamed the countryside.

All through the city—yes, this was still a city, shocking enough—pockets of civilians stood on street corners to watch them and to yell encouragement that Lee ignored. It was a symptom of excitement, nothing more. Excitement did not equate to readiness for battle.

But he supposed Brinly had a point—it was better than a cold, cautious reception.

There was a pattern to the locations where large amounts of people could be held. Back east, where fences were needed to protect against larger hordes of primals, airfields were an obvious choice. Inside the boundaries of a city, schools were the best option. Not too different from Butler, La Junta had chosen to host the influx of newcomers at the local high school.

Abe, along with a tall, bald-headed black man, stood waiting for them at the side of the sports fields, like a pair of coaches surveying new arrivals for tryouts. All around the high school, a massive open expanse of pale dirt and scrub brush occupied an area that must have been several city blocks.

While Lee's MATV and a handful of military vehicles parked themselves at the sports field, the rest of the cars, vans, SUVs, and pickup trucks packed full of armed people, weaved their way into the dusty acreage beside the school.

Lee climbed carefully out of the back of the MATV, eyes going over to the impressive dust cloud created by hundreds of vehicles winding their way through the open landscape, white headlights and red taillights flashing in the sandstorm they'd created.

"Looks like you brought the party with you," a voice sounded behind him.

He turned and looked at the man with Abe, as they stopped by Lee. The man extended one large hand, smiling.

Lee took it. "You must be Jonathan Reeves."

"Yeah, that's right. I keep this little burg running." Jonathan's dark eyes hit Lee's ruined one—he'd forgotten to put his eyepatch on. "And, judging by the fact that you look like an old, battered tomcat, I'm guessing you're Lee Harden."

Lee smiled. "I guess my legendary good looks precede me."

Abe stepped in. "Yeah, I told him you were a one-eyed gimp." Abe grabbed Lee and threw him into a brief embrace. When they separated he looked behind Lee and nodded respectfully. "Madame President. Major Brinly."

Angela and Brinly exited the MATV, Angela with Abby orbiting her and watching Jonathan Reeves with interest.

Lee stepped back and let Abe do the introductions. His own attention was caught by Abby again. She didn't stand in one spot, he noted. She kind of circled around the edge of the gathering, as though trying to take it in from as many angles as possible.

Finally, she came and stood next to Lee, as he was the farthest from the center where Jonathan and Abe were speaking intensely with Angela and Brinly. For a moment, the focus of those four people was so intense, it was like Lee and Abby had been forgotten.

"You trust him?" Abby asked, looking at Jonathan.

Lee watched her until she finally turned her gaze on him. Then he shrugged. "Trust doesn't have anything to do with it. In a way, Abby, at the same time that I don't trust anyone, I trust *everyone*."

She frowned. "That doesn't make sense."

Lee shook his head. "I trust everyone to act like people. Which means they're largely self-centered and opportunistic. This gentlemen?" He bobbed his head discreetly towards Jonathan, keeping his voice down. "I don't need to trust him as an individual. I trust that he's going to act in his own best interests. And right now, that means we're allies."

Abby nodded, as though in the midst of some burgeoning realization.

Lee sighed. Squared himself to the young girl. "Abby, you'd do better not to take life advice from someone like me."

He was surprised when she looked up at him as though she'd expected this. She even had a small smile on her lips. "If I want to live to be an adult, I'd do better to take advice from someone who's kept everyone alive."

Lee grimaced. Felt a strange sensation that he wasn't talking to a kid anymore. "You're forgetting all the people I've lost."

"You're still here," Abby noted, then looked back at her mother. "She's still here. I'm still here."

Angela looked over and seemed momentarily surprised to see Abby and Lee huddled together. Her brow creased for just a flash, but then she put on a smile and motioned him back into the circle.

Lee stepped forward again, and the circle parted to make room.

Jonathan, now acquainted with everyone, turned back to Lee. "Should I get some food prepared for your people? Water?"

Lee shook his head. "No, we've got our own supplies. You should use yours for your own people. Particularly in getting them mobilized. Which leads me to the next item of business: Time is short. We need to be on the move towards Greeley tomorrow. And there's a lot to plan between now and then."

Jonathan cast a doleful glance at Abe. "Well, it's a good thing your boy woke me up and made me pull an all-nighter." He rubbed his eyes. "What's another all-nighter? I can sleep on the road."

Lee allowed it with a smile. "We're going to need a place to meet. Just the command elements. You and two or three people who are going to be your second and third in command."

Jonathan gestured in the direction of the high school building. "The faculty's office, then. I'll gather my folks and meet you in there in, say one hour?"

Lee nodded. "That works. We'll be there."

TWENTY-EIGHT

RISK AND REWARD

SAM STOOD IN THE DARKNESS of the burned-out building, waiting. He had to resist the urge to pace. To fidget. To get some of this manic energy out of his system. But he needed to remain still and quiet. The building was abandoned, and the area was not frequented by the populace or the patrols, but even so, Sam feared being spotted.

It was almost full dark now. It had to be past nine. And still, not a single squad leader had shown up. Every single minute that ticked by sent Sam's mind into the same loop of anxiety, followed by rationalization and mentally talking himself down.

He heard Marie take a long breath in the darkness. He could just make out the form of her, standing near a support pillar, watching the entrance to the building.

"Should we head back?" Sam whispered.

Marie turned towards him. The ambient light from the outside barely cresting the side of her face. "Let's give them a few more minutes."

"What if something happened? What if one of them outed us?"

A long pause.

"Just give them a few more minutes," Marie repeated. "If no one shows in another fifteen, we'll call it."

"Why wouldn't they be here when we said to be here?" Sam hissed.

"Could be a good sign," Marie offered. "Maybe they're being cautious with their approach. Making sure no one is following them."

Sam hadn't considered that. His mind had naturally gone to the worst case scenario.

He was about to continue his worrying when a shadow flitted across the front entrance.

Sam and Marie both whipped around, staring at the silhouette of someone, edging their way into the darkness.

"Hello?" a man whispered.

"Yes," Sam said, stepping forward.

The silhouette jerked as it caught sight of him. "Shit. You scared me. Is that you? Sam Balawi?"

Sam peered at the figure, trying to catch sight of the features. "Who's asking?"

"Christ! You told me to fucking come here!"

Sam approached with caution, stopped a few paces from the man. He could just barely make out the face, but it was one of the squad leaders. "Yeah, it's me—Sam. There's a back room we can move to where we'll use some light, but we need to wait for the others."

"They're here," the man said. "Hang on."

He turned and stepped just outside of the entrance, then waved a hand over his head in two, big, obvious sweeps. Then lowered it. Stood there, looking out at the dark streets.

More figures emerged from the abandoned block of buildings, converging on the entrance. Sam counted them as he spotted them hustling across the street. Three. Four. Six.

The first man drew back into the building and the others followed him in, clustered worriedly around each other.

"Is this it?" Sam said, somehow both disappointed that not all of them had shown up, and thrilled that these seven had.

"Yeah," the first man said. "I didn't hear from the others. We're the only ones that are coming. That I know of."

"Do you trust the other ones not to say shit?" Sam asked, a bit sharply.

"Hell, I barely even know them, man. I barely even know *you*."

Sam nodded. "Fair enough. Follow me."

"What about your friend Nolan?"

Sam glanced at the man. "I wouldn't call us friends."

"Oh." It was difficult to tell in the darkness, but Sam thought he saw an odd expression pass over the man's face.

Sam frowned. "What?"

"Nothing. I thought you guys were friends. You seemed to know each other."

Sam kept watching, sensing that the man had more to say.

The man shuffled a bit. "Well, I saw him."

"Did you say anything?" Sam demanded.

"Well…I…uh…"

"Dammit," Sam spat. "You said something to him, didn't you?"

"I thought he was your friend!"

"Well, he's not! What did you say?"

"I didn't say much. Nothing really. Just asked him if he was going to see you later. You know? To see if he'd received the same invite that we'd received? I didn't tell him anything about the meeting or this place or anything. I swear."

Sam ground his teeth together. "And what did Nolan say when you asked him?"

"I dunno. He just kind of gave me a weird look. Like I was an idiot. And then he said 'no.' That's it."

"He didn't say anything else?"

"No. Nothing else. I swear."

Sam didn't particularly care for how much the man was "swearing." But at the end of the day, he hadn't outed Sam or this meeting to Nolan. He'd asked a relatively innocent question, and Nolan apparently hadn't pursued it.

"Alright," Sam growled. "No harm, no foul. Next time, let's not assume I'm friends with anyone, or that I trust them."

"Okay. That's fine. Sorry."

Sam turned again and continued on. Marie joined him as they picked their way through the darkness to a back room—some sort of receptionist's or security office. They moved carefully so as not to trip over the detritus all around the burned out frame of the building. Collapsed ceiling tiles gone mushy with water and rot. Wires and conduits hanging down, or protruding out of walls that had collapsed.

They felt their way into the back office, swung the door open and waited for the other seven to maneuver their way inside the cramped, dank confines that smelled only dimly now of ash. When they were all inside, Sam closed the door and Marie switched on a small, solar-powered light.

In the thick gloom, the low light was plenty to illuminate the gathering.

Seven worried faces watched Sam and Marie carefully.

"Was anyone followed?" Sam asked.

Glances were exchanged, followed by a round of shaking heads.

"Good." Sam fiddled nervously with his fingers. "I'm going to get right down to it. All of you have expressed a desire to do something about Greeley. I'm here to offer you a chance to put your money where your mouth is. Something is coming down the pipe—something big. It's an opportunity that we can take advantage of, and I fully intend to do that."

"What?" a woman asked. "What's happening?"

"I'll get to that in a minute," Sam said. "First thing's first. How serious are all of you about actually standing up for yourself and fighting back?"

He didn't get a very hearty response from that, but he wasn't sure whether they were hesitant out of caution and mistrust, or if they were hesitant about fighting.

The first man spoke again: "What do you mean by fighting?"

Sam looked at him sharply. "I mean fucking fighting. I mean picking up weapons and using them against Cornerstone in an effort to liberate this city."

"Liberate?" another man scoffed. "There's fucking seven of us. Eight with you. Even with all of our squads, that's only fortyish people. That's not enough to liberate a city."

"No, it's not," Sam conceded. "But what if you were a part of a much larger liberating force?"

"Who are you talking about? Are there others that are willing to fight? Others on the inside?"

Sam shook his head. "On the inside? No, it's just us on the inside. I'm talking about an outside force. I'm talking about…" he hesitated. Then: "An invasion."

Silence.

Followed by a quiet murmur from the woman: "Shit."

"Are you willing to fight or not?" Sam pressed. "If you're not willing to fight, then we leave right now, we keep our mouths fucking shut, and we never speak about this again. But if you're willing to fight, then we can keep talking."

"How big of an invasion force are you talking about?" another man asked.

"Big enough."

More silence as they digested that. But in the glow of the pale light, Sam could see some of the worry in their faces turn to hope. That was good. That was what he needed to see.

"I'll fight," the first man finally said. "I don't have a problem with fighting and killing. But I'm not gonna risk my life or the life of my squad for a lost cause. So I need you to skip over the bullshit right now and tell us straight up what we're talking about. Who is coming and is this a winnable fight?"

Rather than answer him, Sam looked to the others. "Do the rest of you feel the same way?"

More nervous glances. And then they all nodded.

It was time for another leap of faith. It was time for Sam to do what Lee could not—he had to trust these people. It was the only way to move forward. It was a big risk, but without that risk there would be no reward.

"I'm going to tell you guys," Sam said, his voice going low. Getting dangerous in its intensity. "But I will make this promise to you right now: If any of you fuck me over, I will find you and kill you. I can't put it any simpler than that. We're dealing with real shit right now. Life and death. I'm putting my trust in you guys. Do not fucking betray me."

"At this point?" the woman said. "We *can't* betray you. That would require us to explain why we were even here in the first place. And you all know how that'll turn out." Her face grew stern and sharp. "Those Cornerstone motherfuckers will kill us all just for having had this conversation. The risk of letting us go outweighs the value we have to them. We're nothing to them. We're just human trash being put to use."

"Alright then," the first man said after a few grunts of affirmation from the others. "We're in it. No matter what happens, none of us speak a word of this, if for no other reason than self-preservation." He looked at Sam. "Tell us."

Sam looked at each of their faces, hoping that they could see that he meant what he'd said, that he was not the one to screw over. "Lee Harden is coming."

At first, blankness, as they waited for something else. Then, confusion, as the name registered with them. And finally, shock.

Three of them began speaking at once.

"Wait. Here?"

"He's coming here?"

"That's impossible—he's dead."

Sam looked at the last one that had spoken. "He's not dead. I was face-to-face with him last week." He left out the part where he had spoken to him on the satphone recently. He only wanted to mete out the details that were absolutely necessary.

"Are you sure?" the doubter asked.

Sam actually laughed. "Yes, I'm sure. I've known Lee Harden since the beginning of all of this. I was with him in Butler when Greeley invaded."

"So that actually happened," the woman said, flabbergasted. "I thought it was just propaganda."

Sam shook his head. "I don't know what they told you guys, but the truth is, Greeley invaded the UES, and we were forced to retreat. But Lee Harden and several others in charge are still alive, and there are still hundreds of people that are allied with him, and that number is growing every day." Sam stabbed a finger towards the ground. "And they're coming here."

The doubter crossed his arms over his chest. "Hold up a second. Even if we accept what you're saying—that Lee Harden is alive and coming here—he's fresh off of getting his ass kicked out east. What makes you think he's not going to get his ass kicked by Greeley again when he shows up here?"

"Because they're undefended," Sam replied, evenly. "Briggs sank nearly all his military resources into that invasion. He flew them out there, but didn't have the fuel to fly them back, leaving Greeley guarded by a skeleton crew."

Realization dawned on the features of the squad leaders.

"That's why they got so desperate," the woman said. "That's why they conscripted us."

Sam nodded. "I think they have some inkling of what Lee is planning, and they're trying to hold off long enough for that army Briggs dispatched east to travel back from Georgia."

"That shouldn't have taken them this long. They could make that drive in a few days."

"But..." Sam raised a finger. "Brigg's army is trying to catch Lee from behind. Which is why they haven't returned to Greeley yet."

"Alright." The doubter pursed his lips. "I'll play along. You got six squads on the inside—seven, including your squad. I don't know what your background is, but ours certainly isn't military." He looked at the others and they nodded in affirmation—they were untrained civilians with guns. "And besides that point, the only time they give us rifles is when we're on guard duty."

"Right," Sam acknowledged. "But we know where the armory is. Chances are, at least one of us is going to be on duty when the attack starts. Which means we'll have at least one squad of rifles—maybe more than that. If we work together, we can take that armory. It's only guarded by a handful of Cornerstone, and they won't be expecting an attack from the inside."

The man that had arrived first spoke up. "What do we do if we don't have rifles? Throw rocks?"

Sam shook his head. "You let me handle that. Right now, I just need you guys to commit."

"What about casualties?" the doubter asked, looking suddenly uncomfortable with the prospect that fighting might include dying.

Sam stared at him for a long moment. He didn't want to lie to them, but he also didn't want to create unnecessary fear. Sometimes it was best to convince people of their invincibility. The United States military had been doing that with eighteen-year-old infantrymen for generations.

"It's a gunfight," Sam finally answered. "People are going to get shot. What happens when you get shot?"

"You die."

"Wrong," Sam snapped. "You keep fucking fighting. You know how much blood you can lose?"

Silence.

"You can lose about a liter before you're even in danger of losing consciousness. So think about what a liter of blood looks like, and if you haven't seen that much come out of you, then you have no reason to stop fighting." Sam took a breath. "If we hit them hard and fast, if we give them more extreme violence than they can withstand, the better our chances are of coming out of it with minimal casualties. The more we freeze up and hesitate, the more likely we are to lose people. So when we do this, we do it mean. We go into it bloodthirsty and angry."

The doubter seemed less doubtful now. But he still watched Sam carefully. Gauging him. "Have you ever done this before?"

Sam quirked his head to the side. "If you're asking me if I've ever been embedded behind enemy lines and taken down a city? No. If you're asking me if I've ever fought tooth and nail and killed others to stay alive? Yes. Several times. And I can tell you that the amount of aggression you choose to bring to the table is directly proportional to how many of your people are going to walk away from the fight. So don't hold back. You have to go all in."

The gathered squad leaders considered this in silence for a moment.

Sam was surprised when the doubter was the first one to speak up. “Alright. I’m all in.”

***

They slipped away from the burned out building around ten o’clock. They were as cautious exiting as they had been entering. When they were sure that they weren’t being watched, the group dispersed rapidly into the darkness.

Sam and Marie stuck together, hugging the shadows of the buildings. A bright moon was rising, peeking out from a thin layer of clouds that hugged the eastern horizon. It cast the buildings around them the color of bleached bones, the shadows sludgy and thickening as the cold light grew stronger.

“Still got an hour before shift,” Sam noted.

“Maybe you should get some sleep,” Marie said. “Stay at the flat. I’ll cover for you.”

Sam gave it honest consideration. His feet had that feeling about them—that low, chronic ache of having been on them for…how long had he been up and about? He’d lost track. His stomach felt acidic, his chest threadbare, his mind foggy. He could really use that sleep.

But he shook his head. “If it were any other time, I might take you up on it,” Sam muttered. “But right now is the wrong time to draw any sort of attention. I don’t want some Cornerstone fuck taking interest in our squad because we’re down a man.”

“You’re dead on your feet.”

“I can make it.”

"And what happens if shit pops off tomorrow?" Marie asked. "You gonna make it then? What'll that be for you? Forty-eight hours awake?"

It was a real concern. This wasn't just a question of toughness, and Sam knew it. He'd been sleep deprived before. It wasn't a wise way to enter into a battle. After twenty-four hours without sleep, your brain was as inhibited as it would be if you were drunk. Reactions were slow. Judgements were off. Logic fled and emotion took hold.

And forty-eight hours, you might start to hallucinate.

But what option did he have?

"Point remains," he sighed. "I'm not gonna do anything to draw attention."

"I'll tell them you ate something bad and you're shitting your guts out. I'm serious, Sam. Don't go on shift tonight. I'm officially mothering you. Be mothered."

Sam managed a weak smile at her. "What would we do without you, Marie?"

Marie just stared at him. "So, does that mean you're going to listen?"

His smile turned to a grimace. "Maybe I'll cut out early," he said. "After an hour or so, when we can be pretty confident that we're not gonna get a surprise inspection on duty."

Marie made a disgruntled noise. "Fine. I suppose we'll call that the compromise. One o'clock, then. I haven't seen a Cornerstone patrol after midnight, so if you cut out at one, you'll be safe. If they do happen to show up—which they won't—I'll tell them you got the runs."

"Alright," he acquiesced, too tired to argue any more. "I'll take that deal."

God, but he hoped he could actually sleep tonight. The thought of being in the flat alone actually sounded restful. Without the others there to worry about, to listen to their snores and their shuffling about, he might actually be able to turn off his anxiety for long enough to get some shut-eye.

As they rounded the corner to the street where their flat was, Sam pulled to a stop.

"What's wrong?" Marie asked, suddenly alarmed.

Perhaps it was the sleep deprivation muddying his thoughts, but he didn't quite recognize what he was looking at for a moment. Then he hissed out a "Ssh!" and put his hand on Marie's arm, pulling her deeper into the shadows with him.

What was it that he'd just seen?

They pressed themselves into a shallow alcove that had once been the entrance to a coffee shop. The glass doors were boarded up with weather-beaten plywood. He didn't know if anyone lived inside.

He leaned out of the tiny sliver of cover, revealing only the side of his face, which was still in shadows. Down the street. Down the sidewalk. The entrance to the apartment building.

There. That's what he'd seen.

Just a tiny hint of a rifle barrel, protruding. The toes of a pair of boots.

"Someone's standing at the entrance to our building," Sam breathed.

Then, a voice from further behind them shot straight into Sam's heart and froze it. "Sam!" the voice wheezed. "Sam, get your ass back here!"

Sam jerked to look behind him, and barely made out the shape of Jones, huddling behind a derelict dumpster, just a few paces from the mouth of an alley.

Jones's eyes shot out to whoever it was lurking at the entrance to their building. He put his hand out and waved, as discretely as possible, and then disappeared.

But it *had* been Jones, right? Sam's eyes weren't playing tricks on him, were they?

"Was that Jones?" he husked.

Marie seemed to have already come to that conclusion. She moved back towards the alley, towing Sam behind her and sticking close to the shadows. They hustled around the corner, threading themselves through the gap between the dumpster and the wall of the building, and then skidding around the corner.

Jones stood there, plastered to the side of the alley, his knife in his hand, his face sweating despite the cool night air, his eyes wild.

"They came for us!" Jones whispered harshly. "They're in the flat right now, waiting for you!"

TWENTY-NINE

PREDATORS AND PREY

SAM'S INSIDES were a slow-motion train wreck. Everything tumbling over and over, crashing into each other.

"What the fuck happened?" he said, numbly.

Jones's face contorted. "I just told you what happened!"

"I mean…" Sam fought for clear logic. "Where are the others? Were there shots fired?"

Jones shook his head. "No. I was taking a piss off that little balcony in the back when they showed up. I heard them ram the door open, and I just vaulted over. Tried to climb a drain pipe. It didn't work out."

Sam glanced down, saw that Jones's was holding his right leg slightly off the ground, not putting weight on it. Sam's hands went to his head, fingers like claws raking through his thick, black hair. "Shit, shit, shit! Did anyone else make it out?"

Jones shook his head again. "Pickell and Johnson are still in there. I heard shouting, but no gunshots. I think they're still alive."

"Who the fuck did this? Did someone dime us out?"

Jones fixed Sam with a hateful gaze. "My guess is that Gabriella bitch you were talking to! What the fuck are we gonna do now?"

Sam spewed curses, twisting his body back and forth, as though he wanted to run, but couldn't pick a direction. He got the sudden and alarming sensation that they were being pursued, and he slipped breathlessly to the corner of the alley and snatched a glance out again.

Nothing had changed. No pursuers.

One soldier—or Cornerstone operative, Sam couldn't tell—positioned just inside the breezeway. Three stories above, the window to their flat was dark.

Sam jolted back into cover. "How many?"

Jones shook his head. "I have no fucking clue, man! I jumped off a balcony—I was more worried about that!"

Marie approached Sam, holding up her hands. "Slow down, Sam. What are you thinking?"

Sam thrust a finger towards the flat. "I'm thinking we can't leave Pickell and Johnson in there!"

"We can safely assume there's a squad in there. At least five." Marie threw her hands wide. "There's only three of us."

"What about the satphone?" Sam demanded.

"What if they already found it?" Marie countered. "What if it's already burned? You wanna risk your life for that?"

Sam shook his head, though, in that moment, he thought that he very well could risk his life for a chance to recover the satphone, let alone his two squadmates. The more he considered it, and the more he juxtaposed it with disappearing into the dark and leaving them in the hands of Cornerstone, the more he was certain that his mind was already made up.

"We can do this," Sam urged.

"No, we can't!" Marie snapped, though she kept her voice down. "Are you fucking crazy?"

Sam grabbed her by her arms, pleading. "They're not expecting us."

"What the hell do you mean they're not expecting us?" Her eyes widened. "They're waiting for us right now!"

"No, they're waiting to ambush us because they think we're going to come strolling up like a bunch of idiots." Sam dove to his belt, ripped out his fixed blade. "I've got a knife. Jones has one. You have one. We can do this."

Marie searched his face for sanity and looked like she didn't find it.

But Sam could feel himself already hardening off to the risks and the consequences. He couldn't—*wouldn't*—let himself be beaten like this. If he ran, his mission was done. He would not have his satphone. He would not have his squad. He would not be able to coordinate. He would simply have to hole up and wait for Lee to rescue him.

He didn't even have to tell himself it wasn't an option. He knew it in his bones.

He looked at Jones, who seemed much more liable to do something crazy. Then at Marie. And he considered pulling rank, and telling her he was giving an order. But a leader doesn't need to say these obvious things. A leader simply leads.

"We're doing this," Sam husked with complete and total finality.

***

The Cornerstone operative wasn't really a Cornerstone operative.

Well, he supposed he was, *technically*, though he didn't like to think of himself as such. Really, he was a young reservist for the Colorado Army National Guard. But everyone was now lumped under the same command structure, and they were told they were now Cornerstone.

Whatever. It didn't make a difference. New boss, same as the old boss. Etcetera, etcetera.

He just liked to have enough food to eat. If you wanted to have food, and a safe place to sleep at night, well, you had to make some concession. So if they wanted to call him Cornerstone, that was fine. They could call him whatever they wanted, as long as they kept him fed and gave him a bed.

He stood at the entrance to the breezeway of the apartment building. Up above, his squadmates had taken down the traitors and were now holding them quietly in the darkness as they waited for the rest of the errant squad to show up.

Where the hell had they gone? It was less than an hour until their shift. They had expected them to all be present. But only two of the five were.

Had they gotten wind of this and bailed? But then, if they had, why would the other two have stayed? Besides, when they'd busted in the door, they'd seemed shocked as hell. He didn't think they knew it was coming.

So he waited. And as he waited, the tension in his body began to abate. He kept expecting to see the three missing squad members come strolling around the corner from whatever they were up to, but every time he looked out and they didn't show, he got a little more disappointed, and little more bored.

He was getting to the point where he was about to radio his sergeant and ask how long they were gonna sit here and wait, when he spotted a figure approaching from down the street.

It was a woman, he was sure of that instantly. The body shape, the gait—it was obvious.

Hadn't they said there was a woman in this crew? He was pretty sure that had been a part of their briefing. But the one approaching him now was alone. Not a part of a trio, as he'd expected.

He frowned as he watched her approaching, her head down, seeming not to take note of him. She didn't seem overly cautious. Wasn't even looking at the apartment—usually people looked at their destination.

He keyed his radio. "Hey, Sarge. Got possible contact down here. One female approaching. Standby. I'll let you know."

"Roger that," his sergeant replied, sounding similarly bored. "Let us know."

He angled himself in the entrance to the breezeway, so that only half of his body was sticking out, watching her carefully. Damn, but she sure as shit didn't seem too terribly concerned with anything. If she was a part of a crew of traitors, you'd expect her to be a little more circumspect.

But who knew, right? They were amateurs.

As she drew within a few paces of the breezeway, he stepped out, raising his rifle to a low ready but not aiming it directly at her. "You," he commanded. "Stop right there."

Her head came up as though shocked out of a daydream. She glanced around, looking confused. "I'm sorry. Did I do something?"

"Where you headed?" He stepped closer to her.

Her feet seemed rooted to the ground. "I was heading home."

"You a part of a guard squad?"

She shook her head. "No."

He took another step forward. He was now all the way out of the breezeway. He lowered his rifle and stuck his support hand out, waggling his fingers. "Lemme see your ID card."

"Oh. Right." She frowned, looking down at her pockets. "Hang on."

Her hands were in the pockets of a hoodie. She drew them out.

He tensed when she did, his eyes going to her hands. They were shaking.

His grip tightened on his rifle. But that was as far as he got.

***

It wasn't clean, and it wasn't pretty.

Jones snatched the operative into a headlock, and tried to ram the knife into the base of the skull, but the tip hit bone and the knife went slashing through the man's scalp.

Marie grabbed the rifle as the panicked operative brought it up. She jerked the muzzle out of the way, reached through and grabbed the buttstock, and pivoted away, taking the rifle with her.

Jones tried to drag the thrashing body backwards into the breezeway, even as his bloody hands tried to get a new grip on the knife. His forearm was clamped tight over the other man's mouth, but he was still screaming—it was just muffled.

Sam slammed into the man, just a half-second behind the others, and seized the man's right arm as it dove down for the holstered pistol on his belt. He pinned the arm to the man's side, his knife nicking at the man's ribs.

The man started to kick, trying to rear back and hit Sam.

Jones wasn't expecting the sudden movement, and as he was already dragging the man backwards, suddenly lost his footing and all three of them went down in a tangle.

Jones's knife left his grip and want clattering to the concrete.

Sam didn't know what to do, except stab as rapidly and deeply as he could. The man wore no body armor. And so Sam pinned his arm with his thigh and then, in a heavily steeped panic, began stabbing the man in the midsection, his arm pistoning back and forth with the stiff rapidity of a sewing machine.

The muffled screams became high pitched.

"Get him, Sam!" Jones hissed. "Fuckin' kill him!"

For a brief, dissociated moment, Sam felt like he was watching himself. The arm going back and forth. The stiff resistance of flesh against a knife point, which gave way almost immediately to a sickening, frictionless slide, until his fist hit the sodden surface of the man's torso, everything hot and slick.

He saw his own eyes, stretched wide in an animal panic, his teeth bared.

That's you.

"Slit his fucking throat!" Jones wheezed, barely able to hold onto their thrashing victim now.

Sam had heard that if you slit a man's throat he can still scream. So instead, he reached up and simply punched the knife into the man's right carotid, twice. Bright, almost neon arterial spray shot out, speckling Sam's face, warm on his lips.

Two squirts, and suddenly the pressure seemed to abate, like a hose with a kink in it.

The man's thrashing began to weaken.

Sam snapped his eyes to the breezeway, then up to the third floor. He half-expected to see the other Cornerstone operatives there, but the breezeway was empty.

Had they really managed to eliminate the sentry successfully? And without alerting the others?

The thrashing died off to random jerks. The eyes were unfocused, heavy lidded. The neck didn't spurt anymore, simply flowed, and even that flow was ebbing.

Jones still strained to hold his forearm over the man's mouth. His teeth shown in a savage grimace, every vein in his forehead distended.

"Let up," Sam huffed. "He's done."

Jones immediately released, went slack, and flopped back onto the pavement, panting.

The man, still not quite dead, waggled his head nonsensically back and forth, his sightless eyes gazing off into nothingness.

Sam tore his attention away from that face. Visually scoured the man's body. There—to the left of the dozen sopping holes that Sam had punched in the man's shirt—a radio.

It crackled as Sam reached for it.

"Hey, Mikey," a voice drawled. "You keyed up. You okay?"

Shit. They must have accidentally hit the transmit button during the struggle.

Sam reached for the radio, his hands halting as he saw how oddly red they were. Not just streaked with blood, but *coated* in it. Like he'd dipped his entire hand in red paint. If he didn't know that it was real, he would have thought it unrealistic.

His throat tightened. He pushed forward.

Grabbed the radio. "Yeah. Standby," Sam said, hoping that three syllables wouldn't be enough to clue the others into the fact that it wasn't their buddy speaking.

Sam staggered to his feet, finding himself surprisingly wrung out by the brief battle. But there wasn't time to rest. No time to adjust, or to think about what the hell he'd just done and try to come to terms with it. Pickell and Johnson were still up there, still needed their help.

Sam turned to Marie, who stood off to the side with a stricken expression on her face. Sam couldn't tell if it was worry, or guilt, or some strange amalgamation of so many differing emotions. He bent and scooped the man's pistol from his holster, checked the chamber and saw brass in it. Full mag.

"You ready?" he asked Marie.

She snapped her eyes up to him. Then offered him the rifle. "Swap. You're better with a rifle. I'm better with a pistol."

Sam didn't argue, simply traded weapons with her.

He turned to Jones, who was negotiating himself out from under the body. "Jonesy, give us twenty seconds, and then radio in. Sound scared. Ask for backup."

Sam locked eyes with Marie, then jerked his head towards the breezeway and the stairwell up. His pulse was a rampant stampede, his vision constricted. His whole core bore down in the center of him, as though clenching for a blow.

They moved up the stairs as quietly and rapidly as they could, first Sam, then Marie. Sam's legs felt wobbly, the sudden and massive expenditure of energy to fight the dead sentry leaving his muscles shaky and weak. The seconds ticked down, each landing a checkpoint in his brain as he drew closer to the top floor.

He stopped at the second level. Right at an apartment door that he knew was unoccupied. He tested the doorknob and found it unlocked. He pushed his way in silently, waited for Marie to huddle behind him, then eased it closed, one hand still on the knob, the other holding his rifle in a high ready.

He waited. Painfully. Now his muscles seemed to burn, to itch to move. His bladder suddenly spasmed, leaving him feeling like a little kid in a grim game of hide and seek, damn near close to pissing himself with tension.

He held his face close to the door, listening intensely.

The sound of Jones's voice, calling in over the radio—distant, and he couldn't hear the words exactly, but he knew it was Jones.

Then silence.

His heart slammed out the seconds.

The sound of a door above them wrenching open. The tumble of footsteps. A yelp of an urgent voice.

Boots, slamming down the stairwell.

Sam couldn't breathe. Everything in him was locked as though in one massive cramp.

The boots clattered past the door behind which Sam and Marie hid.

Almost…

The sound of them receding down the stairs to the ground level.

A shout.

Sam ripped the door open and shot out, leveling his rifle. He slammed his hips into the metal banister, leaning over. Shapes moving below. He brought the optic of his rifle to his eyes, an unfamiliar reticle hovering over the forms of three Cornerstone operatives as they vaulted onto the first landing below.

"Hey!" Sam shouted.

Their eyes shot up, their feet halting in surprise.

Sam's first shot plowed through a face, yanking the life instantly out of the body and causing it to flop down onto the stairs. He didn't let up—couldn't let up—just kept pulling that trigger, kept that rifle tight in his shoulder pocket as he traced his rounds to the next target, and the next.

Marie's pistol barked, dim in his already deafened ears.

The second operative fell backwards into the wall of the stairwell, trying mightily to bring his rifle up, though Sam's rounds had raked his shoulders and broke the structures inside.

The third operative took a handful of rounds from Marie, spinning around like he couldn't decide where to go to seek cover, until one final round punched the top of his skull and ended him.

Sam pivoted back to the second operative, just as he was sinking down to the ground—putting his back to the floor in order to get his rifle pointed upwards. Sam steadied himself and placed one round into his forehead, halting any further efforts.

"They're down!" Marie squeezed out with a clenched breath.

Sam threw himself off of the banister and mounted the stairs to the third level. His body felt both unstable and unstoppable in the flood of adrenaline. The lactic acid hit him hard, but he could barely feel the pain of it—only the rubberiness of his muscles.

The middle landing. The next flight of stairs. The final landing ahead.

The door to their flat hung open to his left.

He paused at the top step, feeling Marie cinching up close to him.

He sidestepped onto the landing.

He could see straight through that open door, to the back wall of the flat.

Johnson and Pickell, kneeling against the wall, their hands behind their backs.

Sam's eyes struck Johnson's. The other man's eyes widened, flicked off deeper into the flat—looking at the remaining Cornerstone operative? How many were there?

Sam raised his eyebrows, as though to ask the question.

Johnson's eyes went back and forth again—to Sam, and then to the operatives inside, then back to Sam once more. He made the tiniest motion—the barest shake of his head.

The walls of the flat seemed to shake.

A single rifle report.

The wall behind Johnson's head splashed with red, and Johnson fell sideways, dead.

Sam was almost too shocked to move, but then found his feet treading forward of their own volition. He'd seen the angle of that shot—Johnson's last gift to his squad. The operative that had fired the shot was deep in the flat, perhaps in the kitchen…

Somehow, in a flash, Pickell had hauled himself to his feet and then, with hands bound behind his back, he bellowed out a cry that seemed to know it would be his last, and charged into the apartment.

The sound of someone else shouting—alarm, panic—and a loud crash and clatter.

Gunshots ripped through the air.

Sam thrust himself through the door, Marie tight on his heels. By force of habit, he hit the corner hard, his rifle coming around, sweeping across the flat, searching for something to put bullets into.

One step in, one step over, but then he was still moving.

He couldn't see anyone, but he could hear the strangled cries of two people fighting.

A scuffle from the kitchen. The sight of a pair of boots, and Pickell's bare feet, tangled and thrashing behind the kitchen peninsula. Pickell had vaulted himself over the counter and crashed into the operative taking cover on the other side.

He'd given Sam a chance, and Sam couldn't waste it.

Another two gunshots. Sam perceived the rounds slamming into the ceiling above the kitchen, gouts of drywall dust spraying down.

He moved as fast as his feet were able, and yet it felt like he wasn't moving at all.

He plunged around the kitchen counter.

Two bodies.

And blood. Squirting. Painting the linoleum floor. Streaking the low parts of the cabinets.

The bodies thrashed, still fighting, so locked into combat that neither noticed Sam come into view over top of them.

They were on their sides, Pickell trying his best to use his legs to keep the operative pinned, because he had no arms to work with. The operative, sprawled on the floor, was angling his rifle towards Pickell's chest with one hand, while Pickell's bare feet, pale and white and odd in the gloomy interior tried to kick the rifle away.

Sam thrust the muzzle of his rifle like a spear. He slammed it straight into the temple of the operative and pulled the trigger—five rounds in the space of a single second.

He blinked once, almost surprised at the mess at the end of his rifle. Then he snapped back into the moment and fixed his attention on Pickell.

The Cornerstone operative was motionless, but Pickell was still squirming, a low, unending groan issuing from between his clenched teeth, his eyes cinched tight, tears eking out of the corners.

"Dammit," Pickell managed, craning his neck to look down at his torso.

Sam slapped the rifle down on the kitchen counter and dropped to his knees at Pickell's side. "Where are you hit?"

It was obvious, even as the question left Sam's lips. Pickell's torso was a mess, the fabric of his shirt dark, painting crimson smears across the floor. Sam spotted the single, small hole in Pickell's shirt, and smashed his hands down on it.

"Oh fuck!" Pickell gasped. His breath came in short gasps, and then he did something that sent Sam's mind swirling: he laughed. "Same damn place as last time," Pickell seethed, spittle flecking his lips. "Survive that, just to get…" he choked.

"Stop," Sam snapped. "Shut up right now. You're not gonna die."

"Sam?" Marie's voice behind him, the sound of her feet rapidly approaching. Then: "Oh, shit."

Pounding footfalls up the stairs.

Marie whirled, bringing her pistol up.

Jones scrabbled through the door, skidding to a stop in the face of Marie's muzzle. He still held the radio in his hand. Marie dipped her pistol, and Jones immediately turned his attention to Sam.

"We gotta go! They got a call in! Asked for backup!"

"I gotta stabilize Pickell first."

Jones shot around the corner of the kitchen peninsula. "We ain't got time for that, Sarge. We stick around here we're all gonna be dead. We gotta move to safety. Safety first, then we can fuck with Pickell's wound."

Sam knew he was right, but the decision felt rotten. Because he knew that Pickell was bleeding too fast.

"Same fucking place," Pickell marveled, his voice becoming less strained, more dreamy.

"Hey, I told you to shut up, Pickell!" Sam grabbed Pickell's shoulder and wrenched him onto his side. "Jones, gimme your shirt or something!"

Jones shucked his shirt off without questioning it, as Sam whipped out his knife and sawed at the plastic restraints around Pickell's wrists. The second they snapped free, Sam snatched Jones's shirt from his hands and stuffed it against Pickell's belly.

"You gotta hold pressure on your wound," Sam said. "Until we get to safety."

"Not gonna make it," Pickell said, almost resignedly. "God has fixed the time for my death."

"Oh would you stop with that shit!" Sam shot to his feet and hooked his hands under Pickell's armpits. "Jones! Grab his feet! Marie, get the satphone! And don't forget the rifles!"

Marie stuffed the pistol into her waistband as Jones and Sam hoisted Pickell up. Then she ripped the kitchen drawer out, sending it clattering carelessly onto the dead body crowding their feet. She bent down, looked inside.

For a brief, horrific moment, Sam thought the satphone would be gone.

But then she reached in. "Got it," she said. Then she grabbed the dead man's rifle up. "Let's go!"

The next few minutes were a blur of panic. Sam wanted to run, wanted to sprint into hiding, get out of the open before more Cornerstone troops got there to gun them down in the street, but he could only move so fast while burdened with Pickell.

Down the steps, tripping and stumbling, fighting to stay standing, Marie leading the way with the rifle up.

One landing. Past the dead bodies. Marie gathering up the rifles into a jumble in her arms. Stuffing magazines into her pockets. Down another flight. The last landing. Then the ground floor.

An engine roared in the distance.

"Around back!" Sam ordered, he and Jones stumbling out the back of the breezeway, away from the main street. Marie plunged ahead of them through darkness.

"Where am I going?" she demanded.

"Stay off the streets," Sam huffed, all his physicality straining under the weight of Pickell's body and the deluge of adrenaline. "Alleys and backstreets, stick to the dark. Get us to the hiding spot."

He didn't explain what the hiding spot was. Marie already knew. They were heading for the only place of safety they had: the burned out office building.

THIRTY

A GOOD SOLDIER

IN THE DARKNESS OF NIGHT, blood took on many hues.

Griffin stood near the center of Vici, his ears ringing with the ghosts of gunfire that had long-since ceased, and with the wails of those still alive that went on like a background hum. Wives grieving for husbands. Mothers grieving for sons. Sons and daughters for their dead mothers and fathers and siblings.

There were not many men left in Vici now. The women had fought too, and those that had lay with the men, strewn about the streets in whatever pose their body had collapsed to the ground.

In the darkness, all blood looked black. But in the piercing glare of Griffin's weaponlight, the many characters of blood shown clearly. The deep, gelatinous ichor of unoxygenated blood, seeping from opened veins. The neon glow of arterial blood from broken arteries, thick and opaque upon the concrete and blacktop.

Torsos skimmed and ripped by passing bullets spilled their pale contents. Skulls uncapped by large caliber projectiles, leaving empty and nearly-bloodless hollows behind, the gray matter now strewn about like thrown bowls of porridge.

Sightless eyes, scabbed over. Dry tongues lolling in open faces.

His countrymen.

Is this what it was like at Antietam? At Gettysburg? To look out at the wreckage you've wrought and known that you've killed your brother because he was trying to kill you?

The whole of it was more than Griffin could wrap his brain around, and so it became academic to him. A curiosity. A cause for reflection. Emotion was a dangerous thing, to be kept under lock and key, because so often it opposed what you were told to do.

What other course was there? He had not fired on Vici. They had fired on him. And he had responded. How else could he respond? Should he feel guilty because his hand was forced?

All those around him had chosen this as their last stand. Griffin could do nothing for them anymore. Their decision had been final. Surely they'd known it would be.

And many more had chosen not to fight. And they were the ones that filled the air with that scraping, keening noise that buffeted against him whenever his brain chose to focus on it, like wind in your ears that you never notice until you think about it directly.

Is this really what we've come to?

"Sir?"

Griffin snapped upright, realizing he'd been slouching, staring down at a man and a woman who had died, toppled over each other. He blinked away the haze of confusing thoughts and focused on the speaker.

Lieutenant Paige stood watching him carefully. And, perhaps, carefully ignoring the bodies all around them. Willful disregard. Not out of callousness, but out of necessity for one's sanity.

Griffin tried to speak, but the first syllable was a phlegmy croak. He cleared his throat. "Yes, lieutenant?" he said, oddly formal.

"We secured the north end," Paige said, his tone blank. The recitation of a report. Nothing more. "That was the last of the resistance."

"Casualties?"

"Two wounded, one dead. Fifteen confirmed kills." Paige hesitated, then added, "All of them were armed." As though he needed to absolve himself of wrongdoing.

Griffin nodded. "Anyone make it out?"

Paige sniffed, and his eyes betrayed him, taking one single glance downward. He hauled his eyes back up, as though to keep them from processing what they saw. "Yeah. One vehicle got outta Dodge when we closed in on where they were holed up. We fired on it, but if we hit whoever was driving, it wasn't enough to make 'em stop."

"Any idea where they were heading?"

Paige shook his head. "North. That's all I saw."

They stood, not exactly avoiding eye contact with each other, but not holding it either. Maybe they didn't like the look of each other in that moment. Or maybe they didn't want to see the fact that neither of them felt much about any of this.

Academic.

Griffin noticed Paige's demeanor shift as his gaze went over Griffin's shoulder. A flattening of the lips. A heavy-lidded focus, just short of a glare.

Footsteps behind him. Griffin didn't bother to turn. It was like he could smell the newcomer, or knew who it was by the sound of his feet. A certain, stomping, authoritarian quality to the tread. Self-assured and self-righteous. Boots that would pick their way through the bodies like you might casually navigate yourself around bags of trash left to rot.

The footfalls came to a stop, just to Griffin's right. He still didn't look, but despite that, an arm pressed into his view, the hand holding a satphone with the screen lit up green and heartless, the antenna extended alertly.

Griffin didn't immediately take the satphone, but instead dragged his attention around to face Mr. Smith. He looked into the other man's eyes and saw something different. Not the willful suppression of emotions for the sake of mental preservation, but instead the complete lack of them. Or, at least, the lack of any *negative* ones.

Mr. Smith looked vindicated. Satisfied.

The Cornerstone man arched an eyebrow and shook the phone like an impudent customer might shake an empty glass at a waiter. "It's the president."

Of course it is.

Griffin let his rifle hang from its strap and took the satphone. He pressed it against his ear. He could feel the leftover warmth and oily residue from Mr. Smith's own face.

"Yes, Mr. President?"

"Griffin," Briggs snapped, as though he'd been put on hold for an inordinate amount of time. "What's going on?"

"We've subdued the town of Vici, in Oklahoma. We have reason to believe that Lee Harden came through here. There was some…minor resistance. It's been handled."

"Has it now?" Briggs growled. "Because Smith tells me there's still an assload of insurgents standing around. Why are they still alive?"

Griffin's core tightened. Still no strong emotion. How could you have a physiological reaction with absolutely no mental connection? But the connection was there. Way down inside.

"Well, *sir*, those that fought back have been killed in the fighting. We sustained very minor casualties. The rest of the town has been gathered, but they're unarmed and cooperative."

"And did any of them join the fight?"

"I just told you, sir. They're unarmed and didn't fight."

"But they didn't help you either, did they? They didn't try to suppress their own townspeople when they were firing on your troops. Did they?"

"No. It appears the vast majority of them were just hiding and waiting for the fighting to be over."

"Because here's my fucking problem," Briggs continued, as though Griffin hadn't spoken. "I have zero reports—from anyone—that any civilian from Oklahoma, Vici or otherwise, called in or made any effort whatsoever to tell us that Lee Harden had come through their town. Their silence is evidence enough of their radicalization. Choosing not to fight the insurgents that lived right alongside them is still picking a side."

Griffin looked languidly at the gathering of civilians, painted in stark colors and deep shadows by the glow of many headlights that encircled them. "I have neither the time nor the resources to conduct an investigation into their motives, nor do I have the time or resources to take prisoners."

"I'm not asking you to take prisoners, Griffin."

"I came to Vici to gain intel on Lee Harden's movements and what he might be planning to do. At this point, I feel confident in saying that Lee is attempting—"

"I know what the fuck Lee's attempting to do!" Briggs nearly screamed, causing Griffin to wince and pull the satphone an inch away from his ear. "He's trying to swell his ranks and make a move on Greeley! It's fucking obvious! And those people gave him fighters, didn't they? *Didn't they, captain?*"

"I have no idea, Mr. President," Griffin responded icily. "I haven't spoken to them yet."

"There's no need for you to speak to them."

"Intelligence would be valuable."

"You're not hearing me, captain. So pull the fucking fluff out of your ears and listen to what I'm about to *command* you. I am the motherfucking commander-in-chief! The fucking buck stops with me! I'm the one that gives the orders, because I am the fucking President of the United States of America! You are my soldier, and you do what the fuck I tell you to do!"

"I'm aware of the command structure, sir."

"Exterminate the town."

A low hum, like a deep electrical current, trembled up Griffin's spine, all the way up until it engulfed his head and vibrated in his ears. He'd known this was coming. The humming sensation was not surprise or shock. It was the feeling of descent.

"That's not a lawful order," Griffin said.

And he assumed that Briggs proceeded to yell at him, but at that moment Mr. Smith snatched the phone out of Griffin's hand, giving him a withering glare, his lower teeth bared like a growling animal.

Griffin made no move to retrieve the phone back. He didn't want it anymore. He had a massive fucking problem, and talking to Briggs was only going to make it worse.

Mr. Smith was speaking now: "Yes, sir. I'll get it done."

The humming stopped abruptly. Griffin mentally slammed down, no longer descending—he had reached the bottom. The question was no longer hypothetical. It was in his face, right here and now.

He looked at Paige, but didn't really see him. His mind was consumed with the two possibilities. Two divergent paths, and he stood at their intersection, trying to determine which way to go, and what the two destinations would look like.

Defy the order. Yes, it was unlawful. No, there was no oversight. No military tribunal that would exonerate him. There was only Briggs, and his stranglehold on the military that was now more Cornerstone than anything else. He would be labelled a traitor. The destination was this: Griffin on the run, perhaps with others that refused the order, perhaps not. Maybe it would end in a fight between him and Cornerstone, or maybe he would make it out without bloodshed.

And then what?

Ally with Lee Harden? Betray his country?

He could barely even picture it.

Obey the order. No, it wasn't lawful. But that didn't matter anymore. The order had been given. If he obeyed it, he would die, not physically, but mentally. He would morph. Become something else he never intended to be.

But he'd never intended to be a traitor either.

"Sir?" Paige asked, bringing Griffin's watery focus back into the here and now.

"Captain Griffin!" Mr. Smith barked.

Griffin stayed locked into Paige for a moment. Paige had to have known what the order was. He could see it in the lieutenant's eyes. He could also see Paige's loyalty—not to Briggs, not to America, but to him. Paige would do what Griffin told him to do.

"Hey, fuckhead!"

Griffin turned and looked at Mr. Smith. The man's face was all contorted indignation and anger. Griffin considered killing him right there. One shot, straight to the dome. Mr. Smith would be no more. Griffin could deny that the order had ever been given. No one knew about that order except Griffin, Smith, and Briggs.

"You need to think real hard about what you're going to do right now," Mr. Smith seethed. "Because you were given an order. I intend to see that order carried out."

Yes, I have been thinking real hard.

Paige took a step forward. "Captain."

Wasn't this just how things went? Or was that weak of him to think? Where was his strength and honor? Was it aligned with command and control? Or was it aligned with doing the right thing? When had the two become opposed?

Civil war. That's all this is.

Had General Sherman felt this way when he'd burned his way through the South? Or had he simply done what needed to be done to end a terrible conflict as quickly as possible?

Who knows what their actions will lead to? How can you be so confident in your decisions when you never know what the end result will be?

Maybe General Sherman had been conflicted. Maybe he'd felt he was betraying his morals. But what he'd done had crippled the enemy, and brought a quicker end to a hellish war.

What was strength? Was it doing the hard thing that would garner the best results for all? Or was it sacrificing the many for the few in order to save yourself from future nightmares?

Was there even a good way out of this? Griffin didn't think so. But still…there had to be a third option. It couldn't simply be this or that. It couldn't possibly be distilled down to such simplistic terms: Betray your conscience, or betray your country.

Griffin cleared his throat, which turned into a racking cough, like his body had forgotten how to work properly in the midst of a mental struggle. When he regained himself, he didn't look at either Paige or Smith, but instead at the huddled masses in the center of Vici, surrounded by military vehicles, machine guns trained on them.

"President Briggs does not want these people to become insurgents," Griffin stated. "His concern is valid. So we will remove any way they could fight back."

"His order was to exterminate the town," Mr. Smith growled.

"And we will," Griffin replied, suddenly exhausted. "Lieutenant Paige. Mr. Smith. Have your troops round up every weapon and every cartridge. We're taking them with us. Gather all the food. We're taking that too. Drain the fuel from every vehicle in this place, and then disable the vehicles. When you're done with that, burn the town."

Paige's face was stricken. "You can't leave them without food or transport," he said, quietly. "That's just as good as killing them."

Griffin's face contorted into a snarl. "Would you rather gun them all down?"

Paige was silent.

Mr. Smith stewed, a nasty expression on his face, but he didn't fight back.

Griffin drew in a breath that shuddered in his chest. "Do what I ordered. Then burn the town."

***

In the small hours after midnight, Sam existed in a strange dissociative state.

Everything was dark. In the bowels of the burned out building, they didn't dare to flick on a light unless they were huddled in the cloistered confines of the inner office where they'd met before. But he avoided that place. His focus was outward, paranoid, rampant with the conviction that at any moment, the distant rumble of vehicles that he heard scouring Greeley, looking for him and his squad, would suddenly roar down the street outside and they would be surrounded.

Back and forth his consciousness went, unable to cling to any particular reality for long. The paranoia and fear would spike, and then disappear, and he would just be standing in the dark, wondering how he got there, looking at the approaching end of his life in a dispassionate way, as though it were a foregone conclusion.

He saw every action of his life, as though looking at a roadmap from a dizzying height, all the choices that he'd made, starting at the very point that a man named Lee Harden had shoved a pistol in his awkward, childish hands, and asked him if he knew how to use it.

Had he ever possessed any agency over his life? Or did the course of his life follow immovable rails set down for him by fate? Was this destiny? Was this God? Had he ever had a chance to go a different direction, or was he always going to end up in this spot?

Pickell's words lilted through the back of his subconscious, an accusation, a confirmation of what Sam had most feared: *God has fixed the time of my death.*

Pickell had taken courage from that belief. But for Sam, it was a terrifying concept. That he was simply born up on tides that he had no control over, whisked down the river of life without any control. Just another piece of human debris, floating wherever the river took him.

"Sam…"

The word took a moment to make it through his thoughts and into his brain. He knew the voice. Knew what the weak, whispering quality was. It was death. Coming for Pickell, who had arrived at that point in time that God had supposedly fixed.

He looked to his left, and in the darkness could just make out the forms. Pickell, laying against a support column, Marie sitting cross-legged beside him, her hand the only visible motion, gently stroking Pickell's head. A cold comfort for the dying.

Sam moved his feet. They seemed to be made of concrete blocks. He tried to move quietly, but seemed unable. They scuffed loudly through the charred debris of the burned out building. He knelt, his body shaky and weak.

"Yeah?"

Pickell's eyes were just dark, liquid spots. He thought Pickell was looking at him, but he couldn't be sure. He reached out and placed a hand on Pickell's leg.

Pickell appeared to strain, a minor movement in the darkness, as though he were trying to lean forward against the pain of his stomach wound. Then Sam felt Pickell's fingers grasp his hand. They were ice cold and clammy with sweat.

Their fingers wrestled around each other until Pickell managed to establish an awkward grip, and pulled Sam closer.

"Listen to me," Pickell whispered.

"I'm listening, buddy."

"Don't let this take you down. You're fucking..." a wheeze, a painful inhale. "You're fucking Sergeant Ryder. Don't you fucking forget it. Lee trusted you for a reason. He knew. He knew you could get it done."

What the fuck am I supposed to get done now?

"Don't worry about me," Sam husked. "You need to rest."

Pickell shook his head. "Don't be dumb, Sarge. I don't need rest anymore. This is my exit."

Sam felt himself get unreasonably angry. "You shut the fuck up. You're not exiting until I tell you that you can exit. So you just shut your fucking mouth and rest."

Pickell let out a sigh. His hand squeezed Sam's. "You're ridiculous, Sam."

Sam's mouth felt gummy. His spit turned to slime. He blinked and felt the coolness of tears on his eyelashes, and thanked the darkness that no one could see it.

"Exit stage left," Pickell said, nonsensically. "I've done all I could do. This is all good. It's all a part of the plan."

"I don't believe in a plan."

"Don't take it away from me, Sam."

"I don't…" Sam trailed off, feeling his throat constrict.

"It's what I need to believe in. Let me have it."

"Okay, Kosher Dill. You're right. I'm sorry, buddy. Sometimes I just struggle with the plan. That's all."

"Well…" a thready chuckle. "I'm not so much a fan of it myself right now."

"Then don't go along with it." Sam squeezed his hand hard. "Fight back. You're captain of your ship, remember that? Bloody but unbowed."

"Yeah."

A silence took them, and it lasted so long that Sam felt a stab of panic that he was holding the hand of a dead man. But when he squeezed again, Pickell's fingers moved under his.

"Sorry," Pickell murmured. "Don't know where I went there. What were we talking about?"

"You fighting back. Staying alive."

"Nah. That's not for me anymore. I've run my race. I'm good with it now."

"That's bullshit. You can't just give up."

"Hey, man." Pickell's voice was quieter. Just syllables on a breath. "It's gonna be alright. I…" Another lapse of silence. Then: "Oh, God."

"What?" Sam sidled closer, gripped Pickell harder. "What's wrong?"

"Oh, God."

"Hey. Pickell. Talk to me."

Another faint wheeze of a laugh. "Man. We had it all wrong."

"What? What did we do wrong?"

"It's all wrong. But…it's alright, man. He knows."

"Who knows?"

Silence.

A sigh.

"He knows we fuck it all up."

"Who? Lee?" Sam shook Pickell angrily. "Are you talking about Lee?"

"Hey, guys," Pickell said, his voice calm. Barely there. "Guys."

"We're here, buddy. We're all here."

"It's like…It's like a fungus."

Sam frowned at the dark shape before him, wished he could see Pickell's face. He clenched his teeth against any more words. All he could do was let Pickell speak. It was the only thing he could give him.

"You think you love it. But all it does is propagate itself. That's the whole fucking problem. That's why we always fuck it up."

Marie began to quietly shush him, as though his words were too unsettling to listen to.

"Oh, God," Pickell whispered again. "Damn. Wish I'da known."

"Shh. Shh. Easy now."

"Well…That's really kinda funny."

"Incoming."

Sam jolted at the single word from behind him—Jones's urgent hiss. The world swirled in Sam's vision as he turned to where he knew Jones was stationed in the darkness. Small details whirled and melted. Tears in his eyes.

He shot to his feet, raising his stolen rifle. He could just make out Jones's form, slightly backlit by the ambient glow of starlight outside. And further beyond, in the street, a single figure, hustling toward them in a stooped scuttle.

The second that figure breached the interior of the building, Jones hurled himself from the shadows, grabbing the newcomer by the back of the neck and throwing them to the ground, the muzzle of his own rifle jutting into their face.

"Easy!" came the single-syllable yelp. Hands upraised.

Sam had already crossed the distance—hadn't even been aware he was moving until he stood over top of Jones and the person on the ground. He didn't dare flick his weaponlight on—any illumination in this open area could give them away.

"Name, motherfucker!" Jones seethed, all the ire in his voice straining against the low volume he kept.

"It's me!" A man's voice. "It's Evan!"

Evan.

Sam's mind circled the name like a wolf might circle a scared rabbit. Only after a few moments of silence did he lower his rifle from pointing between the two dark pools of the man's eyes.

Right. Evan. One of the squad leaders. One of the rebels.

"The fuck are you doing here?" Jones demanded.

"I…I thought you might be here."

"That doesn't answer my question, asshat! Who sent you?"

"No one sent me!" The man's voice was raising. "I came alone!"

Sam shook himself out of his stupor and nudged Jones with his knee—calling him off from further aggression. "Evan, keep your voice down."

"Sorry," came the whisper.

"How'd you know we were here?"

"I didn't. I just guessed. I heard what had happened—shit! Everyone's heard! Y'all kicked the fucking hornet's nest! They're out to get you guys! They pulled the big red handle, man! What the hell were you thinking? Is it happening? Is Lee coming?"

Sam frowned in a sudden welling of suspicion, though he kept his eyes wide to soak in the minimal light. "Who sent you here?"

"Christ! No one sent me! I heard what had happened and thought maybe you guys were doing…the thing. You know? I thought maybe you'd started and…and didn't tell us?"

Jones looked up at Sam. He couldn't read Jones's expression, but he gave a shake of his head, and that seemed enough for Jones. He retracted his rifle from Evan's face, then seized the man's arm and hauled him up to his feet.

"You said you came alone?" Sam pressed, his eyes shooting out to the street beyond, looking for any other tell-tale movement. Perhaps Cornerstone troops circling, closing in on them. But all was dark and quiet. Quiet, that is, save for the distant sounds of the buzzing hornets' nest they'd kicked.

"I swear," Evan pleaded. "I'm alone."

"Why aren't you on shift?"

"I don't have shift tonight!" Evan's voice was defensive. "I'm off!"

"Where are the others?"

"I don't know. On shift, maybe? What happened?"

Sam leaned close—close enough to smell the man's cool sweat. A strange, foreign musk. "Someone talked."

Evan stared for a long moment. Then his head turned back and forth between Sam and Jones. "Wait. I didn't say shit. Are you accusing me?"

"Should I be?" Sam snapped back.

"Fuck no! I didn't say shit to nobody!"

Nonsensically, Sam thought, *double negative—so you DID talk!* As though they were children on a playground, playing with pedantic turns of phrase. He shook his head as though the thoughts were cobwebs he needed to free himself of.

"Alright, chill out," Sam husked. "Shit's just out of control. We don't know who to trust right now."

"You can trust me."

Like hell I can, Sam thought, but kept it to himself. "Someone talked, Evan. I need to know who."

"Well, I don't know!" Exasperation. "It could've been anybody! But…it wasn't me. I swear."

Jones made an ugly grunting noise. "Yeah, you keep swearing."

"Look." Evan seemed desperate. "I know y'all are on edge. I'm just trying to make y'all understand it wasn't me. I'm with you guys. I'm here."

"Alright, let it go," Sam growled. "If we thought it was you we'd've already killed you. So relax. We still need to know who talked. Do you have any idea who it was? Anybody say some weird shit after we met? Did anybody even *act* weird?"

As much as Sam could see in the darkness, Evan seemed flummoxed. "Hell, man, *everybody* acted weird after that meeting. How could we not act weird? Everyone was fucking keyed up out of their minds. This is big shit."

"But did anyone seem suspicious?"

A long pause.

"Not any of us," Evan said, quieter now. "But…"

"What?"

"I don't think anyone's heard from Gabriella."

There it was again. That ugly, most likely possibility, rearing its head. Why did Sam keep pushing it under like he was trying to drown it?

Because you trusted someone. You trusted Gabriella. And you don't want to admit that it was a giant fucking mistake.

Lee had told him not to trust anybody. Sam had seen it as a necessary risk. But hindsight is always 20/20. ·Necessary risks became tragic mistakes at the whim of the wind. Gotta risk big to win big, except for when the big risk results in a big loss.

"What are we gonna do?" Evan whispered.

Rather than answer, Sam turned away from him. Found his eyes tracking through the darkness to where Marie huddled over Pickell. Their forms were still. Quiet.

"I need to make contact," Sam said, moving now towards Marie. "I need the satphone."

He stopped, just over top of Marie and Pickell. She seemed not to have heard him.

"Marie," Sam repeated. "I need the satphone."

A soggy sniff. The barest hint of motion. Her hand, moving to her side. Then extending, the satphone in it, offering it up to Sam. The starlight from outside caught on her face in silvery streaks.

He didn't reach to take the satphone. His hands felt numb. His whole body felt like it was collapsing in on itself. A physiological reaction, before his brain even came to terms with what his subconscious already knew.

Marie drove it home to him in two breathless words: "He's dead."

THIRTY-ONE

FAITH

THE PEOPLE OF LA JUNTA had been more than generous. Despite Lee's admonition to Jonathan Reeves *not* to wipe out their food stores on feeding Lee's cobbled-together army, many of the residents of La Junta had come of their own accord.

People offered up what they could afford to, as a sign of welcome. Not just food, but many people gave blankets, cots, pillows, hammocks, and even a few small mattresses, as it was obvious that Lee's army slept in their vehicles. They'd grown accustomed to the discomfort of this, but the gesture was appreciated.

There was a strange atmosphere in the place. *Festive* wasn't quite the right word. There was too much anger in it. Too much hunger for vengeance. But there was a hope to it. That was what Lee's army had brought with them. That's what they'd given the people of La Junta.

A sudden light at the end of a dark tunnel that everyone thought they would be wandering in for the rest of their miserable lives. Lee had brought them the possibility of something better.

And that troubled him.

He lay awake in the room that had once been the teacher's lounge of the school they were housed in, reclined in an office chair, with his feet propped up on a large circular table covered with a haphazard collection of maps. Some of them were ripped from atlases. Others were even hand-drawn. They all centered around Colorado, and Greeley specifically—particularly the hand-drawn ones, as they hadn't found a real map of the city that had any detail to it.

On the largest of these hand-drawn maps, rendered partly from Abe's memories of Greeley, and partly from Sam's intelligence reports, a scattering of chess pieces stood—black for Greeley troops, white for Lee's army.

It was these Lee found himself staring at as the hours stretched towards midnight.

That same, quiet, irrefutable fear working its way through his mind, the very same fear he'd had when he was trying to save Butler from its inevitable fall: *It's not enough.*

The people of La Junta, and before them, the people of Lakin, and Cass's people from Vici, were operating on the hope of this promise that Lee had given them, though he'd never really promised them anything. They believed in it nonetheless—that he would win. That he would take down Greeley. That he would end the adulteration of their country, and bring it back to what they remembered from better times, before the world had gone to shit.

He'd only ever promised them a fight. And a fight they would have. But they, perhaps reasonably, believed that Lee would not have undertaken this effort unless he was relatively confident in the chance of victory.

And that's where they were wrong.

Lee was doing this because there simply wasn't another way. But he knew, quietly, secretly, never-to-be-breathed-aloud, that their chances of victory were slim.

Abe knew this secret. And it was likely that Brinly did as well. To an extent, he felt that Angela knew it too. But to breathe it, to give it life by articulating it, was somehow *verboten*. It seemed that they'd all silently agreed to that.

A quiet snuffle of breath drew his attention away from the chess pieces.

Across the room, a pile of figures lay on a series of less-than-comfortable-looking couches.

Deuce shifted around in his sleep, as dogs are prone to do, huffing loudly as he situated himself against Abby. Deuce had made friends with her, as soon as he had discovered Abby could be coerced into giving him bits of food. Abby was only too happy to do it in order to secure her own needs, which was a warm, soft body to cling to in her sleep. A symbiotic relationship, newly born.

Deuce, pressed against Abby, who held him with one arm, still asleep despite the dog's repositioning. And Abby, curled up against the back of the couch, her head on her mother's lap.

Abby had learned to sleep through anything. Kids already had an uncanny ability to do that, but Abby had adapted to all kinds of terrible things. Uncomfortable sleeping arrangements and constant danger were just a few of the things that didn't seem to keep her awake.

Angela, though, slept on a hair trigger, and had come awake with Deuce's stirring. She blinked heavy eyelids, looking down at Abby and Deuce. Her hand on her daughter's shoulder, just like Abby's hand was on Deuce's flank. Her fingers moved, stroking Abby's blonde tangles a few times.

Lee watched her closely as her eyes began to drift off again.

She must have felt him watching her. She glanced up, eyes coming partially awake again, and connected with Lee from across the room. Neither of them shied away from the eye contact. They held it, a whole history passing between them in that protracted moment. A strange intimacy that had grown from shared pain, shared triumph. Experiences carved into their bones.

The moment was shattered by the sharp chime of the satphone.

Lee's core tightened, sending a tremor through the table where his legs were propped. A few chess pieces toppled over.

It had to be Sam. But it was midnight. The timing was all wrong. He should be on his guard shift.

Lee jerked forward from his reclined position. Boots hit the floor. He snatched up the satphone, thumbing it on and pressing it to his ear. He didn't say anything, fearing in that moment that the satphone had been discovered by Greeley, and if he said his name, it would doom Sam to a firing squad…

"Lee?" It was Sam's voice. Quiet. Strangled. Madness lurking underneath that single syllable.

"Sam. What's wrong?"

Angela came upright in the couch. Abby moaned softly and stayed asleep, but Deuce perked up, watching the two wakeful humans carefully.

Angela's expression was one of waiting for an explosion to go off.

A shush of breath in the microphone. It shuddered. Trembled. "I fucked up."

Lee's mouth went dry. His face felt cold. All the blood rushing out of his extremities and gathering in his hammering heart. "Alright. Just tell me what happened."

"I had to, Lee. I didn't have a choice. If I hadn't trusted somebody, we wouldn't have been able to get people to rebel. But it…fuck me, it backfired."

Lee's jaw clenched. *Oh, dammit, Sam! I told you not to trust anyone!*

"We got outted. They came for us. Johnson and Pickell are dead. It's just me and Jones and Marie. We're hiding out, but I don't know how much longer we have. They're looking for us right now. We…we killed some of their people to get away, and now they're tearing the fucking city apart looking for us."

"Alright, alright. Take a breath, Sam. We'll figure this out."

Angela rose up from the couch, padded closer, all the tense muscles in her face giving her a haggard appearance, as though she'd aged twenty years in ten seconds.

"How long do you think you can hold out?" Lee asked.

Hesitation. "I don't know. We have a decent hiding place. The people looking for us, they haven't gotten close yet. But I think they will. We, uh…we have weapons. And there's at least one other squad leader that knows we're here. He's with us now."

"Do you trust him?" Lee said, unable to keep the bite out of his voice, and hating the accusation that it leveled on Sam.

Silence for a long protracted moment. "I don't trust anybody right now."

Lee closed his eyes. "Do you think you can hold out until tomorrow night?"

"I don't know. Maybe. Yes. Yes, we can hold out. I have no fucking clue when they're going to find us, but we can lay low."

"This guy that's with you, the other squad leader…I know you don't want to trust him, and I'm not saying you should, but can he help at all? Is there a way to use him without putting yourself in too much danger?"

"He already knows where we're hiding. If he decides to screw us over? Well. Then we're screwed. So I don't know how to answer that question, Lee. Am I supposed to trust him? Just…Just tell me what to do here. I need you to tell me what to do."

"Alright. Gimme a second…"

Lee smashed his hand over his mouth. His palm was clammy. He stared at the maps, at the chess pieces—*not enough*—and tried to conjure some way out.

Lemons out of lemonade. That was Lee's only option. At this moment, according to Sam's report, Greeley was ass-over-heels, trying to find a group of rebels in their midst. Yes, Sam's life was on the line. But so was everyone's. The fact remained: Greeley was as distracted as they would ever be. While they were hunting for Sam, their attention was turned inward.

Lee had already planned to mobilize on Greeley within two days. What did it matter if he had to move that up a single day? It would take advantage of Greeley's momentary distraction, and if they hit hard enough and fast enough, they could take the heat off of Sam at just the right moment, allowing Sam to do his work from inside.

"Okay, listen," Lee said. "We're mobilizing at first light. We're coming. We're gonna be there by nightfall tomorrow. Less than twenty four hours—" *Oh God, are we really doing this?* "—you can make it that long. *Do not* tell this other squad leader when we're going to be there. But tell him to get whoever he can that's willing to stand up and fight with you. Your hiding place—how many people can you jam in there?"

"As many people as we can get. It's big enough."

"Good. See if you can't assemble a strike team there. Be ready by nightfall tomorrow. You'll know when we hit. Do you have a target?"

"Yes. An armory. I think we can take it…if I get enough squads to help. But Lee, what if someone fucks us over again?"

What if, what if, what if.

"Be ready for it, then. Hope for the best. Prepare for the worst. The only other option is that you kill this motherfucker that's in your hide with you and lay low." Lee frowned deeply. "You're the man on the ground, Sam. You tell me: Is that what you need to do?"

There was a long moment where all Lee could hear was Sam's steady breathing.

"No," Sam finally said. "No, we came here with a mission, and I'm gonna fucking get it done."

"Don't go all heroic on me. Use your head, not your heart. Don't tell me you can get it done if you can't."

"I can get it done."

"Alright, then those are your orders, Sam. Gather who you can. Set your sights on that target. If anyone even looks like they're getting cold feet, you take them out. You understand me? No moral wrestling. We're beyond that. There's too much at stake."

"I understand."

"Then you know what you need to do." Lee felt his stomach squirm around inside of him like all his guts had turned to live snakes. Was he feeding Sam to the wolves? Should he backtrack and tell Sam to just lay low?

It's not enough.

Lee was already against the clock, with less resources than he wanted to have, about to take on a mission that only had a distant glimmer of a chance at success—that ugly truth that none of them could voice. He needed every edge he could get. And Sam was an edge.

"I'll try to call you right before we hit," Lee said, his voice feeling mournful in his head, as though he'd already committed Sam to dying. "But if I don't call you for some reason, you'll know when we hit. You'll hear it. We're gonna come in hot."

"Alright. I got it. I'll get it done."

"I know you will."

But Lee hung up that satphone, knowing that it was a lie. He couldn't know anything at this point. He'd spoken out of a faith he didn't feel. He'd said it for Sam's sake. He'd told the kid what he needed to hear.

He looked up at Angela. “Timeline’s changed.”

She nodded. “I heard. Should we get everybody up?”

Lee shook his head. There was a part of him that wanted to displace some of this exhausted anxiety onto others, to get them up, to get them ready, to diffuse some of the energy. But there wasn’t any point to it. Let them sleep with the blankets and pillows that the people of La Junta had provided them. Let them get one more night of rest. Only God knew when they’d get another chance.

“No,” Lee finally said. “Let them sleep. But I’m gonna need Abe and Brinly.”

Angela nodded again. “I’ll get them.”

***

Sam somehow managed to doze off. That was pure biological imperative. He did it by fits and starts, leaning up against one of the columns, his arms crossed, chilled by the midnight air, but brain inflamed with every permutation of the next hours of his life, and whether or not there would be more after that, or even if there would be that many, and whether or not he could somehow save his squad from that same destiny, or if their fates had been inextricably linked with him.

Then he realized he’d fallen asleep standing up. Though his mind picked up the thread right where it had left off—or perhaps it had never stopped pondering it—he still felt the blessed heaviness of his eyelids, that dissociative apathy of the weary. And so he slid down until his butt was on the cold ground.

And he fell asleep again. And he awoke again, and this time curled onto his side.

It was in this position that he was nudged awake by Jones. His first instinct was to touch the rifle at his side, and as he did he had a strange, contradictory moment where he felt immense relief at the presence of the weapon, and a soul-deep abhorrence that he so badly needed it in the first place.

"Evan's back," Jones whispered.

Sam came upright, looking outwards into the semidarkness. Everything seemed oddly quiet, giving it that breathless, pre-dawn feel. Too early for birds. Too late for insects. Most notably: no engines roaring back and forth; no obvious signs of a search happening.

Evan was picking his way through the office building. His movements looked tired, and yet all Sam could think, pitilessly, was *Welcome to the club.*

He stopped in front of the crouched form of Jones, and the still-sitting form of Sam. Evan's expression wasn't clear, but it was obviously not a happy one. Numbly, Sam waited for the bad news to be leveled on him.

"Everyone's scared shitless," Evan finally murmured.

"Shocker," Sam grunted.

"They're going house to house right now, looking for you, starting in your section and moving out."

Well, that explains the lack of engines. They're on foot.

Had Sam made a stupid mistake in telling Lee that he could make it twenty-four hours? Sure, it was a little less than that now. But as pissed off as Greeley seemed, Sam genuinely wondered if he'd live to see Lee's assault.

And in telling Lee that he could handle it, he'd doomed Jones and Marie to his same fate.

"How close is Greeley to getting here?" Sam asked, picking crust out of his eyes, too tired for emotion.

"I dunno. Maybe by midday?"

"Well, that's not going to be enough time." Sam raised his head, frowned into the darkness. "Is Marie awake?"

He saw movement—a waved hand. "I am now, with you assholes talking."

"Might want to join us."

Marie rose silently and walked a bit clumsily over to them, where she promptly sat herself cross legged next to Sam.

"Evan." Sam returned his attention to the man, who had squatted down in front of them. "You say the other squad leaders are scared shitless. Does that mean…?"

"Um." A cringe. "They're not coming. They barely let me in the door to talk to them."

"I see. Any way to change their minds?"

"They're scared of Gabriella. Scared of some of the other squad leaders that say they've seen them talking to you guys."

Fucking Nolan.

Sam had no hard evidence to prove that point. Maybe he was letting his own personal dislike of the man cloud his judgement. But who else would it be? Who else had known about Sam, but not come to the meeting in the office building?

Fucking Nolan.

Sam pondered all of this for a long moment of silence. He was so tired of trying to see into the future. So tired of playing this chess game, trying to guess three moves ahead of his opponents. He was tired of sneaking around.

To die while sneaking around felt like the greatest antithesis of his life. Or perhaps the most bitter culmination of his own self-fulfilling prophecy—*You can never be scared again.* Everyone around him had died because of his fear, his sneaking around. When was he going to rise up and take the fight to the people trying to kill them? When was he going to stop hiding under the damn stump in the woods, clutching a weapon that was useless if it wasn't being used to kill those trying to kill him?

"They don't trust me," Sam said. Not an accusation, as he didn't trust them either. Simply an observation. "So it seems to me that we need two things right now: We need to get Cornerstone off our back, and we need some faith."

"Faith in what?" Marie asked.

"Faith that they're not gonna be hung out to dry. Faith that their best chance of survival is to fight, and not to hide." He looked at each of his companions. "We only need to give them enough faith to make it to tomorrow night."

"And if we can't convince them?" Jones put in.

"Then we make them terrified to betray us." Sam let that statement hang for a moment, then hauled himself to his feet. "What time is it, Evan?"

"It's around three in the morning."

Sam nodded, hating to be standing. Wishing he could lie back down and go to sleep and wake up in some easier day, where he was relatively safe, out from under the constant threat that loomed while you operated behind enemy lines. To him, in that moment, Lee's assault was home. He needed to get there, to have those lines of friendly troops sweep over him, so that he could be home again. So that he could close his eyes and sleep without a background of terror gripping his mind the whole time.

But not yet.

He looked around him at the defunct office building. Surely it would contain what he needed. "I need markers. Pens. Paint. Anything that we can use to write with."

The others just sat there, bewildered by the off-the-cuff statement.

Sam started working his way towards the closed in office that had suffered the least fire damage. There had to be something in there.

"What do we need those for?" Jones said, rising to his feet.

"So we can send a message," Sam replied. "To help those squad leaders have a little faith." He stopped and looked over his shoulder at them. "But we're gonna have to kill some people too."

THIRTY-TWO

PIECES

EVERYTHING MIGHT HAVE TURNED OUT DIFFERENTLY if Lee hadn't waited to get his ragtag army on the move.

It might have been different if he'd seen the little sedan barreling towards La Junta, and maybe had a chance to intercept it.

Things might have been different if Lee had been able to get to the occupant of that sedan before the news started slamming through their camp like a shockwave from a bomb blast.

Lee had all of those thoughts in the moments immediately after it was too late to do anything about it. But things weren't different. Things were the way they were.

Even as Lee exited the weary tension of his meeting with Abe and Brinly and Angela, it was happening. Stepping out into the cool, dry morning, the stars already disappeared and the sky turned cobalt in the east, all of this seen through his single eye that ached deep in the back of its cavity, it was all hurtling towards him, unstoppable.

Even as Brinly and Abe dispatched their second-in-commands to begin the process of disseminating the orders—Get up, get your shit, be ready to roll in one hour, it's going down—the first sliver of sunlight caught on a distant dust cloud.

As the hush of the encampment turned gradually to the rumble of so many hundreds of people murmuring to each other, stretching legs, wincing at aching backs, taking a morning piss, asking what was happening, is it really going down, are we really doing this, why so sudden?—that little dust cloud culminated in the shimmer of dawn light across the roof of a sedan, hauling towards La Junta, and spotted by a perimeter guard.

As the three miles that separated the sedan and La Junta dwindled, Lee stood over a low, smoky, fire, a soldier in mismatched fatigues breathing life into last night's embers.

As the guard on the perimeter shouted to his buddy down the way, and his buddy used his crappy little two-way radio to call their shift leader, Lee and Abe looked down into the first little tongues of flame, smelling the familiar wood smoke, deliberately ignoring each other's gaze as they spoke in muted tones of the only things they had any control over:

"What's the ammo count for your people?"

"Everyone's fixed with two spare mags, one in the gun."

"I want every man in your outfit to have at least six mags total. I don't care who you have to take 'em from, just get them."

"Alright."

"Sidearms?"

"Couple of Breck's guys. But mostly no."

"Track down some ordnance. I want Breck and Menendez's guys to be rolling fat and heavy."

"What kind of ordnance you thinking?"

"Get 'em ready for house-to-house. All the frags they can carry and still run."

"Sure hope all these civilians can handle it."

"Yeah, me too."

"Well. What we lack in training, we make up for in numbers. Hopefully that counts for something."

"Hopefully."

As the perimeter guard got backup—three fellow guards—and rushed to the main road on which the sedan was approaching, taking cover behind a Jersey barrier that jutted into the road, Brinly joined Abe and Lee around the fire as it began to burn the rest of the half-charred log left from last night.

"The boys are fueled and ready."

A distant whoop, that could have only been a Marine getting excited to break things.

Lee smiled. "Sounds like it."

"Buncha blue-balled motherfuckers," Brinly admitted. "They're hungry."

"Well. They're in for the fight of their lives."

As this muted conversation was taking place, one of the perimeter guards had his finger on the trigger, and was getting ready to send an entire mag through the windshield at the quickly-approaching sedan. But then a hand emerged from the window, waving manically, and one of the other guards, who was respected as a leader of sorts, yelled for them to hold their fire.

The guard took his finger off the trigger, and watched the sedan come skidding to a halt. The perimeter guards all pounced at once. They had minimal training, and with it, minimal self-control. When one of them started shouting, they all started shouting. Some of their commands were contradictory: "Hands up!" "Get out of the car!" "Get on the ground!" "Don't fucking move!"

Lee heard the shouts, but didn't listen to them. They were muted by distance, and mixed with the sounds of talking and hollering, his army awake enough now that the nervous energy was taking ahold of them. The nearer shouts of one nervous person to another could not be distinguished from the far-away shouts of the perimeter guards.

The man in the sedan tried to comply with the commands as best as he understood them, but he had his own mission in mind. No one recognized him when he jumped out of the car with his hands over his head, but if Lee had been there, he would have remembered him from Vici: the salty individual named Dave.

Not so salty now. Gone was the sarcastic confidence and biting dark humor. It had been replaced with a sort of panicked energy. And if he had been a little more controlled himself, perhaps asked specifically to speak to Lee, then maybe none of what was about to happen would have happened.

As it was, Dave went down to his knees, with his hands clasped on top of his head—by now the perimeter guards seemed to be shouting in agreement on that—and then he began yelling over them.

"There's an army coming! Greeley's army just wiped out Vici!"

And from there, the words had been said, and could not be undone.

At the northern end of Lee's encampment, a handful of squads were close enough to that point in the perimeter to watch what was going down, and to hear the words that came out of Dave's mouth.

Most of the people in those squads were Lee's people from Butler. But he'd embedded men and women from Vici in those squads. They stared with dawning horror, and recognized their friend Dave, and heard what he said.

Most of the squads gave no response. But those individuals from Vici looked around and found the faces of their fellows, the other volunteers from Vici.

Their home had just been hit by an army from Greeley.

Then it began to spread through the encampment. Those few individuals embedded with those squads took off at a run, bouncing off of each other like pinballs in a machine, ricocheting around the encampment, finding the other volunteers from Vici, and telling them what they'd heard.

Somewhere in the center of the encampment, Cass heard the news and went white in the face. She had stuck close to Lee and Brinly and Abe and Angela, but knowing that the army was about to start moving on Greeley, she'd gone out to offer encouragement to the people of her hometown.

To her credit, she didn't start spreading the word. She turned and began running, her eyes scanning through the crowded people and their vehicles, looking for Lee Harden.

At the campfire, Lee knelt stiffly, holding his hands over the rising warmth. It wasn't particularly chilly this morning, but his injured left hand was more sensitive to the cold these days. He kneaded at the aching tendons and bound-up muscles.

It was Abe, standing to Lee's right, that first noticed something was off.

He frowned out into the encampment, sensing the change in energy, the movement of people, the sound of their voices turning from nervous excitement to worry and fear.

"Hey Lee," he said, nodding towards the center of the encampment. "Something's going on."

Lee stood up, his left knee popping, his hip jangling treacherously as though it might give out and pitch him into the fire. His eyes came up, and immediately spotted Cass, running full-bore for him.

"What the fuck *now*?" were the last words he said before everything went to shit.

***

Tinnitus is a funny thing.

Lee knew that his ears had suffered a constant barrage of gunshots and explosions. All of which had perforated his eardrums on a regular basis, leaving behind a multitude of tiny scars. It was a physiological thing, he knew, and yet there was a pattern that he'd noticed.

Tension, fear, trauma, stress. All these things regularly sparked his tinnitus. Oh, sometimes it would come and go on its own, not related to anything psychological that was happening. But when it was related to something psychological, he'd taken note that it was far worse.

He stood in the teacher's lounge of the school, the maps still scattered about the table, Deuce making uncomfortable, manic rounds, sniffing every corner of the room, and inspecting the multitude of occupants with a worried glance.

Lee watched the dog moving, and couldn't hear shit that was being said. The high-frequency hum had turned into a pulsing blast of imaginary noise, like uncontrolled feedback from a speaker too close to a microphone. He clenched his jaw, squinting against the squeal of noise and trying to will it to go away.

Deuce completed a full circuit of the room and came back to his side, pressing himself against Lee's injured leg. He could see the way the dog was stress-panting, but couldn't hear the sound of it. He reached down and touched the fur of the dog's head, hoping that it would help to center him, help to relieve the noise in his ears. But it didn't.

He looked up.

Mouths were moving, words unheard. Faces were contorted with a mix of panic and anger. Hands and arms were moving in wild gesticulations. He could see what was happening, even though he couldn't hear it.

Cass and Dave, and two others from Vici, huddled on one side of the table.

Paul and Stephen, from Lakin, Kansas.

Jonathan and Tammy, from La Junta.

Brinly and Abe and Angela.

The volunteers from the towns were beside themselves. And the leaders of Lee's army weren't much better. The volunteers were shouting in fear, pointing out in random directions, as though pointing to their homes, like they could see them burning in their minds' eyes. And Brinly and Abe were shouting back in anger, making a common motion: Fingers pointing down at the floor.

Lee couldn't hear the words, but he knew what was happening.

The volunteers all wanted to leave. Brinly and Abe were trying to get them to stay.

Stuck in a cloud of vicious sound, Lee looked at Angela and found her staring back at him, concern scribbled all over her features. He saw her mouth move—it was his name. She was calling his name. None of the others seemed to notice.

Lee reached up and rammed a finger into his right ear, wiggling it about. Sometimes that helped. He tried to pop his ears like you would after an altitude change. Sometimes that helped too. But none of it worked.

A cold, wet nose on his fingers. A warm tongue.

Deuce, sensing Lee's condition, was trying his best to render aide.

Angela said his name again—actually shouted it. He could see the volume with which she'd expelled it, evident in the heave of her chest and the brief flash of savage lines on her face. The others seemed to jerk, eyes slashing around, first to Angela, and then to Lee.

Angela stalked around the table and stood face to face with him.

He couldn't tell whether he actually heard her words, or if it was just that he could read her lips.

"Lee, you with me?"

"Um, yeah…" his own voice a distant hum in his head. "Ears are being wonky." He glanced up self-consciously at the others. Saw the confusion on their faces. A flash of anger went through him. Like a deaf man, he spoke overly loud—he could feel the scrape of his words in his throat. "Could everyone just shut the fuck up for a minute?"

Abe looked at him with a tilt of his head. More lip reading, but this time with a distant percussion of consonants: "You alright, man?"

"I'm fucking fine," Lee snapped. Defensive measures deploying in his brain. He didn't want them to see him like this. One-eyed. Bum leg. Bum hand. Going deaf. God, when had he become so weak? He hated himself, and he hated them for seeing him like this. He responded to that self-loathing with anger. "I just can't hear with all of you fucking shouting over each other!"

Cass responded by doing more shouting. A slim note of hope: he could hear her shouts, the tinnitus starting to recede like the tide going out, though he still couldn't make sense of the words themselves, and her mouth was all contorted, too wide as it shouted, too much fear in her eyes, too much panic—he couldn't read what she was saying.

Lee lurched to the table, seizing the edge of it, fully intending in that single moment of uncontrolled rage, to flip it over and send it crashing into Cass. He got the table legs about an inch off the ground before he clamped down on his animal instinct. He slammed the table back down.

"Shut. Up."

Deuce barked. A single burst of noise that cut through the whining in his ears. If tinnitus was a fragile plate of glass covering his perception of sound, Deuce's bark shattered it.

He could hear his own breathing now, rushing in and out of his throat. He could hear Deuce's worried panting. Lee issued an irritated grunt, as though to test his own hearing. He could hear the sound inside of his head, and through his ears. They were working again.

He kept his hands clasped on the table edge. Didn't dare release them, because then everyone present would see the violent tremor going through his limbs, like the shakes after a fever suddenly breaks.

A tumult of thoughts. A torrent of words. Single sentences that battered his brain. Declarations, such as, "You can't leave!" and "We can't do this without you!" and "You can't just cut and run the second shit gets tough!"

He shook his head against them. They were all the wrong words. But he couldn't for the life of him conjure up the right ones.

Mixed in with all of this was the background concern of what all these people were thinking about him as they stared, watching, judging. Could they see his weakness? Could they smell it on him? Did they feel like he was already defeated? Did they have any faith in him whatsoever? If they had, he was destroying it right now. But did it matter? Could they even be convinced at this point in time?

He clamped his mouth shut, breathing through his nose. The sound seemed overly-loud now. The tinnitus having released its grip on him, it seemed like every noise was turned up to ten. The rustle of clothing as Jonathan Reeves shifted position. The squeak of a boot as Abe fidgeted. The quiet sigh of Angela's breath. Deuce's panting.

"Cass. Paul. Stephen." Lee dragged his eyes from the maps—his jolt on the table had toppled all the chess pieces. He looked at each of them in turn. "If you leave right now, you're not accomplishing anything. Cass, Vici's already been torched. What the hell do you think you're going to do by going back there?"

She opened her mouth to respond, fire in her eyes, but Lee cut her off.

"Fight, goddammit!" He snapped. "Fight so that this shit can never happen again! What's done is done! If you leave right now, all you're doing is surrendering. You're giving up in the face of Greeley's show of force. If you leave, they win."

"And what about Lakin?" Stephen said. "They haven't reached Lakin yet. It's not a lost cause."

"It *is* a lost cause, Stephen!" Lee shifted his weight off his trembling, aching left side. "What the hell do you think you're going to do by going back? You gonna fight off the whole fucking army? No! You're just going to die with the rest of them!"

"Those are our families you're talking about!"

"Then fight for them! Take Greeley down like you said you would! Prevent this from happening again! You running back home doesn't accomplish a damn thing. The problem will remain. At least right now we have a chance to stop it—to stop Briggs before he massacres any more towns out of spite!"

Stephen looked incredulous. The cold, practical logic of it lost on him in his moment of emotion. "You're asking us to just turn our back on our families. To sacrifice them. For what? For a *chance*? Admit it, Lee! You don't even know if this plan to take Greeley is going to work! And what if it doesn't? What if we get beat back when we try to invade them? Then all of our families will be dead! For fucking *nothing*!"

It was the wrong thing to say, but Lee said it anyways: "Your families are fucked already. Can't you see that? There's nothing you can do. This army—they're the same ones that railroaded Butler!

And we had defenses, and a plan! What the fuck do you think you're going to do?"

"I don't know!" Stephen shouted. "But I have to do something!"

"If the sacrifice is going to be made anyways, wouldn't you rather it be worth something?" Lee didn't like the pleading in his voice. Like he knew he'd already lost. "At least if you stay and fight, there'll be a *chance* that it will all mean something. If you leave, then it's all for nothing."

It was wrong. It was all wrong. And there was nothing Lee could do to fix it.

Stephen shook his head. "I'm not gonna sit here and listen to this shit." He jabbed an elbow into his brother's side. "Paul, let's fucking go."

"No!" Lee shook the table.

Stephen looked at him, his body already turned towards the door, his eyes saddened, terrified, mad. "What are you gonna do, Lee? Shoot me?"

Lee actually considered it. His right hand twitched, still attached to the table. He sensed the tiny distance between his hand and the sidearm on his hip. He could snatch that pistol out and put a bullet through Stephen's head…

And accomplish what?

Everything would devolve after that.

The chaos of the moment would turn to absolute anarchy.

Lee desperately wanted to gain back some semblance of control, but in that tiny moment, staring at Stephen, he knew that he couldn't. This had fallen apart. It was beyond his command now.

Stephen knew that he wouldn't be stopped. And so he left. Without another word, he stalked out of the room, followed by his brother Paul.

If you're going to lose everyone anyways, then why not cap him in the back of the head?

A voice from the past. Mr. Nobody speaking to him from the grave where Lee had buried him.

He heard the sound of the door being thrust open, slamming back on its stopper like a gunshot.

Cass jerked at the noise. Straightened. "We're leaving too."

"Vici's already burned," Lee said, much quieter now.

Cass stood there, facing the door, but still planted at the table for a long, protracted moment.

"Cass," Angela said from Lee's side. "We need your help. I'm so sorry about your town. None of us wanted it to go this way. Make Greeley pay for what they did. Make your town's sacrifice mean something."

Cass bared her teeth at the reality crushing against her. The bottom of her eyes sparkled. She blinked rapidly to clear them. "We've gotta go," she mumbled.

Lee didn't turn to watch them leave.

The silence in the room was so big, so thick, that it threatened to spark off his tinnitus again. Lee could feel it pressing at his eardrums.

A stir to his left brought sound back into the vacuum of the room.

Jonathan Reeves cleared his throat. "Listen…"

Lee shook his head. Looked at the man. "Don't."

Jonathan's face contorted through a mix of things, all flashing through like some nonsensical collage of emotions. Shame. Grief. Anger. Defensiveness. Anxiety.

"This army is on the move," Jonathan said, a slight tremor in his voice. "They're following your trail. Which means it's only a matter of the time before they show up here."

"Mr. Reeves," Angela tried, but Jonathan snapped a hand up.

"Lee. Angela." His voice was stern, even as it shook. "You don't fucking understand."

Lee finally raised himself off the table. The shaking in his limbs had gone. Now everything was heavy. His blood turned to lead. His muscles turned to stone. The breath in his lungs seemed depleted of oxygen. Everything was laborious.

"I think," Lee murmured. "That we understand better than most."

"Then you understand I have to do what's best for my people."

"What's best for your people is to give them a chance at a future."

"They won't have a future if this maniac comes through and massacres them." Jonathan's eyes bounced back and forth between Lee, Brinly, Abe, and Angela.

His wife did not seem as conflicted as he did. Tammy jutted her chin out in a stubborn, immovable manner. Stood tall and imperious. The queen of her little kingdom. "I think it would be best for everyone—safest—if you left. Immediately."

THIRTY-THREE

VENGEANCE

NOLAN STEPPED OUT of the apartment and into the bright, warm morning.

Not early morning, mind you, but nine-fucking-thirty. On his leisurely way to report for his new ten-o'clock guard shift at the ration distribution site. It felt so damn good not to try to force himself to sleep while the sun was peering through every crack and crevice of their apartment. God, but he had hated third shift with a passion.

His crew trundled out behind him, similarly self-satisfied.

Nolan looked at his guys and smiled knowingly. He was tempted to say something along the lines of "See? Stick with me, boys. I'll always find a way." But they knew. No point in bragging too much about it.

His self-control lasted for about a block before his smugness could be contained no longer.

He sighed like a man sated by a hearty meal. Gestured out to the city of Greeley around them, the streets relatively quiet as most everyone had already reported to their shifts. "Just a stepping stone, gents. Yesterday, we were third shift assholes. Today we're running the ration site. Tomorrow, maybe I'll see if we can't get off of this bitch duty and get assigned downtown. Better rations. More respect."

A few chuckles told Nolan that he had reinvigorated his crew's respect for him. Hell, they didn't have any room to doubt—it had only taken him a few weeks to take control of The Tank. But it was good to remind those under you that they owed you for the ease of their existence.

Gabriella had made good on her word. Nolan had pointed her in the right direction for the people that he had already identified as, shall we say, less than loyal to Greeley. Not that he himself was loyal to anyone, but that was neither here nor there. He was loyal to himself, and currently, Greeley was the place to be.

Gabriella had pulled the big red handle on one of those crews—that Sameer-hadji-wetback fuck that had waltzed into The Tank like he owned the place. Big fucking mistake, hadji.

Of course, Nolan had heard the news. Everyone had at this point in time. And it was a bit hard to ignore the Cornerstone troops racing around like wasps defending their nest. Gabriella's operation had gone to shit. But hey, that's what you get when you send a woman to do a man's job.

But it didn't really matter. Gabriella had secured Nolan and his crew the spot that they'd requested—a late morning shift guarding the ration site, so that they wouldn't have to walk around the same damn handful of city blocks all night.

As for the hadji and his little crew, word had it that a few of them had been killed, and the rest were in hiding. If the hadji had managed to survive—and Nolan had his doubts—then he wouldn't last long.

This place was crawling with soldiers looking for him.

And in any case, it wasn't Nolan's concern anymore. He'd gotten what he wanted out of it, regardless of whether the operation had gone to shit. Always an ambitious individual, Nolan decided to put it out of his mind and start focusing on what was next.

There *had* to be some dirt going on at the ration distribution. Food was the currency of Greeley, and so it stood to reason that the old adage "follow the money" would apply, only with rations. Someone who had control of the rations almost certainly would be using it in underhanded ways to get what they wanted from the people that needed the rations.

Maybe it was a Cornerstone operator skimming off the top so he could use extra rations to buy himself other niceties. Maybe someone was giving extra rations to a hot bitch so that he could circle back around after dark and fuck her. The possibilities were limitless, really. All Nolan had to do was wait and watch, and once he had the dirt on someone, he could either use that against them to get what he wanted out of them, or he could out them to the higher ups in exchange for an even better position.

And on the off-chance that everyone distributing rations was squeaky clean—which wasn't likely in Nolan's mind—then Nolan himself would just figure out a way to use the rations to get what he wanted. He'd spotted a few hot bitches himself that looked like they'd be willing to fuck their way into some extra meals. Especially the ones with little kids. Chicks with kids would suck a golf ball through a garden hose to get more food for their little rugrats.

Yes, things were looking up for Nolan and his crew. It was just a matter of time before—

The boom and the splatter of brains hit him at the same moment.

He spun, eyes wide, not quite sure what the hell was happening, wondering if the hot wetness he'd felt on the back of his neck was his own blood…

One of his crew pitched bonelessly right into Nolan, half his head gone. Nolan recoiled, jerking his hands back as the body left a streamer of fresh blood across his chest.

BOOM BOOM BOOM

He felt the rifle reports like slaps to his face. Saw the rapid-fire puffs of smoke. Saw the holes sprout in the chests of two more of his guys, their shocked expressions, like they couldn't believe it.

Nolan was so surprised by all of this that he never even thought to try to run, never thought to try to defend himself or to attack his attacker. When you're always the predator, it's just too damn much of a shift in reality to suddenly be the prey.

A figure strode through the gunsmoke, rifle at the ready, swinging back and forth as it pumped rounds in a cacophony of death into the last of Nolan's men still standing. That last man had managed to spin around and hold his hands up, issuing a weak cry for mercy.

Nolan watched in fascination as the outstretched hands were shredded by a barrage of bullets, fingers flying off, meat scattering, the bullets punching clear through into the chest and neck of that last man, sending him sprawling backwards, trailing ribbons of red out of his neck.

Nolan was so focused on watching his last friend die, that he only wrenched his gaze up to look at the attacker at the last moment. A tiny spark of recognition went through him.

Striding through the blood spatter and the dead limbs of Nolan's friend, rifle pointing right at *him…*

It wasn't Sameer. It was his mouthy-ass friend. The smart-aleck.

"You sonofa—" Nolan issued in a wheeze of breath.

This time he didn't register the rifle reports, only the feeling of being slammed in the chest, like taking three major-league fast pitches all at once. There was a brief slice of time where he thought, *Fuck you! I can survive this! I'll fucking strangle the life out of you!*

He even managed to raise his hands, his fingers curled into claws like they were already around his attacker's neck.

But then he was falling backwards.

How strange.

Oh shit.

He hit the ground, and all the breath went out of him. His head rebounded off the pavement, sending stars and sparklers skittering through his vision like a nightmarish Fourth of July display.

When they cleared, the smart-aleck was standing over him.

Smiling.

"You fucked with the wrong folks," the smart-aleck said.

Nolan actually watched the smoke bloom from the muzzle—how fascinating—

***

Gabriella didn't particularly like what she'd done. But it was one of those duties that had to be taken care of, even if it didn't leave you full of pride afterwards.

The garbage still had to be taken out, whether or not you thought it was a glamorous job. No one wanted to handle garbage, but then again, no one wanted to live in filth either.

She stood at her small kitchen table, in the single-family dwelling that had become hers. Many of Briggs' most loyal Cornerstone operatives had received similar treatment. A house to call their own, in a quiet little neighborhood of small houses, just north of FOB Hampton, where it was easy to walk to work.

No longer did she have to live, crammed in with others. Frankly, she'd grown so accustomed to it, that the little two bedroom house seemed cavernous. But she'd earned it. And she allowed herself to feel some pride for it, even if the quiet confines sometimes gave her the heebie-jeebies.

On the table in front of her, beside a mug with the brown dregs of the morning's "coffee" allowance—which was really chicory, which has no caffeine, and was therefore useless—lay the neatly organized folders of her remaining targets. This was, perhaps, what she had liked least about this entire operation.

It wasn't any outpouring of human compassion that made her not like what she'd done to Sam. It was the fact that her bosses hadn't allowed her to pull the trigger on all of them at once.

In a purely practical sense, she understood their reservations. Much of what she'd gained on these people—the squad leaders that had come to talk to her about how much they didn't like what was happening in Greeley—was hearsay. She lacked concrete evidence. Her bosses, fresh off of having their asses chewed soundly for not having enough guards to post on the perimeters, didn't want to lose a dozen squads that they'd just created. They were worried about how that would make them look to Briggs.

So, rather than let her strike them all down at once, they'd told her to pick the biggest offender and test her theory. If the evidence supported her theory, then she would be allowed to start operations to take down the others.

Well, if last night's debacle was any indication, Gabriella guessed that the evidence was pretty damn sound.

What bothered her was the fact that there were still squads out there with questionable if not downright rebellious leanings, and they all knew that shit was going down. If her bosses had allowed her to take them out all at once, then she could have mitigated the risk of them getting away. Now, they'd be on high-alert, ready to run at the drop of a hat.

Worse than that, Gabriella was not ignorant of the fact that her own life was in danger. The meeting that she'd had with those squad leaders had taken place right here, in this very house. They knew where she lived.

The danger to her life was a fact that her bosses didn't seem to care much about. And she'd been afraid to raise the point for fear of being seen as a coward, and having her own loyalties questioned.

Besides, her bosses weren't dumb. They knew what they were doing. They'd simply decided that they'd rather her life be in danger than their jobs.

She sighed, considering the muck at the bottom of her cup. But she could see the grits in it, coating the white ceramic. She could almost feel their annoying texture on her tongue.

She reached across the table and gathered her carefully recorded documents on these people. Transcripts of their entrance interviews. Notes about what they'd said when she'd met them here. Pictures of them. Their shifts. Their assigned positions. Where they were housed.

Most of them were third shifters, which meant she could hit them right now, in broad daylight, while they were asleep. That seemed to be the best plan. If she waited much longer, they might be down at the ration lines.

No, it was time to put the rest of this into action.

She'd given her bosses a verbal report late the previous night, and, out of an abundance of interest for their own skins, they'd finally admitted that these other squads needed to be eradicated. Gabriella had been given the green light.

She had twelve squads of Cornerstone operatives at her disposal. She just needed to make sure that they all struck simultaneously. Word of Sameer Balawi's take down would have spread to them by now. If the treasonous squad leaders caught wind of an operation against one of them, they'd all go into hiding, and then Gabriella would have to answer for it.

She piled the files on top of each other, shuffled them into a neat block of manila and paper, then tucked them under her arm.

Time to get it over with.

And who knew? At the end of this, she might be in line for yet another promotion. Not that she needed much more amenities than had already been provided for her, but being in charge of the entrance interviews for newcomers was not her idea of a career. Besides that fact, with Briggs ordering the borders closed, there wouldn't be much work in that sector for much longer.

She needed to shine today. She needed to execute with absolute precision and confidence. It was her chance to prove herself, to make a name for herself, and to secure her bosses' good graces, and perhaps come to the attention of Briggs himself.

As she made her way to the front door, she allowed herself a moment of fantasy: being assigned to FOB Hampton—where at least they had real coffee—perhaps with a contingent of operatives under her, or at the very least, some more important responsibility than talking to haggard refugees all day long.

She exited her house, taking a quick scan of the street beyond. It was quiet. Most everyone else in this neighborhood had their own duties to attend to, and had already gone to FOB Hampton, or to the guard outposts and armories, or wherever else they were assigned.

It wasn't them that she was worried about. It was those squad leaders that knew where she lived.

She cinched her right elbow against her side, felt the firm reassurance of the holstered pistol there on her hip.

There was no one else about. No one waiting and watching for her. No suspicious persons lurking about.

She turned, fumbling the key from her pocket as she juggled the file folders. She locked her front door and dead-bolted it—there'd been a rash of break-ins in a nearby neighborhood. It wasn't that she had anything terribly valuable in the house, or that she thought the dead-bolt would really stop a determined burglar. But why not be cautious?

She turned, focused on getting the key back into her pants pocket, and stepped down off the concrete stoop. Only then did her eyes come up, at which point her entire thought life, thoughts of organizing those twelve Cornerstone squads and effectively executing her plan, dissipated like smoke in the wind.

A lone figure stood, right there in the empty driveway—where the fuck had he come from?

Recognition slammed through her hard.

"Sam!" she snapped, in the same moment that the file folders dropped from her arms and she lunged for the pistol on her hip.

Sameer Balawi raised his hand, a pistol in his grip.

Gabriella cried out in panic and rage as her hand squashed down tight on the grip of the pistol and yanked it from its holster…

A single shot rocked the quiet neighborhood street.

***

Sam felt very little in that moment, but knew that it wouldn't last.

His heart slammed in his chest, sure. All the physiological reactions to taking a life. He felt those full-on, as he stepped over to Gabriella's twitching body and pointed the pistol at her head again. The constriction of his blood vessels. The tightness in his chest. The tunnel vision creeping up on him.

But he felt no *emotion*. No victory. No shame. No spite. No guilt.

Just two machines, he and her, crashed into each other. He had come out alive. She had not.

But he dimly knew that his clinical detachment was only forced on him by the mission—*The mission, the mission, the mission! Got to get it done!*—and that eventually he would feel something about this. Who knew what it would be? He suspected it wouldn't be good.

True to the detached state that his mind was in, he took in her jittering body, and assessed whether he should shoot her in the head again. It didn't feel *wrong* to do—dead is dead, whether you accomplish it in one shot or two: They both equate to killing—but another gunshot could hone in already pricked ears. Get him attention that he didn't want.

Sam decided she was dead enough. The twitching was just random. The death throes of an animal that had already passed over.

He stuffed the pistol into his waistband, then jammed his hand in the pocket of his pants and drew out a folded piece of paper, which bore the message that he had written. He stuck the paper halfway into Gabriella's belt line, so that it wouldn't get whisked away in a breeze.

His eyes fell on the stack of folders jumbled off to the side of Gabriella's corpse. One of them had fallen open, some of the papers sticking out of it. He saw an image, printed in low quality. It was a picture of one of the other squad leaders—one of the ones that had met with Gabriella in the very house in front of which Sam stood.

Sam quickly gathered up the folders, becoming increasingly aware that he'd already spent about twenty seconds out in the open since the gunshot. Any more time would put him at undue risk. But he didn't want to leave these folders. They had the look of something that he should take with him.

He stuffed them all under his arm and, without another glance at the woman he'd just killed, he strode through the narrow gap between her house and the neighbor's. He emerged on the other side, onto another quiet neighborhood street on which he was the only pedestrian.

He turned himself west, towards his hideout in the abandoned office building, and walked along, just as casual as you please, while all of his problems gathered behind him like a pack of feral dogs, waiting for the right moment to tear him to pieces.

***

There was nothing out here, Lee observed.

On this lonesome stretch of highway, heading north away from La Junta and deep into the abandoned flatness of the Colorado plains, Lee sat on a jumpseat between the driver and front passenger of the MATV. He stared out the windshield, his elbows propped on his knees, his hands holding up his face, his eyepatch still on because he'd forgotten about it. His one good eye watched the endless miles pass under them.

This place was so brown and lifeless and flat, one could have believed it was the sight of a nuclear detonation that had razed the landscape, if it weren't for the endless line of power poles that passed to their right.

His cramped position, the annoying rub of the fabric patch over his raw eye socket, the ache in his hip—none of it got through to him. Physical pain seemed a dim and easy thing to ignore in the light of the tumult of thoughts that rolled over and over in his head.

The thoughts bore no clear consensus. They clamored at each other like a meeting of divisive politicians, all yelling their own points, none of them listening, none of them truly heard.

Should he have put his foot down? Should he have fought and killed the dissenters?

And what good would that have done? The dissenters were too numerous, too scared for their families. If he had "put them in their place" he would have only hardened their already-made decision to leave. And he might have alienated his own people in the process.

But what were his people thinking now? What did they think about him now that they'd watched him merely cave to the demands of those that were supposed to help them? Did they believe he was weak? He certainly felt weak.

Did they have enough faith in him to continue on? And even if they did, was it even possible to take Greeley now? He'd run this entire course through the American central states, all the way up from the Gulf, operating on the presupposition that he *needed* more fighters, that he *needed* to create a grassroots movement, a groundswell of people willing to stand up against Greeley.

What could he say now? They'd all gone away. Fled back to where they'd come, to die at the hands of the army now chasing Lee down. Could he convince the remaining fighters—all the soldiers and Marines and guerillas from Butler—that their objective was still attainable?

Was it?

The silence in the MATV was cloying, pressing, begging for someone to fill it, but no one had the guts, not even Lee. Because what was there to say? *Good try, folks. We gave it a solid effort, but sometimes shit doesn't work out. Go back home.*

Home to where? They had no home. They were nomads now. They were the barbarian hordes knocking at the gates of Rome. They were the Mongolian horsemen raging towards China. They had no place to call their own except the place they might conquer.

And all the miles between them and the place to be conquered were dwindling—Lee could feel them draining away like someone had opened a port in his veins and was taking the very life out of him.

The silence. The tinnitus whispering in it, keening, threatening to come on strong again.

Lee coughed, for no other reason than to give his ears something to hear. His heart began to pound. His palms against his face felt clammy. His stomach roiled, empty, nauseas—starving but without an appetite. His mouth watered weakly, making an idle threat—Lee knew he wouldn't puke, and had nothing to puke up if he did.

His eyes fixed on a turn off—a single lonely cattle road that led off to the right, out into the nothingness. He needed to stop. They *had* to stop. They were barreling north towards an objective, and Lee was not prepared to come within sight of Greeley, and though he knew there were hours between him and that place, he could go no closer knowing that he had no clue what to do when he got there.

He thrust his hand out over the driver's shoulder. "Pull off there."

The driver didn't question it. The bulky vehicle slowed, then turned off, the hum of the tires on asphalt turning to the rumble of a dirt road.

"Keep going," Lee said. "So that everyone can get off the road. We're calling a halt."

"Yes, sir." The passenger reached and took the radio handset, and transmitted the command back to the convoy.

There was something quieting, calming, about the call-and-response of military commands. It was something familiar that Lee latched onto in that moment, a tiny piece of something to keep him from hurtling out into the void.

By the time the convoy had come to a complete stop, amid the swirling dust storm they had created, nearly five full minutes had passed. And by that time, the tannish dust hanging stubbornly in the windless air, Lee was striding through the ranks of vehicles, eye forward, not looking at the faces through the windshields that watched him as he passed.

Who are you, Lee Harden?

What was this thing in the center of him that wouldn't let him stop? Why did he keep fighting, and fighting, and fighting? From the first time he punched a kid in the mouth when he was in grade school, all the way to watching Mateo Ibarra burn alive, and all the people in between that he'd left dead and broken with his violent hands…what had been going on inside of him?

He wasn't alone. Deuce trotted along at his heels. Brinly, Angela, and Abe followed him.

After nearly a hundred yards, they exited the pall of dust. The day was bright and cloudless. The dry land baking in the sun, the horizon roiling with mirage, as vast and flat as an ocean.

Lee had no specific distance that he wanted to walk. He just needed to be away from prying eyes and ears. Perhaps he walked a little further than was necessary, caught up in his thoughts. But eventually he stopped and turned.

The others gathered around him. Deuce appeared circumspect, and maybe a little disappointed that there was no standing objects on which to piss. The dog let out a grumbling sigh and sat down.

Abe looked back towards the convoy, his head tilted up, taking in the towering dust cloud. "Not a fan of that," he said, nodding towards it. "Like a fucking signal."

Lee considered that. "How close do you think that army is?"

"I have no clue," Abe grunted. "Hopefully not close enough to see that shit. They've been tracking our movements, though. Probably from tire tracks—can't hide the movement of hundreds of vehicles."

Lee sighed, his eyes traveling to the tops of the dust cloud. Like the pillar of cloud that led the Israelites out of the desert. Hadn't Brinly once compared him to Moses? And here he was, in the desert, with his faithless people. Except there was no mountain around on which he could ascend and hear the voice of God.

No, they were on their own.

He reached up and removed the irritating eye patch. Gently rubbed the scarred eyebrow. It relieved a tiny portion of the itch in his socket. He'd learned to mostly ignore that itch. It couldn't be scratched.

Lee let out a slow, tense breath. "I'm at a bit of a loss right now."

There was a moment of quiet, in which they could hear the dim rattle of people exiting their vehicles in the dust, their voices muted, disconsolate, ill-defined.

"Well," Brinly started. "The way I see it, we have two options. We either continue on, or we cut and run."

"Cut and run where?" Abe asked. Not a challenge. Just a question. Everything and anything was on the table at this point, and they all knew it.

Brinly waved a hand at their desolate environment. "We can still do damage. Out here, spread out. Not in one big cluster. It'll be harder for that army to track us down if we split up into core groups. Those core groups can harass, sabotage, steal, wreak havoc."

"To what end?" Angela asked, earnestly.

Brinly shook his head. "To stay alive, I guess. At the very least, we won't be trapped between Greeley and an army."

"This army that's chasing us?" Abe said. "The second they realize we're not pushing on Greeley, they'll just pass us right by and re-enter Greeley. Fortify their defenses. And then Greeley becomes untouchable."

"Sam's still inside Greeley," Angela observed.

"Yeah, I know." Lee dropped his gaze to the dust at his feet. "I know."

"If we scatter, we're effectively abandoning him." Angela's voice was toneless.

"I guess the real question," Abe put in. "Is whether you think our army can actually get the job done."

Lee put his hands on his hips, raised his gaze to the convoy, now a bit clearer as the dust had begun to settle. "Shit. That's exactly what I can't decide, Abe."

"Are the odds too long to take the risk?" Angela said, almost as though speaking to herself. "Dammit, Lee, I don't know what we're supposed to do here either. Part of me just thinks, Do it. There's still hundreds of people in that convoy that think we're heading for Greeley right now. They're here now. They're ready to fight. Are they gonna keep fighting if we scatter? Go into hiding? That might kill any fight they got left in them."

Brinly stretched his neck from side to side, his blue eyes not meeting anyone else's. "At this stage in the game, Lee, it's either we keep playing, or we fold. If we want to keep playing, then we go all in. It's either risk it all, or call it a fucking day."

"Call it a fucking day," Lee echoed with a bitter tone in his voice.

"Lee," Angela said, turning to him. "There's no good call here. There's no safe solution. Any way you cut it, we've got equal chances of getting wiped the fuck out."

"You just thinking out loud?"

She shook her head. "No, I'm telling you what I think. All things created equal, we're fucked. We're fucked if we charge into Greeley, and we're fucked if we don't, although it might take a little longer if we go that route." She reached up and clawed a hand through her blonde curls. "Will another opportunity come along if we're patient and we wait? Maybe. But that's just hoping. That's just crossing our fingers and praying."

"I'm still not clear on what you're saying."

She released her hair, let her hand flop to her side. "I'm saying we go. I'm saying we do this. We made promises. And now we gotta follow through with them. We made promises to these people, that we were going to take the fight to Greeley. 'Greeley or Bust,' remember? And we made promises to Sam. Hell, I dunno how that turns out for us. Maybe we're all fucking dead in a few days. But…but…" She appeared to struggle mightily for words in that moment, then finally shook her head. "Fuck it. I'd rather die fighting than on the run. If I gotta go, I wanna go swinging."

"Hey," Abe said, his tone completely different now.

Lee jerked at the sound of his voice, looked up and saw Abe's hand outstretched, pointing to the south.

"We got incoming," Abe husked.

THIRTY-FOUR

AT THE CORE

Distance estimation?

A mile?

Lee had watched, unable to identify the two figures they'd seen walking towards them. Farther back behind the approaching figures—*two miles, I think*—sat what appeared to be a white pickup on the side of the road.

Why had they left it there? It didn't make a lot of sense to Lee, but he found himself in a sort of neutral mental place. Experience made him dread the newcomers. Were they here to deliver news? Were they messengers from the Greeley army pursuing them? If they were, did that mean that the location of Lee's army was known to them?

Would he kill these messengers to keep the location of his army a secret?

Strangely, none of these thoughts felt extremely pressing. It was like he'd been drained of emotion, so beaten that he'd become numb to it. Now it was all just facts and figures. It was as dispassionate as a math problem.

The two figures, made small by distance, had been proned out on the road. They looked like they had complied without much fuss. It was a squad of

Brinly's Marines that had gone to take them. They'd fanned out across the roadway, two of them approaching and securing each figure in turn. Then they'd hauled them up and piled them in the back of the Humvee, and raced back to the convoy.

Now, Lee and his small inner circle stood, not too far from where they'd walked to have their quiet conference. The Humvee cut wide around the jumble of vehicles parked in the middle of the flat, scrubby plain.

No one spoke as the roar of the diesel engine filled the air and the tires skidded slightly in the dirt as it rocked to a stop, a handful of yards from Lee.

The Marines poured out of the Humvee. It was the open-bed model of Humvee, and Lee watched the two Marines in the back bed, standing over their new prisoners.

The squad leader who had exited the front passenger side nodded to Brinly, and then to Lee. "What do you want to do with them, sir?"

Lee started walking, unrushed. "I'll talk to them."

Brinly, Angela, and Abe fell in behind Lee as he skirted around to the backend of the vehicle. As he cleared the rear fender, he saw the two individuals, seated with their legs kicked out in front of them, hands behind their backs, and backs against the cab of the Humvee.

Lee halted in mid-stride, one hand up on the truck bed. "Well. Holy shit."

Marlin Maclean squinted tiredly at him against the sun. "God. I'm glad it's you."

"Captain Maclean!" Angela gasped as she rounded Lee's shoulder, coming to a shocked halt beside him. "Lieutenant Wibberley!"

Lee raised a hand to cut off any further speaking. Again, it was empty of feeling. Simple arithmetic. "Where'd you come from and who sent you?"

Wibberly's face screwed up and he looked away.

But Marlin simply coughed out a dry chuckle. "That's what I like about you, Lee. Always on point."

"Answer the question," Lee said, flatly.

Marlin nodded. "We came from Georgia, by way of Texas, Oklahoma, and Kansas. Following that army that kicked us out of Butler, who was following you."

"Were you in with them?" Lee asked.

"Christ," Wibberley grunted. "You suspicious wanker. Do you know what we went through to get here?"

"Easy, Buddy," Marlin sighed. To Lee, he nodded again. "You got every right in the world to be suspicious of us. But no. We weren't in with them."

"I thought you were dead."

Marlin's expression went deadpan. "Well the rest of my squad is."

Lee's eye narrowed. "Sorry to hear that."

Marlin studied Lee's face, taking in the raw wound of his left eye, the scars that pocked and slashed his skin. "Looks like we all got our asses kicked in Butler."

Angela took a half step forward and put her hand on the tailgate of the guntruck. "What are you doing here?"

Marlin looked at her. “Are you aware that the army that took over Butler is about one day’s drive behind you?”

“If that,” Wibberley quipped. “Six hours, tops.”

“Yes,” Angela replied. “We’re aware. But that still doesn’t tell me what you’re doing here.”

“Hell,” Marlin tilted his head back as though to stretch his neck. “I guess we’re here, hoping you had some sort of plan.”

Lee blinked a few times. “We did. Until this morning.”

“The fuck happened?” Marlin asked, quietly. “What happened in that town you left this morning? We were outside of it, watching. We weren’t sure if it was really you we were tracking. Then, this morning, everyone starts driving off in separate directions.”

“It was the people from those towns,” Wibberley said, half question and half statement. “The ones that army is burning through right now. They heard about it and cut and run.” Eyes on Lee. “That about right?”

Lee didn’t respond, but he figured his silence was answer enough.

Wibberley hunched forward, rotating his shoulders as though to ease the tension of his bound hands. “What was the plan prior to everything going to shit this morning?”

Angela started to speak again, but Lee cut her off with a grunt. “Let’s stop there. Captain Maclean, Lieutenant Wibberley…I’m glad you’re alive. You might be surprised to learn we have some old friends of yours with us right now.”

Both Marlin and Wibberley looked briefly confused.

Lee turned to Brinly. "Radio one of your squads. I want them to locate Guidry and Worley and bring them here."

Marlin straightened. "Wait…what? You have Guidry and Worley?"

Lee held a finger to his lips and shook his head. "No more talking until we figure things out."

***

"I can't imagine a reason why they would come all this way just to fuck you over," Worley said, looking at the Humvee over Lee's shoulder.

Lee had his back to the Humvee, about twenty paces away. He knew that neither Guidry nor Worley could see their compatriots. Only the Marines that Brinly had ordered to untie them and give them food and water.

Lee looked at Guidry. "What about you?"

Guidry raised his eyebrows and regarded Lee. "I think you're being a little paranoid."

Lee smiled without humor. "Am I? After everything that's happened, you think I'm being paranoid?"

Guidry sighed, shook his head. "I suppose your…suspicions are warranted. But honestly. They fought for you in Butler, didn't they?"

"You know that they did."

"Against our recommendations."

Lee was silent at that.

Guidry pressed his point. "They refused lawful orders from their own command to back you.

And in the process, their entire team got wiped out. All their friends."

"So they say," Lee said, not liking his truculent tone, but there was nothing he could do about it. Again, it was just facts and figures. Was he being paranoid? Perhaps, but not in the emotional way that it seemed Guidry was implying. Lee wasn't ringing his hands and sweating about it. He was beyond such things at this point. He was simply looking at all the possibilities. "Or they got captured by the invading Greeley force—"

"Griffin."

Lee halted, midsentence. "Excuse me?"

Guidry exchanged a glance with Worley. Then nodded at Lee. "That army that kicked you out of Butler and is now pursuing you? It's headed by Captain Perry Griffin. I'm assuming you know him. He was Project Hometown, was he not?"

Lee's jaw clenched, molars grinding. "Yes."

"Well. It's his army."

"And how long were you aware of this?"

"The whole time," Guidry admitted with a tone that implied it wasn't a big deal. "But that fact seemed immaterial."

Lee narrowed his one eye. "You were concerned I would make a rash decision."

Guidry shrugged. "If you knew who it was coming after you, it would have become personal. I believed it would be better for all if you didn't have a face to put to the army. But at this juncture, it seems you should know."

Worley spoke up. "Were we wrong for that, Lee?" The way he asked it, he obviously didn't think they were.

Lee wasn't so sure. His hands were balling at his sides.

Worley noticed. Nodded to them. "Look at your reaction right now. Teeth clenched. Hands fisted. You want to tell me we were wrong to assume that knowledge would make things personal for you?"

Lee relaxed his hands and jaw, almost self-consciously. "No. I suppose you were right."

"And it's neither here nor there," Guidry continued. "Now you know who it is coming after you. It doesn't change things."

It changed everything. It changed the way that Lee saw it. And, though Lee didn't like it one bit, he felt the emotional distance between himself and these facts suddenly wither and disappear. All of the sudden everything was close. Crowded. Right on top of him. He wasn't looking at things from above them, but from within them.

In the space of a few seconds, things *had* become personal for Lee.

Had they ever stopped being personal? Or had Lee just numbed himself to it, rather than feel the pain of it?

He took in a ragged breath. "The point remains the same," he ground out. "They could have been captured by…Griffin's army. Their squads could be held as hostages to get them to cooperate."

"Or it could be exactly as they said," Guidry remarked, curtly.

Lee put his hands on his hips, trying to stuff down that rising feeling in him that threatened to cloud his judgement. God, but Guidry and Worley had been right. "Then explain to me why the hell they would travel halfway across the fucking country to be here right now?"

"Maybe because they want to help," Worley snapped. "They already gave up everything for you. The least you could do is hear them out."

"Help?" Lee growled back. "Two fucking troopers? What the fuck do they think they're going to do?"

Another secretive glance between Guidry and Worley.

It was Worley that made eye contact with Lee again. "We have an inkling. And perhaps this is the right time to go and talk to them. All together."

Lee started to object, but Guidry cut him off.

"What do you have to lose, Lee?" He shook his head. "Griffin's army is a day away from overtaking us. If this was all a fantastical ploy to find your location, then it's already been found. If it is what you fear it is, then you're already fucked. That's the cold, hard truth. You're up against the wall, and you're up against the clock, outmanned and outgunned, approaching a hardened target that you've got a—*maybe*—fifty-fifty chance of beating, and an entire army breathing down your neck that already ruined you once, and likely will again." Guidry tossed his hands up. "So what the hell do you have to lose?"

By the time Guidry finished talking, Lee had already turned away and begun stalking back towards the Humvee. "Alright," Lee called over his shoulder. "You guys coming?"

***

No punches were pulled. Lee was beyond that now.

Guidry and Worley had been absolutely right. Lee knew it. They knew it. Hell, every single man and woman, soldier and civilian, in that convoy probably knew it as well.

They had nothing left to lose. This was the Hail-Mary toss, with two seconds left on the clock. And Lee didn't hold back. Not a single thing. He laid it all out on the line, to an audience of grim-faced envoys from Canada and the United Kingdom, and hollow-eyed Marines, and an exhausted Brinly, Angela, and Abe.

No one stopped him from telling them everything. Brinly, Angela, and Abe all knew their current reality, just as much as Lee did.

Not just *do or die time* anymore. No, it had become *everyone does, or everyone dies*. Not just physical death, but the death of the idea. The death of the possibility of something that Lee had been working for—he now realized with an ugly flush of adrenaline—since the day he'd emerged from his bunker.

His entire reason for being, his mission, his *life* for the past several years, all hinged upon this one concept, this intangible idea, that a fallen country could be resurrected. That if enough people fought for it, they could breathe life back into it. That they could, if they struggled and bled enough, and lost enough, and kept pressing forward no matter the cost, live a life that bore at least some *semblance* of freedom like they'd known in their past lives.

Somehow, all the roads had led to this point. All the decisions, all the blood, all the death, all the friends and lovers lost and buried and left behind—it had all led to this moment, right now, standing around in the middle of an abandoned Colorado plain. The very history of themselves hanging on a razor's edge and teetering, ever so slightly, in the direction of absolute destruction.

It was not lost on any of them, the import of this moment. It was as large as the sky over them, and as weighty as a mountain.

So many times through recorded history, the actors that swung that course of things on its hinges had no real concept of the importance of the individual moments and decisions that they made, almost bumbling through it blindly, relying only on vague morals and ideals to try to puzzle their way through the maze of possibilities.

That was not the case with any of them, huddled around the back of that Humvee. Every single person present, from Lee, all the way down to the lowest ranked Marine, knew that what was decided in this moment wasn't simply the success of a mission, or the toppling of a regime, or the taking of a city. It was the very soul of them.

And when Lee was done talking, his tongue was dry, his heart thudding uncomfortably inside of him, his guts all in a tangle, nerves freshly reborn in the light of their circumstances. A protracted silence overtook the group, and no one made eye contact with any other, but stared into invisible places and distant possibilities.

Wibberley, seated at the edge of the Humvee's bed alongside Marlin, blew a long breath out and squinted into the late morning sun. "Well. That's all a bit of a clusterfuck, isn't it?"

No one replied. The observation was obvious.

Marlin's eyes finally came up from his battered boots and found Lee. "How long can your boy Sam hold out in Greeley?"

"Not long," Lee said. "He's trying to stay alive until we get there."

Worley, with his elbow up on the truck bed beside Marlin, ground his heel thoughtfully in the dirt. "There is another option."

Marlin looked at him, clearly understanding something unsaid. "Donahue?"

Worley nodded.

Wibberley and Guidry both made a face.

"Who's Donahue?" Lee asked. "Another envoy?"

Marlin shook his head. "He's our point of contact for command. Colonel Donahue. CAF. He's parked just north of the border."

Lee folded his arms across his chest. "And what's he doing there?"

"Waiting," Marlin said. "Or at least, he was, prior to us going off the radar. Worley, have you guys been in contact with him at all since you snuck out of Greeley?"

Worley shook his head. "We've been radio silent. Weren't sure how he would take it." A small smirk. "Better to ask for forgiveness, you know?"

Lee glanced between the two Canadian operatives. "What was he waiting for?"

Marlin watched Lee carefully. "He's got a roughly a battalion. Joint task force. Canadian and British. His job was to back our play. QRF if absolutely necessary. But more to show up on a white horse and demonstrate some loyalty to whoever command decided to go with—Greeley or the UES."

Lee frowned. "The UES is dead. Does that mean he's backing Greeley?"

"Not necessarily," Worley answered. "As of two weeks ago, no decision had been made about who Canada and the UK was going to back. I imagine he's holding out for word from us. Certainly, us going dark wouldn't give him any overwhelming sense of trust in Greeley—which is something we were counting on."

Wibberley sniffed loudly. "He won't commit against Greeley, if that's what you're thinking. Not at this point. Let's all just be completely honest here. Command wanted to back the winning horse. The United Eastern States is dead. Not even in the race anymore. Command will back Greeley. In fact, if you guys roll on Greeley, there's a chance they might swoop in and set up shop with Briggs. Which will make the objective impossible."

That was the last thing Lee wanted to hear. In his mind, their chances of success dipped even further. A bubble of anger rose up in his chest and popped like magma. "Then why the fuck is that another option for us?"

Marlin gave Wibberley a severe glance, then held up a staying hand to Lee. "That's an awful big assumption Lieutenant Wibberley just made."

Wibberley turned on his partner. "Is it? Explain to me how I'm wrong."

But it was Worley that answered. "Donahue doesn't like Briggs. He was the one that pushed for envoys to be sent to the UES. Before that recommendation, it was just going to be me and Guidry, down to make peace with Greeley and open the channels of communication."

Guidry appeared to side with his countryman, Wibberley. "If you think Donahue's going to charge in on Greeley, you've gone batty. That's an overt act. Donahue might like to do it, but he's still not in complete control of everything. He's POC—Point of Contact. The people over his head are playing a fucking political game, and they're not going to declare war on the United States of America—and like it or not, that's what Briggs is."

"I get that," Marlin growled. "But what if we managed to get Lee a foothold in Greeley?"

Lee shifted his weight, the anger not yet abated. "How? How are you going to do that?"

Marlin slid down off the bed, seeming to prefer being on his feet at that moment. "Look, we can't make promises. We haven't even talked with Donahue yet. And Guidry and Wibberley are right—Donahue won't commit the entire battalion in an overt act of war against Briggs."

"Then why are we even having this fucking conversation?"

Marlin looked at Lee earnestly, face to face now. "He won't do an overt act. But that means fucking nothing in modern warfare. You know that as well as I do. That battalion is a joint task force, but that means half of it is made up of CAF—soldiers that will do what Donahue says, and do it quietly. We might be able to convince Donahue to commit a few teams—unmarked and unidentified—to infiltrate Greeley."

"A few teams isn't going to swing our chances," Lee said.

"I'd disagree," Marlin shot back. "Greeley's fucking porous as hell—Guidry and Worley can attest to that. A few teams can sneak in quietly.

Secure Sam, and start blowing shit up from inside while we hit from the outside. They could give us an edge. We'd just have to coordinate carefully with them."

"Out of the question," Lee suddenly snapped.

Marlin looked surprised, then pissed. "Out of the question? Hey, beggars can't be choosers, Lee."

Lee pointed a finger in Marlin's face. "I'm not fucking hanging my entire operation on the chance that some colonel I don't know is going to come through for me. You remember Colonel Freeman from Florida? You remember how he fucked us over at the worst possible moment?"

"Donahue is not Freeman," Marlin said.

Lee shook his head. "I don't trust him. I *can't* trust him. Trusting people is what got our shit pushed in in Butler."

Marlin looked genuinely confused. "You're not being reasonable."

"Lee." Angela's voice.

Lee stared at Marlin, feeling everything whirling inside of him, and the sound of it moving was the distant scream of tinnitus, growing, building.

All he could picture was Freeman's convoy, pushing into the gates of Butler. All he could hear past the ringing in his ears was the memory of the radio transmissions, telling him that Freeman's people were firing on Lee's troops.

I can't let that happen again. I won't let that happen again.

Don't. Fucking. Trust. Anyone.

A hand on his shoulder.

He jerked, looked into Angela's clear blue eyes. His brow wrinkled in confusion, eye going to her lips, which were moving with words he couldn't hear. He blinked, shook his head slightly, trying to clear it. His hand went to his temple, finger in his ear, as though trying to pluck the tinnitus out.

"Hang on," Lee said, thickly. "Gimme a minute."

Dammit dammit dammit.

He turned away, unable to look at any of them.

You're not being reasonable.

He realized he was drifting away from them. The visual of floating back towards the convoy. When he glanced down, he was surprised to see his feet moving.

You're not being reasonable because you've lost your fucking mind.

Screeching. Screaming. All encompassing.

Was that tinnitus, or was it the memory of the screams over the radio as his men and women were gunned down by someone he'd thought was there to help them?

The MATV. Dead ahead.

Faces, like mannequins at store fronts, expressionless, watching him from a distance.

He could feel his chest heaving for air, but couldn't hear his own breath.

What the hell is wrong with me?

Was this what dissociation felt like?

Was this what going insane felt like?

All reality was a thin veneer. Lee felt like he could reach out a hand and poke his finger through it, exposing it for the fake that it was. Just a fragile screen beyond which there was only white light and nothingness.

He found himself at the side of the MATV, hands posted on the metal. Warm from sitting in the sun, but not yet hot. It grounded him. He pressed against it, as though testing his theory that it wasn't real, but found the steel solid. Tangible. Immovable.

"Lee?"

He heard it. Crisp and clear sound.

He blinked again. The screaming in his ears was gone all at once, like storm winds that suddenly die into absolute, preternatural stillness. The eye of a hurricane. A tiny respite in the midst of disaster.

He twisted to the sound of the voice, not yet recognizing it until he laid his eyes on the speaker.

Abby stood there at the back end of the MATV, looking at him. Guileless. Earnest. Curious. A bit concerned.

"Hey, Abby," Lee croaked.

Why had the tinnitus vanished so quickly? Why did everything suddenly feel real again?

Abby stepped towards him, but her eyes strayed past him. Towards the Humvee and the collection of people there. Lee could feel them watching him, though he didn't turn to look.

"What's wrong?" Abby asked.

Lee dragged his hands off the side of the MATV. They hung limp at his sides, fingers trembling. It was wrong of him to do, but he was suddenly sucked into Abby, unable to rip his eyes from her. It was wrong, because he was AN ADULT and DIDN'T NEED ANYBODY and she was JUST A CHILD. But she was very real. More real than anyone back at the Humvee.

Abby raised her eyebrows. An expression so much like her mother's. "You don't look so good."

"I don't feel so good."

Abby nodded. Commiserating. "So what happened?"

"The Canadians want me to trust a friend of theirs." Jesus, was he actually talking to her about this shit? But she was so *there* at that moment, like she was the only objective party in the world. The words came out of him, released by some broken levee inside. "They say he'll help us invade Greeley. But I don't know him. They want me to risk everything. But what if he screws us over? What if he betrays us like everyone else has?"

"Oh." Abby frowned. Looked out to where her mother was. Then back to Lee. "Why are you so scared?"

"I'm not scared," Lee said. Knee-jerk response. He cringed at it. Shook his head. "Okay, that was a lie. I'm terrified."

"Yeah." Abby didn't seem surprised at all. "I think everyone's scared."

"Yeah."

"But why?"

"Because I'm afraid of losing everyone."

"But it sounds like they're trying to help."

"Maybe they are. But they don't know if this friend of theirs will actually come through for them. And if he doesn't then everyone's going to get killed."

"What about Sam?"

Lee clenched his jaw.

Abby continued to watch him. Still so neutral. Like none of this actually affected her. Was she as scared as everyone else? It didn't seem like it. Lee didn't know what she had, but he wanted some of it.

"So…" Abby picked at her fingernails. "If you don't trust their friend, will that mean that we win and everyone lives?"

"No."

"What if you trust him? Will we win then?"

"Maybe."

Abby looked a little confused. Pondered her fingernails for a moment. Chose to bite a cuticle off. Spat it out. "Well. I always like 'maybe' more than just plain old 'no.'"

Lee sniffed. Tore his eye off the girl. All those faces watching him. Standing outside of their trucks and cars and vans and SUVs. Uniforms. Camouflage. Plaid shirts. Civilian clothes. Rifles slung on chests and backs. Pistols on hips. Waiting. Wondering.

Lee put his back to the MATV and leaned against it. His eye wandered along until it found Angela. And Brinly. And Abe. Also watching him. Waiting for him. Wondering what he was going to do.

"Abby," Lee said, glancing at her. "Why are you talking to me now?"

She frowned. "What do you mean?"

"I mean…" He fought for the right words, and again, found himself just being flat-out honest. "I killed your dad. You hated me. For years, you would barely even talk to me. You were afraid of me."

She didn't seem inclined to object.

Lee gestured to his face. "I thought that when I got my face shredded…"

"You thought I'd be even more scared of you?"

He nodded. "So why all the sudden are you not afraid of me anymore?"

She tilted her head, inspecting him boldly, eyes ranging across his scarred face. "I guess…I guess you never seemed human before."

Lee chuffed at the brutal frankness. "I've always been me."

"Yeah, I know. But now? You seem…realer. Before, you were just so hard. And now you seem…"

"Weak."

"No." She crossed her arms, thoughtfully. "Not weak. Just…vulnerable."

Lee squinted at her. "That's a big word for an eleven-year-old."

A smile. "I read it in a book." She turned and leaned her back up against the MATV, mirroring Lee's pose. "So I guess that's why you seem realer to me. And that's why I'm not afraid of you anymore."

Lee puzzled over that for a few moments. Over how that made him feel. On the one hand, it hurt some source of pride in him, that an eleven-year-old was no longer scared of him—what kind of a fragile piece of damaged goods did he seem like now? But at the same instant…why would he want a child to be afraid of him?

"Can I ask you a question now?" Abby said.

"Sure. Why not?"

"Why do you keep doing this?"

Who are you, Lee Harden?

Lee found himself at the precipice of realization. And he couldn't tell if he even wanted to know anymore. But the thoughts kept coming. Demanding to be figured out, like a riddle that piques your curiosity.

What's at your core? What motivates you to do the things you do?

Lee gritted his teeth, hissed air through them. "Abby, I'm not even sure I know."

"Hm." Abby fidgeted, looking out towards the Humvee where Angela and Brinly and Abe still stood. Lee followed her gaze and watched them watching him. Angela in particular, looking at him, looking at her daughter. Like she didn't understand why they were standing there, speaking together, thick as thieves.

The thoughts kept on circling, like Abby's question had stirred a whirlpool in his brain, and it was all funneling down towards that secretive center of him that he'd never quite puzzled out. Closer and closer to touching the truth.

"Hoo-boy," Lee muttered.

"Yeah," Abby agreed.

"Abby?"

"Yeah?"

"I'm gonna call Sam. You wanna talk to him?"

"Yes."

THIRTY-FIVE

THE MESSAGE

SAM SAT ON THE DESK in the dark inner office of the building. He held the pistol in one hand, the satphone in the other, pressed to his ear. "Lee?"

"It's me." Abby's voice. She didn't need to say so. Sam recognized it instantly.

And everything went very still inside of him. All the roiling tension and second-guessing and thoughts of his imminent death, inching closer to him. He stared at the pistol, the dull black frame of it, the anodized black slide. The imagery of placing that shot into Gabriella played on a loop in his brain, but his mind turned away from it at the sound of Abby's voice.

"Abby, is something wrong? Is Lee there?"

"Yeah. He's right here with me. I just wanted to talk to you."

Sam wasn't sure what he felt in that moment. Any semblance of guilt that he might have felt for executing Gabriella...well, that had never even shown up. If he'd had it in him in the first place, it had been covered up with a crust of rage, thinking about Johnson and Pickell, dead and dying. Because of her.

No, he didn't feel guilty at what he'd done. But he did feel surprised.

He pictured himself in that moment, very different from what he now was. He pictured himself from years ago, in a very similar position, huddled beneath the roots of a downed tree, with a pistol given to him by Lee that he had no idea how to use outside of "point it at the bad guy and pull the trigger." Terrified of the possibility that that might happen, that he might be forced to do it. Terrified of the sounds of death and screaming and gunshots in the distance as Lee destroyed the people that had destroyed his father.

Terrified that he would never have the guts to do what needed to be done.

That version of him was gone. Dead. He wasn't afraid of it anymore. He wasn't afraid of it poisoning him now.

Somehow, Abby had become linked to that childlike version of him. He'd met her so soon after his world had crumbled, and they'd been close, all through the formation of Camp Ryder. Two kids just trying to survive. And there was a time when he'd been scared to be around Abby, or Angela, for fear that they would drag him back in time to that worthless little kid that was frightened of everything.

Now, hearing Abby's voice, he found a smile on his lips. Wan, and lacking joy—it's very difficult to feel joy when you think the end is so close. But he wasn't afraid anymore. Abby couldn't drag him back in time to that other version of himself, because it was dead.

Sam had grown up. And Abby had too.

"Well," Sam said, his voice a little thick. "What did you want to talk about?"

"I didn't really have anything to talk about," Abby said. Her voice was calm. Frank. "I just wanted to hear your voice and tell you that I love you. You know. Like a big brother."

Sam coughed out a dry chuckle. "Yeah, I know, Abby. And I love you too. Like a little sister."

A single shush of breath over the line. Almost like Abby was relieved.

"Okay. I guess that's it," she said. "Lee wants to talk to you."

"Okay, Abby. Be good."

"I will."

Shuffling.

Lee's voice: "Sam. How you holding up?"

The smile fled from Sam's face. "We lost Pickell last night. But…"

He looked at the pistol in his hand, half expecting it to tremble in his grip. But it was still. Everything in him was still. Quiet.

"But what?" Lee asked.

"We took down the people that betrayed us," Sam said, keeping it short and sweet. "I wanted to send a message. The people that were willing to rebel, they got cold feet. I wanted to give them something to have faith in. So we killed the people that tried to kill us, and we left a message."

"You left a message?" Concern. "What do you mean?"

Sam gritted his teeth together. "Don't be pissed."

"Sam…"

"They needed to know that they're not alone. They needed to know that someone's going to have their back if they stand up and fight. I know that you wanted to keep the operation a secret to the last minute, but Greeley already knows, Lee. They know what you're planning."

"Christ, Sam. What'd you say?"

"We left papers on the bodies. And Marie wrote it on some walls, down near where the conscripts are housed." Sam took a deep breath, knowing that he had, in some way, betrayed Lee's trust, but also knowing that he hadn't had an option. He'd done what needed to be done. "We told them 'Lee is coming.'"

A long, uncomfortable silence. Long enough for Sam to feel a seed of doubt begin to sprout, ugly and black inside of him. Had he ruined things by sending that message? It hadn't been a thoughtless decision—he'd pondered it before doing it. It had felt, in the moment, like the only thing he could do to bolster support inside of Greeley. But Lee's silence was nerve-wracking.

Sam's fingers ached from clutching the satphone so hard. He forced himself to relax. A new concern flitted through his mind on insect wings. "You *are* coming, aren't you?"

"We lost a lot of support," Lee replied, quietly. "Greeley has an army down south of us. Same fuckers that took over Butler. They've been on our asses the whole time. They burned through some of the settlements that sided with us, and the people we got to support us lost faith and cut and run."

Suddenly, the fears came crashing back into Sam. Not the old fears of his old self. The new ones. Being stuck behind enemy lines. All alone. No one coming. It set his heart to racing again like it had when Gabriella had stepped out of her house.

"Lee," Sam said, his voice a little shaky. "I made promises to people. I trusted you. And they need to trust you too. Please tell me that you're still coming."

"It's a long shot, Sam. Do you understand that? We have half the manpower we thought we'd have. Even if everything went the way I'd planned, even if those settlements were still backing us, it *still* would have been long odds."

"Lee, it's always been long odds. We knew that. Every person you spoke to on that road when we evacuated Butler—they knew it was long odds too. And they had faith in you. They *still* have faith in you now. Remember what you said. Remember what you promised them, Lee. You promised them a fucking fight. You promised them you'd take it Greeley. Bloody but unbowed. That's the only reason they came with you. Because they're fighters. And fighters don't give a fuck about the odds."

"It's my job to give a fuck about the odds."

"Lee," Sam snapped, surprised at his own anger. "You told me, outside of that fucking gas station when I thought everything was going to shit because I'd lost my squad, you told me that this is what leaders do. They worry about the people under them. But they understand that some of them are gonna die in the process. That's the nature of war, you said. You told me that you couldn't obsess about it. You couldn't let it break you. *Don't ever let it break you!* So was that all fucking bullshit? Have you let it break you, Lee? Because you can't. You fucking can't! I didn't let it break me, and now it's time for you to take your own goddamned advice!"

"Alright, shut the fuck up," Lee growled, but it lacked the heat that Sam had expected in response to his mutinous tone.

Breath rushing in and out of his throat. Heart beating in his ears.

"You said you could hold out for another twenty four hours," Lee said. "Is that still true?"

Sam looked out the open office door, through the atrium, where Marie and Jones stood quietly, watching him, backlit by the daylight pouring in through the front of the building. Greeley hadn't given up on finding them. The search parties were getting closer.

Sam had no idea if he could actually make it twenty-four hours. But he realized that everything hung on his answer. He'd leveled the charges on Lee, and now Lee was levelling them back. Just as Lee needed to take his own advice, so did Sam. He had to remain unbreakable. And sometimes, in the face of seemingly impossible odds, you just had to believe that you'd see the other side of it.

"Yeah," Sam said. "We can hold out."

A long sigh. "Alright, Sam. There might still be a chance. I've got to go out on a limb and do some shit I am highly fucking uncomfortable doing, but I don't think we have an option right now. If you can hold out for another twenty-four hours, I will try to get a team of operatives into Greeley to support you. They won't be from our people. And I can't even guarantee you that they're coming. I have to talk it over with some folks. But…I'll try."

"So you're coming?"

Please don't make a liar out of me, Lee.

"Yes, for fuck's sake. I'm coming. *We're* coming. Hell or high water, Sam, we're gonna get you out of there are we're gonna die trying."

***

What is your core? What is this thing at the center of you?

Lee stalked back to the gathering at the rear of the Humvee. The Marines on guard had inched closer, and the four envoys were huddled tight with Brinly, Angela, and Abe. Their voices were urgent, but not loud.

Lee figured they were talking about how to knock some sense into him.

Brinly was the first to spot him approaching and fixed him with a gaze that Lee could read all too well: *Does he have his head on straight or is he still off the rails?*

Lee didn't even have the inclination to be miffed by this. He had his reasons for struggling with this decision—good reasons, reasons that were bathed in the blood of his memories, reasons that had the evidence of so many catastrophic betrayals to back them.

But it didn't matter anymore. They might be good reasons, but there was one thing that everyone in that little worried huddle had right, and Lee had wrong: There wasn't another option.

As Abby had so aptly pointed out, "maybe" was always better than flat out "no."

Why did he do the things he did? Why did he keep going, in the face of seemingly insurmountable odds? What was it that moved him, animated his actions, made him into who he was?

And he thought he knew. He was close enough now to it that he could see a glimpse of it, like the answer to that riddle, the way it just *fits*, and you know it only at the moment when you realize it, that it connects all those disparate, seemingly-contradictory things.

Yes, he was violent. Yes, he killed people. Yes, he was vengeful.

But that wasn't the whole story. Those were just the manifestations of the same thing that kept him fighting. The same thing that made him punch that kid back in grade school. The same thing that made him join the military. The same thing that made him join Project Hometown, and violate protocols, and wage war against a man who claimed to be the president.

It was all the same thing. All branches of the same tree, that was connected to a central tap root that went deep down into the center of Lee.

This world is broken. It's off-kilter. It always has been. Maybe it always will be.

But sometimes, in flashes, between sleep and waking, Lee could see the pieces. He knew how they fit together, because he'd seen how they fell apart.

The world needed people that were willing to try, were willing to die, were willing to do violence, to put it back together.

I want to fix it. That's what lays at the center of me. That is the core of me. That is what animates my actions. That is the source of my anger, of my willingness to do violence. I want to put the pieces back together—I need to put them back together so that something out of all of this makes sense again.

I need to fix it.

They all turned and looked at Lee as he stopped at the edge of their circle, the air between them all as taut as a steel cable threatening to snap.

Lee had no time for anything but plain language and clear commands.

"Worley," Lee said, looking at the Canadian. "Do you have a way to get into contact with Donahue?"

Worley nodded at once. "I still have our satphone."

"Call him. I don't give a shit what you have to say or what you have to promise, get him to commit whatever he can, however he can manage it. I need his people inside Greeley *by tonight*." Nothing else to be said about it. Lee looked to the others. "Brinly. Abe. Angela. I need every squad leader rounded up so we can lay out our plan of attack. We might not have what we wanted to have, but we're going to adapt and overcome. Strategy meeting in thirty minutes. I want to be on the road north in two hours."

Everyone stared, as though waiting for the other shoe to drop.

Lee raised his eyebrows. "Questions?"

All seven heads shook.

"Then let's get to it."

***

Thirty minutes later, as a ragtag jumble of rebels gathered for a strategy meeting in the middle of Colorado, hundreds of miles to the north, Colonel Donahue had a meeting of his own. Much smaller. And much more secretive.

He stood in the center of a command tent, half plywood walls, half camouflage netting. A few rows of folding tables and folding chairs. Computers and communications equipment left abandoned because he'd ordered everyone out.

The only people in the command tent with him now were four uniformed men with very curious faces. Two captains, one lieutenant, and a master sergeant. They were the leaders of the four special forces units that Donahue had under his command. And they were the only four people that Donahue truly trusted.

They knew about opsec. They could keep their mouths shut.

Donahue decided not to stand. The four operatives were already sitting, leaning forward, their faces intense. And Donahue's legs suddenly felt tired, like he'd just finished a nightmare ruck up a mountain.

He grabbed a folding chair from the table behind him and sat down with a sigh. Propped his elbows on his knees, and leaned in, just like the men across from him.

"I'm gonna ask you to do some shit," he said, his voice steady, but quiet. "There's no way around the fact that it's an absolute crap shoot. And you know what I mean when I say that."

They knew what he meant.

Dangerous. Some of them would not be coming back.

"You can't breathe a word of it to anyone outside of your teams and the people in this room. And you have to get to it the second we're done with this meeting. Also, you cannot be identified as CAF, and if anyone asks me, I'll deny that this fucking meeting ever happened." Donahue laced his fingers together, meeting each of his operatives' eyes. "I'd ask you if you were willing, but that's probably a dumb question."

One of the men, a chunk of dip bulging in his lower lip, spat into the dirt between his boots. "We driving or flying, and how much ordnance do we need to pack?"

Donahue smirked. "Flying. And lots."

THIRTY-SIX

GUILT AND JUSTICE

EVERYTHING WAS HAZY. Indeterminate. Alien.

Griffin moved through the world like a man in a bubble, as though nothing could touch him, and none of it was real. Of course, he held no such illusions of invincibility, or that the people that he ordered killed would indeed be dead, human lives gone up in smoke.

No, it was simply the sensation of completely breaking with any emotion that was, in every other time in his life, a touchstone for the moments that he had lived.

As he walked through the field of tire tracks, right outside the high school in La Junta, he wondered if he would even remember any of this with any particular clarity. Death, destruction, burning, screaming. All just special effects, it seemed like. All the universe a big fakery, and he the lone conscious being, the sole audience.

Oh, he would remember it. But it would all be colorless and bland. Snapshots in his mind, rather than full clear memories with real people and real feeling. The images just thumbnail sketches. The moments just footnotes to a larger objective.

Where'd you go, Lee? Why are you making me do this?

If he could have one wish, it would be that Lee would stop hurling himself northward at Greeley, and turn and duke it out with him for all the marbles, and then all of this could end, and Griffin could get his life back.

But until that happened, Griffin was sequestered in this strange mental place of lifelessness.

A defensive mechanism, to be sure. But he'd long ago stopped trying to question his brain's inner workings. It was best to let the brain block what it found too offensive to hold onto.

He scuffed the toe of his boot along the tread pattern of a tire left in the dirt. Smudging it out. Erasing it like it had never been there, though all the tracks still converged on a single point, and from there, Griffin was sure, led northward.

"So," Griffin said, flat and quiet. "What to do about you?"

He heard the intake of breath behind him. A decidedly feminine quality to it. When he turned and looked, it was the man named Jonathan Reeves, and his wife, Tammy. She clung to him, distressed. He stood there, resolute, trying his damndest to not look terrified, and failing miserably.

Reeves swallowed hard. Took a step away from his wife—her fingertips clinging to his shirt sleeve until they were plucked from her grasp. "Do what you will with me. But leave the people alone. They weren't a part of this. I made the decision to allow Lee Harden to stay here. Everyone else didn't want it. Including my wife—"

"Jon..." she uttered.

"—so if you're going to punish anyone, punish me."

Griffin stared at him, eyes half-lidded. "That's very heroic of you."

Another dry-looking swallow. "No, sir. Just the truth. I swear it."

"That's fucking bullshit," the devil's voice said from beside Griffin.

Griffin closed his eyes—a painful wince, like the voice was the sound of metal squealing. That teeth-rattling noise that a metal filing cabinet made when you pushed it across smooth concrete.

He turned. Opened his eyes.

Now. Here was some emotion. Dim, like the heat of a fire you're standing several feet away from: Repugnance. Disgust.

Mr. Smith stood there, all eager bloodlust. He was looking at Jonathan Reeves, not Griffin. Was that the tiniest smirk at the corner of his mouth? A greasy, sweaty hunger written all over him. God, but he actually got off on this shit. He *liked* to see people terrified.

Griffin had a flash of imagination: Mr. Smith in a black, leather trench coat, hunting for Jews hiding under floorboards. He would have made a top gestapo agent.

"It's not bullshit," Reeves answered, hollowly. Unconvincing.

Mr. Smith glared, acting affronted, when in fact, this was the game he loved playing the best. "That's not what my operatives tell me. In fact, my operatives tell me that you damn near threw Lee Harden a ticker tape parade when he came in. People lining the streets. Waving. Cheering. They *wanted* him here."

"He's gone," Reeves tried. "We kicked him out. What more evidence do you need? We're lucky he didn't turn on us when we told him to leave."

"Oh, yes," Mr. Smith nodded. "He's a dangerous animal, that one. And when you play with dangerous animals, sometimes you get bit."

"He's gone," Reeves repeated.

Griffin took in a long breath through his nose, his eyes straying from Mr. Smith and Reeves, to the soldiers all around them. Army. Marines. A lot of Cornerstone operatives. All of them—or at least most of them—with the same hollow expressions that Griffin knew was on his own face.

"It's too late for all that," Mr. Smith said, his voice low and seething. "You should have done the right thing when he arrived in the first place. You want me to give you credit because you begged him to leave when you found out that you might have to face consequences for your actions? Well, that boat don't float, my friend. You provided assistance to an enemy of the state. That makes *you* an enemy of the state. And do you know what we do with people like you?"

Reeves nodded. "I know. And I accept it. Do what you're gonna do. But leave the people out of it."

Mr. Smith laughed. "You're not in a position to make demands."

Griffin listened, placidly. His eyes hopping from one face to another—a soldier here, a Cornerstone operative there. Some of them caught Griffin's eyes, and they couldn't hold his gaze. Guilty. Every last one of them guilty as sin.

Guilty as Griffin was.

Ah, well. War is hell. I'm sure General Sherman felt the same way. Probably why he said that.

Mr. Smith was going on again. He was really on a roll. Feeling his oats. Reveling in the misery he caused. Feeding off it like a vampire. Griffin didn't really hear his words, just his feigned, self-righteous indignation.

Mr. Smith was fake too. Fake to his core. Nothing real about him at all.

Back beyond the Reeves, and the soldiers and operatives that surrounded them; more people, and more soldiers. The citizens of La Junta. Not all of them, but a good chunk, come to see what was happening. Some of them had come willingly, others—the ones that seemed squirrelly—had been rounded up and disarmed. Not a shot had been fired. Yet.

All around those civilians, guntrucks with their turrets trained on unarmed people. Soldiers standing around with their rifles at a low ready. In the backs of pickup beds. Striding slowly about the perimeter.

"Captain Griffin!"

He winced again at the voice. That disgust a little stronger now. "What?" he snapped.

Mr. Smith was looking at him. "I said something to you."

"Oh, you did?"

Mr. Smith squared himself to Griffin. "Yes, I did."

"I didn't hear."

"I said—"

"And also, I don't take orders from you."

Narrowed eyes, just dark little glints of malice through the thin slits of his eyelids. "Yes. You've made that abundantly clear. But that doesn't change the fact that justice needs to be done here. President Briggs expects you to *do your fucking job.*"

Griffin's mouth stretched in a mirthless smile that didn't even get in the same hemisphere as his eyes. "Justice?"

"Yes, justice! You may not take orders from me, but you do take orders from your command-in-chief. And I will ensure that President Briggs's orders are carried out. The guilty parties need to be punished."

Griffin sighed. "Yes. Of course."

He faced Reeves, hand slipping to his pistol. His eyes weren't on Reeves, though. They were still scouring the faces of the soldiers and operatives. As he drew his sidearm, they watched. Brief flashes of discomfort. Disappointment. They looked away.

Griffin had one job, and that was to command this army.

The guilt on the faces of his men—yes, even the Cornerstone men—told him all that he needed to know. He'd already made his decision, but now he was much more comfortable with it.

He met Reeves' eyes.

"Guilty parties have to die," Griffin said, almost apologetically—*Hey, I don't make the rules; I just enforce them.*

Then he lifted his pistol.

And blew the back of Mr. Smith's head out.

Every single person jerked in unison. Reeves jolted backwards. His wife made a tiny cry. The soldiers gaped. The Cornerstone operatives lifted their rifles—but only a little bit. And then they stopped.

By the time Mr. Smith's body hit the ground, all was still again.

Griffin watched the Cornerstone operatives carefully.

They wrestled with it. He could see that. And he could also appreciate it. When you spend your whole life as a part of the system, you shudder to see it trip and fall. You think, *maybe I should do something about this, maybe I should prove my loyalty to the system...*

But then you realize that you're relieved.

And that's what Griffin saw on the operatives' faces.

Relief.

Not a single one of them pointed their rifle at Griffin, or moved towards him, or even shouted out with incredulity. If they were being honest, they weren't even surprised. Hell, they'd probably been hoping for it.

They were a whole pack of assholes, those Cornerstone boys. But there's only so long you can walk down a dark road before you either let it swallow you whole or you become desperate for a chance to turn around.

Guilty, every damn one of them. But not too far gone, Griffin thought. Otherwise, he figured he'd have been shot.

"Mr. Reeves," Griffin said, holstering his pistol. "I'm putting you in charge of gathering every firearm and every cartridge in this settlement. They now belong to me. You're also going to gather half of all your food, water, and medicine. Those belong to me too."

Reeves' mouth opened, as though to object.

Griffin held up a finger. "Your cooperation is the price for your people's lives. I'm sure it's not too much to pay."

Reeves blinked a few times, then shook his head. "No. No, it's not too much."

Griffin nodded. "I didn't think it was. Please have the requested items loaded into my convoy within two hours. Lieutenant Paige will direct you where to put everything. We're done here."

***

"Twenty-four hours," Jones said, sitting cross-legged with the rifle in his lap. "Sure. Yeah. Why not."

As if to challenge the likelihood of that, a boom trembled the floor. A grenade. Sam wasn't experienced enough with them to know if it were a flashbang or a fragmentation grenade. He only knew that it was close. Maybe a few streets over.

Jones, Marie, and Sam, all looked out at the afternoon light pouring in from the front of their hideout. Shadows already tilting away from the sun, but not fast enough. Lips were tensed and flat. Hearts were beating faster than necessary. Guts were watery. Palms clammy.

Time inched by at a painful pace.

"Lee says they'll be in by nightfall," Sam replied.

"So he hopes," Jones commented. "And even if they get into Greeley, that doesn't mean they find us by nightfall. And we can't really start making our move until Lee hits anyways."

"No. But we can sure as shit defend ourselves. And we will."

Jones met his gaze, bereft of humor. "They're frag and clearing. What? Two blocks over? How long you think it's going to take them to get here?"

It wasn't an actual question. Jones's point was obvious in his tone: *Not long.*

"Heads up," Marie said, rolling from her sitting position and bringing her rifle up to her shoulder.

Jones and Sam came up, stomachs in throats, but then immediately relaxed.

It was Evan.

"Knock knock," Evan husked as he picked his way quickly into the building.

He stopped, not far from the entrance, his hands up.

Sam's grip tightened on his rifle. "What's up, Evan?"

Evan tossed his head behind him. "Got some people that want to come in."

Jones shifted his body towards a nearby column, ready to spring for cover.

"Yeah?" Sam said, not daring to hope, only jumping to the worst possible conclusion. "Who?"

Evan made a grimace that Sam didn't like. "I'm sorry Sam…"

Sam almost shot him right then and there. He raised his rifle to the point that the optic was just below his line of sight.

Evan recoiled. "Christ! Wait!" The next sentence tumbled out about as fast as you'd expect someone to speak when they knew their words were the only thing between them and a bullet. "I was apologizing because I was only able to convince two of the other squad leaders! My squad is outside, with the two other squads."

Stillness.

Sam's heart felt brittle and overworked. He nearly gasped as he lowered his rifle. "You fuck. Don't do that to me."

Evan winced. "God. You guys are high strung."

"Yeah, you're damn right we're high strung," Jones snapped. "You should be too. Your life's on the line just as much as ours. You understand that, right?"

Evan nodded. "Yeah, I understand that. Can I signal them to come in?"

Sam stood up, hands still gripping his rifle, the muzzle pointed somewhere south of Evan's feet. "Humor my paranoia for a second and don't get offended. But if it's anyone but who you say it is, you die first."

Evan actually managed a smile. "Good thing I'm not lying. And you know what? I'm glad you're a fucking hard ass, Sameer. I'd hate to throw my life on the line with a pushover."

Sam nodded. "Go ahead and signal them. But stay right where you are."

Evan turned. Craned his neck to the side a bit. Waved his hands like a stranded motorist.

Out of the abandoned building across the street emerged a figure. Then two. Then three. They sprinted across, one at a time, looking both ways down the road as they did and stumbling breathlessly into the dim tomb of the hideout.

They gathered silently around Evan as more continued to skitter across the street. Only nods of greeting, and then eyes on Sam and what remained of his crew. Watching them and waiting, as the rest of the dissidents scrambled in behind them.

Sam counted heads. Fifteen total. But none of them armed.

"Folks," Evan said, once they'd all made it across. "This is Sameer, for those that haven't met him before. He's the one I told you about. Sameer, these are your new friends."

"Anybody have weapons?" was the first words out of Sam's mouth.

Glances traded around.

"Knives," one of the guys said, to a general nod of agreement.

Sam almost laughed. "Well. Guess that's better than nothing."

One of the others that Sam recognized as a squad leader took a hesitant step forward. "We saw the signs. Shit, I think everyone saw the signs." He shook his head as though bewildered. "Y'all done pissed 'em off, dintcha?"

Sam nodded, his grip on his rifle relaxing. "Well, it got you here, didn't it?"

"Is it true?" a woman asked, shouldering around Evan. "Is Lee Harden really coming?"

"Yeah," Sam answered. "He's coming."

"How long?"

"Twenty-four hours. Little less now."

The woman blanched. "Twenty-four hours is a long time."

Sam shrugged. "Yeah, well. It's better than twenty-five."

THIRTY-SEVEN

TIDES

THE LIGHT WAS FAILING NOW.

Lee glanced westward and saw only an orange smudge where the sun had been. The clouds still hung onto its light, creating a diffused amber glow across the landscape.

Only twelve hours now.

One more sleepless night.

There was no rise in the land. No hill. No high vantage on which to look out at his objective. All was flat. All was desolate. But there was nothing between him and Greeley anymore, except for twenty miles of road.

The horizon to the north showed nothing. No sign of the city he had his sights on. Not a glow of electric light. Not a pall of smog. Nothing. Lee could almost imagine that it didn't actually exist.

And yet, knowing that there was nothing in his way, that twenty miles might as well have been nothing. The lack of barriers made the distance insignificant.

He worked the fingers of his damaged left hand. The ache had gotten stronger. Something to do with the weather, he assumed. Or maybe it was the tension and the lack of sleep.

He put his hands on his hips and stared at that horizon line, picturing his objective, his desires, his strategy, his hopes, his anxieties, every bad thing that might happen, and the distant glimmer of what he could possibly accomplish, all overlaid on top of one another in a jumble of blood and loss and spectral victory, troop movements, chess pieces, areas of operations, and a broad, poisonous sense of rage that coalesced around an image of what Briggs would look like when Lee finally kicked down his door.

That twenty miles might as well have been nothing.

Lee was on the doorstep.

Only twelve hours left.

One more sleepless night.

***

Far to the south, in the full dark of the freshly fallen night, the Alpha did not have to wait any longer.

The tide that had been building was now rushing through them, like the wind that thrashes the trees ahead of a storm, carrying with it destruction.

The Alpha had no pack any longer. They were *all* his pack. So many of them that the clear, cold light of the moon across their bare shoulders created a landscape of its own that stretched in all directions, as far as the Alpha could see.

This territory was dead. That was what the Alpha understood, in his own vestigial way. The Easy Prey had left, and so the Alpha and all of his packmates, and all of the Omegas, and all of the Strange Ones that led them, knew that they had to pursue.

The Easy Prey had fled to the place where the sun touches the earth.

And where the prey go, the predator must follow.

The scent was heavy on them now, communicating far more than the grunts and cries with which they conversed. It told the Alpha that their time had come. Their hunger had been sated—for now. Their numbers had swelled. Their strength had been built back from the lean months following the rutting and the mating. The Omegas, every one, had begun to grow new life in their bellies.

The scent told them that they must follow their prey or be destroyed.

It seized the Alpha with an urgency that seemed to come out of his bones. The need to move. To cross great distances. To sniff out the places where the Easy Prey would be. To go to any lengths to preserve the many that were his packmates now, and the many more that would arrive very soon.

They had to go. And the time was now.

A single Omega, only a few body lengths from the Alpha, let out a quiet hoot, and began to move forward.

And the rest followed with her.

FOR UPDATES ON THE LEE HARDEN SERIES, MAKE SURE TO FOLLOW D.J. MOLLES AT

FACEBOOK.COM/DJMOLLES

AND SIGN UP FOR HIS FREE NEWSLETTER AT

http://eepurl.com/c3kfJD

(If you're typing that into a browser, make sure to capitalize the J and D)

ABOUT THE AUTHOR

D.J. Molles is the New York Times bestselling author of *The Remaining* series, which was originally self-published in 2012 and quickly became an internet bestseller, and is the basis for his hit *Lee Harden* series. He is also the author of *Wolves*, a 2016 winner in the Horror category for the Foreword INDIES Book Awards. His other works include the *Grower's War* series, and the Audible original, *Johnny*. When he's not writing, he's taking care of his property in North Carolina, and training to be at least half as hard to kill as Lee Harden. He also enjoys playing his guitar and drums, drawing, painting, and lots of other artsy fartsy stuff.

You can follow and contact him at:
Facebook.com/DJMolles
And sign up for his free, monthly newsletter at:
http://eepurl.com/c3kfJD
(If you're typing that into a browser, make sure to capitalize the J and D)

Printed in Great Britain
by Amazon

71651222R00303